CORRECTIONAL

NJ CROSSKEY

Legend Press Ltd, 51 Gower Street, London, WC1E 6HJ
info@legendpress.co.uk | www.legendpress.co.uk

Print ISBN 978-1-80031-003-2
Ebook ISBN 978-1-80031-004-9
Set in Times.
Cover design by Kari Brownlie | www.karibrownlie.co.uk

Printed and bound by CPI Group (UK) Ltd, Croydon CR0 4YY

N.J. Crosskey lives with her husband and two children in the seaside town of Worthing, West Sussex. She has worked in the care sector for almost twenty years, but has always yearned to be an author. In 2014 she finally found the courage to chase her dream, and began by writing short fiction which has since been published in various ezines and online literary magazines.

Her first two novels *Poster Boy* and *Overdrawn* were published by Legend Press in 2019.

Visit N.J. at
www.njcrosskey.com
or follow her
@NJCrosskey

*For my awesome son Riley. Thank you for bringing
so much love and laughter to our lives*

It's just another Saturday evening. Up and down the country, families gather on their sofas ready to devour the entertainment provided for them by the gods of prime time. Snacks are gathered, drinks are poured. Guesses are made, opinions are shared. The nation waits in anticipation; the bookies take their final bets before the broadcast begins.

It's just like any other Saturday evening, except tonight I'm watching too. Tonight, I'm on the spectator side of the screen. For now. Reclining in my chair, beer in hand and a bowl of peanuts resting on the arm, waiting for the spectacle to begin, just like millions of others.

From John o' Groats to Land's End, wives shush husbands, and parents hurriedly usher children to bed as the adverts draw to a close and the commentator finally speaks.

"Twelve inmates. One chamber. Who will face justice tonight? Their fate is in your hands as we join Mo Wilson and the guards at Whitefield Prison for this week's *Juustiiice Liiive*!"

I turn the volume up as Mel saunters in, tutting.

"Really, Cal?" She plucks the glass of Merlot from the coffee table. The one I poured for her. "On your holiday?"

"What can I say?" I smile, slightly. Willing her to lift the wine to her lips. "I guess I'm a workaholic."

The theme music kicks in, a deep beat overlaid with jazzy electric guitar. The logo *Justice Live* – written in a jagged neon-blue font – sweeps across the screen at a jaunty angle before settling in the middle. CGI prison bars descend in front of it.

Then it's the mugshot montage. Twelve monsters, all in a row. Unwashed, unkempt, every scar and pockmark accentuated by the sickly yellow light. A rapist. A murderer. A paedophile. Each one holding a letter board that gives their name, their crime, and the number to call to cast your vote.

Some of them are instantly recognisable to the public, even without the prop. I guess you'd call them notorious, or infamous. However you want to put it, they're the images you see when you think of evil. Like Harvey Stone, whose picture comes last in the montage. His letter board reads *Child Killer*, but nobody needs to be told that. His round, greasy face and beady eyes are as familiar to the nation as any celebrity's. The Playground Slasher. Seven little girls, seven different parks, one serrated blade. A reign of terror. A nationwide manhunt that lasted three months but ended abruptly, with a disappointing lack of bloodshed or drama, when he was arrested while buying a packet of digestives at a Tesco Express in Walthamstow. That was ten years ago now, but the memory of his crimes, and the innocent faces of his victims, are burned into the collective consciousness. Some things are so heinous, so painful, that we need to keep poking at them to remind ourselves they're not just myths.

The parade of pariahs ends and Whitefield itself comes on-screen. The hairs on my arms prickle, ever so slightly, at the sight of its barbed-wire-topped walls and lookout towers. I glance over at Mel, who's now settled in her favourite armchair, knees to the side with her feet almost tucked under her. I wish I could do that – contort my limbs to fit my whole self into a chair as if it were a cocoon. But my legs are too long, too straight, and not at all flexible. I worry that she'll notice the goosebumps on my arm, that my own flesh will rat me out, but she's not looking at me. As much as she professes her disgust for the show, she can't take her eyes off it.

We all stare a little too long at the things we hate, and not long enough at the things we love.

The camera zooms in, over the walls and on to the exercise

yard. But the basketball hoops and workout benches have been cleared away, and you can't see the courts marked out on the concrete, because of the crowd. They swarm around the raised platform in the centre, each holding an oversized umbrella, emblazoned with the *Justice Live* logo, to protect them from the autumn drizzle.

Mo Wilson emerges from the main building, via a door I know to be the entrance to the camera runs, though they've moved all the wheelie bins that are usually there. The audience erupts into applause and he raises his hands in the air, fingers splayed as if trying to absorb their adoration into his skin. He's all bleached teeth and slightly too orange spray tan. A walking Wotsit – as Dax likes to put it.

One of the show's runners jogs up to him, hands him an umbrella. Wouldn't do to get that perfectly coiffured greying hair flattened and frizzed up by the misty rain.

He steps up onto the platform, smiling wide and white. When he holds up his free hand, the crowd settles to a dull roar. He addresses the camera. "It's Saturday night. The lines are open, the guards are pumped, and the inmates are quaking in their boots!"

The crowd roars, almost feral in their excitement. Rabid dogs who've caught the scent of blood on the breeze.

"And so they should be," Mo continues, "because I've had a sneak peek at tonight's chamber program, and let me tell you, ladies and gentlemen, it… is… a… doozy!" More roars. Cheers. They'll all be hoarse by the first commercial break if they keep this up. "As always, it's up to you guys at home to decide which of Britain's most despicable criminals should face justice – live! But before you make up your mind, let's catch up with what's been happening at White-field this week. And I warn you, it's not for the faint-hearted! They may be called in*mates* but there's no love lost between our contenders."

Mel shakes her head slowly, biting her bottom lip. She's judging me, I can feel it. Even though she doesn't take her eyes off the television, I know that the raised eyebrow and soft clicks of her tongue are as much aimed at me as at Mo Wilson and his pithy one-liners.

But that's Mel all over. Reclining in her faux-leather chair, watching the world with faux outrage as she cradles the ornate glass in her palm, tapping the edges of it unconsciously with her slick, glossed fingernails – those are faux too. She can't help it, everything she's ever been surrounded with has been faux. Until she met me. At least that's what I like to think. I like to think she was overcome by me, instantly attracted. I like to think I was the first real and raw thing in her life, and that's why she fell in love with me. I don't like to think that maybe I was just a bit of rough at first, just a boy from the wrong side of the river to satisfy her desire.

She grew up in a house full of false niceties and polished veneers, went to a school that gated itself off from the real world, took up a job in which appearance is everything. Even her supposedly profound experiences are artificial. Like the latest fad. She spent three months in the Himalayas last week, courtesy of a VR gift card her boss gave her for her birthday. She actually thinks she had a spiritual awakening, or some such cliché. The fact it was all pixels and code, when you get down to it, doesn't register.

Mo cuts to pre-recorded footage. Highlights of the week include inmates squaring up to each other over a pot of hair cream, and the infamous Manchester Maniac bragging about having sex with his victims – after he'd slit their necks.

"Christ, Cal," Mel says, looking at me for the first time since the show began. "Really?"

"You don't have to watch," I say, turning up the volume again, "if you find it too distasteful."

She just tuts, and we sit through the rest of the week's highlights in silence. I feel a shiver of excitement as my eyes dart to the clock.

"I honestly don't know what's worse," she says, topping up her glass. "The show itself, or the audience."

I know what she means. Of course I do. It's sickening. The primal, hate-filled bloodlust on the crowd's faces. Worse still will be what comes next. The pure delight, the whooping and cheering, when the votes are all counted and the tortures begin. The irony of it is lost on them.

"So don't watch," I say, and she frowns even more. She wanted me to agree, to launch into a debate about the cruelty of human nature like we used to when faced with such stark evidence of man's obscene treatment of man. But not any more. We don't agree any more.

I never intended to be a part of this, of course. It wasn't what I signed up for. That I ever wanted to work at Whitefield at all was incomprehensible to her. But *Justice Live* isn't Whitefield. Or at least, it's only a tiny part of it. The part that makes the rest of it possible. I didn't expect to be anywhere near this sick carnival of twisted punishments. I never dreamed I'd even set foot in the max wing. The guards of max are stars as much as they are correctional officers. All of them look like they could bench-press a double-decker bus without breaking a sweat. And, of course, they're all ruggedly handsome, boasting a range of decidedly deep and masculine regional accents between them. All of them except me.

I'm still in all the calendars and posters, of course. But I know I'm the joke addition –physique-wise. There are no teenage girls swooning over me like they do over Dax. All the women swoon over Dax. Even Mel.

When she catches me staring she flashes a small smile, and I wonder how we got here. I think she still loves me. I know I still love her. This distance between us isn't irrevocable, it can't be. If I thought these walls between us could never be breached, I don't know what I'd do. Even though the world she comes from turns my stomach now, even though the air of superiority she can't seem to control sometimes makes me seethe, even after everything that's happened, she is mine. My Melody. My soundtrack.

I've loved her for so long that I can't remember how it felt not to. And it's because I love her that I don't tell her how empty and vacuous the world she inhabits seems to me now. It's because I love her that I don't mar her psyche with the things I've seen. It's because I love her that I don't tell her what I've seen her do. It's because I love her that I slipped the Valium into her drink tonight, so she won't have to look. Won't have to know who I've become, or learn what I know. She won't have to watch me destroy Dax Miller, and bring the whole fucking house of cards down with him.

When you love someone, you keep them from harm.

She drains the rest of her spiked Merlot as the chamber preview begins. Tonight's virtual reality scenario is the reason why more people than ever are tuning in. The details have been 'accidentally' leaked online to generate interest. You've always got to think about the ratings, that's what the producers tell us. And for once, I'm completely on board. I want every pair of eyes in England glued to a screen. Every pair of eyes, that is, apart from hers.

She shuffles slightly in her chair. Yawns. Her lids are growing heavy, starting to droop. She fights it a little, curious about the chamber despite all her protestations. But she can't hold off for long. When she succumbs to sleep, I grab the blanket from the sofa and place it over her gently. Before I head for the door, I kiss the top of her head.

"I'm going to fix it, Mel. I'm going to fix it all. I promise."

PART 1

DON'T DRINK THE WATER

1

I was seven years old when the taps were turned off and we were plunged into poverty. Although there have been many accidental twists of fate that have led me to where I am now – and I won't pretend that some of them weren't my own fault – it was the events of that day that first set me on my path to Whitefield. I, like millions of others, saw my life change and my future dissolve almost overnight, and we were powerless to stop it. We were victims of a catalogue of circumstances that conspired to seal our misery.

If the ship had been just a few miles further out, if the wind had been blowing in another direction, if the tide had turned, or if the authorities had been able to identify what they were dealing with a little earlier, then perhaps my life would have been very different.

Little Josef Rodgers, his face covered in blisters, grabbing at his throat as he suffers through his final breaths with the white residue of the Mr Whippy ice cream he'd been eating smeared across his cheeks, is of course the most iconic image from that day. But it wasn't the first one I saw. Instead it was the footage of ambulances and army trucks lining the coast roads and men shrouded in bright yellow biohazard suits frantically handing out gas masks in front of Brighton pier that first alerted me to the fact that something was very wrong.

I asked my parents what was happening, in between

mouthfuls of spaghetti hoops and chicken nuggets, but they had no idea either.

"Must be an industrial accident," Dad said. "Loads of factories round that way, aren't there?"

"But it's not just there," Mum replied, scraping her dinner into the bin. She seemed to have lost her appetite. "It's the whole south coast. Jenny's cousin lives in Devon, and she's been told to stay inside, Jenny says. Keep doors and windows shut and all that."

It soon emerged that it was a national emergency, on a scale not seen since wartime. A scale I couldn't possibly comprehend at my tender age. An unidentified cargo ship carrying biological and chemical weapons had caught fire, just a few miles off the south coast. The authorities didn't know which country had been transporting them illegally in our waters or why, and I didn't really understand the technicalities at the time, of course. All I knew was that a lot of people down south were very sick. There was something in the air that could kill them, so they were being moved inland. It was an awful thing that had happened to people who didn't deserve it, and I hoped they'd be alright. But I had no clue that soon it would impact my little world too.

For a few days, life went on as normal, apart from all the worried chatter from the adults. The school had a collection – old clothes and toiletries, things like that, to be sent to the displaced children who had had to flee their coastal homes in haste, but that was as far as it went. Until the morning I turned the tap on to brush my teeth, and nothing came out.

"Muum," I called out, "the bathroom tap's not working."

"Oh, for God's sake." She rushed in tutting and shoved me out of the way, but fiddle as she might not a drop emerged from the tap. She pushed the button on the toilet, and smiled in satisfaction when it worked. But her relief was short-lived when the swirling flush ended abruptly, without the churn of the cistern refilling.

"Must be a burst pipe or something," she said. "I'll call the water company later and find out. In the meantime, you still need to get dressed for school. Don't look so worried, Cal. It's just a water outage, not the end of life as we know it."

She didn't know how wrong she was.

* * *

The water wasn't back on by teatime. It never came back on again, but we lived in hope for a good few months until the reality of the situation slowly dawned on us. Along the coast, the water had stopped running almost immediately after the accident – the plants used safety valves, which automatically shut off as soon as the contamination was detected. As an emergency measure, neighbouring counties had rerouted some of their supplies to assist, but now the reserves were gone. With the groundwater, and rainwater, potentially contaminated by toxins, the powers that be felt it was too dangerous to allow people to consume water from the southern quarter of England, at least until they could ensure these new biological threats were completely eliminated in the treatment process.

The air may have been breathable again down south, but the water wasn't drinkable (neither, as we would later discover, was the land farmable, or the sea and rivers fishable). No one could precisely pinpoint the exact location where natural sources were no longer at risk, so a line had to be drawn somewhere – and that somewhere was the Thames.

Every water source south of the Thames was potentially unsafe, the experts declared, and therefore every tap, pipe and drain went dry. But we were assured that solutions were being found, it was just a matter of time. "Just keep on keeping on," the cheerful local news anchor said with a wink. "Help is on its way. Let's pull together, and see this through."

For the first few weeks, the government trucks rolled in every day, filled with bottled water. Kind and concerned people from across the river filled bottles, buckets and old milk containers from their own taps and brought them to us. Although there was no longer anybody alive who had lived through the Second World War, there was much talk of 'Blitz spirit' and a rosy, almost nostalgic sense of community and togetherness.

But the love-thy-neighbour attitude didn't last long. As the weeks went by, fewer and fewer people made the trip across the river each day with supplies. Local shops began stocking bottled water from floor to ceiling, at extortionate prices, which all the adults scoffed at – to start with. "Does that cheeky twat down the corner shop think I'm going to pay through the nose for some Evian rather than walk to the town hall?" Mum laughed. "Does he think we've all got more money than sense? Stupid fool." But when the trucks stopped coming, the cheeky twat had the last laugh.

Somewhere in the heart of London, no doubt in buildings with plush décor and an abundance of water coolers, our fates were sealed by financial advisors and government think tanks. It wasn't 'cost-effective' to build new pipelines in order to bring safe water to the southern counties. Neither was it 'cost-effective' to treat the poisoned rivers and reservoirs. Moreover, it wasn't 'sustainable' to keep sending supplies, given that there was no longer any end in sight. Instead, we would have to learn to be 'self-sufficient' and 'take charge of our own needs'. So the trucks made one last journey, this time to deliver a free water butt to every household and a 'starter pack' of small dissolvable tablets that we were told would make the water safe to use for washing, but not drinking. After that, the government decided it had fulfilled its obligations and we were on our own.

Dad attached the water butt to our guttering, and purchased three more. Mum would boil, treat and cool the water for us to wash in, and for the laundry, but there was never enough. Suddenly there were no more Saturday outings to the cinema or bowling alley, no more Friday night dinners of pizza or fish and chips. No more of the little luxuries that I had come to take for granted.

But kids are resilient, and a major change can become their new way of life incredibly quickly. It was harder on the adults, to have worked so hard for so long to achieve a comfortable life, only to see the cost of everything soar overnight and be left scrabbling just to put food on the table. Looking back, the sense of loss and unfairness must have been almost too much to bear.

It certainly was for Dad, who withdrew almost entirely. When he wasn't at work, he was in bed. And often he was in bed when he should have been at work. I didn't know about things like depression, or stress, back then, and I didn't realise Mum's ultra-enthusiasm and permanent toothy grin were her way of making up for my dad's effective absence. Her way of trying not to let their problems affect my childhood, I suppose.

But it was always inevitable, from the moment that ship caught fire and unleashed its illegal cargo on to the winds, that my life would be swept up in the quicksand of its repercussions. When everything around you changes, you have to change too.

2

Hallow, as the area in which we lived came to be known, crept up around us over the next few years. More and more high-rise apartment blocks were built to house the families who had fled the south coast once its industries had collapsed and its rich business owners had taken their enterprises north, now that land and property along the coast was practically worthless. Those who could afford to moved beyond the river, but those who couldn't, thanks to the catastrophic decline of their assets, found themselves here.

With them came the need for more of everything. More schools, more hospitals, more shops and amenities. The parks and playgrounds where I had learned to ride my bike, hunted for conkers in autumn, and torn across in frantic flight from whoever was currently 'it' became multistorey car parks or public baths. Class sizes doubled, queues at the checkouts trebled, waiting lists at the doctors quadrupled.

At first, my school friends and I hated the 'coasties'; we saw them as a plague that had swarmed north and settled around us, making everywhere crowded and robbing us of our outdoor spaces. It's hard not to be influenced by the chatter of the adults around you. They blamed the new influx of residents for everything – from unemployment to the prevalence of the rats on the streets. Coasties were poor and dirty, everyone knew that. In reality, a lot of the new residents in our area had been far more affluent than we were before the accident. Some of them had fled beautiful country homes, or three-storey beach houses, and wound up living in pocket-sized flats surrounded by rubbish. But children don't see things that way. My friends and I sneered and held our noses if they dared approach us for so much as to borrow a pencil. We were clueless and cruel, not caring that these kids had lost way more than we had.

It felt like they were an invading force, and we couldn't find the compassion – or perhaps the desire – to welcome them into our community. But nothing unifies people like a common enemy, so when the border went up, we all came together in our shared hatred.

The youngsters nowadays are furious at our lack of action back then. Why didn't we stop them, they ask. Why didn't we protest, rage? Why didn't we set up barricades, chain ourselves to bridges? Why did we allow ourselves to succumb to this fate? But the truth is that we simply didn't know. No one tells you that the measures you submit to in a time of crisis will become the new normal, even when the crisis is passed. That's the trouble with living through a major historical event, you don't realise that's what's happening. There's no neon flashing signs or blaring alarms alerting you to the fact that everything you know is about to change, forever. There is no understanding of how what happens today will impact tomorrow. There is only one event, and then another and another – each in response to the last, each seeming, at the time, a perfectly natural and inevitable progression.

* * *

The border went up overnight, with no prior warning. We awoke one drizzly Wednesday morning to the news that, while we had been sleeping, the authorities had been busy turning the arbitrary line that the experts had drawn across the country into a very real, very controversial one. Half of the bridges across the river had been shut completely, the other half were now manned by patrols. Reports soon came in of fences and checkpoints that had suddenly sprung up in the west to mark the edge of the safe-water zone beyond the end of the Thames.

It was a necessary action, the government declared, once they had been forced to admit what they were doing. A regrettable but vital measure for everyone's protection, to prevent theft and the sale of black-market water. Desperate families without the means to afford the ever-increasing cost of bottled water had been making their way across the river to fill containers and buckets from public fountains and bathrooms. Low earners who worked in the city but lived south of the river had been filling flasks from their employers' taps to bring home to their families. Overnight these means of survival had been criminalised, and the country had been irrevocably divided.

There were no 'coasties' any more. There were no Cornish, no Kentish, no Sussex or Surrey residents. We were all lumped together – the unfortunate victims of our geography. Forgotten residents from the arse end of a country that no longer cared about us. Now, there was just them and us. We didn't hate the newcomers any more, all our anger and frustration was directed across the river.

I don't remember where the term 'razzles' came from, or exactly when it became part of everyday vocabulary, but soon it was the slang we all used, usually with a sneer and sometimes even with a spit, to describe everyone north of the Thames – everyone who lived with the luxury they mostly took for granted, the luxury of running water. We similarly lost our previous identities and were all lumped together as one, stuck in the newly formed Hallow. I don't know who coined the name, or why. I've heard it said it's a mixture of Hell and Fallow – in reference to the fact the land could not be used until it had recovered. It seems fitting, so I like to assume it's correct.

As teens in Hallow, we were served rage and despair over

breakfast, lunch and dinner. Our parents, our teachers, even the adults we passed as we walked to and from school, could not contain their anger at the injustice they had been dealt. Words like 'abandoned', 'hopeless' and 'forgotten' swirled in the air everywhere we went. The movies on television were full of people whose lives were nothing like ours, the books we read in class filled with protagonists we couldn't relate to. The world outside Hallow didn't acknowledge our way of life. The idols on the screen didn't have to boil and treat their water, they all jumped in the shower, or turned on a tap to grab a drink or wash their hands. They were nothing like us, which meant we didn't belong in their world, and could never hope to.

My school, like all the others, was underfunded, overcrowded and staffed by teachers who themselves were struggling with a new, harder way of life. My dad managed to get a better-paying job, which meant we could at least afford food and clean drinking water (something that had become an either/or choice for far too many families). But it also meant he had to travel across the river for work six days a week. The border checks added at least an hour to his commute, so he would leave home at 7am and return around eight in the evening, tired and pissed off. Like thousands of others who had been forced to compete for positions that were only marginally better paid in order to survive, he became almost an absent parent. Hardly ever home, and too exhausted from work and despair to have much to do with me when he was.

Mum still worked only part-time at the local supermarket, but the added time and effort involved in doing daily chores like laundry and cleaning without the benefit of running hot water left her exhausted each day. She never asked if I needed help with homework any more, or even whether I'd done it. Dad would slink up the stairs straight after dinner, collapsing into a snore minutes later. She would boil another pan of rainwater to wash the dishes, cursing under her breath as she wrestled with the greasy plates and pans at the sink – the dishwasher sitting dormant in the corner of the kitchen as if to taunt her. Then she would sigh, pour herself a small sherry and shuffle up the stairs, reminding me to switch the lights off when I went to bed, but without the breath or care to nag me not to make it late.

It wasn't long before I began to despise being at home, craving instead the company of my peers – the only people in this godforsaken place who seemed to still exist in technicolour. We thought we were alone, misunderstood. We wanted to find something worth doing, and feeling, in this world that seemed to be disappearing into decay and despondency, just as we were getting ready to inherit it. We were angry, we were horny, we were reckless and short-sighted.

We were the first generation of Hallow teens, and it's fair to say we paved the way for what was to come.

3

It was Jay who first introduced me to VR booths. He turned up at my door on the morning of his fifteenth birthday, wearing a grin and his best faded leather jacket.

"Get those fuckin' rags off," he said, pointing to my uniform which hadn't been washed in nearly two weeks because of the summer drought. "We're bunking today."

Jay and I had become friends by default, the only two boys in our form with a modicum of intelligence, or so we liked to think. He'd moved up from Sussex eight years before, immediately after the accident. His parents had been savvy enough to sell before it became clear that house prices were going to continue to go down. He used to have a double-barrelled surname, Billington-Smythe, but he dropped the hyphen and his mother's maiden name in favour of plain old 'Smith' and that was really just Jay all over. No airs and graces. His family had more money than most in Hallow, but he didn't make a big deal of it. He didn't flaunt his intelligence either. In fact, he barely even used it.

"What are you on about?" I said, stuffing my maths book into my backpack while trying to consume a piece of toast.

"It's my birthday!" Jay proclaimed, throwing his hands in the air with a flourish, as if that explained everything.

"Okay… happy birthday?" I replied, unsure what he was getting at.

"Precisely! Happy birthday to me, and happy fucking day for you too. For, by virtue of being one of only very few human beings I can actually tolerate the company of, I have decided that you, Calvin Roberts, are to join me on this most haw-spicious of occasions. Whereupon, we shall shake off the shackles of the education system and seek out untold delights!"

"I... what?"

Jay rolled his eyes and exhaled loudly. "We're bunking off and having fun. Got it?"

I was a little dubious, but definitely intrigued. "What kind of fun?"

Jay's grin doubled in size and he pulled a handful of banknotes out of his pocket. "Thought it was about time discerning gentlemen such as ourselves got to check out those new VR booths across the river."

"No. Way." Double maths could go whistle. I'd been dying to experience the latest in virtual reality ever since I'd seen the adverts online, but I never thought I'd really get to. "Where the hell did you get all that?"

"Present from my uncle." Jay shrugged, like it was no big deal. "Mum says it's him rubbing our noses in how much more successful he is than Dad. But I just say ker-ching! I'm gonna take this little token of my uncle's esteem and show my boys a good time."

"Boys?"

"Figured we'd take Curly," Jay said. "Don't fancy his chances walking home from school without us, and Christ knows he's never gonna get a girl outside of VR. It's basically a public service."

I frowned. It made sense, but I didn't much like the idea of trying to look inconspicuous with Curly in tow. At six feet tall with a shock of ginger hair and a mouth that seemed compelled to voice every random thought that crossed his mind, he wasn't exactly the most discreet and mature of adventure companions. Harry 'Curly' Kerlwith was as dense as they come, and barely literate. But he had a heart the size of a mountain and would give you his last penny if you needed it. Jay and I had the sense to appreciate that in a friend, and we looked after him. He was the type who could easily be manipulated if left to his own devices. Fortunately, he had us to make sure that didn't happen.

"Okay," I said, feeling guilty that I was disappointed it wasn't going to be just the two of us. "You're right."

"Course I'm right," Jay said, throwing his arm round my shoulder as we headed down the street toward Curly's flat. "It's gonna be the best damn day of your life, Cally baby!"

He was right. In all the days that have come and gone since, I can't recall a better one. And yet, now that the story has played out, I wish it had never happened.

4

We waited by the corner shop for Curly – his mother always watched him from the window until he was out of sight and we didn't want her to see us out of uniform.

"Shit," Curly exclaimed when he spotted us loitering, Jay with a cigarette hanging casually from his lips. "Is it mufti?"

"No, you dappy mare," Jay replied. "It's my birthday. And you, dear Curly, are invited."

Curly raised an eyebrow and looked us up and down. "To what?"

"Adventure!" Jay leapt up onto the short brick wall that separated the shop's driveway from the garden next door. "Intrigue! A quest to sample the carnal delights of the upper classes."

Curly just stared at me in confusion. "We're taking the train into the city to try out the VR booths," I translated.

"Oh," Curly replied. "Well, why didn't you just say so?"

"So." Jay slung his arm around Curly's shoulder. "You in?"

"Yeah, I'm in." Curly grinned.

"Excellent," Jay replied. "Just need to get you both cleaned up a bit, then we're city-bound!"

"Cleaned up?" I asked.

"No offence, lads, but we all reek of Hallow. We can't smell it on each other, of course, because we're all so used to stinking like a nun's bunions. But the razzles will whiff us a mile off. When was the last time you guys had a bath?"

"I scrubbed last night!" Curly protested.

"Yeah," I said, "me too."

"I'm not talking bits and pits in a bucket of water," Jay said. "I mean a real bath. Deep and hot."

I shook my head. It had been months since we'd had enough left over in the butts for a whole hot bath. And even then, I'd gone third after Mum and Dad and the water was murky and tepid. Curly screwed up his face, and sniffed at his arms.

"Right," Jay said. "I think a trip to the bathhouse is in order, are we agreed?"

"No." Curly looked positively terrified. "Uh-uh, Jay. My mum says you'll get verrucas and typhoid if you go in there. Plasters and pubes floating in it, there is. Plus people piss in it."

Jay rolled his eyes. "What do you take me for? I don't mean the pauper baths for the tower-block plebs. I'm talking about the *real* bathhouse. The swanky one up on First Street, where they give you heated towels and everything."

I whistled. I'd never been to The Bathhouse, but I knew all about it. In fact, we'd studied its owner, Kurt Massey, in our business class. "An example of a true entrepreneur; a man who sees opportunities where others see only problems," Mr Warner had told us. Another way of putting it would to be to say that he was a greedy scumbag who capitalised on other people's misfortune. He was the owner of a nationwide chain of hotels, which was still his main business north of the river. But after the accident, he saw a gap in the market.

All of Hallow's old swimming pools had been turned into public baths, and Curly's mum wasn't wrong in her assessment of them. Filthy, festering pools of tepid water collected from government-owned properties where those who lived in apartment blocks and couldn't have their own water butts could have a daily wash, for a nominal fee.

Frankly, they probably came out dirtier than they went in. But Massey realised that for the more 'discerning' (that is, wealthier) residents of Hallow, there was still no alternative but to treat and boil their own water and painstakingly fill a bathtub bucket by bucket. An effort and inconvenience he deduced that people would pay to avoid, if they could.

So, he struck a multimillion-pound deal with a northern water company, and converted all the Massey Inns south of the river into luxury bathhouses. Massey water tankers started to roll through Hallow in the dead of night, always heavily armed.

As much as I disliked the man, I had always wanted to see the inside of a Massey Bathhouse for myself. And it had been an age since I'd soaked in hot, soapy water. "That's awesome, Jay," I said, suddenly feeling guilty that I hadn't even thought to get him a present. "Really. I can't believe you're spending your money on us like this."

"Don't be soft," Jay said. "Who else am I gonna go with? Come on, you daft sods." He skipped ahead, throwing his hands up to the air. "Let the birthday shenanigans commence!"

* * *

The Bathhouse was exquisite. We spent over an hour just floating and luxuriating in the scented, rippling water. I'd forgotten the serenity of it, or perhaps I'd never appreciated it back when a bath was a nightly ritual. I was mesmerised by the deep wrinkles on my fingertips, and the way they felt numb yet exaggerated at the same time. How many years had it been since I'd been in water long enough for my skin to resemble a sultana? Curly's cheeks turned red as he lay on his back in the centre of the pool-sized bath, just staring silently at the ceiling.

"So, what's next then, Jay?" I asked, though I would have been content to stay right where I was.

"Next we head to the station, catch us a train to the city."

After we'd hauled ourselves out of the bath and got dry,

Jay handed Curly a bag of clothes he'd taken from his dad's wardrobe. "Don't want to rock up to the VR booths in school uniform, Curly," he said when the offering of over-starched trousers and an itchy-looking green jumper was met with a grimace. "Some of those programs are age-restricted."

Curly obliged, and we headed to the station, where we were frisked for weapons and asked to state the purpose of our visit before being issued a day pass and allowed to board a train out of Hallow.

It really was another world on the other side of the river. Everything was so bright, so vivid. I hadn't noticed the thin layers of grime that had built up so slowly around me in Hallow; not until I saw life without them. Cars and buses gleamed, almost offensive in their ostentatious colour. Street signs were white – not yellowed or grey – and the bold black letters on them seemed to shout the information they bore. The people walking past were scurrying clouds of long-forgotten scents. Cloying musk, light bursts of floral sweetness, sickly clouds of deep vanilla – all moving through the air, mixing and mingling. It was like being Dorothy when she opened the black-and-white door to Oz and found herself assaulted by technicolour.

But if the vibrancy of the city was a shock to my senses, it was nothing compared to the mind-blowing euphoria of experiencing the VR booths for the first time.

5

When we arrived at the plush, glass-fronted entertainment club, Jay tried to head for the *XXX* section, but was quickly stopped by a burly guy in a suit that looked a little too small for his well-built torso. Unsurprisingly, the adult VR booths required ID to enter, which meant Jay wasn't going to pop his virtual cherry on his birthday as he had hoped. I feigned disappointment, but I was relieved. As far as I was concerned, the adventure programs boasted far more enticing experiences.

"What about *Space Dash*?" Curly suggested as we perused the list of available booths.

"Aliens and lasers?" Jay screwed up his nose. "Nah, that's kids' stuff."

"*Wyrdworld*," I said, pointing to the huge poster on the wall that depicted a band of adventurers fighting a three-headed hydra. "I've heard it's the bollocks."

"Alright," Jay said. "I guess I could be up for that."

We handed our cash to the booth operator, who opened the door to the *Wyrdworld* chamber. "Adventuring together?" he asked. We nodded, and he gestured for us to take our seats.

The VR recliners looked like black leather versions of the chairs you get at the dentist, except that they had wires coming out of them in several places, and Velcro seat belts. The booth attendant gave us each a small handheld touchscreen device on which we could choose our characters. I played it pretty standard, and went for an assassin bedecked in a scarlet tunic and black leather trousers. Curly chose a wizard and opted to go for the full-on stereotype: flowing black robes and a long grey beard. Jay fiddled with his little screen the longest, but wouldn't tell us who he'd chosen to be.

"Alright," the attendant said, taking our devices away. "I'll just upload these character files and you'll be all set. The program starts you off in a safe village, mostly so you can acclimatise. Any questions?" he asked. We all shook our heads. "Okay, so I just need to go through some safety advice."

"Safety?" Curly looked a little pale.

"Relax, Curly boy," Jay said. "You're strapped into a bloody chair, how much safer could you be?"

"Most importantly," the attendant continued, "I need to let you know the safe word. If at any time you experience pain or dismemberment, or a sense of all-consuming terror or total amnesia, you must immediately say the word 'octograph', which will end the game and alert us that you are in need of help."

"I'm not so sure this sounds like fun any more," Curly said, his fingers running along his seat belt, seeking the join.

"Oh, don't be daft," Jay said. "Why octograph?"

"Why not?" the attendant replied with a shrug. "It was chosen as a word that isn't commonly used, but will be easy to remember in an emergency."

"Yeah," I said, "speaking of that. You said to say octograph in case of 'total amnesia', but how would I remember if I had total amnesia?"

He sighed and rubbed his temples. "Look, mate. I'm basically just reading off a card here. I'm not a bloody game designer. I have to say it, so I've said it. It's never happened, and it probably never will. It's just red-tape health-and-safety bollocks, alright?"

I nodded.

"But," he continued, "the pain thing is *very* important. I don't mean a cramp in your leg or whatever, I mean if you start to feel pain from events in the game. Like, if you bang your elbow on a table and it actually *hurts*, not the weird pins and needles you're supposed to get to let you know your character's been injured, but actually hurts like it would if you did it in real life."

I swallowed hard. "Does that happen sometimes then?"

"Not often. Very rare. But the fact is that some people are more suggestible than others, see? So, some people's brains are so convinced by the virtual reality that they even start to send pain signals. Now, it's not so bad if it's just a splinter, or a scraped knee when they've hopped a fence, so some players just ignore it. But what happens when something really bad happens? Like, what happens when you're stuck through with a sword, or a demonic crow pecks your eyes out, and you really feel it? I've only seen it once but, Christ, it was harsh. Dude was sat right in that chair," he pointed to Curly, "and he just starts screaming. Like, howling. When I switched off the game he couldn't even speak. Just sobbed and hugged me."

Curly clawed at his belt. "I wanna switch seats!" he yelled.

"Don't be a div," Jay chided. "It was the guy's brain that did it, not the seat."

"Exactly right," the attendant said. "And it was his own fault. He'd had this talk, same as you, but he chose to ignore it. Then, a ruddy great griffin swept out of the air, tore his chest open with its talons. He couldn't ignore that one. So, do yourselves a favour – if you feel pain, you hit me up with a nice yell of octograph, right? No excuses."

We all nodded and the attendant grinned. "Perfect," he said. "Now, it's up to you how you play it, of course, but I'd recommend you stay in the village for the first night."

"The first night?" I enquired. "How long is this game?"

"Well, you've paid for two hours, so in VR time that's about a week," he replied. "It's all down to the way your brain perceives time, the brainiacs have fine-tuned it so that it works a bit like a dream does. Something to do with neural transmission, or is it neuron transmission? I can't remember.

Anyway, the simulation is effectively 'downloaded' into your brain via the headset, so what seems like an hour happens in just a few seconds. Of course, they could give you even longer for your money if they chose to, but it wouldn't be good for repeat business if you completed the whole year of gameplay in one sitting. So, they give you a week per session."

A week? A week away from Hallow, adventuring with my friends. It seemed too good to be true. We were handed our headsets and I eagerly put mine on. They looked nothing like the old-fashioned extended goggles I had seen at my local amusement arcades. These were more like leather hoods with built-in earphones, and pliable criss-crossed metal strips sewn into the top so that they could be smoothed down to fit neatly across your skull.

Once we'd got them fitted correctly, the attendant began the countdown.

"Okay, lads," he said. "I'm going to fire up the game. Don't worry if you feel a little disorientated for the first few minutes. Right. Have fun in *Wyrdworld*, guys, your adventure begins in three... two... one..."

6

With the VR headset on, I was in total darkness. My heartbeat thundered in my ears, my limbs feeling limp and large. Then the tiniest buzz: high-pitched and insistent, as though a rogue mosquito had found its way into my headgear. The whine grew louder and deeper, morphing into a whooshing noise like waves breaking all around me as the black nothingness was broken by stark maroon lettering that filled my entire vision.

WYRDWORLD (2.0)

© Heraldgamesinc

No matter which way I turned my head, the title stayed in front of me, even when I closed my eyes. Because, I came to realise, I wasn't seeing it with my eyes but with my mind. I started to wonder if the game had glitched, or failed to load, when suddenly the innocuous letters disappeared, along with reality as I knew it. No one forgets their first real VR. That's what the adverts say, that's what the gamers and enthusiasts say. But what they don't say, because it's hard to find the words to even come close to doing so, is why.

In an instant I was standing in a dusty, noisy village square. Thatched buildings lined the edges, a horse and cart passed by me, people bustled all around holding baskets of goods or draining tankards of ale. I don't know what I'd been expecting. I suppose I thought it would be just a more immersive first-person game, perhaps with better graphics. But these weren't graphics. Not in the way I'd ever have envisioned. There was no sheen, nothing artificial. It was fantasy so realistic that it didn't seem like fantasy at all. I could feel the breeze, smell the horse shit. It was both thrilling and disconcerting, and I wasn't sure at that moment which feeling would win out.

"Cal." A stern, gravelled voice interrupted my thoughts. "Cal, is it you?"

"Curly?" I spun round to meet a robed torso. Looking up, the wizard (who was even taller than real-life Curly) loomed over me, eyes a piercing blue and a beard so long he could have tucked it into his belt.

"Yes," he replied in a booming, authoritative tone. "It is me."

"Christ," I said, squinting at him. "You sound like Gandalf."

"Never mind that. Where's Jay?"

"I…" I scanned the people in the village square, realising that we had no idea which character Jay had picked, and therefore no idea what he would look like. I guess I'd assumed it would be obvious to spot a 'real' player amongst the computer-run characters, but it wasn't. "I don't know. He could be anyone."

"Looking for someone?" A deep, rich voice beside us made us jump. We turned to see a young man with flowing blonde hair and disconcertingly white teeth. He was wearing a green tunic and tights, with a lyre strapped to his back.

"Jay?" we asked in unison.

"In the flesh! Well, in the pixels technically, I guess. Handsome fucker, aren't I?"

"You're a bard?" I asked, a little thrown off guard.

"Always fancied myself as something of a rock star," Jay replied. "Drowning in groupies, that kind of thing. This was the closest I could find."

It didn't take long to get the hang of the game. By the next morning we had procured some weapons and supplies, booked ourselves rooms at the local tavern, practised our skills at the training grounds, and were ready to go exploring. What followed was six days (or so it seemed) of pure adventure. From slaying monsters in swamps to sneaking through guarded towers to rescue damsels in distress. I don't think I had ever felt so alive.

On our last night we camped out under the stars, roasting the carcass of a sabretooth tiger that we'd worked together to kill. We talked over our escapades, laughing at Jay's failed attempts to seduce noblewomen and Curly's disastrous attempt at casting a love spell for him (somehow he managed to mix up the incantation, and Jay found himself pursued through the village streets by a randy sow – much to the farmer's dismay). Tears rolled down our cheeks as we did our best impressions of the amorous pig and its hot-headed owner. But when a new constellation appeared in the sky, our mirth turned sour.

"It's an hourglass," I said, holding my finger up and tracking its outline.

"Yeah," Jay sighed. "It's the countdown. Time's nearly up."

We sat in silence for several minutes before Curly said what we were all thinking. "I don't want to go home."

"Me neither, bud," Jay replied, squeezing his shoulder in a rare display of affection.

"It's not over." I stood up, a sense of determination overtaking me. "It can't be over. We have to come back. Promise, guys?"

"Sure," Jay said. "Maybe next birthday, eh?"

I shook my head. That was too long, I didn't think I could wait. Though I knew I had very little choice. "I think this is the happiest I've ever been," I whispered, half-afraid Jay would call me soft. But he just smiled.

"Me too," he replied. "You two are pretty decent to go adventuring with. Even if you are wankers."

I laughed, "Takes one to know one, Jay," I said as the

colour started to fade from the world around me. Slowly, ever so slowly, until everything was black.

I felt total disorientation as my headgear was unceremoniously removed and the bright fluorescent lighting of the VR chamber flooded my sore eyes. The attendant said something. We said something back. But it was just white noise. We gathered our things, took the complimentary bottle of water and cookie we were offered, and left the building in a fog of melancholy.

At the station we were frisked, patted down by officious, calloused hands that removed the untouched water bottles from our pockets, and then we were shouted at by their petty, uniformed owner who accused us of trying to smuggle. That was the world we'd come back to. A world that wouldn't let us take a simple drink of water, that we had neither begged nor stolen, on a train home.

We parted ways outside Jay's house with just a nod and a 'see ya', because there was nothing we could say here that could begin to convey everything we felt. By the time I crawled into my bed, after a supper of beans on toast and a dispassionate ticking off from Mum for being late home from school, I couldn't decide if I wished I was still in *Wyrdworld*, or if I wished I'd never been at all. It may have been the most exciting and exhilarating experience of my life, but it just made everything else seem desperately bland and pointless.

* * *

Life carried on, the daily routine slowly chipping away at the memory of my first VR experience, until I could no longer envision it as clearly, or remember precisely how it felt. At first Jay and Curly had talked about nothing else, but as the months rolled on, our determination to revisit seemed to dwindle, and we stopped saving every spare penny, opting to grab a Snickers bar or a packet of crisps when we felt like it instead of squirrelling our allowances away.

Perhaps if Mum hadn't got sick we never would have gone back. Perhaps we would still be friends to this day, or perhaps we would have drifted apart naturally and amicably; Jay would have got a high-profile job and a trophy wife, I'd have worked for a big corporation in the city and raised kids in Hallow just like my dad. And Curly... Curly would have found himself a sweet, homely girl – someone who valued true love and honesty over anything else, and he'd have given her so much laughter, loyalty and adoration that she'd have been the happiest wife in Hallow, and he the happiest man in anywhere.

7

Mum passed on a Thursday afternoon, taking all the light and love in our house with her. Perhaps, if we had had the good fortune to live across the river, the cancer would have been found in time to halt its progress. But we were at the mercy of Hallow's ill-equipped and underfunded hospitals, and after the six months it took for her to get the tests and scans needed to identify the problem, it was already too late to do anything other than ease her pain as she died slowly before our eyes. We were both sitting by her bedside when she took her final breath. Dad lifted her hand to his mouth and kissed it, right on her wedding ring, before reaching across and gently sealing her eyelids shut with the tips of his fingers. He patted me on the shoulder, but did not speak. In an instant he was a different man; a broken man.

* * *

It's strange how the bricks and mortar of a house can stay the same, yet feel completely different. Like the change in a room's acoustics if the furniture is removed, Mum's absence left an echo in our home. The words I spoke seemed to hang unfinished and unheard, not finding their ear. Dad withdrew from the world, and embraced the bottle. When I woke in the mornings, he had already left for work. There was no one to rouse me gently from my sleep, or make sure I had breakfast or clean clothes. I could have skipped school every day if I wanted, but instead I got there early. I couldn't bear to be in the soulless house alone.

Jay had found some older friends, and I didn't see as much of him as before. He still hung out with us from time to time, always acting as if there was no one in the world he would rather spend his time with, but his presence was fleeting and for the most part it was just Curly and me now. But I couldn't have wished for a better friend. I took to going home with him most days, and his mum would give me the concern, and even the nagging, that was missing from my own home.

I don't think I've ever met a more wonderful woman than Patty Kerlwith. It didn't take many evenings spent as a guest in her ramshackle apartment to make me deeply ashamed of any snobbish thoughts I'd ever had about Curly's family or situation. As soon as she realised I dreaded going home, she gave me everything she could, from home-cooked meals to hugs and a shoulder to cry on. There hasn't been a day in all these years that I haven't thought of her. And it hurts. It hurts beyond endurance to think of her, because I cannot bear the knowledge of what I did. I destroyed that woman, that wonderful, vividly compassionate and fiercely kind woman. I tore her heart to shreds because of my own selfish greed, and she never even knew it was me who was to blame.

8

Everyone who lives in Hallow is trying to escape it, one way or another. I know that now. I know it in spades. Everyone has their own desperation, their own craving, their own ways of getting through a life of hardship and drudgery. But in the months after Mum died, I felt as though no one could be as trapped and unhappy as I was.

There was only one thing I started to desire, only one way I could see to bring a little light into my life, and that was to revisit the happiest of my days – in *Wyrdworld*. I broached the subject with Curly, and he was just as eager as I was. But, of course, there was the ever-present obstacle in our way.

"It'd be awesome, Cal, don't get me wrong," Curly said as we sat on the wall outside the corner shop devouring a packet of Wotsits between us. "I deffo want to. I loved being a wizard, made me feel all powerful and like... useful. But," he held up the empty packet, "I just spent my last 50p on these. Won't get no more cash till God knows when, and it'll be nowhere near enough when I do."

"I know," I sighed. "I haven't got any money either. Christ, Curly. I just... I just really need this, you know? I can't..." I could feel my voice starting to shake, and a sharp prickle made me swipe at my eyes. But I never had to worry about being macho around Curly, he never cared about stuff like that.

"I know," he said softly, touching me on my shoulder

with his Wotsit-stained hand. "I know, mate. We'll think of something. I promise."

I smiled at him. I didn't think we would, but he was trying his best. As we sat on that little stone wall, our fingers and lips covered in cheesy crumbs, I knew the guy beside me was the greatest friend anyone could have. Unfortunately, if he felt the same way about me, he was wrong.

Later that evening, I was taken by surprise when Jay knocked on my door. Dad had already returned home from work and retreated to his bedroom, and I was wrestling with quadratic equations at the kitchen table. I ushered Jay in and as he cast an eye around the room I suddenly became aware of how we had let the place go since Mum had been gone.

"So," Jay said, "Curly came to see me earlier."

"Yeah?"

"Yeah." Jay clicked his tongue, shifting awkwardly from one foot to the other. "Listen, man. I just wanted to say I'm sorry."

"What for?"

"I've been a shit friend. I haven't been around as much as I should have. I… well, I've been busy, and I should have made more time to check in with you. It's shit, losing your mum. I should have come around more, taken you out more. I know Curly's been looking out for you, but… I should have been too."

I felt a lump in my throat, and swallowed hard against it. "Don't sweat it," I said. "Like you said, you've been busy."

Jay shook his head. "Not fucking good enough. I see that now. Curly made me see it, of all people."

"What exactly did he say?"

"Proper laid in to me, he did. Told me I'd abandoned you, right when you need me most. I've never seen anything like it. Never knew he had it in him. Christ, Cal. You shoulda seen him, he was ranting and raving and stabbing his finger at me, and his cheeks went all red – looked like a fucking psychotic tomato."

I laughed. I couldn't imagine Curly getting angry like that. But I was deeply moved too. To think he got so worked up, just for me.

"Anyway," Jay continued. "He's really worried about you, mate. And so am I. He told me what you'd said, about needing money, and it just so happens, I might be able to help with that." He pulled out his wallet and produced a stack of notes.

"Christ on a bike, Jay. What did you do, rob a bank?"

"Nah." He grinned. "Let's just say I found myself a little part-time hustle. Curly thinks I'm working at the supermarket, he's been asking me to put in a word for him. But you can't make this kind of dough stacking shelves. Look, this has to stay between us, you can't tell Curly. But if you're serious about making money, I can get you in."

"In where?"

Jay rolled his eyes. "In on the gravy train, you dense twonk. But *just* you, not Curly. I'm serious. He can't be involved. If I let you in on this, you have to swear you won't say a word to him."

"Alright."

"Swear it, Cal."

"Okay, okay. I swear I won't say a word about it to Curly. Christ, Jay. What the hell is this job? Anyone would think it was MI5 or something, the way you're carrying on."

"Is your dad home?"

"Yeah, but he's fast asleep upstairs."

"Okay, well, I'll show you."

I stared at the small foil packets as Jay pulled them from his pockets and deposited them on my kitchen table.

"Is that—"

"Spice," he said, picking one up and carefully pulling the edges apart to show me the substance inside. It looked like the weird dried-flower crap Mum used to fill little glass bowls with, but it didn't smell like it. "Hallow's drug of choice for those long, painful lives of poverty."

"Jay," I said, images of the emaciated and zombie-like

people in the anti-spice posters at school flooding my mind, "you're not *using* it?"

"Course not." He looked genuinely offended at the suggestion. "What do you take me for? Some shit-for-brains Hallow-lifer? This stuff's the quickest way to make sure you never get out of here. I've got my eyes across the river, you know that. I'd never use it, I'm just selling it, to the kids at school."

I couldn't decide whether I was relieved or disgusted. It certainly explained why Jay had been hanging about with so many new people. "Selling it? Why?"

"For. Mon-ey," he said in a slow, sarcastic tone. "Why else?"

"I know that," I snapped. "I meant why, when you know how dangerous it is?"

"Pfft." He waved his hand. "It's not dangerous. Christ, you don't believe everything they stick on a poster, do you? It's basically just souped-up weed. I just wouldn't touch it because I'm not a deadbeat, directionless moron who wants to bake his noodle."

"But what about the kids you sell it to?"

"They're deadbeat, directionless morons already," he said. "C'mon, Cal. You really think the likes of Zack Tucker are ever going to do anything other than work crappy little jobs and have crappy little lives?"

I thought about Zack slouching at the back of the maths class, chewing gum and carving swear words into the desk with his compass. "No," I admitted. "No, I don't."

"Exactly!" Jay's eyes lit up now, and his hand gestures became more animated. "He'll die here, Cal. So will ninety per cent of the kids we know, and our teachers, our parents, the woman in the grocery shop and the man who sweeps the streets. They're here for life, and they know it. Open your fucking eyes, mate. Everyone here needs a crutch. Whether it's the bingo on a Saturday, a bottle of Jack of an evening, a bit of spice to numb the pain, or even the occasional trip to the VR booths." He raised his eyebrow at me. "Think about it. You know you've got the brains to make it out of here, but even you can't bear the thought of the next few years without your own little drug to keep you sane."

"That's not fair," I protested. "I've had a really shit time. I'm grieving."

"Yadda, yadda." Jay rolled his eyes, and I contemplated socking him. "There's always a reason. I'm not playing it down, Cal. I know your mum dying is shit as hell, and a bigger reason than most, but the point is everyone's got something that makes their days even harder. And everyone needs something to get them through. Your choice of escape is a smarter one, but it's still the same principle. If they weren't buying it from me, they'd just be buying it from someone else."

"And where are you getting it from?"

Jay sighed. "It's best if you don't know. Plausible deniability and all that malarkey. But, I can tell you it's a safe source, and a well-established business model…"

"Drug lords, in other words?"

"Nothing lord-like about 'em," Jay replied. "But yeah, if you like. Trust me, it's a well-oiled machine. It's a totally sweet deal. I just pick up the gear from some middle-manager guy, sell it to the idiots at school and return the money – minus my cut. See, smart guys like us need opportunities. If there aren't any on offer, we have to get creative."

"Or criminal."

"Fuck me, when was the last time you saw any coppers round here give a toss about drugs, Cal? You could sit outside the station and skin up, they wouldn't give a shit. They haven't got the time to go chasing harmless little hustles like this."

He was right. Of course. Drug use was almost as low down on the priority list as littering. There were far worse things happening every hour in Hallow, and the underfunded police force could only do so much.

"So," Jay continued, "now that we've taken care of your moral and legal objections, you want in or not?"

"Me? Sell drugs?" The thought was abhorrent… initially.

"Well, duh. Why d'you think I showed you? You said you wanted money, and this here is a bona fide business opportunity. Look, you wouldn't even need to ever meet the suppliers. I can shift twice as much with you helping, I'll just split my cut with you – unofficially. They never even need to know your name."

It *was* the only option on the table, apart from slogging through the next few years without any kind of respite at all – which was a prospect I couldn't bear to contemplate.

"I'll think about it," I said.

And I did. I did think about it, long and hard. I lay awake most of the night, wrestling with my conscience. But it turns out that kind of soul-searching doesn't always lead to you making the right decision.

9

By the time I heard Dad stumble down the stairs and out of the door the next morning, I'd talked myself into it. It's amazing what you can allow yourself to justify if your want is urgent enough. After all, Jay was right, wasn't he? They'd only get it from someone else if not from us; a cog in a machine is not responsible for its ultimate function.

What I hadn't expected was the thrill. Walking right past the teachers with the goods tucked in my trouser pockets, exchanging them for money in playground corners, whispering with Jay in class about when the next supply was due, it all gave me a buzz. Walking those dreary halls I felt like *someone* in a sea of no ones. It was heady, and seductive.

Having a secret with Jay was exciting too. Jay was colourful and exciting, and to be the focus of his attention – to be his equal and confidant – made me feel as though I too was someone to be admired. Something I never felt with Curly.

And that's the rub. I was ashamed of Curly, always had been. I loved him behind closed doors, when we shared our deepest fears and laughed so hard that we snorted. But in public, he was an embarrassment. Always clumsy, graceless and tactless. Always blurting out things best left unsaid and making himself the butt of jokes, always being too loud and drawing attention. Always being the most honest and authentic person I've ever met.

How quickly I forgot everything he'd done for me, how quickly the memories of him beside me in my darkest days faded when I was having my brief time in the sun. His face fell every time I made some cock-and-bull excuse why I couldn't come for dinner, and I *did* feel bad, but I justified giving him the cold shoulder for most of the week by reminding myself that we were funding his trips to the city. He got suss about that too, of course. He may have been a little intellectually challenged, but he wasn't blind.

"How have you suddenly got all this dosh, Cal?" he asked me one Saturday while we were waiting for Jay to meet us outside the bathhouse. "I know Jay's got a job, but you haven't, have you?"

"No," I said, not looking him in the eye. "No, I just had a little windfall. Great-uncle passed away, never even met the guy but he left me some money."

Curly just frowned, the creases on his freckled forehead meeting in a point above his nose. "Seems like something you would have told me," he said. "But then, you never seem to tell me anything any more. I don't like it. You and me, we've always been... what's that word? Simpa... simatic?"

"Simpatico?" I offered.

"Yeah. That. But you and Jay don't seem to want me around any more. I mean, I get it, nobody really wants me around. I'm used to that with everyone else, and if you've had enough of me I could understand that, but why are you taking me to the city all the time if you don't like? That's what I don't get. Am I your friend or not?"

My throat felt dry. He was calling me out. What could I say? How could I explain that even though he was the kindest, most loyal friend I had ever had, I was embarrassed by him? How I could I defend that? I couldn't, because it was indefensible.

"Well, how about that shit?" Jay's voice suddenly interrupted my struggle to find the right words. I hadn't even heard him approach. He wasn't wearing his usual carefree smile, he looked out of breath and pissed off. "Talk about ungrateful!"

"I wasn't asking you, Jay," Curly squeaked. "I was having a private talk with Cal."

"Oh, a 'private talk'. Oh, well, excuse me then," Jay snapped. "Only it sounded to me like you were complaining about being given a free fucking ride, Curly boy. Didn't your mama ever teach you not to look at a gift horse's arse in case you get kicked?"

"Jay." I thought about correcting his use of the phrase, but decided against it. He looked as though he might bite my head off. "Jay, it's alright."

"No, Cal." Jay squared up to Curly, staring straight at him. "No, it is not alright. You want to know the truth, Curly boy? We feel fucking sorry for you, so we take you with us out of the kindness of our hearts. But it's not enough for you, is it? Instead of being thankful, you just whine because you want more attention. Grow the fuck up, you're pathetic."

Curly's lip trembled as he looked at me. "Are you going to let him speak to me like that?" he asked, blinking quickly.

"Curly…" I didn't know what to say. Or do. Jay seemed to have fire dancing behind his eyes, I'd never seen him so worked up. I didn't want to piss him off any more, I needed him. "Curly, I…"

"Right," Curly said, swiping at his eyes with the sleeve of his oversized tartan jumper. "I see how it is." He turned away from me and headed off back towards home.

"Curly!" I called after him. "Curly, wait." But he didn't turn around.

Jay grabbed my arm. "Forget him," he said. "He's dead weight. Who needs Gandalf the ginger anyway? We'll do better without him."

"That was a bit harsh, Jay," I said. "I think you really upset him."

Jay just laughed. "Me? He expects a bit of stick from me. Nah, Cal. It was you not telling me to shut up that really stuck the dagger in. I swear I actually heard his heart break."

I knew he was right, and it made me want to vomit.

"Oh, c'mon," Jay said, "I'm only messing. Let's go and have a bath."

He still seemed rattled. I had a feeling he'd been upset by something more than just Curly's questions, but when I asked him he just said, "Everything's peachy, Cally baby. Everything's peachy," and grabbed a towel from the warming rack in the Massey lobby.

10

Curly stopped talking to us altogether after that day. He would avoid even making eye contact at school, and it made my stomach flip over every time I saw him. I didn't blame him, he was owed an apology but I was too weak and self-serving to give it. Instead, I tried to pretend I didn't care, tried to convince myself I was better off with Jay, that he was a better friend than Curly anyway. But I knew that was horseshit, even before what came next.

It was a crisp, chilly morning in February when Jay turned up late for school sporting a cut lip and a graze on his cheek. He mumbled an insincere apology to Ms Dixon and slouched into his seat beside me. "What happened to your face?" I hissed under my breath.

"Tripped," Jay said. "Stupid bloody trainers." He stretched his leg out and wiggled his foot to show the worn soles that were starting to come away at the front. "Need to talk to you at lunch, got an errand I need you to do."

I frowned, wondering what it could be and whether I wanted to do it. It wasn't like Jay to send me on errands, either we worked together or he conducted business by himself. He liked to be in full control. I guessed it couldn't be anything too important if he was giving me the reins on it.

"So," he said when we'd finally got our chips from the

canteen and found an empty table to eat them at. "We need to expand."

"Expand?"

"Yeah." He picked up a chip and swirled it in ketchup before biting into it. "It's the nature of business. Speculate to accumulate, evolve or die, all that jazz. Suppliers are very pleased with the customer base we've built up, but they say we need to grow, to stay competitive like."

"It's selling drugs to schoolkids, not a burger franchise!" I protested.

"Doesn't matter, Cally baby. Principle's the same in all businesses. It's just the logical next step."

"Expand where?" I asked, feeling a bit uneasy at the prospect. I never envisioned doing more than just selling to my peers here, on home ground.

"Oakbridge Grove," he said, with a mouthful of greasy potato and sauce. "To start with."

Oakbridge Grove was the closest high school to ours, just a mile or so further along the river. "And you want *me* to go? What am I supposed to do? Just rock up and start offering people spice?" My blood ran cold at the thought.

"No, you doughnut. It's all in hand, I've already set it all up. I know a guy there, see? Jake, his name is, he's one of the football players so everybody knows him. He's spreading the word amongst the kids, all you have to do is wait under the big tree by the back gates and the customers will come to you! Piece of piss, even you can handle that much on your own, surely?"

"So why aren't you gonna come with me?"

"Too risky. My dad knows the headmaster, they're in a quiz team together – down The George every Friday night. If he saw me hanging around he'd be bound to mention it, and then Dad would get suss."

I shook my head. "I'm not sure this is a good idea."

"It's not up to us, though, is it?" Jay said, rolling his eyes. "Without a supply coming in, we haven't got a business.

So when the boss says jump, we jump. Otherwise he'll go elsewhere. There's plenty of people lining up to take our spot."

I sighed. He was right, of course, any number of kids would give their right arm for our positions. And they'd happily do as they were told, being smart enough to know that there were no other ways for a fifteen-year-old to earn money. So it was sell at Oakbridge, or don't sell at all. No more money, no more status, no more VR. I couldn't bear the thought of losing the only things that made life bearable for me.

"Alright," I said. "If you promise it's that easy."

"Scout's honour," Jay said, making a finger signal that looked like a cross between the Nazi salute and a Vulcan greeting. I guess he'd never actually been a scout.

So I took the extra packets of spice that Jay had brought in to school with him and stashed them in my pockets. I had to skip last lesson in order to make it to Oakbridge before their gates opened and the students started spilling out. I was nervous as hell when I positioned myself on the east side of the large oak at the back entrance, just as Jay had instructed me to. But it was all just as easy as he'd promised. A tall kid in a football jacket approached me and introduced himself as Jake, and from there the customers rolled in, just as Jay predicted. Jake hung around, keeping a lookout for any faculty or passing cops, and the whole thing was over in less than fifteen minutes. I had a pocket full of cash to take back to Jay, and hardly any spice left.

"Hey, thanks, man." Jake shook my hand vigorously once all the stragglers had departed and the street was clear. "I know we all appreciate it. Good quality shit is hard to come by round here, what with the zoning. And we're tired of getting ripped off by the Berkleys, y'know?"

I had no idea what he was talking about, but I smiled and said, "Yeah, totally," before heading back towards home. In truth, I was buzzing. It was the first time I'd ever sold to new clients without Jay there do to the talking, and I'd smashed it. These kids had welcomed me onto their turf like I was a rock star. I felt accomplished, and a little smug.

I was anxious to get back and crow about my success to Jay. So I decided to cut through the disused industrial estate to shave a bit of time off my journey. The wind was getting up. It whistled and shrieked around the empty buildings while old tin cans rattled across the cracked concrete, heading in no particular direction. I was halfway across, just passing the gates of the old timber merchants, when I spotted Curly riding towards me, his face beetroot from the effort of pedalling against the wind.

I thought about calling out to him. Here, where there was nobody but the two of us – no Jay to get in the way. Maybe I'd be able to make peace, add another little victory to the day's inventory. So I tried to make eye contact as he approached. For a split second, his gaze met mine and I started to open my mouth to say hello. But almost instantly he raised his head and stared behind me, setting his face in a frown.

He was pretending he hadn't seen me. *How fucking childish*, I thought. *Screw him then. Stupid little prick.* I sped up, I had my own business to attend to. No point wasting time dwelling on Curly and his pathetic strop.

I was passing the boarded-up windows of what used to be an electrical wholesaler when someone hit me from behind and I lurched forward, splaying my hands involuntarily to keep from smashing my face as I plummeted to the ground. Between the noise of the wind and the crest of arrogance I was riding, I hadn't heard the footsteps behind me. Hadn't realised I was being followed.

A pair of vice-like hands grabbed me by my shoulders, yanked me to my feet and spun me around, slamming my back into a brick wall. There were two men, both much larger than me. Older too; they must have been about nineteen or twenty. They were dressed in ripped jeans and leather jackets. The tallest had a scar that ran from the corner of his right eye down to his chin, the shorter one had a snarl on his face and a spliff in his hand.

They had me trapped against the wall. Scarface tilted my

chin, making me look him directly in his sewage-green eyes. "And where the fuck do you think you're going, buddy?" he growled.

"H-home," I replied, frantically trying to work out what they might want or what I could say to get myself out of this situation.

"Guess again." The shorter one laughed and blew smoke in my eyes.

I coughed, and tried to stop my bladder from betraying me. "What do you want?"

"What do we want?" Scarface smiled, eerily. "Why, we just need to send a message. To your boss."

"I-I don't have a boss," I protested.

"Now don't start fucking around with me." Scarface's voice got deeper, and his grip on my collar got tighter. "I am not in the mood, you little shit. I already told your shitty little 'colleague' the deal this morning. I don't repeat myself. I have better things to do with my time than chase after school brats who think they're gangster."

"I-I'm not. I don't. I don't think I'm gangster, I swear. I don't know what you're talking about."

He reached into my pocket and pulled out the cash and the spice and waved them at me accusingly. "Oakbridge is in Berkley's zone," he said, his face so close to mine our noses were almost touching. "And you ain't one of Berkley's boys. I'm betting you're one of Fisher's, just like that little prick we caught trying to deal there this morning. We warned you. And you only get one warning." He pulled a knife from his belt and I felt all the warmth drain out of me.

In an instant, I realised how dumb I'd been. Jay had lied to me. Tripped over his trainers, what a crock of shit. He'd been late for school because he'd been trying to deal at Oakbridge, and he'd run into these two. How could I be such an idiot? I thought I was just dipping my toe, but I was in this up to my neck. I knew nothing about the politics and etiquette of the world I'd allowed myself to be sucked into. I didn't even know who our boss was, I'd always thought that was a good thing – until now.

"I don't know," I squeaked. "I don't know who we work for, I swear. My friend, my friend Jay, he's the one who deals with the supplier." I didn't have a moment's hesitation in dropping Jay in it, considering I'd just learned that he'd sent me walking unarmed into the lion's den. "And he didn't tell me about your warning, I promise. I'd never have gone there if I'd known."

"Know what, kid?" Scarface said, cocking his head to one side sympathetically. "I actually believe you. I do. You look like a smart kid. Too smart to mess with Berkley on purpose. I don't often buy what people tell me when they're at the end of my knife, but on this occasion, I do."

I exhaled with relief. It was then that I noticed something out of the corner my eye. A flash of ginger. It was Curly, crouching behind a wall a few feet away, his messy curls just visible above the bricks, blowing in the wind. That was why he'd stared beyond me, he'd seen these two following me. He must have ditched the bike and sneaked back to check on me. My heart soared a little, despite the panic that was only slightly fading now.

"Unfortunately," Scarface continued, "it doesn't actually matter whether I believe you or not. It's not you, or that shitty friend of yours, I need to get the message to. It's Fisher."

"I can do that," I said, chancing a sideways glance to see Curly creeping towards us. "I can give him a message, I swear I can."

"Yeah, you can," Scarface nodded. "But I'm afraid there's only one language Fisher understands." He pushed my shoulder into the wall with one hand, and drew back the knife with the other. I scrunched up my eyes and braced for the end.

"AAAAHHHHHHHHH!" Curly's battle cry pierced the air, and instead of being hit by a blade, I was knocked to the ground by a leaping ginger missile. His full weight crushed me into the concrete and the back of my head hit the wall.

"Fucking run!" the shorter guy yelled as I became aware of the shriek of sirens in the distance.

My assailants fled in a flurry of curses and I tried to catch my breath, but Curly was crushing me. "Curly," I croaked. "You saved my life, dude. They're gone, Curly. Curly, you can get up now." I pushed up his shoulders so that his face was looming over mine. His eyes were wide and his face ashen. He opened his mouth to say something, but instead he coughed and blood poured out, covering my chest.

"Curly!" I managed to wriggle out from under him and scramble to my feet. "Curly!" It was only when I turned around to see him lying face down on the concrete that I saw the blade protruding from his spine.

11

"Curly!" I shook him in desperation, cupping his chin in my hands and staring helplessly at his bulging, lifeless eyes. "Curly, wake up! Please! The sirens are coming, Curly. You're gonna be okay if you just wake up. Please, Curly, please!"

A hand touched my shoulder and a deep but soft voice spoke. "He's gone, kid. I'm sorry, but he's gone. And you need to go too."

I looked up to see a willowy, greying man dressed in overalls that were splattered with green paint. I didn't know it in that instant, but that man would turn out to be one of the biggest influences in my life, and one of the best.

"Who are you?" I asked, refusing to let go of Curly even as the stranger tried to gently pull me away.

"My name is Ben," he replied calmly, holding his hand out for me to shake, as if he was introducing himself over a meeting table, not over the corpse of my best friend. "I'm working in that building over there." He pointed to a red-brick building with graffiti all down one side. "Those sirens, that's the police. I called them when I saw those guys grab you. I think you got yourself into a bit of trouble there." He nodded towards the foil packets of spice that were still scattered on the ground. "Am I right?"

I nodded weakly. "But that doesn't matter," I said. "Not now. Only Curly matters."

"Curly's gone," Ben said matter-of-factly. "Nothing can

change that. Now you need to go, get yourself inside. See those brown doors? You go run in there and wait for me."

"But… But I need to talk to the police! Those guys killed my best friend."

Ben nodded. "That's as may be, kid. But I'm telling you now that if you speak to those officers in the state you're in you'll regret it. A boy from Hallow running drugs, you're an easy target. They'll twist your words, use your grief against you. Confuse you and get you to say things you don't mean. You need to think about what you're going to say very carefully, or this could be the afternoon that defines your whole life."

There was something about him that was so genuine, so in control. My head was spinning with a thousand different thoughts at once, I barely knew up from down – let alone what the right course of action was. So I nodded and headed for the door he'd pointed to, speeding up when the sirens got really loud.

I made it through the brown doors just as the first cop car rounded the corner into the estate. My heart thundered in my ears, and I leaned against the wall feeling as though I might puke. Curly. Of all the people in all the world, why Curly? It should have been me on the receiving end of that blade, it *would* have been me, if it wasn't for that big-hearted idiot throwing himself in harm's way. How could I ever live with it? How could I ever face his mother? What was I going to say to the police? Or anyone for that matter.

The air in the large, dark room was bitter with paint fumes. The same green colour that splattered Ben's overalls was glistening on two of the walls, paintbrushes dumped back into the pot in haste and a smear across the wooden floor where Ben must have trodden in a spillage. I briefly wondered what it was he was trying to achieve; no businesses ran round here now. The costs of any kind of manufacturing were prohibitive in Hallow, and no amount of fresh paint would make the warehouse an attractive economic prospect.

I crouched below the large, filthy window that looked

out across the trading estate and risked a peek over its sill. Ben stood beside Curly's body, deep in conversation with several police officers. They nodded and tapped at their tablet screens as Ben gesticulated and pointed. One of them prodded at Curly's lifeless arm with the tip of his boot, and it made hot rage burn in my guts. Eventually, an ambulance pulled up – without any blue lights flashing. The paramedics quickly covered Curly up, strapped him to a gurney and wheeled him inside, slamming the doors and stopping to share an anecdote or two with the police. The emergency workers laughed, slapped each other on the back and got into their respective vehicles. As they all drove off, Ben headed back inside.

"I'm sorry you had to see that, son," he said as he entered the building. "Let me get you a cup of something sweet, for the shock." He walked over to a dirty rucksack that lay abandoned in a corner and pulled out a bottle of water which he used to fill an old kettle sitting on what used to be a trade counter.

"I-I'm Cal," I blurted out, not knowing what else to say.

"Pleased to meet you, Cal," he replied with a smile. "Though I wish it were in better circumstances."

"Why did you help me?" I asked, suddenly feeling suspicious of this stranger's motives.

"You're just a kid," he said. "Too many like you round here. Kids living without hope, getting mixed up in things they're too young to fully understand, and paying for it for the rest of their lives. That's exactly the type of thing I'm trying to fight against here."

"What do you mean?" I asked.

"Never mind that right now," he replied. "You've got more immediate things to worry about. I've just lied to the police, told them all I saw was those thugs attacking your poor friend out there. As far as they're concerned, you were never here. I need you to go along with that, for your sake and mine."

"But-but…" My mind swirled. Was he saying I should just pretend I had nothing to do with this, that I didn't even know it had happened? That it wasn't my fault for being so bloody stupid, and greedy, as to follow Jay's lead? "Won't they tell them? The guys who killed Curly, I mean. When they're caught, surely they'll mention me?"

"Cal." Ben looked me directly in the eyes, and spoke softly. "Son, they won't catch them. They won't even try to. Do you know how many kids wind up on the wrong end of some thug's knife in Hallow? The gangs are out of control. They'll just assume your friend was involved somehow, that he brought it on himself."

"But he didn't!" I yelled. "He wasn't! It was me. I was the idiot, I was the criminal."

"I'm aware of that," he said sternly. "And it goes without saying that that stops right now, yes? I haven't lied for you just for you to go throwing your life away. Because you will end up in a cell, or with a knife in you, if you don't change course quick smart, got it?"

"I didn't ask you to lie! I didn't want you to lie!" I was trembling now, trying to fight back the tears. "I'm going to the police, right now. I'm going to tell them the truth. Curly was a decent guy. The best guy. His mum deserves to know that." I started for the door.

"Will it bring him back?" Ben called out.

"What do you mean?"

"It's a simple question, Cal. Will it bring him back? You rotting away in young offenders, and then prison. Will all those years behind bars bring Curly back to life, or ease his mother's pain? It might ease your conscience, but will it stop that poor woman from having to put her son's body in the ground?"

I just stared at him, biting my lip hard as my jaw trembled from the effort of trying to hold back the tears. "Why do you care?" I snapped at last.

"I can't bear waste," Ben said. "What happened to that poor boy – it's a terrible waste, no doubt about that. But it's done now. He's gone. He was a hero, I saw it with my own eyes. He saved you, so however much you hate yourself right now, you have to realise that he thought you were worth saving. I think you have a responsibility to him to prove him right. The only decision you have to make now is whether you're going to wallow in your guilt, or whether you're going to turn yourself around and become a force for good in this world."

12

I didn't go to the police. I didn't go to the funeral either. I couldn't face seeing Patty, or any of Curly's family. The next few weeks were some of the hardest of my life. I lay awake every night, running images through my head of her being told that her beloved boy had been murdered, torturing myself by imagining her sweet, kind face twisted in unimaginable pain and grief.

As for Jay, I never told him what had really happened, but he must have guessed something close to the truth, else he'd have demanded his money. I simply stopped talking to him, declined his calls and shouted "Fuck off!" through the letter box when he banged on my door. I had a thousand rants I wanted to unleash on him, and a myriad of names I wanted to call him, but I couldn't trust myself to speak to him without blurting it all out, and Ben had impressed upon me that it was vital not to tell anyone the truth.

I spent my days with my head down, concentrating on my school work and avoiding conversations. I stopped caring about VR, or making money and the status and prestige that came with it. Somehow, none of the things that had driven me before seemed important any more. I no longer looked for a way out of my reality, choosing instead to do my best to change it both by knuckling down at school, and by throwing myself into a more altruistic pastime.

Every day after school I made my way to the abandoned trading estate to help Ben with his renovations. I had been right about one thing – the warehouse was no good as a business prospect. But Ben had a bigger vision for the dilapidated building than that, he was looking for a way to help the community – a way to give the next generation an alternative to drugs and gangs. Slowly but surely over the coming months, we painted walls, fixed and reglazed windows, carpeted floors and crafted furniture from the dregs of the stock abandoned and left unsecured at the old timber merchant. We added curtains, bookshelves, a kitchenette and a pool table. Ben lobbied the council relentlessly for funding, and eventually they agreed.

So it was that Ben found himself in possession of the finances and permissions required to launch a youth centre, right in the middle of one of the most deprived and dangerous parts of the country. The day the funding came through, he was waiting for me outside the newly replaced door with a wide grin and a six-pack of non-alcoholic beer.

"We did it, Cal!" he yelled out to me as I approached on my bike, my school jumper wrapped around the near-bare saddle to stop the worst of the chafing. "We got the green light! We can open whenever we're ready!"

I'd never worked so hard for anything in my life. Months of sanding, sawing, sweeping and painting, getting more blisters and splinters than I could count, never knowing if it was all just a pipe dream. The feeling of achievement was like nothing else on earth. I took a cold can and clinked it against Ben's before taking a long slug – nothing had ever tasted sweeter before. Nothing had ever tasted so much like victory before.

Later that evening, after we'd ordered a celebratory pizza and chatted for hours about the types of activities and projects the centre could host, Ben's expression turned serious. "I want to show you something, Cal," he said, wiping tomato sauce from his mouth and grabbing his jacket. "Will you come for a little walk to see it?"

I nodded and got to my feet. "Of course," I said. "What is it?"

"It's what we're up against," Ben replied solemnly.

We strolled north, past the school and through the small shopping parade that housed a mixture of second-hand shops, pound stores and takeaways. Ben led the way up the dingy stairwell of the tallest multistorey car park that now stood where the park I used to play football in as a kid had been. From its summit, we could see the bright lights of the city and all its hustle and bustle. But that wasn't what Ben wanted me to see.

"You see that construction site, just along the river past the power station?" he asked, pointing to a large plot of land that was currently filled with half-finished walls, bulldozers and scaffolding poles.

"Yes." I nodded, confused. What was so important about a building site?

"That's Whitefield. Or it will be. The largest prison in the country, by a long chalk." He put his hand on my shoulder and held my gaze. "And they're building it here in Hallow for a reason, Cal. Do you know what that reason is?" I just shook my head. Ben seemed fired up, and deadly serious. "You've been chucked in a hole, your generation. Through no fault of your own, every kid trying to make something of themselves in Hallow is doing so against insurmountable odds. Your lives were thrown off course. Your parents all saw everything they worked for become almost worthless in the blink of an eye, and you've had to suffer deprivation and struggles that no other generation ever has. You think the teens are making bad choices now? You wait until they realise the way out of Hallow is blocked at every turn. No way to make money in Hallow, and no way to get out of Hallow without money. They're doomed to work themselves into early graves, just to earn enough to put food in their bellies so that they can work some more. You're all spiders in a bathtub. You'll scrabble and scramble to get free, wearing out your bodies and souls with the effort. But even if you could get a foothold, the bastards with their hands on the taps don't want you to. You horrify them, you disgust them. And if they see you making headway, they'll flush your spindly arse down the drain and call themselves heroes. Do you get what I'm saying, Cal?"

"I... I'm not sure."

"The kids of Hallow, they're already incarcerated. Poverty and hopelessness are a form of prison in themselves, and too often they lead youngsters to make desperate, dangerous choices. Just like you did when you agreed to sell with Jay, right? You wanted to escape reality. Well, so do thousands of kids just like you. But outside Hallow, they don't care about the cause of our despair, they only care about treating the symptom. Whitefield is a prison within a prison, a way to lock up the kids that go bad, instead of trying to stop them going bad in the first place. And it's a trap far too many round here are going to fall into. That's why the centre's so important, Cal. I know we can't help everyone, but if I can save a kid – even just one kid – from that fate it'll be worth it, right?"

"You already did," I said, squeezing Ben's arm. "You saved me."

PART 2

ZERO TOLERANCE

1

From the very first moment I laid eyes on Mel, all I wanted to do was to keep her from harm.

I'd managed to make it to my early twenties, and through college, with relatively little trouble, considering how Ben's prediction had proved correct and disorder in Hallow had climbed to new heights once my generation had come of age. If anything, I was doing my bit to improve matters by working at the centre, which had become a hub for kids who needed guidance, a shoulder to cry on, or even just somewhere safe to hang out after school. I'd volunteered for years but, as if by providence, Ben received extra funding just as I finished my course on common law, and was able to take me on full-time. I loved the job, and was relatively happy with my life. I'd even put aside any notions of getting out of Hallow. Here I was making a difference, people needed me and that felt good. I fell into a pattern of working all week and then spending most of my money at the bar with friends on the weekends. It wasn't much, but I was content. I no longer craved escape, or yearned for anything more, until the evening that Melody went wandering where she shouldn't and changed everything.

* * *

Sometimes, something enters your sphere of vision that's so out of place, so alien, that it shocks you and causes you to catch your breath. When I leapt up from the stained, ragged sofa of our usual dive bar to chase the mysterious girl in the designer coat down the street that night, the guys thought I was just drunk and horny. But it wasn't attraction, not then. She was beautiful, don't get me wrong. Christ, she was probably the most beautiful girl I had ever seen outside of a VR booth. But that wasn't why my heart started pounding when she walked past the smeared windows. It was because it was *wrong*.

It was like seeing a polar bear in a desert, or a fish on the pavement. People like her don't walk down the streets in Hallow, especially not at night. She was rich, it was obvious. From her immaculately styled hair, to the crisp new clothes she wore, to the fact that she was carrying a handbag, everything about her made her a target. She looked lost. But then she'd have to be, to be in Hallow. Everyone was, one way or another.

Rich. Alone. Lost. And heading towards the Moorings.

"I've got to stop that woman." I slammed my half-drunk pint down on the table, and shuffled my way along the seat and out of the booth.

"Easy, lover boy," Lars slurred, wiping the foam from his Guinness off of his greying stubble. "You ain't got a chance with a razzle like that."

"Likes 'em posh, I reckon," Jez joined in. "Hey, Cal. See if she's got a sister, eh?"

I ignored them and pushed through the crowd at the bar, knocking someone's pint in my haste. I didn't care that the guy was shouting obscenities at me, all I could think about were the Frank Street Boys, and the things that I knew went down at the Moorings after dark.

By the time I got outside, she had already turned the corner. All the shops were closed now, their graffiti-covered shutters locked down for the night. With half the street lights broken, the only obvious sign of people was coming from across the water, past the Moorings. If you were lost, it's where you'd head. Down to the banks, across the bridge and towards the bright lights of the more affluent side of town, with its array of restaurants and nightclubs.

But there were people between here and there. People who gathered in the shadows. And she'd be heading right for them.

As I raced down to the banks, the stench of the polluted water grew stronger. She'd picked up her pace, probably because she'd heard my footsteps thundering towards her and assumed she was being chased by a madman. I called out, "Miss! Miss, please stop. It's not safe that way," and she glanced behind her, wide-eyed, before breaking into a run. I couldn't blame her. A scruffy, breathless and wheezing man shouting at you on a dark street should rarely be obeyed.

She reached the dirt track by the line of dilapidated boats and took a sharp right, heading for the bridge. She didn't see the youths gathered in the shadows of the old shack that used to be a riverside café, but they had seen her.

A tallish lad dressed in a black hoodie stepped out in front of her, forcing her to skid to a halt. She tried to dash around him, but he blocked her way and shook his head. "Uh-uh," he said slowly as his cohorts stepped out from behind the shack and lined the path beside him. "Not so fast, little diamanté girl. We're gonna have a little chat, yeah? Real friendly, alright?"

I recognised the voice. Thank God. Struggling for breath, I came to a stop a yard or two away from them. "Vincent Felton," I yelled in my best teacher-esque voice. "Is that you?"

Vincent pulled off his hood and leaned forward, squinting into the darkness at me.

"Beanie?" he said, frowning. "What you doing here, man?"

Beanie was the nickname the kids at the centre had for me, short for 'beanpole'. A not-too-subtle play on my height, and lack of girth. I chose to believe it was meant affectionately. With kids like Vincent, you've got to find any positives you can.

"Who's with you?" I said, ignoring his question. "Harry?

Jock? Spooner? Christ, are you dealing out here still? You know Ben can't keep you out of Whitefield if you get busted again, right?"

The three lads next to Vincent stepped forward, mumbling apologetically. I just shook my head. The Frank Street Boys weren't regulars at the centre, but they came in when they needed legal help – which was often enough. I wish I could say they weren't really bad kids, the way people do when they know and love a juvenile delinquent. But they were. They were bad kids. Sure, they had their redeeming features, no one is rotten all the way through. In Vincent's case, it was his love and loyalty for his younger brother Danny, and for his 'crew', that really stood out. I was an important part of Danny's life, which is why I knew it was safe for me to intervene. Vincent had nothing but respect for anyone who helped his friends or his brother.

"I weren't gonna do nothing, Beanie," he said. "I was just playing."

"Well," I said, "you're not a kid any more, Vincent. That birthday you had was the end of any leeway, in the eyes of the law. Time to put the toys away, eh? If you can't do it for yourself, at least think of Danny. He needs you, how would he cope if you went to jail?"

That did it. I knew it would. Vincent may have been a drug-dealing, store-looting, knife-toting gangster on the outside, but he was never late collecting Danny. That says a lot about a person, or at least about where their true priorities are. He loved that kid. How could he not? I loved that kid too. At fifteen, he was nothing like his older brother. There was a nervousness to Danny, and a kindness about him, that made adults want to protect him and nurture him just as much as it made his peers want to attack and ridicule him. I always felt a little anxious if he hadn't emerged through the squeaky door of the centre by 4pm.

Sometimes, he'd turn up with a black eye, or his bag ripped. He never wanted to talk about what had happened, he'd just shrug and smile and say, "Never mind that, Beanie. How's about I whoop you at pool again?" At first I used to worry that his notorious sibling was inflicting the beatings. But from the way Danny gushed about his older brother, and the stony, resolute look on Vinnie's face whenever he spotted a new injury on Danny, I knew he wasn't the perpetrator. Frankly, I felt scared for whoever was.

At the mention of his younger brother, Vincent sighed, put the blade back in his pocket and held up his empty palms as he stepped aside to let the woman go on her way. But she didn't move. She was just staring at me, frozen. "Alright, man," Vincent said. "Have it your way, bro."

"Good." I smiled, and gestured to the trembling woman to come to me. "It's alright, Miss. Would you like me to take you home?"

She stepped forward, nodding. That's when I saw her properly for the first time, her delicate face tear-streaked and bathed in moonlight. She stumbled a little, then bent down to examine her foot. The heel on her bright red shoe had snapped as she'd tried to flee. When I held out my arm for her to take hold of, she smiled at me.

And that's when my recollection gets hazy. I think the Frank Street Boys said something more, I think I asked her if she was alright, I know she told me her name, but all the details are blurry. There's practically a soundtrack to my memory. I'm not sure exactly what it is, some kind of concerto I guess, I never was very up on my classical music. But it's dramatic, all full of crashing drums and urgent tubas. Something bombastic and magnificent. Something life-changing.

We walked toward her side of town, she told me how she'd been distracted while talking on her phone and got off a station too early. "I don't usually take trains," she said, almost apologetically. She asked me how I knew her attackers, I told her about my job, and she was enthralled by the drama of it all, by the tales of lives so different from her own. She invited me into her apartment for a drink. A real drink, poured from a bottle kept on a high shelf into a delicate glass. A delicate glass rinsed with running water from a working tap. We talked for hours. There seemed to be no end to the stories we had to tell. An almost uncontrollable urge to pour every part of ourselves out for the other's consumption. With such different lives, everything we had to say was new and intriguing to the other's ears.

By the time I made it home that night, I was already in love.

2

New love is urgent and greedy. It sweeps through your life, planting its roots quickly before its bloom begins to fade, obliterating anything that might dissuade you from allowing it to grow.

Within two months, I'd moved in to her apartment. Within six, we were having lunch every Sunday with her parents at their country club. Mel's father was none other than the ludicrously wealthy Doug Fanning, a man who ran so many successful businesses I don't think even he knew the names of all of them. Yet he seemed to have no objection to his daughter's choice of boyfriend. In fact, he almost fell over himself to include me in family events and social engagements.

By the time the year was out, Mel and Cal (always that way round. Always.) fell from people's lips like salt and pepper, or rock and roll. *Her* people's lips anyway. I didn't see much of Jez, or any of the others any more. I shopped at the uptown precinct, not the old high street. I bathed in huge tubs of warm water drawn directly from a tap, not boiled and cooled and carried in buckets from stove to bath. But it felt right. I wasn't concerned that my life was morphing into something else. I wasn't losing myself, I was finding a better version of myself. Evolving. And most importantly, I slept each night beside the sweetest, most perfect woman I could ever have imagined, and I was blissful.

I was Cal Roberts, a man with a life that most would envy. I had a job that gave me purpose, and satisfaction. An occupation that was grounded enough that I could tell myself it offset the obscene luxury I now lived in. So I was dining on steak while Danny and kids like him scrabbled in the back of the cupboards to find some out-of-date cereal to assuage their hunger – so what? I'd spent all day doing everything I could to help the disadvantaged youth, that was more than most. Besides, it wasn't *my* money and luxury to distribute. I was just in receipt of it.

The first two years of our relationship were like some technicolour dream of happy ever after. Which I guess made me a sort of lanky, semi-macho Cinderella. I was a humble, hard-working and compassionate hero, swept up in the arms of my true love, welcomed into the bosom of her wealthy family and transported to a life of comfort and ease. It would have made a good ending, if it wasn't for the fact that it was only the beginning.

There are few people more naïve than a young man who has convinced himself that he deserves everything that life has gifted him. The invites kept on coming: champagne breakfasts, society weddings, skiing in Aspen, snorkelling in the Bahamas. And I kept on taking, convincing myself I belonged. Certain that Mel's family loved me for who I was, maybe even appreciated the social value of what I did for a living. I'd forgotten the stark reality behind so many fairy tales. Sooner or later, there's always a royal wedding. And when the time comes, the princess' father wants a prince, not a pauper, at the end of that damned aisle.

Arrogance wasn't a cloak I was used to wearing. Somehow, during the heady days of our new love I'd slipped it on, revelling in the feel of it, without realising how it can blind you to what others really think. Even when Mel's dad made some spurious excuse to get his wife and daughter to leave us alone at the club one evening, I didn't see it coming.

"I've been meaning to have a chat with you, Calvin," he

said, once Mel and her mother had left and we were alone, sipping Scotch by the fireside. "I've been meaning to ask you about your plans."

I grinned, like the fool that I was. "You want to know when I'm going to make an honest woman of her, eh, Doug?"

"Oh, no," Doug chuckled, insincerely. "No, not quite the angle I was going for. Do young people even still get married these days? No, I'm not a dinosaur. I'm not concerned about her honour or anything like that. I was more thinking about your goals."

"Goals?"

"Your long-term plan. Your ambition. Come on now, Calvin. You're a bright, energetic young man. You must have one."

"Well, I'm pretty happy with the way everything is right now, to be honest, Doug."

"So you're intending to continue to allow me to keep Melody in the lifestyle to which she has become accustomed forever, instead of stepping up to the plate yourself?"

The sudden change in tone shouldn't have taken me by surprise, but it did. In an instant, all the confidence and arrogance I had been luxuriating in disappeared, like the emperor's new clothes. I should have been expecting this. No amount of charm and goodwill will sustain a man forever, not without the cold hard cash to command respect.

Anger coursed through me. "Mel and I have never asked for your money," I snapped. "We can support ourselves. I took your offers of dinners, holidays and all this sugar-coated nonsense to be gifts. I thought you invited us because you wanted to spend time with us. But don't misunderstand, Doug. We love each other, we have everything we need without your 'generosity', particularly if it comes with strings attached."

There, I thought. *That showed him.* I rose from my seat, downing the remains of the Scotch in my glass – it might be the last time I got to indulge in such an expensive tipple, after all – and gestured to the maître d' to fetch my jacket.

Doug just reclined in his chair, and lit a cigar. "Melody's monthly income is higher than yours, but it doesn't even cover a quarter of the rent on her apartment," he said, smiling.

"What?" I sank back into my chair, stunned, just as the wiry, moustachioed cloakroom attendant rushed over with my coat and deposited it in my lap. "I-I didn't…"

"Don't suppose you ever thought to check exactly how the bills were paid, did you, Cal? I don't blame you. Who looks a gift horse in the mouth? A beautiful young lady with a magnificent apartment right in the centre of the city. Well, I bet you're too scared to pinch yourself in case it's all a dream. But, pinch yourself you must, I'm afraid."

"You make it sound like we're freeloaders. I work, she works."

Doug sighed. "My daughter rearranges pictures of obscenely thin models wearing the ridiculous costumes that pass as fashion these days, and posts them on a website. It's a decent job for a young lady, but it's not a provider's job. It's not a penthouse-in-the-city job. Did it never occur to you that your neighbours, whose apartments pale in comparison to yours, are CEOs and investment bankers?"

"No," I whispered, all the fight gone from me.

"So, you don't want my 'generosity', as you put it?" Doug smiled slowly, and I could tell he was exactly where he wanted to be – in possession of the upper hand. "I respect that. A man should want to pay his own way, after all. And, as you say, you both work. In the current climate, you should easily be able to afford a small high-rise on the edge of the river by the Moorings. If love is truly enough, then I'm sure Melody won't object to the smell, or travelling all those miles to work on a crowded train full of the great unwashed. I'm sure she won't even mind the lack of new clothes or holidays. Just you and her and *love*."

He reached across the table, poured me another drink.

"Don't go thinking I'm not a romantic, Calvin," he said. "I'm a great believer in love. But I'm also a realist. It's a long, hard life without a little comfort and entertainment to see you through. And love – even the greatest, most passionate love – struggles when times are hard. I like you, Calvin. I like you very much, in fact. I'm not telling you any of this to dissuade you from her, quite the opposite."

"Then what, Doug? What is it you want?"

"I want you and Melody to have a happy life together, and to want for nothing. So, I'd like to offer you a position in my company. I'll pay you three times what you're currently earning, as a starting wage, and I will of course continue to pay for the apartment until such time as you are earning enough to take it over yourself."

"I don't want to leave the youth centre, Doug. The kids there, they need me. We're making a real difference to their lives. That means something to me. More than something."

Doug just sighed. "I didn't want to have to go down this road, Calvin. But, I'm afraid I don't think the centre will even be open much longer."

"What do you mean?"

"I know you've been busy mooning over my daughter these past two years, but Henman's plans can't have escaped your notice?"

Henman was the newly elected prime minister. The youngest in history. A great showman, full of charisma and confidence. The ladies loved him, the men admired him, and after decades of wishy-washy politicians spouting nothing but hot air, his assured and to-the-point rhetoric had made him a shoo-in for number ten. With crime the biggest problem facing the country, it was his Zero Tolerance campaign that dominated all the headlines. But for the life of me, I couldn't see what that had to do with the centre. We were part of the solution, helping to steer the disaffected and vulnerable youth away from crime. Prevention is always better than cure, surely?

"I don't see what you're getting at?" I said.

"I've had the privilege of meeting him, you know? He's a man who gets things done. A man who directs resources where they are most needed, if you get my drift. Realistically, Calvin, how many kids do you actually manage to keep out of trouble, long-term? A handful, if that? In a place as riddled with crime and decay as Hallow, it doesn't even scratch the surface. Wouldn't it be better to fund more... effective initiatives?"

"Not everything is about money, Doug."

He laughed. A deep belly laugh. "Yes, it is. I'm sorry to burst your bubble, but that's exactly what everything is about. You can spend your life wishing it weren't the case, but you won't change it. Money may not be everything, but everything requires money. Even idealistic schemes like your centre. What leaders, true leaders, have to do is decide how best to spend that money, and where it will have the greatest effect."

"You're telling me he's going to close the youth centres?"

Doug shrugged. "Maybe not today, maybe not tomorrow, but..." He raised his palms in lieu of finishing the quote, and leaned forward in his chair. "You didn't hear it from me. Consider it a heads-up, from a concerned family member."

"How do you even know? Aren't you just making assumptions?"

"Let's just say, I've got my fingers in a lot of pies. I make a lot of investments. And recently, I was offered the chance to get in on something so huge, so revolutionary, that I just couldn't say no. I've seen the plans, and I'm a convert. Henman is going to clean up this city, starting with Hallow. But, for you, my boy, it's time to jump ship. If you don't do it of your own accord, you'll be sunk sooner or later anyway."

My head was swimming, and not just because of the Scotch.

"This is a lot to process, Doug," I said. "I don't really know what you want me to say."

"I want you to say you'll come work for me, of course," Doug chuckled. "But I don't expect an answer right now. Impulse is the enemy of good decisions. Take some time, talk it over with Melody, it's an open-ended offer."

3

Walking into the lobby of our apartment block, everything already seemed tainted. I felt out of place in a way I never had before. When the doorman nodded and called me 'sir', it occurred to me that he probably made more per hour than I did, and I felt ashamed. "It's Cal," I said, stopping to shake his hand instead of walking past like I normally did. "Just Cal. Not sir."

He nodded, looking slightly confused. "Have a pleasant evening, Cal."

By the time I reached the top floor, I was feeling sick. The Scotch sloshed in my belly, and Doug's revelations pounded in my head. There was only one person who could make me feel better.

When the doors opened onto our neutral-toned, climate-controlled and thickly carpeted open-plan living space, the sight of her was almost too much of a relief to bear. My Melody, serene and beautiful even in her fluffy pink dressing gown and slippers.

"Cal!" She put the book she was reading down on the arm of her chair, and sprung towards me, arms open. "Are you alright? What did Daddy want to talk to you about?"

I drew her close, loving the way she fitted neatly into my embrace. So compatible, so perfect. "You're never going to believe this," I said, my mouth brushing against the top of her golden hair. "He offered me a job."

She pulled back slightly, looking me straight in the eyes. "Oh my God," she said raising one hand to her mouth. My perfect Melody. I knew she'd understand the conflict swirling through my mind. "Oh my God, Cal. That's… that's…"

"I know," I sighed and squeezed her shoulder. This was what I loved about us the most, the way we knew each other's hearts and thoughts, the way we could communicate so much without words.

But then her face erupted into a smile. Not just any smile, *the* smile. The one that made her eyes shine bright and her cheeks flush pink. The one she wore when she was so full of joy and excitement that she couldn't conceal it if her life depended on it. The one I had fallen in love with.

"Oh Cal, this is *it*! I can't believe it. He doesn't do this, you know? Don't go thinking it's nothing to him, or that he'd do it for just anyone. This means he likes you. Like, *really* likes you." She gasped, and hopped a little on the spot. "This means he sees what I see in you."

"And what exactly is that?" I asked, not liking where this was going.

"Potential, Cal. I see the man you could be, I always have. From the first time we met."

So it was never me, or at least not the me I currently was. She fell in love with the man I could be, the man she thought she could shape me into. It was suddenly so obvious. I'd let her direct me. Let her dictate what I ate, where I went, even what I wore. And now here I was, the perfect canvas to be dressed in a monkey suit and taught to be a pillar of high society.

"Did it never occur to you that I might not want to be that man?"

She snorted. "What, you don't want to be successful? You don't want to have money in the bank, a nice place to live, the chance to raise children who can have opportunities? What exactly is it about all that that you don't want?"

I ran my fingers through my hair. She was infuriating me. "It's not that I don't want that, it's that I want to do something that means something! I don't want to give up on those kids, Mel. I *won't* give up on them."

"This is about the centre, isn't it? Oh, Cal, I'm sorry. I should have known. I know it's more than just a job. But, sweetie, you've paid your dues. You don't have to keep giving back forever."

"Paying my dues? Is that what you think I've been doing?"

She took my hand, so gently and with so much grace. "Yes," she said, pulling me down onto the couch beside her. "I think you feel you owe it, even if just subconsciously. You think that centre saved you—"

"It did," I interrupted. "I'd be one of them now, Mel. One of those lost youths drifting into crime, or else I'd be dead in a ditch somewhere."

"Okay." She nodded, but I could tell she thought I was being overly dramatic. "But tell me, Cal," she continued. "What is it you want for those kids?"

"A better life, of course," I replied. "A chance. A future."

Mel just nodded sagely, the way she always did when she was building up to her point. "What you really mean is you want them to get out of Hallow," she said. "You want to help them grow wings, so they can fly away."

"Well, that's a rather poetic way of putting it. But yeah, I guess."

"And when they grow those wings, would you want to clip them?"

I had no idea what she was driving at. "No, of course not."

"If that kid… what's his name? Danny. If Danny managed to break free would you want him to refuse because he felt indebted to you? You always say you were the first kid the centre saved. But did it really, if you still can't leave Hallow behind?"

"You don't know what you're talking about," I snapped, storming into the bedroom. Anger blurred my vision and made my hands shake as I pulled my thick winter jacket from the wardrobe. Irrational, misplaced anger – at Mel. Because she did know what she was talking about. She'd hit on a truth I didn't want to acknowledge.

"I need some air." I walked out of the apartment without looking at her, scared that the water forming in my eyes would show her she was right.

4

I caught the train back into Hallow, Mel's words running through my mind as I walked the littered streets. Her comments about Danny had hit me hard, and when I pushed open the door to the centre and saw him sitting at the table chatting with Ben, I realised she was right. I didn't want that kid to still be here in five years' time, let alone ten. I didn't ever, ever want him to feel like he owed anyone anything, and I certainly didn't want him to clip his own wings out of a sense of misplaced loyalty. If he wasn't as far away from this dump as he could get by the time he turned twenty-one, I'd feel like it was all a waste of time.

"Hey." Ben smiled and put down the cloth he was holding. "Did you forget something?"

"Maybe," I said. "Late one for you tonight, Danny? Vincent not come to pick you up yet?"

"No." Danny stared at the ground. "He's not. I mean, he won't be."

"It seems Vincent might be in a spot of bother again," Ben said. "Something about a weapon on his person. One of those 'random' stop-and-searches that seem to happen disproportionately to him."

"It was only a bloody Stanley knife," Danny chipped in, clearly upset. "He weren't even doing anything wrong, just lending it to someone."

"Well," Ben said. "If that's the case I'm sure it'll all get straightened out. But the long and the short of it is that Vincent is in custody again, so Danny is going to stay with me tonight."

"Where's your mum?"

Danny just shrugged, looking doleful.

"Okay," I said. "Well, it's a good excuse for a sleepover anyway. Between you and me, I happen to know Ben keeps the really good biscuits at the back of his kitchen cupboard, so don't let him fob you off with digestives."

Danny laughed and Ben pretended to be cross. "I actually just wanted a quick word with you, Ben," I said, "if you've got a minute?"

"Course." Ben chucked his car keys at Danny. "Go start her up for me, would you?"

Danny nodded and headed out to the car park.

"What's troubling you?" Ben asked as soon as the door closed.

"Ben." I sat down at the table opposite him, but didn't look him in the eye. "Am I a disappointment to you?"

"What?" Ben sounded confused. "Why would you ask that? Have you forgotten to order the loo rolls again or something?"

"No. No, I'm serious. Me still being here, it's not what you wanted for me, is it? I mean, you put so much time and effort into helping me when I was a kid, you must have thought I was worth more."

"Worth." Ben clicked his tongue. "It's a funny old word. And I'm not sure I like it. See, when people talk about their 'worth' they tend to think it's something measurable, or worse, they get it confused with money. They tend to forget that value isn't always quantifiable at all – least of all financially."

"I didn't come here to argue over semantics," I said. "You know what I'm driving at, you're just being deliberately obtuse."

"Yeah, I know what you're driving at. The answer's no, Cal. No, of course I don't think you're a disappointment. But something tells me that's not going to be enough to calm whatever storm you've got blowing through your mind, is it? So why don't you tell me what's actually going on, eh?"

Ben sat back, arms folded, and I poured it all out for him. Doug's warning about the future of the centre and his job offer, Melody's unwanted psychological analysis, my own swirling doubts and indecisions. He listened in silence, until I asked him what he thought.

"Well," he sighed, "I think you have a choice to make."

"Jesus Christ, I know that! I'm asking you wha—"

"You can choose to resign, or you can let me fire you."

"What?"

"I can't get these kids out of Hallow, Cal. Half of them don't even really want to go, at least not enough to truly work for it. And of those that do... well. You were the brightest kid I ever had come through those doors, and even you aren't getting out because of your brains. There are blocks at every turn, you know that. None of these kids can afford a decent education outright, and a Hallow postcode makes student loans impossible to come by. All I can do is try to help them stay out of trouble – to make as good a life as they can for themselves. I'm not trying to get them out of Hallow, I'm trying to keep them out of Whitefield. I realised that a long time ago. Now here you are, with a real chance to rise above it all. Think about it, Cal. After all, I can think of some kids that you could really give a future to if you go for it."

"Which kids?"

Ben reached across the table and put his hand on my shoulder. "Your own."

5

So it was that when Monday morning came around, I put on the expensive suit that Mel had picked out for me and headed to the imposing tower block that housed the headquarters of Fanning Corp ready, but not entirely willing, to join the legions of corporate wage slaves. The immaculately dressed receptionist sent me straight up to the top floor. "Mr Fanning is expecting you," she said with a slight edge to her tone that made me think I ought not dawdle. I took the polished glass elevator up to the penthouse office where Doug conducted all of his most important deals, and found him ready to greet me with a hearty handshake and a beaming smile.

"Come in, come in, Cal," he said, ushering me to a seat beside the large aquarium that he'd had installed adjacent to the 'rustic' fireplace. Apparently, you can tell how successful a person is in business by how closely their office resembles a living room.

"I'm so happy you decided to accept my offer." He pulled out a cigar and offered one to me; I politely declined. "I promise you, you've made the right choice."

"So what it is you want me to do, Doug?" I asked. "I'm a quick learner – at least I think I am. But, you know I've never worked in an office before."

"I know." He grinned. "And I also know you think the

corporate, suit-and-tie world is a soul-crushing, meaning-less abyss."

I laughed nervously. He was right, but I didn't want to offend his lifestyle by being too emphatic in my agreement. "I guess you'll show me I'm wrong," I said.

"Oh, no," Doug replied. "You're absolutely right. A man like you will wither and die in an environment like this. You know it, I know it. And I actually like that about you, Cal. It's refreshing. Most of the people I'm surrounded with would break out in hives if they had to do 'real' work. You're a man's man, Cal. And you need a man's job. Trouble is, they don't value real men like they used to, not financially at least."

"I get that, Doug. You already gave me that speech, that's why I'm here. To be a provider, just like you said. And I'm sucking it up for Melody's sake – so we can have the future she deserves."

"You've impressed me," Doug said. "You're prepared to take a job you know you'll hate because you love my daughter. That's next-level kudos right there, Cal. That's you getting my blessing, should you ever ask for it, and a whole heap more besides. But I'm not going to ask you to spend your days behind a desk, I've something far more up your street in mind. I've got one hell of a proposal for you, and I'd bet my uncle's toupee you're going to be biting my hand off for it."

Before I could ask any questions, the door to Doug's office flew open and two security guards grunted and groaned as they manoeuvred a large VR chair inside. "Ah, perfect timing." Doug jumped up from his seat and ignored the two guards as he made a beeline for the tall, weedy man in glasses who had now entered the room behind them. "James!" he exclaimed, shaking the man's slender arm so vigorously it seemed to make his whole body wobble. "Thank you for coming in at such short notice. I have someone very important that I'd like you to meet." He gestured to me to stand up, and I duly obeyed. "This is Cal Roberts, he's going to be an integral part of the project. Cal, this is James Leary. He's one of the top boffins at VirtReal."

I shook James' proffered hand. "Actually," James said, "I'm a senior development engineer; and also the project coordinator for the Whitefield Initiative. It's sort of my baby."

"VirtReal and *Whitefield*?" I was confused. What possible collaboration could there be between the leading manufacturer of VR booths and Whitefield Prison?

James frowned at Doug. "Mr Fanning, sir. What exactly does Cal here know about the project?"

"Absolutely nothing!" Doug beamed. "But it's right up his alley, trust me. I wanted to leave the presentation to you, it's your baby, after all. I just want to see his face."

James didn't look convinced. "Forgive me," he said, "but what part exactly is Cal here going to play?"

"I'd like to know that myself," I chipped in. "Along with about a million other things."

"First things first," Doug said. "Show him the tech. Then give him that spiel – sorry, the pitch, you gave me. This is going to knock your socks off, Cal. Trust me."

"Alright." James plugged the VR chair into an empty socket on the wall and handed me a headset. "Would you like to take a seat, Cal?"

6

I hadn't been in a VR chair since my last trip to the booths
with Jay nearly a decade before, even though they'd become
much more prevalent, and a good deal cheaper, since VirtReal
had all but monopolised the market. The truth was, I hated
VR because I blamed my addiction to the booths for my
involvement in Jay's drug-selling scheme, and therefore for
Curly's death. I blamed the booths because it was easier to
live with than blaming myself.

But with Doug and James waiting expectantly for me
to get in the chair, I couldn't think of a single excuse that
wouldn't make me look like a moron. So I took up my seat
and secured the headset, trying not to feel claustrophobic as
James fastened the belt around my waist.

"Alright," James said. "Ready to boot up."

"Wait!" I tried not to sound panicked. "What's the safe
word?"

"What?" Doug chuckled. "It's VR, not BDSM, you know."

James tried to suppress a snigger. "I take it it's been a long
time since you used VR, Cal. All those little quirks and faults
our competitors' machines used to have are no longer an issue.
Nobody feels pain in VR any more, unless we want them to."

"Why would you *want* them to?"

James just smirked a little and started pressing buttons on

the remote console in his hands. "Let's just begin the program, shall we?"

"Wait." The wrist straps suddenly felt very oppressive. "What is the program?"

If either of them gave me an answer, I didn't hear it. Reality flew away and I was plunged into darkness. I waited for a logo, or a title screen, to appear but there was none. Instead I found myself in a large brightly lit auditorium, standing in front of a row of sinks and toilets that looked comical and out of place lined up against the wall. A greying man with faded blue overalls appeared next to the third toilet from the right, sporting a huge grin.

"Welcome to plumbing 101! Or as I like to call it, sinks and shitters." He had a thick northern accent and laughed a little too hard at his own joke. "Now," he pulled a small circular disc that I recognised to be a washer out of his work bag, "can anyone tell me what this is?" His eyes scanned the whole hall as if he was surveying a crowd, yet I was the only one there. "Come on," he said, "I know you're a useless bunch but one of you must surely know?"

"Um," I ventured, "a washer?"

"A washer, *sir*," he corrected me. "But yes, lad. You're quite right." He held the washer aloft and slowly moved it from side to side as though to allow the non-existent audience to see it more clearly. "This is a standard washer. Quite how you've all made it to this point in your lives without encountering one is beyond me. But never mind. After today you'll be able to identify them and replace them. And by the time your first year in the job is out, I promise you you'll be sick of the sight of them."

It suddenly clicked. This wasn't a VR game, or even an experience programme. This was a training course. They were going to use VR to train Hallow's incarcerated youth in skills that were actually beneficial. No wonder Doug thought I'd be interested.

"This is brilliant!" I exclaimed.

"Calm down, lad," the instructor said. "If you're getting this excited about washers, I'm not sure you'll be able to contain yourself once we start on septic tanks."

"Not the washer," I said, gesturing to thin air, "this! The concept, the initiative, the positive impact it will have on their futures."

"Well, you'll all be able to deal with your own leaks and overflows, that's for sure."

I shook my head. "No, that won't do. You'll need your AI adjusted, you've been programmed by a razzle."

"I'm not following you, lad."

"They don't have working sinks and flushable toilets in Hallow. You chided them for not knowing what a washer was, but half of them have never even encountered a dripping tap."

"I don't know what you're getting at, lad, but I'll thank you not to keep holding up the class. May I remind you that your presence on this course is a privilege, and if you continue to interrupt the programme unnecessarily, you will be removed and required to serve the rest of your sentence in full without eligibility for rehabilitation release. Now, I'd like you all to locate the number two spanner in the toolbox in front of you and choose a sink to work on."

This was incredible. Beyond incredible. For so many years I had despaired at the lack of constructive choices available for the disadvantaged kids in Hallow. Time after time I'd watched them throw all their potential away by resorting to crime in order to feed themselves, or joining a gang in order to feel like they belonged. Then, the systems that failed them in the first place locked them up and in doing so stripped away even the meagre glimmer of hope for their future. A Hallow ex-convict is about as likely to get a legitimate job as they are to marry into royalty. The only thing they learn in Whitefield, apart from how to commit a more serious crime next time, is how much the establishment hates them. I thought I'd been screaming into the void, I thought nobody cared about the unending cycle. But VirtReal had come up with a real solution, and Doug was funding it.

Wait. I tried to focus on unscrewing the tap in front of me, but I was so caught up in my thoughts that I almost dropped the spanner. *Doug was funding it?* That couldn't be right. A scheme like this couldn't possibly produce any financial profits worth his while? And VirtReal? It was widely known that they used every loophole in existence to avoid even paying their fair share of taxes, why on earth would they sell their technology to Whitefield? It can't have been the highest bidder. There had to be more to this than I was seeing.

7

I got as far as learning how to remove a U-bend before James ended the program. "Well," Doug said before I could even remove the headset. "What do you think? Amazing, eh?"

"VR training programs for offenders?" I replied, squinting a little as my eyes tried to adjust. "I think it's an outstanding idea."

"We have pretty much any vocational course you can think of," James chipped in. "Plastering, bricklaying, carpentry, mechanics, we've even got catering and hospitality, and military training, of course. It's our vision, no, more than that – it's our *mission* to help these wayward offenders get back on the straight and narrow and offer them a real shot at making a better life for themselves."

"Why would you do that?" I asked. They both stared at me in confusion for a few moments.

"Well," James said, "these people are trapped in a cycle of poverty and criminality. If we can help them to break that, the benefits for society as a whole will be enormous. Hallow will become more prosperous, the problem of gangs that are beginning to creep across the river will be lessened. Not to mention, the use of VR means that training programs can be completed in a fraction of the time they would take in real life. Inmates displaying good behaviour can opt to complete a vocational course and receive time off their sentence as an incentive."

"Not to mention the pièce de résistance," Doug interjected. "The National Service initiative."

"Ah, yes," James smiled. "The jewel in the crown. Less serious offenders can choose to complete a two-year National Service programme – which takes just one week of real time, instead of serving a custodial sentence. Whitefield's overcrowding issues will be a thing of the past!"

"I've got to say," Doug said, "I'm surprised at your question, Cal. I thought you would be able to see the benefits for yourself."

I nodded slowly. "Better training and education, breaking the cycle, giving them a real future – of course I can. But that wasn't my question. Those would be the reasons *I* would do it, but I asked why *you* would?"

"Well," James blustered, "I'm not sure I know what you mean by that."

Doug chuckled. "Oh, I do," he said, clapping me on the back. "Cal here wants to know about the bottom line. He's a little too cynical to believe this is pure altruism, right, Cal?"

"Got it in one," I said. "Besides, it doesn't make sense. Why not offer these courses via the schools and colleges in Hallow? Why wait until someone commits a crime to give them a free education?"

"You're quite right," Doug said. "Everything costs money, after all. Even if we weren't looking to make a profit, we'd still have to cover the running costs, and they're not cheap. No school board could afford to purchase this technology en masse, especially not the schools in Hallow."

"But Whitefield can?"

"Not yet, but it soon will. As of next week, Whitefield will no longer be run by the national prison service, it will become a privately owned correctional facility. And guess who the proud new owner is?"

"You." I nodded. "I knew there had to be something like that going on. What is it, tax write-off?"

"More a government service." Doug smiled. "Henman's Zero

Tolerance policy made him popular, but the overcrowding in the prisons is biting him in the arse. I offered to take White-field off his hands and run a little experiment to see if I can't solve that issue for him. VR technology is expensive, but not as expensive as building new prisons left and right. If the programme goes well, it could be the start of a national initiative."

"But how are you funding it?" I asked. "I know you, Doug, you didn't get where you are by just throwing money at things with no thought of a return."

"It has to be paid for, yes," Doug replied. "But I'm not the only investor. Whitefield will be jointly owned by three wonderful, hugely successful and community-minded companies. A golden triumvirate, if you will. Fanning Enterprises, VirtReal and UView."

"UView? The TV network?"

"Lots of money in television," James piped up. "And UView's most popular shows are in the true crime genre."

"You can't seriously be telling me that you can make enough to fund this scheme, and generate profit, just by filming a documentary."

"Well." James shrugged a little. "*Justice Live* is more a reality show than a documentary. People love to see behind the scenes, and the general public is absolutely fascinated with the criminal mind."

"*Justice Live*? I smell a rat here, Doug. It sounds to me like you're going to be exploiting these kids rather than helping them. I'm not sure I want to be involved, after all."

Doug just sighed. "You've got it all wrong, son. Look, I didn't mention the show before because it's not relevant. It's just a necessary evil in order to fund the great work I want to do. You thought it was a great idea, right?" I nodded. "Well, everything has a price. But believe me, the only people who will be paying it are the ones who truly deserve to."

"What do you mean?"

"James." Doug pointed at the large flat-screen TV on the wall. "Show him the pitch VT, will you?"

8

The promo video was less than a minute long, a teaser trailer designed to pique interest and generate buzz. It began with a montage of old headlines concerning various serial killers or other violent criminals, accompanied by shocking, often graphic stills taken from police archives. Then, as twelve mugshots were flashed up on-screen, a gravelly-voiced narrator proclaimed: "Twelve inmates. One chamber. This autumn, for the first time in television history, justice will be *live*."

"Compelling, eh?" Doug grinned at me. "Tell me you wouldn't be desperate to know more if that popped up in the middle of your favourite show. Tell me you won't tune in when it premieres. I defy anyone not to."

"Yeah," I said. "Of course I'm curious. But I've still got more questions than answers."

"I told you, the only people paying the price for this are the ones who truly deserve to," Doug said, flicking through the promo footage and pausing on Harvey Stone's mugshot. "You know who this bastard is, I take it?"

"Of course," I said, shivering a little at the glassy, steadfast look in the Playground Slasher's eyes.

"Ripped up seven little girls, end to end." Doug ran his finger from his navel to his throat and I felt a little queasy. "Ain't nothing in the realms of hell that son of a bitch doesn't deserve to suffer. What about this guy." He skipped forward to a mugshot of a bald, butch man whose mouth seemed to be set in a half-smirk.

"I don't think I recognise him," I replied.

"A little before your time, perhaps," Doug said. "His name's Edward Redvers. Otherwise known as Eddie the Eater."

"Oh God." I'd heard of Eddie the Eater alright. A notorious cannibal who'd been incarcerated since before I was born. Over a period of two years he'd lured twenty-eight young men to a storage locker just outside the M4 by pretending he had a vintage motorbike for sale. He drugged them, chained them up and then proceeded to eat them – while they were still alive. The locker itself is a macabre tourist attraction now. Some joker scrawled *Eddie's Larder* above the door and people stop to take photos in front of it for their socials.

"Yeah," Doug said. "Your classic sicko, that one. Course, he looks a bit different now. Lost a lot of weight, and gained a lot of wrinkles. He's got false teeth too, hasn't he, James?"

"Well, he has now," James replied. "But he went years with no teeth at all. Knocking them all out was the first thing the other inmates did when he was sent down. Don't blame them really. I mean, imagine trying to sleep in a cell with him, knowing all he's had for supper is prison food. Doesn't bear thinking about."

"No," Doug agreed, "it doesn't. And you must recognise this guy, Cal." The next face was that of Finn Tulley, the monster who had raped and mutilated six-year-old Jessie Barnes just a couple of years ago. When she'd gone missing, the whole country had been looking for her. She had distinctive emerald-green eyes – everyone was sharing her photo all over the internet to aid the search. But Finn brought any hope of finding her alive to an abrupt and grizzly end when he posted those very eyes to her parents in a Jiffy bag.

"What point are you trying to make?" I snapped, trying to stop myself from imagining those eyeballs dropping through Mr and Mrs Barnes' letter box.

"These men are monsters, Cal. Monsters. Human rights

don't apply. I know you're a bleeding heart, and I'm not criticising you for that, but surely you must agree that if they have to suffer in order for us to provide the opportunities those wayward Hallow kids sorely need, then it's a small price to pay."

"Suffer how?" I asked, the whole 'live justice' concept was unsettling me. What exactly did they mean by that?

"VR," James piped up. "All completely virtual, no physical damage whatsoever. We've several programs already, and more in production, designed mostly to elicit the type of terror their victims would have suffered."

"An eye for an eye," Doug said, gesturing at Finn's face which was still dominating the screen, "as it were."

"Wait," I said, remembering James' comment to me just before I entered the plumbing 101 programme. "You said no one feels pain in VR 'unless we want them to'. You've found a way to make it hurt, haven't you? You're actually going to torture them, aren't you? And what, televise it?"

"In a manner of speaking," James replied. "We are able to stimulate certain nerve endings electronically, yes. And, combined with the next-level realism and immersion we have developed, the participant's brain will interpret those pain signals as a direct result of what is happening in the program. The electric stimulation itself is relatively mild, it's the user's brain that produces the terror required to… well, to make the sensation more intense."

"And you think people are going to *watch* this?"

"Yes." Doug smiled. "Even you. Oh, you'll shake your head and tut, I'm sure, but you'll watch it nonetheless. It's rubbernecking at its peak. Think about it, it's not a new concept. Justice has been a spectator sport throughout history. From the Colosseum to hangings in town squares – heck, even Jesus Christ himself was on full public display up on that cross."

"And Court TV is immensely popular," James added. "People love crime – as a form of entertainment, that is. We've commissioned a whole new maximum security building to be constructed at Whitefield to house twelve of the country's most prolific and disturbing violent criminals. They'll be filmed twenty-four-seven and the public will be able to get a real glimpse into the criminal mind. Think about it, some of those old reality TV shows ran for a decade or more – and all they were doing was watching people in a house, or celebrities eating bugs on a glorified camping trip. Not to mention the public fascination with crime, three quarters of the evening schedules are some form of investigative documentary or detective dramas. *Justice Live* will combine the two most popular television genres – true crime and reality TV, with the added spice of audience participation."

"Audience participation?"

"Phone-in voting," Doug said. "The public will get to choose which of the inmates will go into the chamber."

"And we've plans to allow the viewers to submit their own ideas for the VR programs, once the show is established," James smiled. "It ticks all the boxes for a ratings behemoth."

"It's gonna be huge," Doug replied, unable to keep the grin from his face. "There won't be a person in England who isn't talking about it. I wouldn't be surprised if it proves to be the biggest television event of all time."

I didn't doubt it. Doug was right, of course everyone would watch the premiere, including me. How could anybody not, even if just out of morbid curiosity?

"But it's all by the by, Cal," Doug said. "I'm not asking you to be involved in the *Justice Live* aspect of the project. I want you purely focused on the new re-education and rehabilitation initiative. I want you on the ground as my eyes and ears. My inside man, keeping me up to date with how my big investment's going."

"What exactly is it that you're asking me to do?"

"I want you to get a job at Whitefield, as a correctional officer. You'll be able to use your passion and experience to work with the disaffected youth again, but you'll still be able to pay your bills. A blue-collar job for a white-collar wage. Not a bad deal, eh?"

"Doug, I appreciate what you're trying to do but—"

"Think about it, Cal. Think about it seriously. I know you miss the centre, but this is an even better chance to really make a positive impact on the future of Hallow."

"By being a screw?"

"Uh… 'correctional officer' is the correct term," James interjected.

"Call it whatever you like," Doug said, waving his hand dismissively. "But this is no ordinary prison, or at least it won't be once these programs are up and running properly. So you have to do a few guard duties, big deal. You'll also get to help with the rehabilitation. Think what you could achieve, the lives you could turn around. Far more effective than chatting to the odd kid who happens to wander in, and let's face it, the kids who bothered to turn up to your centre probably weren't the ones that could have benefitted from it the most. This time you'll have a captive audience, so to speak."

"I don't have any experience," I protested. "Why would they even employ me?"

"You'd be an asset! You know how to talk to these… types. You've done it for years. This is a new direction for Whitefield, they'll need forward-thinking people like you. Anyway, James here can pull some strings on my behalf, I'm sure. I am their biggest investor, after all. What do you think, James? Can you get him in?"

"Are you kidding? They're desperate for new recruits, he'll be snapped up without any intervention on our part. Let's face it, he's literate and doesn't have a criminal record, that's better than half the existing staff for a start."

"Well, there we are then! Look," Doug pressed the intercom and summoned his PA, "I'll even get Greta here to download the application form for you. But, this has to stay between us. I don't want anyone at Whitefield to know that you're working for me as well, this is strictly undercover.

I want you to be able to tell me what really goes on behind slammed bars, so you need to be inconspicuous."

"Excellent idea, sir," James said. "VirtReal will appreciate the insight as well, I'm sure."

"No need to kiss my arse, James," Doug laughed, "I've already handed over the money. So, Cal, what do you say? You fancy a job that really matters? Or are you going to spend your life being worn by that suit?"

9

Doug didn't need an inside man. He didn't crave any insight into the day-to-day running of Whitefield any more than he cared about the petty goings-on at any of the multitudes of factories and offices he owned. As long as his investments made him money, he couldn't care less what they were up to – he had managers for that. He'd created this position for my sake, I knew that. A way for me to earn a wage good enough for his daughter without having to succumb to corporate slavery. I supposed it was his way of showing me he cared – money and love were one and the same to Doug Fanning. I chose to take it that way anyway, and I'll admit it was flattering to know he cared about my happiness as well as my ability to provide for Mel.

Looking back, I wouldn't be surprised if my little Melody had been singing in his ear. I'd struck gold – yet again. A three-figure salary for an entry-level position to a profession that I knew, even then, to be chronically underpaid. (Once I realised how tough the job actually was, I'd have gone so far as to call it criminally underpaid – if it wasn't such a terrible pun.) I was undoubtedly one jammy son of a bitch, no two ways about it. My outrageously good fortune didn't help with the first-day nerves, though.

"What the hell do I know about being a screw?" I whined to Mel, who was lounging on the bed watching me wrestle with the stiff buttons on my new uniform.

"That's what training's for," she replied with a wink. "Silly boy. No one expects you to know anything yet. Anyway, they wouldn't have given you the job if they didn't think you were up to it."

"They would have given the job to anyone with limbs and a pulse," I snapped. "That James guy from VirtReal said as much."

"Well, there you go," Mel said, rising from the bed to slip her arm around my waist and nuzzle my back. "Can't be too hard then, can it?"

"You're infuriating," I said, turning round to kiss the top of her head.

"No, I'm *right*. You always seem to get those two words mixed up."

"Ha, ha." I tried to sound sarcastic, but I couldn't help smiling.

"You'll be great, Cal. You know why?"

I shook my head.

"Because you actually give a shit. I reckon that's half the battle."

She wasn't wrong. It wouldn't take long for me to discover that there were two types of guards at Whitefield: the ones who wanted to do a good job and the ones who just wanted to do as little as possible. And there were way more of the second type than the first. The majority of my colleagues cared only about their pay cheque, and seemed to view doing the absolute minimum required not to get sacked as a career goal. Throw a stick in Whitefield and you'll hit a lazy-ass CO who'd rather come up with some spurious excuse to keep their landing locked down than do anything to help rehabilitate their inmates. The decent, motivated guards were few and far between. But, as luck would have it, I met two of them before I even got through the door.

The interview (if you could call it that, I was barely asked a question beyond 'when can you start?') had been held in the warden's office which was located in a separate building to the prison itself, so when I arrived on my first day I hadn't yet been through the ominous wire-topped gates and into Whitefield proper. They don't give tours to interviewees, I guess they don't want to risk putting them off before they even start.

The guy in charge of the barrier didn't even look at me when I pulled up alongside his booth. "Good morning," I said, rolling down my window, "It's my first day, can you tell me which door I ought to head to?"

"Pass," he said, without looking up from his phone.

"You don't know?"

"Your. Pass." He tapped the thick glass and I noticed the scanner protruding from under the window.

"Oh, right." I waved my security pass at it and the device beeped as the barrier arm rose up, so I drove through without getting an answer from the abrupt security guard.

I followed the faded signs and bore right into the small gravelled yard that served as a staff car park. There were no demarcations, but I took a spot that was furthest away from the main doors – I didn't want to tread on anyone's toes by unwittingly taking their 'usual' space. A light grey Ford, slightly battered round the bumper, pulled up a few spaces away from me, and as I got out its owner – a young guy about my age, I guessed – bounded toward me, all shaggy blonde curls and oversized smile. He looked simultaneously nervous and enthusiastic, like he didn't know whether to lunge forward or slink back – just like my aunt's cocker spaniel whenever the doorbell rang.

"Excuse me," he said, the smile never fading even when he spoke. "Could you please tell me which building I ought to be heading to? It's my first day and I'm supposed to go to the training centre. I'm Bodie, by the way. Bodie Matthews." He stuck out his hand for me to shake.

"Cal," I replied. "Cal Roberts." His hand was warm and moist and I struggled to resist the urge to wipe my own on my trousers when he finally relinquished his slightly-too-tight grip and let go. "But I'm afraid I can't help you – it's my first day too and I'm just as lost as you are."

"Oh." His smile grew even broader. "Oh, that's even better. We can find it together, I'll feel less of an idiot if we're both lost!"

"Sure," I said, returning his smile before heading toward the main doors.

My first impression of Bodie was that he talked too much, and gave too much of himself away. His heart wasn't so much on his sleeve as plastered all over his face. He was a short man whose personality made him seem taller in recollection. He trotted, rather than walked, next to me as we made our way across the car park, and he chattered incessantly as though leaving a moment's silence would cause him to implode. It irritated me slightly, and I hate that about myself now. I wish I'd seen more clearly from the start – I wish I'd appreciated the value of the man beside me back then. Things might have been very different.

"Do you reckon we're supposed to go through there first?" Bodie asked, pointing at the large double doors marked *Reception*, where several uniformed COs were milling about.

"I guess," I said, trying not to roll my eyes at the inane question.

"New recruits, I take it?" A female voice behind us made us jump. We hadn't heard her approach and were caught off guard (which, as I soon realised when I got to know the tall, dark-haired CO who now smirked at our surprise, was precisely her intention).

"Yes," Bodie said. "Yes, ma'am." She raised her eyebrow at that, but I don't think he noticed. "I'm Bodie, and this is Cal." He thrust his hand out again. Her eyes flicked down to stare at it, but she didn't shake it. "Pleased to meet you, Miss…?"

"You will address me as CO Tanner," she snapped. I already knew from the glint in her eyes that she was playing with him, but Bodie seemed oblivious.

"Oh." Bodie's face fell. "Oh, yes. I'm sorry, CO Tanner, of course."

She let out a splutter, as though she had been choking, and erupted into laughter, leaving poor Bodie looking utterly bewildered. "I'm *shitting* you," she said, patting him playfully on the shoulder before shaking his hand. "I'm Erin."

For once, Bodie was lost for words so I stepped in. "Pleased to meet you, Erin."

"You Roberts?" she asked me, looking me up and down.

"Yeah."

"Thought so. I saw your name on the rota. You're up on threes with me this afternoon."

"On the landings?" I asked. "That can't be right, I'm supposed to be training."

"That's this morning," she replied. "And the training centre's over there, by the way." She pointed to a small building covered in scaffolding. "This afternoon, you're mine." She said it menacingly, but the wink she gave me let me know she was kidding. I liked her already, and that was before I realised just how good she was at her job.

"Thank you, Erin." Bodie had found his voice again. "I hope we'll be a good addition to your team."

"Yeah," she said, sounding unconvinced. "Just what this place needs – more razzle guards."

"I'm from Hallow," I said quickly, suddenly realising that she was too. She frowned a little, and I felt embarrassed at how *un*Hallow I must have looked now – with my daily showers and wet shaves, and the little bottles of expensive products Melody lined up for me on the shelves of our – fully-functioning – bathroom. "Originally, I mean."

"You might want to show it a bit more then," she said. "The inmates, they give the razzles more shit than the Hallow guards. I guess they feel like they can't relate to them. Odd that." She winked at me and I smirked at our shared understanding.

"Excuse me," Bodie interjected. "Isn't it, y'know, a little

un-PC to use the term 'razzle'? I mean, some people might be offended. Not me, of course. But, some people could be."

I winced. How like a razzle.

"That's a good point," Erin said, though she was still smirking at me. "Unfortunately, it's a very common term among the inmates here, and I don't see that changing. But I do have a piece of advice that I give to every guard who comes from north of the river if they feel offended by it."

"Oh," Bodie said. "What's that?"

"Go cry about it in your shower."

10

"I don't think she likes me," Bodie said as we headed to the half-constructed building that Erin had directed us to.

"Why?" I asked. "Because she called you a razzle?"

"Well, yeah. That and the fact I put my foot in it. I didn't realise, I mean we were always taught that 'razzle' was an offensive term. I know the inmates are going to use it, I'm not stupid. But, I didn't expect it from the staff."

"Where were you taught that?" I asked. "At your school with working toilets and drinking fountains?"

"Well…" Bodie paused, frowning a little. "When you put it like that."

"It *is* offensive," I said, pushing the buzzer on the door to the training building. "It's supposed to be."

"But," Bodie said, "I get how hard it is in Hallow. I do. But it's not our fault, is it?"

"That it happened?" I replied, "No. But that it continues… maybe."

"How?"

"What would happen if everyone north of the Thames turned their stopcock off, and refused to turn it on again until Hallow had running water? How much money would the water companies lose then? How quickly do you think it would suddenly be 'cost-effective' to re-establish our supply? Razzles may not be the reason why Hallow is in the state it is, but they could do something about it if they truly wanted to."

"I'd do it." Bodie looked steely-eyed and sincere, nodding profusely. "I'd turn my water off in a heartbeat if it would help. But, it wouldn't do any good – not unless everyone did it. One person wouldn't make any difference."

"That's what every razzle says," I said, "but in your case I think I actually believe you would." He looked confused, like he didn't know how to take that. "It's a compliment," I assured him. "I get the feeling you mean what you say. That's not something you get much of north of the river."

"Thanks." His face erupted into that enormous grin again. There was nothing to dislike about the guy, not really. But I did wonder how the hell he was going to cope with Hallow's criminals when a casual comment from a fellow guard had upset his equilibrium so easily.

"Yes?" A gruff voice emanated from the intercom.

"Oh, good morning." Bodie leaned in close to the small microphone, talking too slowly and too loudly. "Bodie Matthews and Cal Roberts here, reporting for training."

The voice didn't reply, but a loud buzz and click indicated that whomever it belonged to had opened the door for us. Inside, the training centre looked more like a building site than a functional workplace. The reception desk was unmanned and covered in wrenches, spanners and screws. Computers were still in their boxes, lined up against the wall, and blue tarpaulin separated the large entrance lobby from the rest of the, mostly unfinished, building.

"Sorry." A stocky guy with three days' stubble and thick spectacles emerged from behind the hanging tarpaulin, holding an oversized mug emblazoned with the phrase *Live long and prosper*. "Late breakfast," he said, brushing crumbs off his chest and wiping his hands on his dark jeans. "You're the new recruits?"

"Yes," I said, "are you the trainer?"

"Me?" The guy laughed a little. "No, I'm the programmer.

Nate, Nate Hughes. Excuse the mess, it's supposed to all go live in three weeks but I can't see it happening. They haven't even started on the main training areas yet, and the rooms they *have* built haven't got doors on. Bloody noisy it is too, when they actually turn up. I've been coming in early just to get some work done before the banging starts. Course, it's gone eleven before they actually pick up their tools most of the time." He stopped suddenly, and looked a little embarrassed as if he'd said too much. "Which one of you is Roberts?" he asked.

"Me," I replied.

"Ah." He stuck out his hand and shook mine. "Right. Yes, sorry about that little rant there. I'm just a workaholic, you know? Total perfectionist. But everything's fine, totally on schedule, I'm sure."

For a moment I was confused about his change of tune, but then I realised why. He knew who I was. No one here was supposed to know that I was working directly for Doug, and yet within ten minutes of setting foot on-site I was already being treated like the spy I was. I wanted to question him, find out how and why he was privy to my secret task, but I couldn't do it in front of Bodie.

"Anyway," Nate said, "follow me, I'll get you started."

We followed him through the unplastered corridor and down to a small room which contained two VR chairs and a couple of computers, and it suddenly dawned on me why Erin had said she'd see me this afternoon.

"VR!" Bodie exclaimed, stroking the chair as though it were a pet cat. "Our training is in VR!"

"Well, of course," Nate replied, "far more efficient this way."

"I love VR," Bodie gushed. I was starting to wonder if there was anything this guy wasn't enthusiastic about.

"You're from VirtReal?" I asked Nate.

"Yeah," he replied, "but don't hold that against me. I'm a nice guy, I promise. I actually designed all the vocational programs – including the plumbing one. I was hoping you'd give me some tips, Calvin. I know you have a lot of experience with the kids from Hallow, I gather my AI isn't quite right for them."

He'd heard about my criticism. "James?" I asked. Nate nodded. "Of course I will." I glanced over at Bodie, worried he might be confused, or intrigued, by our exchange, but he was too busy mooning over the equipment to notice. "I didn't mean to be critical," I said.

"Oh, I'm not offended," Nate said, "quite the opposite. I really believe in this project, I want it to succeed. I'll take any help I can get."

"What about *Justice Live*?" I asked. "Do you believe in that too?"

"You mean am I designing the chamber programs?"

I nodded.

"I'm programming supervisor," he replied. "I don't really get a choice in what I supervise. But there's a whole team for that particular endeavour, so I'm hoping I can focus on this side of things. I'm the only one programming the rehabilitation machines. Most of the guys wanted the more exciting tasks."

"Sounds about right," I said.

"In fact," Nate said, "you two are the first real recruits to undergo your training via VR."

"You mean it hasn't been tested?"

"No, it's been tested by existing guards, but you'll be the first to have your actual induction done this way. And it's infinitely better than the traditional course, even if I do say so myself."

"How so?" Bodie asked.

"Well," Nate said, "I suppose there's not much difference in the first half – that's all just theory. Classroom stuff, you know. Except of course it takes a fraction of the time, which is a massive bonus from the company's point of view. But the second half is gold. Think about it, normally the practical side of training is all role play. Instructors pretending to be inmates, or trainees taking it in turns to act out scenarios. None of it is realistic. When the shit hits the fan on the job, it won't really help you. But with VR, the practical sessions are actually *in* the prison, not in some cosy classroom. The inmates are played by actual inmates, the environment is the actual environment you'll be working in. I got everything perfect, down to the last detail. Even got some of the inmates to provide the voices!"

As he talked about the training program he'd created, his passion was obvious. His whole face seemed far more animated than it had before, and his words came out so fast that I had trouble keeping up with what he was saying. My first impression of him had been entirely wrong – this was a guy who truly loved his work, and was very obviously proud of his creations.

"I see what you mean," I said. "That does sound like a much better introduction to the realities of the job."

"Yep." Nate grinned. "In fact, it's so effective that the governor is happy for recruits to go live as soon as they pass the course."

"What does that mean?" I asked.

"No need for a shadowing period," Nate replied, looking very proud of himself. "New officers can be part of the official team from the get-go. Saves hundreds in staffing costs, normally recruits are supernumerary for several weeks after training."

"You mean, we're going to be part of the official staff numbers straight away?" Bodie sounded panicked, I knew how he felt.

"As in, this afternoon?" I asked. "Shouldn't we at least shadow another guard for a shift or two?"

"You won't need to," Nate assured us. But I was starting to think his passion was morphing into overconfidence. "You'll run through a whole host of nightmare scenarios on the 'practice shifts' built into the induction. Trust me, every shift you ever work for real is going to be a cakewalk compared to what you'll do on training. If you pass this course, you'll be as experienced as any CO on those landings."

To say I was dubious would be an understatement. I didn't think that any VR program, no matter how well designed, could ever compare with actual, real-world experience. Back in *Wyrdworld*, I'd got pretty adept at slaying demonic necromancers with broken-off branches, but that didn't mean I'd feel confident enough to snap off a bit of birch and leap into the fray if things got supernatural at the local cemetery. I didn't think a VR simulation could ever be realistic enough to rival reality. But I'd not yet fully experienced one of Nate's immersive programs.

11

"Okay, it's all pretty self-explanatory once you get in there," Nate said as we settled ourselves in the chairs and secured our headsets. "Just go with the flow, and remember the program is constantly calculating your progress, so it'll adjust the pace accordingly. I'll start you off together, if your learning speeds are vastly different, the program will automatically separate you. If you're near enough the same, it will march at the pace of the slowest. Alright?"

"Great," Bodie said. "Hope I can keep up with you, Cal!"

From any other razzle, I'd have found that condescending. They tend to view people from Hallow as intellectually inferior, due to the notoriously bad education system. But in Bodie's case, I felt that he meant it sincerely. Hell, he meant *everything* sincerely as far as I could tell. It was as admirable as it was annoying. I just smiled back at him, and Nate started the program.

"Welcome to your Prison Officer Entry Level Training course." An overly cheerful female voice broke the darkness. "On behalf of Whitefield and VirtReal, we would like to thank you for your interest in pursuing a career in corrections, and wish you every success. Remember, at Whitefield, you are more than just a number."

The classroom was about as sterile and generic as you could get. A whiteboard at the front, pale green walls, the sweet scent of coffee and furniture polish in the air. I was sitting at an impossibly shiny wooden desk, a pen and paper set slightly too far back so that I would have to actively pull them toward me if I wanted to use them.

"Cal?" I turned to my right to see a young man with short dark-brown hair sitting at the desk beside me.

"Bodie?" I asked. He nodded. "You look completely different."

"So do you," he replied. "You've got a moustache!"

"Must be generic avatars," I said. "Makes sense, I guess, it's not like it matters much."

A tall, uniformed CO wandered in and introduced himself as our instructor. Bodie hastily picked up his pen and started making notes, but I couldn't see the point seeing as how we were in a computer simulation. As Nate had forewarned us, the classroom stuff was pretty dry. Mostly just policies and procedures, health and safety and the like. After each topic, we were handed a small touchscreen and asked to answer the questions that appeared on it. I assume we were both answering correctly, as the program didn't separate us.

After our seventh mini-assessment, a small chime rang out and a loading screen appeared along with the message: *Congratulations, you have passed Section One.* I had lost any sense of time, I couldn't tell you whether Section One had taken an hour or a day. In reality, of course, it had probably only taken ten minutes – the whole twelve-week course would be over by lunchtime, after all.

Not having clearly defined 'days' within the program was disorientating and confusing. We were simply ploughing through an endless day, with no breaks for meals or rest because we hadn't physically been in the simulation long enough to need them. Mentally, however, I could really have used a half hour respite after the stale, statistics-based module on data protection.

Fortunately, the rest of the classroom sections were a lot more engaging. We learned about the different categories of prisoners, protocols, routines, chains of command, emergency procedures, and even a little bit about criminal psychology. It was all a lot more interesting than I had expected, and I'll admit I started to feel pretty excited about the prospect of life as a CO.

The final theoretical section was all about the upcoming innovations, and it could just as easily be described as propaganda instead of training. We watched a recording of Henman's impassioned speech on Zero Tolerance, followed by a virtual tour of the new rehabilitation wing – or at least what it would look like once it was actually finished. It became instantly apparent to me that I would have little or no involvement with rehabilitation. A CO's role in the process was simply 'running' (escorting inmates from one part of the prison to another). When free flow began each morning, the long-term inmates would move to their work assignments as usual, but those who were completing programs in exchange for early release would instead be taken to the new wing for the day.

Moreover, the ultimate grand plan was to drastically reduce the overcrowding problem the new crackdown had created by allowing less serious offenders to bypass spending time in a cell altogether. 'Day Stayers' (as they would come to be known) would simply arrive at the gates at 7am and complete their National Service program in one day, gaining their release papers without ever having set foot on a landing. I would never even see them, and I wondered how many Hallow kids I once knew would come and go through the system that way without my ever even realising. I was a little disheartened, my dream of being able to help with rehabilitation had been entirely taken over by VR.

But it was still going to be a hell of a lot more interesting than inputting data and scrutinising spreadsheets at Doug's office. Plus there were all the long-term inmates, and the opportunity to make an impact on their lives. I decided I just had to adjust my perspective, let go of the notion of being some sort of self-appointed counsellor for Hallow's wayward teens and embrace the life of a CO.

"Oh, man," Bodie whispered to me as the instructor bid us farewell and the room faded away, replaced by Whitefield's looming walls. "The practicals! I'm so nervous, are you nervous?"

"A bit," I replied as we walked through the gatehouse, depositing our valuables and collecting our keys and walkie-talkies as we had been instructed. Then the doors to the wing were opened and I could hear the dull roar of hundreds of inmates chattering, swearing and laughing in their cells. "Okay," I conceded, "a lot."

Nate had warned us that the simulation shifts would be nightmarish, full of every possible worst-case scenario. But still, we barely had time to acclimatise to the stench of sweat and cabbage before the first fight broke out. The CGI inmates were lined up by their cells for morning count, Bodie and I diligently clicking our devices to register each one as we had been taught. But, without warning, a large, bearded prisoner with dodgy tattoos launched himself at a smaller, bespectacled guy from the adjacent cell. We rushed toward them, ready to put into practice the restraint techniques we had been shown in the classroom, but before I could reach the fray, another inmate thrust himself in front of me, blocking my way.

The dude was six foot eight, at least. In my own body I'd have come up to his chin, but in this avatar I was nose-to-chest.

"Out of the way, inmate," Bodie squeaked at him, but he just laughed and pulled a rudimentary shiv made with a toothbrush and a razor blade from his pocket and pointed it at my throat. Bodie backed up and pressed the emergency button to summon assistance, just as he should. But it was too late.

"Fucking screws," the inmate spat in my face, and I looked up at him to see a ragged, cross-shaped scar on the underside of his chin. He laughed manically as he drew his hand back and plunged the blade into my throat. The last thing I saw before the screen went black was his smiling face.

In a flash, we were back at the end of the landing and the inmates stepped out of their cells for morning count.

"Redo," I said to Bodie, whose avatar was frowning. "It's put us back at a checkpoint, just like in a game."

"But, what did we do wrong?" he asked. "We followed protocol."

"I don't know." I thought hard for a second. "But we know what's coming up now, so let's disarm him first, rather than rushing to break up the fight."

"Agreed," Bodie said. "Cell thirteen, right?"

I nodded, and before the inevitable fight broke out, we both headed down the line towards the cell where the guy with the shiv would be. Except this time, he wasn't there. This time, when the bearded guy jumped on the speccy inmate, we were attacked from behind by the shiv-wielding psycho and Bodie got stuck in the stomach before I even reached the emergency bell.

"Fuck," I said as the scene reset again. "That was even worse!"

"I'm starting to think we're not cut out for this," Bodie replied, looking despondent.

"To be fair," I said, "we were trying to cheat."

"What do you mean?" he asked.

"Well, you don't get do-overs in real life, do you? If it played out exactly the same then it wouldn't teach us anything. This is supposed to be training, after all. Look for the lesson, there must be something we need to learn from this."

"Don't rush in?" Bodie offered. "Like, don't be in so much of a hurry to deal with the fight that we don't notice what else is going on?"

"I bet that's it," I agreed. So this time, when Beardy leapt on Speccy, we stood back completely, scanning all the other inmates for Shiv Guy. But Shiv Guy just stood still, meek as a lamb watching the fight. And we watched too as Beardy's fist mashed Speccy's face and his boot shattered his skull with a sickening crack.

"Okay," I said when the simulation started over again. "So doing nothing is *not* an option. Not unless we want a dead inmate on our hands."

"I've got it!" Bodie bounced on the spot excitedly. "Clear the area!"

"What do you mean?"

"Well, the psycho only attacks once we make a move towards the fight, right? So, we lock the cells again before we intervene. Remember what the instructor said, about not turning your back on an inmate or leaving yourself vulnerable?"

"Of course!" I agreed. "That's what this is trying to teach us. I can't restrain Beardy without leaving myself vulnerable."

"Inmates will exploit any moment when your guard is down." Bodie repeated the instructor's words verbatim. "Cal, for all we know the fight is just a distraction. Beardy and Shiv Guy could have planned the whole thing!"

"Never assume you know all the facts about a situation," I said, remembering the points the instructor had written on the board. "He told us that, a lot."

"But we didn't apply it to this situation," Bodie sighed.

"Right, let's do this," I said, feeling determined. We began the count as before, but this time when Beardy jumped I shouted, "Lockdown!" The other inmates stepped back into their cells and Bodie hit the button that locked all the doors on the landing. Now, Shiv Guy was behind a cell door and we were both free to tackle Beardy together. We restrained him without much problem, and called for runners to escort Speccy to medical to get his jaw checked out, and to take Beardy to segregation.

"We did it, partner!" Bodie held up his hand for a high five, and although it was cringey as hell I couldn't leave him hanging.

"Yeah, and it only took four attempts," I laughed. "Christ, I dread to think what's coming later in the simulation if that was test number one!"

But the rest of the first simulation shift went smoothly. We ran through all the daily procedures, and managed to accomplish everything we ought to with only a slight scuffle over bacon rashers in the dining hall to contend with. But we had learned our lesson the hard way from Shiv Guy. Not once did Bodie or I let our guard down, not even for a second. When the inmates moved along the landing towards their work assignments, or back from lunch, we stood with our backs to the wall as we supervised. And when one of them stopped to ask us a question, we barely made eye contact with them, so busy were we scanning the others to make sure we weren't being deliberately distracted. The incident had made us paranoid and suspicious – which was exactly the point of it.

There were seven more simulation shifts on the main wings. Each one contained an incident which we had to deal with correctly, and we never knew when they would occur or what they would be. From being covered head to toe by faeces and urine thrown from a cell (a so-called 'dirty protest') to a whole-prison lockdown when an inmate couldn't be found, we took everything in our stride. With the exception of a bag of heroin smuggled in by a visitor, and an ensuing OD in the shower block (Bodie's post-visit cavity search hadn't been up to scratch), there were no more fatalities or do-overs. And we never once let ourselves get blindsided again. Even when a young inmate slashed his wrists in his cell, despite our panic, we remembered to lockdown the other inmates and summon help before rushing in to stop the bleeding and leaving ourselves exposed.

After the main wing shifts, we undertook simulations in the hospital wing, psychiatric ward and in seg. Those were a little more harrowing and Bodie struggled to keep the contents of his stomach down when we had to deal with the inmate who had peeled off large sections of his skin and smeared the wounds with his own shit. I told him that at least he now knew not to request a transfer to psych or medical – but he wasn't in the mood to see the bright side of that one.

In seg, most of the inmates were so violent that they had an 'unlock' in place, which meant a certain number of officers (usually three, but sometimes six or seven) had to be present whenever their cells were unlocked. For the most part, this made seg pretty easy. But of course, this was 'nightmare scenario' training, so even with six officers in riot gear in front of us, a deranged inmate managed to sink his teeth into my arm and I had to demonstrate that I knew how to fill in all the correct paperwork. That was always half the test – not just dealing with the situation but filling in the paperwork in triplicate afterwards. No wonder Nate had said it was the most realistic training possible – half a CO's damn life is paperwork.

The final shift in the training program was back on the main wing, and we were jumpy as hell about it. "You know it's gonna be bad," Bodie said. "The last test. Why put us back on main wing for one more shift otherwise?"

"Yeah," I said. "The shit's going to hit the fan, no doubt. The only question is which direction it's going to come from."

We instigated a random cell toss and scoured every inch of the wing for contraband, we frisked every inmate on their way to and from work and meals, we eyed everyone with increased suspicion, I nearly jumped out of my avatar's skin when someone dropped a plate by accident, we were nervous wrecks for the whole eight-hour shift. Yet nothing happened.

"I can't believe it," Bodie said as we filed our shift reports and entered the staffroom to collect our coats and bags from our lockers. "Is that it? I mean, I'm glad it's over but it feels like a bit of an anticlimax."

"Don't knock it," I replied, still scouring our surroundings even though we were in a sterile area. "Let's just be thankful."

We were heading for the gatehouse to relinquish our keys and clock off when the alarm sounded.

"*Code red. Code red.*" The walkie-talkie I was seconds away from handing over to Marie in the lobby shrieked at us as the piercing siren assaulted our ears and elevated my heart rate. "Multiple prisoners armed. Disturbances on F, G, B, H and J wings. Officer down on H wing. Officer down on B wing. Shots fired on F wing. Lockdown in progress, all officers report, stat."

"A riot?" Bodie's eyes were wide.

"Sounds like all the wings at once." I could feel myself panicking. "Must have been meticulously planned."

"We should get gear." Bodie started running for the armoury and I followed. This was big, we needed riot gear and weapons, and we needed them now. But as we turned the corner, dozens of inmates had already broken through from the wings into the sterile zone and rushed towards us wielding shivs, broken pipes, bottles, and even a prison-issue gun. There was no way we could reach the equipment. We were unarmed, and the inmate leading the charge had stolen a fallen guard's key card as well as his gun, meaning the prisoners now had access to all the shields, tasers and guns in the armoury, and could unlock any door we put between us and them.

I pressed the button on the walkie-talkie, trying to communicate with fellow officers around the prison, to let them know how great the danger was, but it was dead.

We died seventeen times trying to quash the riot with no weapons or backup. No matter where we ran to, the only officers we came across were dead or incapacitated. F wing was up in smoke, G wing was under siege. We hurtled from wing to wing, trying to find more officers or a working telephone. But no matter which way we went, we were always stuck with a knife, or incinerated by a Molotov, or shot in the back as we tried to scurry to safety. By the eighteenth redo, we'd given up all hope of controlling the riot and tried only to stay alive until the police arrived.

By this point, the only place we hadn't already fled to was the seg. We sprinted through the prison grounds, knowing by now where the inmates with guns were going to be and darting under parked cars in the lot to avoid detection. When we reached the seg, the doors were all open and the inmates nowhere to be seen. Senior Officer Bates was slumped across his desk at the end of the corridor, a blood splatter on the wall behind him where the bullet had pierced his brain and blown a hole in the back of his skull.

"There's no one here," I whispered to Bodie. "Let's just hide here, until the authorities come. That must be what this is, a test of survival. Two officers can't stop a full prison riot on their own."

"Agreed." Bodie was panting as we entered one of the cells and squeezed ourselves under the bed. "We just have to survive to pass."

"Ooopsie then." A sing-song voice made us jump and we peered out from our hiding place to see a tall inmate with long grey hair smiling at us from the doorway. "Looks like you've failed, boys!"

The door to the cell slammed shut, and the laughing inmate squirted liquid through the serving hatch. "Oh my God," Bodie said when the smell hit our nostrils. "It's petrol!"

The inevitable lit match followed, and we found ourselves trapped in a burning cell, struggling to breathe as the flames surged toward us.

"This can't be done!" Bodie shouted, almost sobbing. "There's no solution, there's nothing we can do to beat this!"

"You're right," I said. "There's nothing we can do." A thought struck me suddenly, a memory from a childhood spent watching old movies and devouring sci-fi. "That's it!" I jumped up, smiling, gesturing emphatically at Bodie. "There's nothing we can do! That's the answer!"

"Are you crazy, Cal? How is that an answer?"

The flames were almost on us now, and the thick smoke made every breath painful and arduous. But I knew I was right. Nate was a sci-fi geek, it was obvious. So obvious, I couldn't believe I hadn't predicted this.

"Bodie," I said, "it's a Kobayashi Maru!"

12

"A what?" Bodie asked.

The screen went black for a second, and then we were back in the lobby with the walkie-talkie screeching "*Code red*" at us again. This time, instead of instantly fleeing from the lobby and leaving poor sweet little Marie at her desk looking terrified, I opened the store cupboard to the left of the reception desk and gestured to her to get in. "Just stay there," I whispered as I shut the door. "No matter what. I'll send help."

The first of the inmates would be here in seconds, their footsteps were already thundering towards us. "Come this way, Marie," I shouted, hoping they could hear me and would assume the mild-mannered receptionist had followed us. Bodie just stood looking puzzled, still waiting for an answer to his question.

"A Kobayashi Maru," I said, grabbing his arm and pulling him back towards the staffroom. Once we reached it, we slammed the door behind us and pulled a couple of the lockers across it to buy us some time.

"What's that when it's at home?" Bodie panted from the effort of lugging more furniture towards our makeshift barricade.

"It's from that old-time sci-fi show, *Star Trek*," I replied. "Nate's a fan, didn't you see his mug?"

"*Star Trek*?" Bodie asked. "Is that the one with the Ewoks?"

"No." I rolled my eyes a little. "But it doesn't matter, the point is this *is* unwinnable. It's an unwinnable test."

"What's the point of a test you can't pass?"

"To see how you deal with defeat," I said. "Look, in the movie they made the cadets do simulations – just like this. One of them was unwinnable, deliberately. They were supposed to rescue the crew of a ship, the *Kobayashi Maru*. But they couldn't. There was no way to rescue them without dying themselves. The test wasn't about winning; it was about grace in defeat."

"So we just have to be graceful?" Bodie asked. "What does that mean? Shall we get out the good china before we die?"

The barricade started to shake as the inmates on the other side of the door charged against it. We didn't have much time.

"No," I said. "But there's got to be something. We have to show our professionalism, show our honour. It's a test of character. If we accept that we're going to die – and soon – what can we do with our last few minutes that will be helpful after we're gone?"

"File a report!" Bodie exclaimed, looking a bit more chipper now. "We've been everywhere, we know who's got weapons and where. We saw the ringleader, we can describe him. We could send a report to the authorities, maybe even a schematic – it could help save lives when the riot police arrive."

"Paperwork is king." I quoted the instructor again. "I think you're right. We just need a computer, and enough time to send the information before we die."

"The library," Bodie said. "There's a small office next to it that the SOs use to do their weekly evaluations, it's our best shot."

There were two more doors out of the staffroom. One led to the main clerical area, which would be full of computers but was also way too close to the impending stampede of inmates, the other led to the staff shower room. I quickly locked the door to the clerical area, hoping they would assume that was where we had gone, and we fled into the showers leaving the door behind us wide open to throw them off the scent (who'd be stupid enough to leave the door open behind them in our situation, right?).

I boosted Bodie up to the high window and he wriggled

through before turning around and pulling me up. We dropped down into the exercise yard below and stayed close to the walls, semi-crouched as we ran behind the rows of benches at the side until we reached the door to the library. Hidden by bookcases, we made our way across unseen by the inmates who were fighting each other, as well as any guards they came across on the other side of the long Plexiglas window that separated the library from the main corridor. On the other side, just past the scruffy beanbags that were haphazardly arranged in the so-called 'reading corner' (more often used for drug deals or the giving and receiving of blow jobs than for appreciating literature), we sneaked into the small one-man office and pulled the monitor and keyboard down under the desk so that we weren't visible from the door.

I wrote down everything I could think of that might be of use – from a description of the ringleader, to where I'd hidden Marie and even the weapons the inmates had access to. I downloaded a prison schematic from the internal network and marked the last known location of all the armed inmates we had encountered, and even which wings were currently on fire. I sent it to every relevant email address I could think of – the police, the governor, even Doug.

"What now?" Bodie asked when I'd hit send. The library was filling up with inmates who were gleefully setting fire to books and smashing windows. "Sit under this desk and wait for them to find us?"

"We could," I said. "Or, we could go out fighting."

Bodie grinned. "Second option," he said. "Blaze of glory and all that."

"Alright," I said. "Let's do it."

We looked around for anything we could use as weapons, but the small office was ill-equipped for a siege. We decided it didn't matter, we were resigned to our fate, after all. So, brandishing staple guns and hole punches, Bodie and I emerged from under the desk, screaming a war cry as we held our budget stationery aloft and charged forth into the library. I didn't even hear the bullet that got me.

13

This time, after the screen went black the simulation did not reset. Instead, I opened my eyes to see Nate, Trekkie mug in hand, grinning at me.

"Brilliant job," he said, unfastening first Bodie's headset and then mine. "Absolutely brilliant. How cool was the bonus simulation, eh?"

"Bonus simulation?" I asked.

"Yeah, the riot. Pretty nice epilogue, eh? It's not part of the test, I just put that in for fun."

"Fun?" Bodie said. "That was supposed to be *fun*?"

"Well, yeah. I thought you'd get that – I mean a riot so well planned that it breaks out on all wings simultaneously, that would never happen. Crims aren't that organised. It was just light relief."

"So we passed?" I asked.

"Oh yeah, totally," Nate said, pressing a button on the large monitor to his left that caused the printer to whir into life. "Congratulations, correctional officers. I'm just running off your certificates now."

"Were you watching then?" Bodie asked.

"Yes and no," Nate replied. "I mean, you just did twelve weeks of training in four hours – it's all recorded on the computer but it's too fast to see in real time. I need to slow the footage down if I want to watch it properly. And who's got time for that? No, it'll be filed away so it can be watched if needed, but it never will be – unless you request a copy or unless you do something terribly wrong on the job. If that happens they'll find the relevant footage to prove you had the correct training, so you can't claim you didn't know any better. But no, it's those reports you had to file at the end of each simulation that you get graded on. Those come up on my screen, and I pass or fail you on each section accordingly. You're all good to go."

"Thanks," I said, taking the newly printed certificate that Nate had handed me. "Where do we go now?"

"Well, if I were you, I'd grab some lunch at the canteen. You're due up on the landings at one. Just head to the gatehouse, Marie'll sort you out."

"I feel like I know her already," Bodie said.

"Well, yeah, that's kinda the point," Nate said. "To familiarise you with your surroundings. Oh, just out of curiosity, how did the prison smell?"

"Like sweat and cabbage," I replied.

"Like bleach," Bodie answered simultaneously. We looked at each other, confused.

"Why was it different?" I asked Nate.

"Ah, well, that's the really cool bit," he said, his eyes lighting up like a toddler gleefully explaining what each of the seemingly random squiggles on his latest drawing represent. "See, there is no smell. Not really. I mean, VR is good, but we can't actually tap into your olfactory system. It's pure suggestion."

"There's no smells in VR, ever?" Bodie looked a little sceptical. "That can't be right, I've done dozens of VR holidays – the smells of the ocean, the barbeques, even the chlorine in the pools, they're definitely there."

"The petrol," I said. "When the inmate poured liquid through the door, we knew it was petrol from the smell."

"No," Nate said. "You *assumed* it was petrol because of the situation. I mean, what else was it likely to be, given that they were setting fire to stuff left and right? It's all just suggestion, you smell what you're expecting to smell. I can make you smell what I want you to smell to a certain extent – if it's important, I'll put enough visual clues in to steer you in the direction I want, but I can't actually create smells in the program."

"The Molotovs," I said, thinking out loud. "You made sure we saw inmates holding Molotovs so that we knew they had access to flammable liquids."

"Got it in one." Nate grinned. "From there, you subconsciously filled in the blanks and created your own aromatic experience! That's how immersive this tech really is, it can even reach beyond its own limits."

"It's clever," I said, "I'll give you that. So, why did we experience the prison differently?"

"I didn't bother trying to influence your nasal perceptions on that score," Nate replied. "Wasn't important enough. So you just smelled whatever you were expecting to. Think young Bodie's expectations about the standard of cleanliness inside might be a bit too high, though!"

"So," Bodie said, "it doesn't smell like bleach in there?"

Nate shook his head. "It's more BO and urine, to be fair," he said. "This is Hallow, after all. Two thousand crims locked up with no running showers or flushing toilets, it's never going to be a treat for the nostrils, is it? I'm told you get used to it, though, after a while."

Bodie screwed up his face a little. "I hope so."

"Well, I think we ought to get going," I said. "Thanks for everything, Nate."

"Sure." Nate shook our hands with gusto. "And don't be a stranger, Cal. I mean it, I'd really like some input on the training programs from someone from who grew up in Hallow. Any time you like, I'll be here if you fancy dropping in and giving me some tips."

I promised I would, and meant it. Perhaps I would have a chance to get involved in rehabilitation, after all.

"C'mon." Bodie's bouncy enthusiasm was back, and he pulled my elbow towards the gatehouse. "Let's go do it for real!"

14

Neither of us felt like eating, the sudden dopamine crash from exiting the simulation had left us feeling nauseous. So we decided to head to the staffroom and load up on caffeine before our first real shift began.

I'd only known Bodie for four hours, and yet we'd spent three months together. That's the strange intensity of VR, it can create a unique bond between people who were unaware of each other's existence just hours before. As we walked to the gatehouse together, we felt like old friends – comrades, even. I already knew his turns of phrase and sense of humour, could already anticipate his reactions. I knew, for example, that discovering that in-the-flesh Marie was nowhere near as congenial (or attractive) as her cyber counterpart would come as a bit of a blow.

"Wow," he whispered to me after we'd been scanned and scowled at by a decidedly spiky and abrasive Marie. "Guess Nate Photoshopped her face a bit, eh?"

"Yeah," I laughed. "Reckon he Photoshopped her personality too."

"I think we might be in for a few surprises," Bodie said. "I mean, Nate said the guards have played the simulations through to test them, right?"

"Yeah." I wasn't sure what he was getting at.

"Well, he must have been... how shall I put it... *flattering* in his depictions of them, mustn't he? I mean if he knew they'd be testing the simulations. He wouldn't have wanted to piss them off by immortalising them with spots, or bad hair, or a horrible personality."

"Damn it, you're right," I said. "People don't want to be confronted with what they're actually like. Plus they'll have posed for their avatars and stuff, and recorded the voices. They may have given Nate the completely wrong impression about themselves in the first place."

"I suddenly feel like I don't know any of them, even though we've met them all," Bodie said.

"Well, we met that Erin in real life," I said. "So we know her."

"Great," Bodie replied as we headed for the staff room. "The only person we've actually met and she hates me."

"No, she doesn't," I said. "She was just having a little fun at your expense."

"Oh, well, that's alright then," Bodie replied sarcastically. "I'm full of confidence now."

In the staffroom, a rather portly-looking guard with a lazy eye was lounging on the sofa, watching the TV screen that hadn't existed in the simulation.

"How do," the guard said without looking away from the screen. "You the new recruits?"

Bodie introduced us both with his usual zeal.

"You're Matthews?" the guard asked, finally dragging his gaze from the TV to Bodie's face. "I'm Wilkes – but you can call me Squinty. Everyone else does. You're on twos with me today. Roberts, you're with Queen Bee. Not sure where she is, but she'll be along soon enough."

"Do you mean CO Tanner?" Bodie asked. "We've already met her."

"Yeah, that's 'er," Squinty replied. "Full name's Queen Bitchmouth, but HR got the hump about that so now we just call her Queen Bee. Stupid really, she never cared. Everyone's nicknames are insulting, it's the whole point."

"There weren't any nicknames in the simulation." Bodie looked crestfallen. I already knew he hated being unprepared. "How will I know who everyone is?"

"Don't stress. They're not exactly inventive. Lardarse, Specs, Ginger Ninja – it's hardly rocket science to work out who's who. Think of the most unacceptable way to describe someone's appearance and you'll probably guess them. The guys here are about as literate and sophisticated as preschoolers. Just don't use nicknames in front of SOs, or the guv of course. He's called Captain Wanker for a reason."

"Doesn't it bother you," I asked, "being called Squinty?"

Squinty shrugged. "It'd bother me more if they didn't – you only get an offensive nickname if people like you. This place is perverse like that. Ah, here comes the queen now."

Erin burst through the door looking flustered. "There you are, Roberts," she snapped. "I went to the canteen looking for you."

"Sorry," I replied. "Wasn't hungry."

"Doesn't matter," she said, tapping Squinty on the legs and plonking herself down on the sofa next to him when he obligingly moved over. "We've still got time for a coffee. Kettle's over there." She pointed at the small kitchenette and I realised she was expecting me to make her one. "White with two, and a tea for Squinty."

I nodded and set about making drinks while Erin and Squinty stared at the television.

"Anything?" she asked her fellow guard.

"Nah, nothing from Hallow this morning. Couple of Essex lads sent down for arson, but they'll go to Belmarsh, I expect."

"What is it you're watching?" Bodie asked them.

"Court TV," Squinty replied. "It's basically a 'coming next' for us. All the major cases are on it, gives us a heads-up if any problem prisoners might be heading our way."

"Squinty here's addicted to it," Erin said. "I reckon he likes that female judge with the wispy beard."

"She can bang my gavel any time," Squinty said, and the

pair of them burst out laughing. Bodie and I just watched bemused.

"Inside joke," Erin told us. "If you'll pardon the pun. Right." She downed her coffee and stood up decisively. "Let's go, Roberts. Afternoon count awaits."

Squinty didn't seem to be in any rush to get up, so I bid farewell to Bodie and followed Erin out of the sterile area and through the double-locked doors onto G wing.

Nate wasn't kidding about the smell. Sweat, piss, vomit and mould all mingled together to create the distinctive eau de Whitefield. I tried not to gag, but Erin didn't flinch so I guessed Nate was right on that one too – I'd get used to it eventually.

"So how was training?" Erin asked as I followed her up the metal staircases through the landings.

"Intense," I replied. "But thorough, I think."

"Okay, well it should be a pretty straightforward afternoon. Threes have got exercise this afternoon, so we'll get some freshish air at least. Oh, except for Holmes in cell six, he's got his court case so a runner will come for him shortly. And number twelve is on an unlock, so no exercise for him until an SO shows up – if they ever do."

"Wait," I said. "If someone hasn't been sentenced yet, shouldn't they be in the remand centre? And why is there an unlock in gen pop? Shouldn't he be in the seg?"

We reached the third floor, and Erin smirked at me before shoving her key in the lock that opened the door to the landing. "Ah, poor starry-eyed newbie," she said. "Everything may be done by the book in the training simulations, but you ain't in Kansas any more, Alice."

"Shouldn't that be Dorothy?"

"Expect the unexpected," she said with a wink.

I stepped onto the landing and instantly realised that I was totally unprepared. In training, there had been two men to a cell, but in reality there were four or more in most of them. Some were lying on the cold stone floor for want of a bed to rest on or a chair to sit on. They were squashed together like battery hens, with barely enough room to move.

"Oh my God," I whispered to Erin. "There are so many."

"It's called overcrowding for a reason," Erin said, and I felt a bit stupid. It'd been all over the news, it was the whole reason for the Whitefield Initiative, and yet I hadn't really considered the reality of it. "It doesn't help that seg's full, so guys like Jones in twelve have to have a whole cell to themselves. He's too dangerous to put in with anyone else, unless they want to solve the numbers problem by letting him murder a few. I've worked in corrections long enough that I wouldn't even be surprised."

"What's he in for, this Jones?" I asked, imagining he must be a convicted killer or a gang leader.

"Petty theft," Erin replied. "Got caught shoplifting." I must have looked confused, because she tutted at me. "Real-life lesson number one," she continued. "Never judge a crim by their conviction. All that tells you is what they got caught for, for all we know Jones could have beaten seventeen people to death and just never got collared. He's the most violent prisoner on the wing, and he's managed to extend a three-month sentence to a decade with all the shit he's done since he got here. You get a new prisoner in for pickpocketing, don't assume he's an easy ride, or that he won't stick you in the guts given half the chance. Likewise, you could get a guy who's gone down for GBH and he could be a total pussycat. You don't know the circumstances. There's a guy down on twos, likes playing mah-jong and painting watercolours. He shuffles about, head down, polite as you like. Never so much as said 'boo' to anyone here. He's in for smashing his wife's face to a pulp with a brick."

"That's horrific!"

"Yeah, it is. And he deserves his time, but he's no danger to anyone else. She was having an affair, he snapped. Never been violent before or since, and probably never will be again. You need to realise that prison is its own world, and all that matters here is what goes on here. Let the courts judge the crimes, but we need to take the inmates as we find them – not get hung up on why they're here."

The bell rang to signal afternoon count, and we duly opened the cells and got busy with our clickers. Apart from the far larger number of inmates, it was all much the same as the simulations had been. Though I'll admit that, as realistic as Nate's program was, it was a lot more unsettling to be so close to so many convicted felons in the flesh. A few of them jeered at me a little, with comments such as "Fresh meat" and "Baby screw" being bandied about, but Erin didn't pay any mind so I figured it was nothing to worry about. I was struck by how many inmates muttered a polite "Afternoon, miss" or gave her a respectful head nod as she passed them.

"Hey, miss," a rather mouthy young lad from the end of the landing yelled out. "Who's the new screw? He your boyfriend?"

There were sniggers and whistles from the others, and a few made obscene gestures or thrusting motions with their hips.

"This is CO Roberts," Erin addressed the whole landing in a tone that was both authoritative and friendly at the same time. "It's his first day, but no need to go easy on him, lads. He's a big boy."

"How do you know, miss?" Mouthy Kid yelled to more sniggers and whoops. "You been checking out his dick?"

"I don't need to check it out to know it's bigger than yours, Fisher," Erin addressed the loud-mouthed inmate directly. "By the way, that enlargement kit you ordered didn't make it through security, sorry about that."

The inmates laughed and clapped, Fisher included. I was a little taken aback.

"Wasn't that a bit risky?" I asked Erin as the inmates began filing out towards the exercise yard. "Winding him up like that?"

She just laughed. "I *know* them," she said. "No amount of training and protocol is a substitute for that. Fisher loves a bit of banter, and he's a good sport. The lads enjoy our exchanges, it's almost a pantomime now. It defuses tensions, makes them all pay attention at count. This life is monotonous for them, absolutely mind-numbing. Trust me, anything that gives them a bit of a smile in their day is golden. Bored, stressed-out prisoners are trouble."

I nodded, and made a mental note to pay close attention to Erin's methods – I hadn't yet seen the other guards in action outside of the simulation, but I already had a suspicion she was one of the best.

Out in the yard, Erin and I watched closely as the inmates took advantage of their exercise time. A few of them played a rather haphazard game of basketball, while others used the workout benches or running track. Some simply sat and chatted in pairs or small groups, and those were the ones Erin instructed me to watch more closely.

I was just starting to relax a little and appreciate the warmth of the lurid afternoon sun on my skin when a tall inmate broke away from a group in the far corner and jogged towards us. As he got closer, I recognised the jagged scar slightly protruding from under his chin. "It's Shiv Guy," I whispered, involuntarily taking a step backwards.

Shiv Guy noticed my reaction and stopped a couple of feet away from us, erupting into laughter.

"Oh my God." His voice was several octaves higher than it had been in the simulation and bordered on squeaky. "Oh, your *face*!"

Erin tried to stifle a giggle. "I take it you encountered Greavsie's avatar then, Roberts?" she asked.

"'Ere, 'ere, shall I do it? Shall I do the bit?" Greavsie's almost ultrasonic register was a total contrast to his tall, stocky stature. He cleared his throat, exaggerated his posture and affected a deeper voice as he came closer to me. "Fucking screws," he boomed in his put-on butch tone, before bursting into laughter again.

"Very good, Greaves," Erin said, giving a little clap.

"Next stop Hollywood." She turned to me, the amusement obvious on her face. "Greaves is nothing like the character he portrayed in the simulation," she said. "Obviously. We were hardly going to reward the actual troublemakers with a day off work assignments to pose for VirtReal, were we?"

"I guess not," I replied, feeling naïve again.

"Oh, that was brilliant. Brilliant," Greaves squeaked. "Proper made my day, that." He held out his hand. I glanced at Erin and she nodded, so I shook it. "Thanks for the laugh, sir. I promise not to shiv ya."

"Thanks," I said. "I'd appreciate that."

"Ha!" Greaves seemed to find that hysterical. "Oh, he's funny, in't he? We got a funny one. That's sweet, that. I likes a laugh I do. Don't I, miss?"

"You certainly do," Erin replied. "Was there something you wanted, Greaves? Before Roberts here gave us some entertainment?"

"Oh, yeah," Greaves said. "Yeah, there was, as it goes, miss. I was just wondering what's for dinner?"

"Monday night, pie and mash night. Same as always."

"Great. That's great." Greaves moved a little closer to Erin. "My favourite, that is. I do like a good relaxing meal."

"Me too," Erin replied, her smile gone now.

"Did I tell ya, miss, I got a letter from my cousin the other day, crazy bastard that he is?"

"No, you didn't," Erin replied. "What did it say?"

"He reckons he's going to start a little recycling business. Says it's amazing what people throw away."

"That's fantastic," Erin said, sounding very sincere. "Thanks for sharing your news, Greaves."

"No bother, miss." Greaves smiled at us before turning around and jogging away.

"That was odd," I said. "Is he a bit… unusual?"

"Damn it," Erin said, ignoring my question. "We've got to do a cell toss."

"Eh? Why?"

"Didn't you hear that?" she snapped. "Something's going to go down at dinner. Someone's hidden something in one of the bins on the landing, my guess is a weapon."

"You got that, from *that*?"

"You'll learn," she said. "Greavsie's cousin's letters are always informative."

"There is no letter, is there?" I asked, suddenly realising what was going on.

"There isn't even a cousin," she replied.

"So, Greaves is a rat?"

"I wouldn't put it like that." Erin scowled at me. "Greaves, like most of the inmates, just wants to do his time without any hassle. An incident means we have to lock down, which means more time stuck in their cells. An incident at dinner means they might not get fed, and will definitely lose their evening wash and movie. There's fuck all pleasure or comfort to be had in here as it is, he just doesn't want his life made even bleaker by some idiot who thinks he's hard and wants to cause trouble. And he wants to stop other people getting hurt, I happen to think that's pretty damn decent."

"Okay," I said, feeling ashamed of myself. "Rat was a bad choice of words."

"Fucking right it was," she said, turning away from me.

I felt terrible. Clearly it was a sore topic for Erin, and I'd gone and put my size tens in it. "I really do want to do a good job here," I said. "And I really want to learn. I've spent my whole life viewing Whitefield, and the police and screws and courts, as the enemy. Now I'm on the other side and it's hard to adjust."

"It's not you," Erin said. "I'm just sick of the macho, boys-will-be-boys, honour-among-thieves crap. Hallow's full of it, that 'us and them' mentality, and where does it get us? I respect anyone who goes out of their way to help another human being, no matter who they are or what bullshit 'code' they've broken to do it. And frankly, some of the people in here are on the wrong side of the bars."

"Guards?" I asked. "You mean some of the COs?"

She sighed and didn't look me in the eyes. "A kid bled out in the washroom a couple of months ago," she said, her gaze fixed firmly straight ahead. "Got his throat slashed with a razor over a carton of orange juice. Greavsie saw the other inmate stash the blade in a bar of soap. He tried to tell Lardarse, but the fat fuck wouldn't listen. Told him he didn't need telling how to do his job, then he punched him in the stomach and locked him back in his cell for 'causing trouble'. The kid was nineteen, he only had a week left on his sentence. But his parents had to throw a wake instead of a parole party."

"Shit," I muttered, unable to find anything more eloquent to say.

"Some of them think the inmates must go easy on me because I'm a woman." Erin scoffed a laugh. "They think that's the reason I have fewer incident reports to my name than they do. But that's bull. After what happened last time, d'you think Greaves would have told Lardarse about the weapon in the bin today if he was on duty?"

I shook my head, and Erin continued. "Course not. So there's an incident right there that's not going to happen, not because I'm a woman, but because I *listened*. Just, treat them like people, Cal. Okay? Don't let the power go to your head. It takes a real man to stay kind in a job like this."

15

"The thing you have to remember," Lardarse proclaimed loudly as we walked past the cells on twos the following morning, "is that you're dealing with scum."

The inmates in the cells jeered and booed, someone down the end shouted, "You should know, tubby," and Lardarse strode to his cell and banged his baton on the door.

"No breakfast for cell three," he boomed, and the inmates inside groaned and swore at the offender. "As I was saying," Lardarse turned back to me, "any one of these cunts would stick you in the back soon as look at you, so never give them an inch."

I opened my mouth to disagree, but thought better of it. Now probably wasn't the right time to go pissing him off, seeing as I was stuck with him for the next eight hours.

"It's no good going soft on them," he continued with his unwanted monologue, "they'll run rings round you. Just look at Queen Bitchmouth, bet you had a hell of a shift with her, right?"

"Well, actually, it was pretty good," I said.

"Pfft," Lardarse snorted. "Well, you wait and see what you think of 'er once you've had a shift with a real professional," he said. I wanted to ask where I might find one of those, but bit my tongue. "Don't you go taking no notice of all her airy-fairy 'treat them like lost little boys' nonsense. It's bollocks. Look at what happened yesterday, some fucker got a screwdriver onto the wing, right under her nose! That's what happens if you're fucking soft, mate. She's lucky it didn't end up in her skull, or up her cunt. Though that might have screwed some sense into her, eh?"

I started to worry I might not make it to coffee break without smacking his greasy, smug face in. Not only was he crass, offensive and downright bigoted, he was also completely wrong. We'd found the screwdriver taped to the inside of a wastepaper bin during a cell toss, thanks to Greavsie's tip-off, and therefore averted what could have been a serious attack, or even a fatality. It had to have been there since before we came onto threes, which meant it was probably smuggled in under Lardarse's nose, seeing as he'd been supervising visitation that morning. But clearly, he wasn't one to let facts and logic get in the way of a good sexist, self-aggrandising rant.

By lunchtime, it had become patently obvious why Lardarse had more serious incidents to deal with on his shifts than Erin did. He caused half of them, either by deliberately winding the inmates up or by simply ignoring warning signs, such as the little rumble of discontent in the game room. That could have been defused easily, had Erin been around to step in and take the tension down a notch with her well-placed banter. But Lardarse didn't step in until things were already out of hand, so a small argument over a missing Queen of Clubs escalated into a fist fight that resulted in an inmate going to medical with a nosebleed.

"Think of it as a practical demonstration," Erin said when I relayed the incident to her in the staffroom. "The what-not-to-do portion of training."

"He's an incompetent bully," I said.

"I have to agree," Bodie, who had the good fortune to be on shift with Erin that day, chimed in. "Honestly, when I worked with him yesterday I thought I'd made a huge mistake taking this job if that's how guards are supposed to behave."

"There's good and bad," Erin said. "He's about the worst.

Just do the exact opposite of everything he does and you'll be fine."

For all Nate's bluster about the training program being so efficient that shadowing wouldn't be required, it was several weeks before Bodie and I were paired together instead of with an experienced CO. By that time I'd worked with just about every CO on the wing, and fortunately Lardarse was indeed the worst of them. Most of the other guards were competent and reasonably amiable, but Erin and Lardarse stood out as the two polar extremes. Johnson (aka Ginger Ninja) was pretty decent to work with, less intuitive than Erin but equally professional. He impressed me because his no-nonsense attitude towards troublemakers was combined with a calm empathy. He didn't stand for any shit, but equally he listened to the inmates instead of just assuming he knew the score.

As the weeks rolled by, I started to feel at home at Whitefield. My favourite part of the job wasn't officially a part of the job at all. Whenever I had an early finish, I would go over to the rehabilitation centre to help Nate. I undertook every course he had created, giving feedback to help him improve the AI. As a nice little consequence, I found myself well-versed in basic carpentry, plumbing, electrical work, cookery and even laying wood flooring. Mel nearly had a fit when she came home early and caught me with all the carpets up one afternoon, but she was impressed with the end result.

Working with Nate made me feel like less of a fraud when I met with Doug each Friday to give him a weekly update. If it wasn't for my involvement in the VR creations, I wouldn't have had anything to tell him at first. As Nate had speculated, the rehabilitation was taking longer to get up and running than anticipated. Not least because the vast majority of the allocated workmen were commandeered for the *Justice Live* project. While Nate and I sat on upturned boxes, trying to work with computers that didn't yet even have a desk to sit on, the new maximum security unit was taking shape just a few yards away.

It was difficult to see exactly what was happening on the construction site. The whole unit was walled off from the rest of the prison, it even had its own entrance. But the roar of machinery was relentless. There had to be fifty men, at least, working twelve-hour days to get the buildings finished. Nate, on the other hand, was lucky if a couple of guys showed up to do some plastering for an hour a week. There was no doubt where VirtReal's priorities lay.

"To be fair," Nate said, "they need *that* to fund *this*, so I guess it makes sense to focus on it first."

I conceded the point, but I was still a little dubious. Whitefield was at breaking point. More and more inmates arrived every day, four and sometimes five to a cell. The kitchens couldn't cope, the laundry couldn't cope, the staffing numbers were so dangerously low that most days we couldn't unlock for more than an hour – meaning that tensions were rising among the men. The prison was a pressure cooker, and it needed the help VirtReal had promised before the lid blew off.

Despite the stress of the ever-increasing inmate population, I really did enjoy the job. As I became comfortable with the daily routines, I relaxed into the role and got to know the long-term inmates so that I could anticipate their behaviour, and soon the other guards stopped treating me like the new guy. After a couple of months I even got a nickname. Or rather, I regained my old one.

16

That some of the kids I knew from the centre would one day turn up on the wrong side of the bars was sadly inevitable, and happened sooner than I expected it to.

There was no real order to the categories of prisoners in Whitefield, it was far too crowded for that. Petty criminals bunked with murderers, inmates with psychiatric needs were squeezed in with gang members for want of enough beds on psych. The governor was simply trying to keep things ticking over until the new rehabilitation programs could deliver the reduced population they promised. While the prison had been constructed with the aim of keeping those awaiting trial separate from those serving their sentence, the remand wing had burst at the seams long before I arrived, and its contents were now spilling into every section of Whitefield.

So it was on my eighth week in the job, I heard a familiar voice call out to me from within a cell stuffed with rapists, arsonists and killers.

"Beanie? Beanie, is that you, man?"

I stopped abruptly, and scanned the cell. A young guy with a shaved head and wild eyebrows jostled his way to the front, grinning at the thrill of having spotted a familiar face in such an unfamiliar environment. I recognised him instantly as one of Vincent Felton's crew.

"Spooner?" I asked. "When did you arrive?"

"Last night, man," Spooner said. "They got me for trafficking. Bullshit it is, I was only hooking up a couple of friends. Half an ounce over the bloody limit it was. Typical, eh?" He shook his head and tutted, as though he was a victim of fate and not the cause of his own misfortune. "Anyway, enough about me, eh? I can't believe you're a fucking screw! I thought you went off with your posh skirt to do some la-di-da big job in the city. That's what Danny said anyway."

Danny. My heart sank a little at the mention of his name. When I'd left the centre, I promised him I'd be back to visit and I really meant it, at the time. But I'd been so caught up in my new job and helping Nate with the programs that I hadn't found the time.

"How is Danny?" I asked. "And Vincent?"

"Ah, you know Vincent." Spooner shrugged. "Ducking and fucking like always. Danny's sound too, Vinnie's doing right by him."

I wasn't sure what Spooner's interpretation of 'doing right' might be, so I wasn't exactly put at ease by his comments. "What are you looking at, sentence-wise?" I asked.

"Lawyer's gonna get me one of those VR sentences," Spooner replied. "National Service, he reckons. Fucking sweet as, he says I'll get a job out of it too."

"You're going to join the army afterwards?"

Spooner nodded enthusiastically. "Yeah, Beanie. I wanna get out of Hallow, see the world. Plus," he ran his palm across his head, "I've already got the haircut."

"The VR programs aren't up and running yet," I said. "It'll be a few weeks yet." Trials were quick for Hallow's less serious offenders, they rarely waited more than a week to be sentenced for straightforward crimes. Especially when the defendant was pleading guilty.

"Yeah I know," Spooner said. "But my brief's real smart. He's coming up with all these bullcrap reasons to delay the trial so I can be one of the first to get VR."

"Sounds like you got lucky with your lawyer there," I

replied. Hallow lawyers were notoriously uninterested in their clients, there were so many trials going on every day that having a lawyer present had become more of a formality than a defence. They rarely even read the case file before going to court. "Don't blow the chance, eh?"

"I won't, Beanie," Spooner said, crossing his heart. "Scout's honour. I'm out, man. I'm done with all that gang shit. The cops are so on our arses, I swear they'd bust us for fucking sneezing. I can't go back to Frank Street, not now I've been banged up once. I'd be in here for fucking life if I went down again. Plus it's all getting too shady with the Ringers."

"The Ringers?"

"Malachi's gang," Spooner replied. The name rang a bell, I must have heard it from Danny, or Vincent, in the past. "Real nasty cunts. They want the Moorings, but Vinnie's not standing for it. It's going to go down soon, I reckon."

"Roberts," Johnson shouted from the other end of the landing. "What's the hold-up?"

"Sorry," I called back. "I'm coming."

"I'll catch you later then, Beanie," Spooner yelled as I hurried towards Johnson.

"Beanie?" Johnson looked at me in confusion.

"A nickname from a previous life," I replied.

"It suits you," Johnson smirked.

After I spoke to Spooner, I resolved to head into Hallow after work and see if I could find Danny. But when I gathered my belongings at the end of my shift, there was a message on my phone from Mel asking me to hurry home. Concerned, I said a hasty goodbye to Bodie who was changing into his bicycle shorts ready to ride home and made it back to our apartment as quickly as I could.

She greeted me at the door with a glass of a champagne and a soft kiss.

"What's going on?" I asked.

"We're celebrating," she said, pointing to the dining

table which had been adorned with candles and an array of expensive hors d'oeuvres from our favourite takeaway.

"Celebrating what?"

"Four years ago today, you swept in and rescued a damsel in distress, and made her fall helplessly in love with you."

"Oh shit," I said. "Anniversary? Oh God, I'm so sorry. I forgot."

She shook her head and tutted playfully. "Well," she said, taking my hand and pulling me towards the bedroom. "In that case dinner will have to wait until after you've made it up to me."

I followed her into the bedroom and lay down beside her on the new silk sheets she had bought. All thoughts of Danny and Vincent were banished by the heady scent of Dior that seemed to emanate from her body and the feel of her warm, soft skin on mine.

* * *

The next morning, I arrived at work dishevelled and a little hung-over and Marie on reception eyed me with uncontained disgust.

"Well, if it isn't Beanie." Erin prodded me in the back as I picked up my keys and walkie-talkie.

"Oh good," I said, turning around to see her playful smirk. "I'm glad that's caught on."

"Could be worse," she said. "Take it from Queen Bitchmouth, you've got off lightly."

Lardarse strode in and chucked his bag at Marie without so much as a good morning. She scowled a little, but he didn't notice. We were all heading into the staffroom to join Squinty for a quick coffee and some Court TV when Bodie appeared huffing and puffing, his cheeks bright red and his forehead dappled with sweat and marked with a red line left by the neon-yellow cycle helmet he'd just removed.

"Running late this morning, are we, Sweat Sack?"

Lardarse guffawed and pointed at Bodie's tight Lycra cycling shorts, which were sporting an unfortunate wet patch right on his groin.

"Sweat Sack!" Squinty exclaimed. "That's a good one. 'Ere, Sweat Sack, put the kettle on, will you?"

"Oh great," Bodie mumbled. "That's just great."

"See what I mean, Beanie?" Erin said, touching Bodie's arm sympathetically. "Next time you're feeling sorry for yourself, just spare a thought for poor old Sweat Sack here."

"I'm never wearing these shorts again," Bodie whined.

"I don't think it matters now." I tried to stifle a laugh. "The damage is done."

"Don't stress," Erin said. "I happen to think those shorts are quite flattering." She gave a slow wink and a playful smile then headed over to the sofa. Bodie flushed and fumbled awkwardly with the taps as he tried to fill the kettle.

"You've embarrassed him," I whispered to her. "He's gone all shy."

"I know," she grinned. "Sweet, isn't it? He's got a little crush on me."

"How do you know?"

"That'd be telling," she said.

"Hey, shut it, will you?" Squinty said, pointing the remote at the TV and pressing hard on the volume button. "Something big's happened."

17

We stopped our chatter and turned our attention to the TV. The aging news anchor looked sombre as he addressed the camera. "Devastating scenes from North Hallow this morning as authorities try to deal with the aftermath of the blaze that claimed the lives of several children and at least one member of staff at the Church View Residential Home last night. Our reporter, Sian Lewes, is live on the scene."

The broadcast cut to a mumsy-looking middle-aged reporter gripping a small, fluffy mic as she stood outside a row of terraced houses, one of which had all but collapsed and seemed to still be smoking. "Thanks, Stephen," she said. "I'm here outside the charred remains of the Church View Residential Home for Children in North Hallow, which this morning is coming to terms with its devastating losses. Church View has been a vital part of its community for over thirty years, providing long-term and respite care for children with life-limiting conditions. Neighbours say they were first alerted to the blaze at around 2.04am, when the home's fire alarms woke them from their sleep. Several onlookers tried desperately to help with the evacuation of the children, some of whom are now being treated for burns and smoke inhalation themselves."

"Do we know anything yet about how the fire started, Sian?"

"As yet, the authorities are reluctant to speculate as to how the blaze began, but I have been informed by police on the scene that they are not ruling out foul play. The number of fatalities is not yet clear, and several children and two members of staff are still fighting for their lives in intensive care. However, we do know that at least three children tragically lost their lives last night, among them six-year-old leukaemia sufferer Kayla Williams. The other victims, including a member of nursing staff, have yet to be named."

"Thank you, Sian. Tragic news. Our hearts go out to all involved." He paused briefly before breaking into a smile. "And now, it's time to take a look at what the weather has in store for us over the next few days."

"Holy shit." Erin shook her head. "Those poor kids."

"Sounds like they were half-dead anyway." Lardarse shrugged. "All cripples and cancer kids, weren't they? Probably better off."

Erin slammed the coffee Bodie had handed her down on the table and leapt to her feet, looking Lardarse right in the eye. "You watch your fucking mouth, you incompetent piece of shit," she snarled before storming out of the staffroom, leaving him staring after her.

"Jesus, Lardarse." Squinty picked up a newspaper from the coffee table, rolled it and whacked Lardarse on his overfed buttock. "Have a bit of fucking sensitivity, will you?" He looked at me and Bodie. "Her kid's in a wheelchair, in case you didn't know."

"I didn't even know she had a kid," I confessed.

"That's hardly my fault, is it?" Lardarse replied. "I'm still entitled to my opinion."

"You really *are* a piece of shit, aren't you?" Johnson shook his head in disgust, and we all followed him out of the room leaving Lardarse alone muttering something about us all being snowflake, simp fags.

When we headed toward the wing for our first shift as a duo, Bodie and I couldn't help but notice Erin emerging from the ladies toilets, her usually pale face blotchy and puffy. I didn't know whether to go over to her and offer her a sympathetic word or to leave well alone in case she was embarrassed. I turned to ask Bodie what he thought we should do, but his face was ashen and his lips almost trembling.

"Are you okay, man?" I asked.

"I'm taking him down," he said, stone-faced.

"Who?"

"Lardarse. I'm telling you now, I'm taking him down."

"No offence, mate," I said, "but he's got quite an advantage, size-wise. I wouldn't put money on you in a fight."

"Not a fight," Bodie said. "I mean he's gone. I'll have him fired. I'm gonna watch that bastard's every move, I'll get him. He shouldn't be here, he's a disgrace."

"I don't disagree with you," I said. "He's an unprofessional twat. But, this is prison. No one likes a rat, even among the guards."

"I don't give a shit what anyone likes or doesn't like," Bodie snapped, with a ferocity I didn't think him capable of. "All it takes for evil to triumph is a good man to do nothing, isn't that how the saying goes? Well, I may not be a popular man, Cal, but I am a good one. At least, I try to be."

His face was flushed red from the passion of his resolve, and an unwanted memory flashed through my mind. 'A psychotic tomato' – that's how Jay had described Curly's passionate out-of-character fury. Suddenly, the man in front of me now seemed more familiar than ever, and I couldn't believe I'd never noticed it before. The naïve friendliness, the heart on his sleeve, the loyalty and desire to do right by everyone. No wonder I'd felt so connected to him so quickly, no wonder it seemed as though I knew him so well after such a short time. I'd known a man just like him before.

"You are a good man," I said, knowing it was true. "*That* I'd put money on."

18

Lardarse wasn't in the staffroom at lunchtime, and Erin breezed in looking as though nothing had ever happened. Bodie hastily got up from the sofa and dashed into the kitchenette offering to make her a drink.

"Your boy's got it bad, I reckon." Squinty nudged me and nodded his head toward Bodie.

"Yeah," I said, watching him try to get Erin's favourite mug from the cupboard only for her to snatch it herself before he could reach it. "I think you're right."

The hourly news round-up began and Squinty shushed me, leaning forward to hear the broadcast. It was a different anchor this time, a woman with peroxide hair and a string of pearls that only partially covered the wrinkles on her décolletage, but the top story was still the children's home fire.

"In the last few moments, police have released a statement confirming that they now believe that the fire was started deliberately. They are launching an appeal for witnesses, and asking members of the public to come forward if they may have seen anyone suspicious in the area at the time of the attack."

Squinty whistled. "Looks like we might have a child-killing arsonist on our hands in the near future then," he said.

"Good," Erin replied. "I hope they catch the bastard, and put him on G wing. I'd happily turn a blind eye to whatever Lardarse wants to do to that scumbag."

"It'll be high profile if they do," Squinty said. "Press will be over it. He'll probably have to be in with Vulnerable Prisoners. Or maybe they might even put him in that new max wing."

"Nah," Erin said. "They've already filled their twelve slots, so I've heard. You're right about the VPs, though. Fucking joke, isn't it? The worst criminals get the special treatment."

"I hear there's working showers in the max," Bodie chimed in. "And the cells are huge."

"That's not possible," I said. "There's no mains supply into Hallow at all."

Bodie just shrugged. "It's only what I heard," he said. "I bumped into Nate when I took a couple of the inmates over to clean the toilets in the rehab centre. He was fuming about it."

Bodie must have got it wrong, I thought. There was no way anyone in Hallow could have running water, least of all a bunch of serial killers. He must have misheard, or got the wrong end of the stick. But it played on my mind, so after my shift I headed over to rehab to ask Nate directly.

He was digging in to a box of cream doughnuts when I walked in. Pink frosting was smeared around his lips, making his stubble look like spiky candy floss.

"Cal." He beamed and held the box out to offer me one. I shook my head, remembering how Mel always referred to the sugary, almost luminously iced deep-fried treats as 'pre-packaged diabetes'. I didn't have much of a sweet tooth anyway. "Perfect timing," Nate continued. "I'm celebrating."

"Celebrating what?"

"I've just finished making the final adjustments to the woodwork program. I am done! Every training program fully functional and ready to rock. We can be up and running as early as next week!"

"That's fantastic," I said. "And not a moment too soon, people are gonna start suffocating in those cells if we cram any more in."

"Well, fear not. Help is at hand," Nate replied. "The governor's getting all the release papers ready, I've got fifty inmates scheduled for National Service on Tuesday, and another eighty for vocational programs on Wednesday and Thursday, all with early release as the incentive. It'll be like a ghost town in there in a few weeks, you won't know what to do with yourself."

"I actually came to ask you something," I said, remembering the purpose of my visit. "Bodie's got this crazy idea from somewhere that the max has working showers?"

"Oh." Nate picked up a paper serviette and wiped fruitlessly at the congealed goop around his mouth. "Don't even get me started on that. I'll blow a gasket."

"Wait." I couldn't believe what he was suggesting. "You mean it's true?"

"Yep." Nate nodded. "Disgusting, isn't it? There's me having to wait for inmates to come and empty my chemical toilet, once a week if I'm lucky, while UView just swan in and get everything they ask for."

"How?" I asked. "How is it even possible?"

"Everything's possible if you throw enough money at it," Nate replied. "And trust me, the money Fanning's throwing at that project is unbelievable. He's paid the water company a small fortune to tap into one of their reservoirs across the river, and that's not even the half of it. It's like a bloody palace in there. Here's me trying to change hundreds, no *thousands* of lives for the better in what amounts to a shack, and all the while they're putting on the Ritz for twelve murderous bastards and a bloody camera crew. Screwed up, it is, and you can tell your father-in-law I said that if you like, I don't care because it's the truth."

"I can't believe it," I said. "Doug never told me he was going to run water pipes!"

"To be fair," Nate seemed to have climbed down a little now that he'd got his rant out of his system, "I don't think he intended to. It's UView, or more specifically that bitch from hell, Aisling Swann. They've got Fanning Corps and VirtReal over a barrel."

"Who's Aisling Swann?" I asked.

"A bloody nightmare," Nate said. "She's the executive producer for *Justice Live*. Never bothered to set foot on-site until a few weeks ago, then suddenly she waltzed in making all these demands. And now we can't get rid of her, got her nose in everything, she has. They're bringing in hand-picked guards and production staff from all over the country, and they're housing them on-site so the filming can go on twenty-four-seven. But, they won't put up with living without running water and Aisling insists her 'stars' need to be taken care of. Between you and me, I think Doug and James are regretting ever signing with UView. Aisling holds all the cards, see? Fanning and VirtReal have already invested millions in this, and if she decides to pull the plug on the show they've got no way to recoup their losses. So, she says jump they say how high."

"Jesus," I said. "What else has she demanded?"

"The moon wrapped in cellophane from what the guys working on the chamber programs tell me," he said. "Honestly, the facilities in there," he pointed to the *Justice Live* compound, "compared to what you've got in there," he gestured to the main Whitefield building, "would make you sick. In fact," he opened a drawer and rummaged around, finally pulling out a lanyard marked *Visitor*, "don't take my word for it. Put this on, I'll give you a little tour."

19

"Just follow my lead, and go along with whatever I say," Nate said as we approached the tall, heavily guarded entrance to the *Justice Live* compound. I nodded, wondering why a small maximum security unit which didn't yet even contain any prisoners needed more staff on its gates than the main Whitefield facility with its population of nearly two thousand.

"Afternoon, lads," Nate greeted the three security guards congenially.

"Alright, Nate," one of them replied. "Who's this?" He nodded his head toward me.

"Security consultant," Nate lied. "Pinched him from Whitefield for the afternoon, their governor wants one of his staff to do a quick check."

The guard grunted and opened the gate. Inside the compound, there were people everywhere. Workmen in hard hats manned cement mixers and scaled scaffolding, young men and women in smart suits dashed in and out of the caravans that were parked on the grass, and guys in overalls were slapping paint onto the benches that lined the outer perimeter. There were three main buildings which were slightly angled to form a triangle around the large asphalt centre on which a raised platform was being erected.

"For the live stuff," Nate told me. "It's a stage, for the

presenter to do all that filler nonsense from. You know, 'we're coming to you live' and all that crap."

"Okay," I said. "So which of the buildings is the actual prison?"

"That one there." He pointed to the largest of the three concrete oblongs. "And to the left is UView's control centre. The ground floor is offices and the studios where they do their editing and mixing or whatever. Staff and stars have their apartments on the first, second and third floors."

"Stars?" I asked.

"The guards. Well, twelve of them. There's only twelve who will ever be on camera. Aisling hand-picked them herself, one for each prisoner. There's others, of course, to cover night shifts and days off, but they're just ordinary Joes, they won't be in the show."

"What about when they're off duty?" I asked. "Aren't they filming all the time? What if something big happens when their 'star' guards aren't around?"

Nate just shrugged. "I guess they know what they're doing," he said. "I don't much care about the theatrical side of it. Now, that building on the right is where the justice chamber is. Well, actually there are four chambers, but the public won't know that. They have to have enough to be able to test run the various programs throughout the week, and they won't know until the votes come in which one will be used. On the first floor is where all the programming gets done. Officially, that's where I'm based, but I avoid it as much as possible. Reynolds is perfectly capable of managing the office by himself, and we don't exactly see eye to eye so I'm happy to leave him to it. He's in his element with this project, got a really sadistic streak, he has."

"But, you're technically his boss?"

"Technically," Nate said. "He doesn't see it that way, though. Fortunately, I don't give a shit about petty little power plays. I'm more than happy to leave the high-profile stuff to him and work by myself away from this circus. And as long as I leave him to it, he's got no cause to come gunning for my position. It's a win-win. Anyway, there's no need to go poking around in there, it's the prison facilities you wanted to see, not some office full of geeks and brown-nosers."

We made our way toward the main block, but as we approached its front doors flew open and a short woman with a severe black bob strode out, ranting incessantly and gesticulating wildly. A young woman with a clipboard hurried after her, trying to keep up.

"Oh, shit," Nate said. "It's Aisling."

"I mean, the sheer incompetence is actually mind-blowing." Aisling lit a cigarette and thrust her lighter at her scared-looking assistant who hastily put it in her pocket. "I am dumbfounded. Have you ever known me to be lost for words before, Jessica?" The young assistant shook her head.

"Afternoon, Miss Swann," Nate said when Aisling and her bewildered sidekick almost bumped into us.

Aisling didn't return the greeting. She looked straight at me with one eyebrow raised. Her eyes were rimmed with thick black liner which accentuated her emerging crow's feet, and somehow made her seem even more formidable. "Who is this?" she barked.

"Oh," Nate replied. "This is Cal, he's a… uh, content, I mean security, consultant. He's here to, well, to consult."

She narrowed her eyes and smiled slightly with only half her mouth. "Sure," she said in a sarcastic tone. "Well, whoever you are, Cal, I want you to settle something for me."

"What's that, ma'am?" I asked, figuring it was best to be ultra-polite.

"Tell me, Cal, have you heard of Ollie Barnes?"

"No," I replied, confused. "I'm sorry, I haven't."

"Exactly!" She threw her hands up in the air. "Thank you. That's exactly my point." She turned to her assistant again. "Write that down, Susie." She stabbed her finger on the clipboard. "Cal the… what are you really, Cal?"

"A CO," I replied sheepishly.

"Perfect." She took a long drag on her cigarette. "Cal, the C bloody O, no less, has never heard of him! And if Cal the C bloody O doesn't know who he is then it's patently obvious that neither will Karen the hairdresser, or Abdul the ticket clerk, or Jasmine the bloody checkout girl." She let out an exaggerated sigh, then turned back to me. "He's a murderer. Poisoned a hedge fund manager."

I had no idea how I was supposed to respond, so I just shrugged and said, "Okay."

"Precisely," she said. "That's precisely it. Who gives a shit? Good for him, right? Hedge fund managers are pricks. No one knows, and moreover, no one cares. He can't be on the line-up, Lara," she said to her assistant. "He just bloody can't."

Aisling strode off across the asphalt towards the largest and most luxurious caravan, her harassed assistant scuttling after her.

"So that's Aisling," Nate said. "Don't know her assistant's name. But then, neither does she by the sound of it. No point in learning it really, she gets through them so quickly. Come on, let's slip in through the camera run."

"Camera run?" I asked.

Nate led me round the side of the max building to a small, unmarked door. "It's like a secret passage," he said as we stepped through into what amounted to a small, dark corridor. "Except it's not very secret. Everyone knows the camera men are in here, watching and filming through all the two-way mirrors, but they have to remain out of sight, for authenticity. There's cameras mounted on all the walls, but you get better angles from here, see?"

A few steps along the passage, we came to a large viewing window that looked on to a communal area full of tables and chairs.

"So, this is where they will eat," Nate said.

"They're going to be eating together?" I asked, shocked. These men had committed worse crimes than the majority of the inmates in seg. "Surely they should be kept apart?"

"What kind of television would it be if they were all just

locked in separate cells all the time?" Nate replied. "Over in gen pop, you do everything you can to prevent trouble. But in here, it's going to be actively encouraged. Ratings are God. And two serial killers punching each other's lights out over a pudding cup is prime footage."

"Jesus," I said. "I can see their point, but it goes against everything we're taught."

"That's why she's hand-picked the COs," Nate replied. "Mind you, I doubt it was hard to find guards with a sadistic streak. I bet even you've met one or two."

"Yeah," I said, thinking of Lardarse. "I have."

We carried on down the camera run until we came to the main living area. A large, square room with a television and a pool table, several upholstered leather chairs and a couple of smart, art-deco-style tables. There were shelves holding books, board games and even games consoles. It would have looked like quite the bachelor pad, if it wasn't for the cells lining its edges.

They weren't like the cells in Whitefield. Our cells had grey steel doors with lockable hatches; these had only bars, like an old-fashioned county jail from a spaghetti western. Every cell looked on to the main lounge area, and every cell was visible from any angle in the room. Which meant every prisoner would be able to see, and be seen by, every other inmate at all times. They each held nothing inside except a bed, sink and toilet, there weren't even any shelves or cupboards for belongings.

"Hang on," I said, doing a mental count of the cells. "There are only eleven. I thought there were going to be twelve inmates?"

"Ah, yes. Well spotted," Nate said. "There's a twelfth cell, but it's separate."

"Why?"

"Remember when I said they'll all be living and eating together? Well, I should have said all except one. The main attraction has his own, more isolated, cell."

"Who's the main attraction?" I asked.

"Harvey Stone, of course. There's no camera run behind his cell," Nate said, pulling a bunch of keys from his pocket and unlocking a small door that led out of the passage and into the wing. "We'll have to go inside the actual block to see it, same with the showers. No cameras at all in *there*, much to Aisling's disappointment. Quite a row about that there was, apparently."

"Why?" I asked, stepping through the door and into another corridor.

"Difference in opinion on the tone of the show," Nate said. "Aisling argues that the main demographic is middle-aged women, and she wanted to give them some eye candy. But the UView execs said no, it was a step too far. They're all for torturing these bastards live on air, but they don't want anything that could be considered 'pornographic' – so no wet, naked serial killers on national TV."

"So they do have *some* standards then?" I joked.

"Yeah," Nate chuckled. "You can broadcast a guy getting his guts ripped out, but not washing his crack. It's a fucked-up kind of morality when you think about it, but there we are."

We were in a short, brightly lit corridor with a locked door at each end. The door behind us led back into the main cell block. Nate fumbled with his keys again to open the way ahead. "Harvey's cell is down this way, past the showers," he said, and I followed him to the washrooms.

"I never thought I'd see the day," I said, stepping into the large wet room that housed five rudimentary showers and a row of sinks and mirrors. "Working showers in Hallow."

"Well, now you know what you've got to do to get one," Nate said. "Just off a few people, eh? Sorry, I know it's sickening. I mean, I'm not from Hallow so I can't really understand, but I can imagine."

"Yeah, well," I said. "You get a thick skin for unfairness when you grow up in Hallow. I'm not going to dwell on it."

"Wanna see Harvey's crib then?" he asked. I nodded and

we carried on down the corridor until we came to a single cell, set apart from the rest of the block.

Harvey's cell was barred like the others, but his had shelves and a cupboard inside. "He won't be able to use the facilities the others can," Nate said. "So they're going to have to let him have books and stuff in his room. There are six wall-mounted cameras." He pointed to the small devices, one in each upper corner and two on the floor angled towards Harvey's bunk. "More than in the other cells, because of the lack of camera run."

"Yeah," I said. "About that, why isn't there a camera run behind his cell?"

"Because he's the most dangerous, manipulative bastard to ever walk this earth." A gravelled voice behind us made us both jump. I turned around, not knowing I was about to come face to face with Dax Miller for the first time.

20

He was tall. Not as tall as me, but taller than most. Dressed head to toe in black, his ripped, faded jeans and dangling keychains made him look more like the leader of a motorcycle club than a correctional officer. His rough three-day stubble was tinged with grey and the half-smile he wore was slightly lopsided. You could see the bulge of his muscles even through the thick leather of his jacket as he stood with his feet a little too far apart and his arms folded. He looked every inch the archetypal 'bad boy', even down to the splintered silvery scar that snaked down one side of his neck.

In contrast, the short, clean-shaven man standing beside him wore a shirt and tie, and looked as though a stiff breeze might knock him over.

"Reynolds?" Nate addressed the smaller man. "Who is this, and what are you doing in here?"

"Well, I might ask you the same thing." Reynolds smirked a little, and I already hated him. Maybe it was just because I knew Nate couldn't stand him, and I'd grown quite fond of the slobby, straight-talking programmer, but there was something so slimy and self-satisfied about Reynolds' manner that it made my skin crawl. "This is Dax Miller, Harvey Stone's personal officer. He's arrived ahead of the rest of the guards to help advise us on how best to handle

Harvey's incarceration. And who is your…" – he looked me up and down with a sneer – "guest?"

"This is Cal," Nate said. "The Whitefield governor sent him to check security protocols."

"Is that so? And are we up to your high standards, Cal from Whitefield?" Reynolds' sarcasm made me seethe.

"So far, so good," I said, not trusting myself to say anything more.

"He was asking why Harvey doesn't have a camera run," Nate explained. "Perhaps you could enlighten us further?"

"Like I said," Dax replied, "he's a manipulative bastard. You can't let him talk, to anyone, alone. You put some sappy son of a bitch with a camera behind that wall," he pointed to the back of Harvey's cell, "and he'll get in his head. That's what he does. It's like some supernatural shit or something. Like hypnosis. He can sense weakness in a person, and he whispers away at them. Chip, chip, chip until he's in *there*," Dax put his finger to his temple and rotated it slowly, "twisting and changing them. Telling them up is down and black is white. Before you know it, he's got a little disciple and then everyone's in trouble. We lost two good men the last time Harvey was allowed to get close to someone."

"As you can see," Reynolds interjected, "we are extremely fortunate to have the benefit of Dax's years of experience with Harvey, to help us avoid any pitfalls. I know I speak for everyone at VirtReal when I say how grateful we are to you." He smiled at Dax, but Dax didn't return the gesture. "We were just heading over to the chambers to get Dax's opinion on the opening night program," Reynolds continued. "Perhaps Cal would like to 'inspect' that too?"

Nate looked at me, and I nodded. I'd come this far into the *Justice Live* compound, I might as well see the main draw.

We stepped outside and Nate and Reynolds headed for the chamber building, chattering between themselves. Dax stopped for a moment to let them get ahead of us before turning to whisper to me. "If that guy Reynolds gets any further up my arse he'll see what I had for breakfast," he said.

"Yeah," I replied, "he does seem a little sycophantic."

"He's a turd," Dax continued. "Can't stand a man who kisses my arse. He's even invited me for dinner with him and his wife. Reckon he might live to regret that."

"Oh?"

"Wedding rings turn me on," he said with a salacious wink. I wasn't sure which man I disliked more: Reynolds with his slimy brown-nosing or Dax with his arrogant swagger. No wonder Nate preferred to keep away from the compound.

The four chamber rooms were identical to each other, just as Nate had told me. Each one was painted black and grey and had nothing inside except for a large VR chair with far more wires and restraints than a recreational machine. A small operating booth containing two screens, a small switchboard, keyboard and headphones was located next to each chamber, and it was one of these booths that Reynolds showed us to.

"So this is the command centre for chamber one," he said, gesturing to the nearest chamber. "From here I can view the simulation as it's running, whilst simultaneously observing the inmate in his chair. And of course that means I can make the necessary adjustments to the electronic stimulation he receives."

"And by electronic stimulation, you mean pain, right?" I shuddered a little, picturing Reynolds with the power to inflict agony at his fingertips.

"Yes," Reynolds replied. "Well, in a sense. The stimulation causes a sensation akin to a small electric shock, but the VR is so immersive that the recipient's brain interprets it as pain caused directly by whatever is occurring in the program."

"Well," Dax said. "Just you make sure you crank that dial up and rip off the knob when you've got Stone strapped in that chair."

"I think you'll find that won't be necessary," Reynolds replied smugly. "The program is designed to elicit terror.

Harvey's whole body will be in a state of panic, to the point where even a very mild shock will feel to him as though he is enduring quite unspeakable agony."

"Is that so?" Dax raised an eyebrow, sounding dubious. "Only I don't think Harvey's the suggestible type."

"Oh, trust me." Reynolds grinned. "The research that has gone into this is unprecedented. Every single aspect of the chamber experience, from the lighting to sound and even the temperature of the room, is pitched perfectly to trigger a biological adrenaline-inducing response."

"So what happens then?" I asked. "In this program?"

"Well," Reynolds spoke matter-of-factly, "given the nature of Harvey's crimes, we've gone for a very gory, very unpleasant butchery theme. The aim is first to induce panic and terror – to that end we have created a truly horrifying creature who will pursue Harvey through a series of dark, eerily lit tunnels until he is ultimately trapped in a room resembling an abattoir, whereupon he will be strung up on meathooks and sliced open slowly."

I felt queasy just at the description, but Dax didn't look impressed. "What if he doesn't run?" he asked.

"What do you mean?" Reynolds looked dumbfounded at the suggestion.

"You said he'll be chased by this 'creature', but what if he doesn't run? What if he just stands there and stares the fucker down? He knows it's not real, he knows you want him to 'perform' for the cameras. And one thing I know about Harvey Stone is that he doesn't kowtow to anyone's orders. He'd fucking love it – ruining the big premiere, making you all a laughing stock."

Reynolds frowned. "Perhaps," he said, "if I showed you a little of the program? You'll see for yourself. He'll run. Anyone would run."

"By all means," Dax said. "I ain't getting in that fucking chair, though."

"Of course not," Reynolds looked appalled at the

suggestion. "I can run the simulation with just a generic avatar. When the chamber experience airs, the viewing public will see a split-screen. On the left-hand side, they'll be able to watch a first-person view of the program – essentially they'll be seeing what the inmate is seeing. But on the right-hand side of their screen they'll see a close up of the subject's face, allowing them to watch him suffer."

"If he does," Dax remarked, but Reynolds ignored him.

"Unlike most VR simulations," Reynolds continued, "the chamber programs run in real time, allowing us to televise the experience as it happens. So, let me just cue up the program." He tapped at the keyboard, cranked up the speakers and angled the large screen towards us. "And voila. Gentlemen, welcome to Harvey Stone's nightmare."

21

The stone walls of the tunnel were tinged green with moss. A small grate overhead allowed just enough light through to create shadows that danced and flickered as rodents scurried through the rivulets of brown sludge underfoot. The constant drip, drip, drip of water from the ceiling morphed slowly into a heartbeat until it seemed as though the very tunnel itself were a living being. The scuttling of the rats grew louder and faster as they ceased their ambling and hurtled forward as one, fleeing from something. The same something that now approached, not yet visible, save for a slight ripple in the darkness.

A distant scream was followed by the chink of metal on metal. It was impossible to tell which direction the noises were coming from.

"This is all part of the build-up," Reynolds said, pausing the simulation. "The sounds are perfectly configured to elicit fear responses. Our bodies respond to certain stimuli in certain ways, it's utterly involuntary. Everything in this part of the simulation is designed to signify danger, and activate the 'fight or flight' instinct which causes the body to tense in readiness for potential battle, which in turn will make the pain responses more severe. Note the patterns of the moss on the walls here and here." He tapped the screen. "The clusters are porous, full of tiny little pocks and holes. They're designed to stimulate a strong aversion known commonly as 'trypophobia' – the holes and bumps subconsciously remind us of diseased skin. It's not something that you will have picked up on, of course. But taken as part of the whole, it adds another layer of unease and increases the subject's negative biological reaction to his environment."

"Bloody hell," I said, shuddering a little at the thought of someone being so dedicated to causing the suffering of another. "You really have thought of every little detail."

He took it as a compliment, and thanked me with a smug smile before restarting the program.

The figure in the shadows slowly came into view, and it was every bit as horrifying as Reynolds had promised. Around seven feet tall with elongated limbs, its elbows were what I noticed first as it came into the light. They seemed to point in the wrong direction as though its creator had misread the assembly instructions, and as a result, its sinewy silver-blue arms bent away from its body.

Another step forward, and its face was illuminated by a shard of light. I was surprised at first at how human-looking it was. Aside from the deathly pale skin, blue-tinged lips and intensely dark circles under its eyes, at first glance its features were simply that of a very average-looking man.

"You can keep all your monsters, demons and aliens," Reynolds said when he noticed my confusion. "Our research shows that human flesh, when it is in a state of decay, dismemberment or severe deformation, will trigger a greater fear response than any amount of tentacles and teeth you can flash on-screen."

I looked closer at the face as the creature lumbered slowly forward. Its ashen skin rippled, ever so slightly at first, and its eyes were covered in a milky sheen. It tilted its head to one side, taking a long, audible breath that bubbled and rattled in its chest. As it exhaled, the skin on its face began to undulate, and dozens of tiny maggots dropped from its nose onto the murky ground below. It blinked slowly as more of the tiny, wriggling larvae emerged from its eye sockets. I glanced at its unclothed torso and almost swore out loud when a small handprint appeared, pushing out against its flesh. Then another, and another, as though this cadaverous wretch were pregnant with overdue septuplets all trying to force their way out.

"The hands of Harvey's victims," Reynolds explained. "It was faces originally. The faces of the seven little girls he killed, all pressing against the skin with their mouths open, like they were screaming. It was much more disturbing than a few hands, truly horrifying, it was. But the execs said we couldn't use the girls' images like that, said it would be too distressing for their families." He shook his head sadly. "Shame. It was one hell of a creation, would have scared the shit out of him – all his victims trying to burst forth from the belly of his tormentor. It was practically art."

"Thank God you cut it," Dax said sharply. "Look, I'm sorry, Reynolds, but you're barking up the wrong tree by bringing his victims into this. The guy has *no* remorse. Zero. He thinks they deserved their fates. You put their tortured faces in a VR simulation and he'll smile, not scream."

Dax's point was crude, but valid. Stone had famously shown nothing but disdain for his victims, and their grieving families. In fact, he'd stated in court that he had performed a public service by ridding the world of 'seven little sluts' – a statement that had solidified his status as the most hated man in England.

"Aside from that, though," Reynolds shuffled awkwardly as he spoke, "don't you agree that the creature is terrifying?"

Nate and I nodded, but Dax just clicked his tongue. "Well, I wouldn't want to meet it in a dark alley," he said, "and I'm sure it'll be a crowd-pleaser. But you're not dealing with an ordinary man here. Look, I'm not trying to piss on your party, I'm just saying. Harvey Stone isn't scared of monsters; Harvey Stone *is* the monster."

"Perhaps we better leave the demonstration there then," Reynolds snapped, turning off the monitor with an exaggerated flounce like a petulant teenager. "Clearly, it's not up to what you were expecting. Though I'm not sure exactly what I'm supposed to do with your feedback. Opening night is less than two weeks away, I haven't got time for anything beyond minor adjustments now. We're still working on the programs for the other inmates, they take weeks to prepare."

"Hang on," I butted in. "Are you saying Harvey's is the only one that's fully ready?"

"Yes," Reynolds cupped his forehead in his hand and massaged it, "the workload is immense. And I seem to be having to bear the brunt of it almost entirely by myself." He shot a dark glare at Nate.

"But," I continued, "I thought the public were going to vote on who goes in the chamber? Isn't that the whole point? How do you know he'll be picked on opening night?"

"Oh, you're a green one, aren't you?" Reynolds chuckled a little, giving me another one of those smug smiles. "Trust me, we *know*."

"You mean the vote is rigged?"

"Of course not," Reynolds replied. "That would be fraud. People pay to cast their vote, after all. Let's just say that Miss Swann's quite unrivalled experience in the area has given her the benefit of insight into the behaviours of the viewing public. UView know exactly how their audience will vote. That's not a concern. What *is* concerning me now is Dax's theory. If Stone doesn't respond the whole thing will be a disaster. Upwards of ten million people are set to tune in to watch the Playground Slasher scream for his crimes. If he doesn't, we're all in the shit."

"I didn't say he was Superman," Dax said. "I said he wasn't scared of monsters, but he'll react to pain just like anyone else. I'm telling you, just crank that dial up. Give him all the juice you can, he'll scream then. Trust me." He winked at Reynolds.

"It's not the same," Reynolds whined. "The public want to see terror in his eyes. They want him to feel the mental anguish his victims suffered."

"They won't know the difference," Dax replied. "At the end of the day, a scream is a scream. They'll get what they want."

PART 3

BEHIND THE BARS

1

"I can't believe I've got to go to this bloody launch party all by myself." Mel held her hair up out the way as I wrestled with the fastening on the silver diamond-laced necklace her parents had given her for Christmas. "It's going to be hideous."

"Oh, come on," I said, finally managing to get the tiny clasp shut and patting her shoulder to signify it was done. "You'll have a great time. Champagne, hors d'oeuvres, your dad getting drunk and giving one of his speeches – you won't even notice I'm not there."

She let go of her hair and her long golden curls cascaded over her shoulders. "Of course I will," she said, frowning at me. "I don't even want to go. It'll be the usual bunch of sycophants from Fanning Corp sucking up to Dad, and a whole new bunch of egotistical twats and sycophants from UView and VirtReal. Who am I going to talk to? I mean, *really* talk to?"

"Your mum'll be there," I replied. She just rolled her eyes.

"You know you're the only thing that makes these functions bearable for me," she said. "If I'd known this new job would mean we couldn't be seen together in public then…" She cut her sentence short, leaving me to wonder what she'd stopped herself from saying. She'd have forbidden me from taking it? She'd have told her dad not to offer it to me? I seethed a little that the thought had crossed her mind, even if only briefly.

She still saw herself as the one in charge of us. Of me. It was starting to wear a little thin.

"I just…" She sank into my arms and I returned the embrace, even though I wasn't sure I wanted to. "I just wish we could lock the door, get in our pyjamas and watch a movie or something instead. Just me and you."

"Me too," I said, but I was lying. G wing was having its own little launch party and I was oddly looking forward to it. In truth, I hadn't considered the social implications of accepting the post as Doug's spy in Whitefield either. But, unlike Mel, I was pretty pleased about the fact I could no longer attend high-profile functions with her. All it would take would be one pap snap of me and her at the launch party and my connection to Fanning Corp would be there for all at Whitefield to see. It hadn't been an issue until now; prior to his involvement in the *Justice Live* project, Doug had managed to stay pretty low-key by virtue of his lack of vices. While everyone knew of him, no one was particularly interested in the ins and outs of his life. He didn't have affairs, or avoid taxes, or say outrageous things. He was rich, but essentially boring. The papers don't care about soirees at country clubs, but they did care about the launch of *Justice Live*.

"Plus I hate having to pretend I'm single at these things," she whined. "It makes me a target for all those slimy gold diggers trying to get in Daddy's good books."

I tensed a little, imagining all the young, rich executives from UView and VirtReal schmoozing up to her, flirting with her. Anger twisted in my stomach. I wasn't angry at them, they were only doing what any man would in their position, I was angry at her. Why would she say that? Why would she force the mental images of would-be suitors throwing themselves at her stilettoed feet onto me? She was trying to hurt me, to make me jealous.

I wanted to call her out, to tell her how low her tactics were, but it would only end in an argument and somehow she'd twist it until she came off as the victim and me the jealous, overbearing aggressor. So I left her applying mascara in the bathroom, still pouting about having to take a limo to an extravagant party at which she would be fawned over and adored, and headed to work.

By the time Bailey waved me through the gates with only a cursory glance in my direction, I'd all but forgotten about Mel and her attempts to make me jealous. Life at Whitefield had become a breeze since the rehabilitation programs had started running less than a fortnight before. With so many eligible inmates jumping at the chance for early release, the prison population had almost halved within the first week. G wing was functioning as it should, and the lightening of the workload meant that we were actually able to do the odd thing to make prison life a little less stagnant – like tonight.

The whole country was excited about the launch of *Justice Live*. Even though opinion was divided as to whether it was a great idea or a total abomination, it was without doubt the hottest topic in every home and workplace in the country, if not the world. Whitefield was abuzz. The most anticipated television event of the century, and it was happening just metres away. Erin had proposed that we make an event of it, get the big projector screen up in the canteen and allow the inmates to watch. With the population so much reduced, it was doable as long as enough of the COs didn't mind coming in for a few extra hours to help out. Everyone volunteered except Lardarse, who claimed he had a date. Nobody was upset that he wouldn't be joining us.

It was my first workplace event since starting at Whitefield, and it was definitely more my scene than one of Doug's soirees. Erin had already started rearranging the tables and chairs in the dining hall when I arrived, and Bodie was happily following her directions. I went to pick up a stack of chairs, but Squinty stopped me.

"Never mind that, Beanie," he said. "You haven't seen it yet."

"Seen what?"

"The madness," Erin said.

"Come on." Squinty started for the door. "Come up on the roof and have a look."

I glanced at Erin and she smiled and waved me along. "Go on," she said.

I duly followed Squinty up the landings and through the locked door to the small, flat roof above the reception area.

"Here," Squinty said, gesturing toward the *Justice Live* compound, "look at 'em all. I've never seen anything like it."

From our vantage point, we could see over the ten-foot barbed-wire-topped walls that surrounded the compound and into the heaving throng of spectators gathered under the gaudy floodlights surrounding the stage. So many people, all jostling for the best positions. Some held banners, but I was too far away to read what they said.

"You'd think it was a bloody rock concert or something," Squinty said, shaking his head in disapproval as a helicopter began circling over the compound, shining beams of light down onto the crowd.

"Well." I shrugged. "It is the television event of the century, as they keep telling us. I suppose being able to say you were there will be quite something. I mean, the whole country will be watching."

"Not me," Squinty said. "Fucking disgusting, it is. Grown adults baying for blood. And they say it's the crims who are the monsters."

"You're really not going to watch?" I asked.

"Nope." He shook his head. "I promised to help because Queen Bee asked me to, but I told her straight: I'll help set up and afterwards I'll stay for lock-up and to get the inmates settled, but when the show starts I'm gonna be in the staffroom. Kinda my little silent protest, I guess. I don't know why but it just feels wrong to watch, like I'd be condoning it or something."

"I get that," I said. "I think it's horrific too, but I'm still gonna watch."

"You and half the country," Squinty said. "That's why they'll make a killing out of it. At the end of the day they don't care if people love it or loathe it, as long as they watch."

He was right. The only effective form of protest against *Justice Live* would be not to watch it, no amount of criticism or controversy would do anything other than boost its ratings. I knew that, but I was still going to watch. I told myself it was vital for *Justice Live* to succeed in order for the rehabilitation programs to keep running. A necessary evil, as Doug liked to put it. I told myself I had legitimate reasons to be interested in the show, but deep down I knew it was just morbid curiosity like everyone else.

True to his word, Squinty slunk off to the staffroom as soon as the inmates were all seated in front of the projector screen. They were hyped up, like kids at a party, but the atmosphere was one of excitement, not hostility. Even the most confrontational among them, like Sanders and Fuller, seemed content to stay seated and watch.

"Here we go, lads," Erin said as she switched on the live stream and the pre-show advertisements began. "Don't make us regret doing this for you, will you?"

They all clapped and cheered. Greavsie shouted, "Thank you, miss!" and a few of the others made approving comments about us being "alright as screws go". The chatter faded as the commercials came to an end and the announcement began.

"And now, exclusive to UView, we are proud to present the highly anticipated launch of *Juuuussstice LIVE!*"

Whitefield itself came on-screen, an overhead view from the helicopter, and everyone cheered.

"Hey, hey, where are we on there?" Hollington asked and Greavsie, who was in the front row, shuffled forward and pointed to G wing, his finger creating a blanched circle on the screen.

"Wahey," Jones cheered. "I've never been on telly before!"

"You're not now, you nonce," Fuller said, rolling his eyes.

"Well, I'm behind that wall there," Jones replied. "That's good enough for me."

"Maybe we should wave out the windows," Greavsie suggested, and a few of the inmates started to get to their feet.

"You'll do no such thing," Johnson barked. "If you do, *we'll* get it in the neck and trust me, you'll regret that."

"There'll be no more nights like this if we get into trouble for it," Erin added. "So sit down and shut up."

They all muttered apologies and sat back down. Erin flashed me a knowing smile and I grinned back, sharing her satisfaction with the situation. Her methods had proven correct, give a little, get a little. The inmates knew we were doing them a favour, and they had enough respect for that not to push their luck. It was a rare moment of kinship across the bars.

The helicopter-cam was now circling the *Justice Live* compound, and the floodlights illuminating the audience flashed from green to blue to red, making it look as though the spectators were at a disco. The crowd cheered, waved, jumped up and down and thrust their handmade banners and placards skywards towards the camera above. The camera zoomed in on them, and I was at last able to read their slogans.

Most were pretty mundane. *Welcome to Justice Live*, *Hello Mum*, *Gav woz ere* – that kind of thing. But in amongst the banal, jovial placards there were some more unsettling messages.

AN EYE FOR AN EYE!

Rot In Hell Murder Scum

Gut The Bastards

The camera paused on a portly, mumsy-looking woman who held a sign proclaiming *Make Them Scream!* She waved and smiled, blowing kisses with her free hand.

"Jesus," I whispered to Bodie, who was standing next to me. "It's all a bit sick, isn't it?"

2

The two-hour launch special followed the same tried-and-tested formula as dozens of other reality shows before it. First the glamorous host, in this case Mo Wilson with his sequined suit, fake tan and even faker smile, whipped the crowd up into a frenzy with hints and teasers about what was to come. Then, he cut to pre-recorded footage of himself exploring the max wing prior to the prisoners' arrival, pointing out the blindingly obvious purposes of each room ("This table is where our deadly inmates will eat their prison gruel", "These are the cells where the inmates will spend most of their time, trapped like the rats they are.")

He lingered on the isolated cell that I knew to be Harvey Stone's, even going in and sitting on his bed. "Let me tell you, ladies and gents," he said, bouncing his bottom on the bunk. "This has to be the hardest, lumpiest bed I have ever seen. And I've stayed at a Premier Inn!" The audience roared with laughter at his terrible joke, and I wished they wouldn't encourage him. "So, a lot of you may be wondering whose cell this is and why it's separate from all the others. Well, don't worry, all will be revealed in part two when we meet the inmates and learn a bit more about the terrible crimes that brought them here. But, ahead of that, I've got someone very special here with me to tell you a little about the inhabitant of this unusual cell. Please welcome Correctional Officer Dax Miller!"

Dax swaggered on-screen, taking a seat on Harvey's bunk

next to Mo. He waved and smiled at the cameras and the audience cheered and wolf-whistled.

"Now, Dax," Mo said. "Am I right in thinking that you are the personal officer for the inmate who will be living in this cell."

"Yes, that's right Mo," Dax replied, his face set in a smile. He looked a little more tanned than he had in real life, and I wondered if they'd put make-up on him.

"So what can you tell us about the man behind these bars?" Mo quizzed him.

"I can tell you he is the most dangerous, disgusting and repulsive criminal in the country, Mo."

"Mmm-hmm." Mo nodded. "That's right. He's a man whose crimes have shocked the nation, isn't he, Dax? And I believe you have a personal connection with him, is that right?"

"Yes I do, Mo. In fact, I've known him ever since he was a child."

"Well, say no more now, Dax. Because all will be revealed after the break when we meet the inmates! Once all of our dirty dozen have been introduced, the phone lines will open for you at home to cast your vote to decide who will be the first to enter our justice chamber later tonight. But for now, please enjoy these messages from our sponsors and we will be back in three!"

We handed round some crisps and popcorn to the inmates during the commercial break. Erin's idea, of course. "Keeps them from getting bored, and rowdy," she said. "Works with all males, I find. Especially my son."

Bodie was just staring at her in awe as she weaved her way through the prisoners exchanging banter and giving out snacks. I felt sorry for the guy. He had it bad, but she didn't seem interested in him beyond throwing him the odd crumb of attention or asking him for favours.

When the show came back on, it was time to introduce the twelve inmates and their personal officers, all of whom would be celebrities by the time the broadcast finished. The sweatboxes had arrived two days before, under cover of darkness, bringing the country's most notorious criminals together from far and wide. The night security guard (who was a hell of lot more friendly and on the ball than his daytime counterpart Bailey) had seen them drive into the compound, and was so excited that he'd hung around long after his shift ended to let us all know that max was now full. Not that it made the blindest bit of difference to us really, we had nothing to do with the goings-on over there, but it did feel a little eerie knowing that the very worst killers in the country were just behind that wall.

Each of the twelve inmates had a ten-minute introductory section, and each followed the same formula. Footage of their 'walk of shame' across the compound from the transport van to their new cell was interspersed with newspaper headlines regarding their crimes, and narrated by Mo who gave grisly details of the atrocities they had committed. Then, families of their victims gave short, tearful sound bites about their grief. Finally, the inmate's personal officer was introduced with a montage of pictures of them going about their daily life (supposedly, though in reality the photographs were highly staged) and then a short interview in which they told the viewers about their personal connection to the monster they were assigned to.

First out of the van was Bruce Knox, commonly known as the Sussex Strangler. A butch-looking man in his fifties, the newspaper headlines that flashed up on-screen detailed a spate of murders he'd committed twenty years ago. All young blonde women that he had stalked relentlessly before strangling to death and dumping in woodland. Teary-eyed parents clutched tissues on floral sofas as they recalled how full of life their deceased daughters had been.

Bruce's personal officer was Marv Wilson, a correctional officer previously working at Belmarsh. His montage included pictures of him volunteering at a soup kitchen and cuddling his large shaggy dog while shooting a smouldering smile at the camera. In his interview he talked about how he'd been a rookie cop at the time of Bruce's murder spree, and how Janice Rippon, Knox's third victim, had been the first murder scene he'd ever attended. As part of the team that eventually tracked him down and brought him to justice, he'd apparently been so traumatised by the state of the victims that he'd decided to quit the police force once he'd solved the crimes. "I felt like this was too much. I knew then and there that I'd made a mistake joining the force. Dealing with Bruce's victims, and their families, I just couldn't handle the horror of it. I started having nightmares, and I knew they wouldn't stop until Bruce was stopped. I wanted to quit, as soon as I saw Janice's body, I wanted to quit. But I couldn't, not then. Because her family, they didn't have the choice to just walk away from the case, so I felt I owed it to them to see it through."

Next came Francis James, known as Franco. A young man from a wealthy, possibly slightly inbred, aristocratic line. He'd been responsible for the murders of six rough sleepers in Oxford during his time as a student there. When questioned as to why he did it, he claimed it was 'euthanasia' and freely admitted that he was disgusted by them. He famously described his crimes as 'a cure for idleness' and was immediately disowned by his family, probably because he was simply parroting the attitudes they had taught him, and they wanted to distance themselves from the consequences of their own bigotry.

Franco's personal officer was a well-built, olive-skinned young man named Carlos Fuente. The connection between them was spurious: they had grown up on opposite sides of the same town. But the rippling abs Carlos was sporting in his VT made the reasons for his inclusion very clear. The producers had chosen to show him working out, rather than seated on his couch for an interview like most of the others. Presumably, they thought that the sight of him bending, stretching and lifting wearing nothing but some very tight spandex shorts would distract the viewers from his painfully boring 'about me' monologue playing over the footage. They were right, he was quickly voted 'Hottest Guard' in all the teen and celebrity magazine polls, and was soon drowning in offers for modelling contracts.

He was swiftly followed by Finn Tulley, the evil bastard who had kidnapped little Jessica and posted her eyes to her parents. In his late twenties, he was the youngest of the bunch and had a habit of pushing his floppy blonde fringe out of the way to glare at the camera as though he were trying to intimidate the viewers with his cold stare. The headlines on-screen read *Pure Evil* and *Stone-Hearted Killer* and his demeanour in the arrival scenes seemed to qualify them. He ambled through the compound, defiantly refusing to keep step with the unnamed guards escorting him to his cell.

The CO charged with being Finn's officer was known simply as Titch, and he looked to be little more than a child. Short, wiry and fresh-faced, his cheeks were slightly too big for his head, as though he hadn't yet grown into his own bone structure. In his tearful interview, he confessed that he understood the pain and grief that Jessica's family had been through more than most. His older sister had been murdered by her boyfriend when he was a child, leaving his parents grief-stricken. Her killer had never been caught, choosing instead to end his own life with a leap from a multistorey car park just minutes after he had squeezed the life from his girlfriend's neck. "So I guess I understand the need for justice in a very deep, personal way," he said, dimples on display for the viewers. The mums in the crowd loved him and his little-boy-lost demeanour.

Another commercial break, during which the prisoners of G wing proclaimed that the new max inmates were 'pussies' and boasted about how easily they could 'do' them if only they could have a moment alone with them.

"I'd rip that Finn fucker's balls off and stuff 'em down his throat," Sanders declared. "They should let me have a go at him, that'd be good telly."

"I'd kick the cunt to hell and then rip his fucking eyes out and eat them in front of him," Holt joined in.

"What good would that do?" another inmate chimed in. "He wouldn't be able to see you eating them if you've ripped 'em out, would he?"

"Alright, I'd do one at time then," Holt retorted, "real slow. Make him wish his mother had never opened her fucking legs."

There was a roar of agreement from the others. Finn had got their rage up more than any of the other inmates so far, and it wasn't hard to see why. You don't hurt kids. That was the fundamental golden rule even amongst the most violent and despicable of the criminals. There were no child killers or paedophiles on G wing, or in any of the gen pop wings. They wouldn't last five minutes on one of the landings, so they were sent to the Vulnerable Prisoners wing to serve their sentence amongst their own kind. Breaking into the VP cells and wreaking bloody justice on the 'nonces' was one of the most commonly discussed fantasies on the wing, next to breaking out altogether, of course.

After the break, the introductions continued with notorious cannibal Edward Redvers. Time behind bars had taken its toll on Eddie the Eater. In the mugshot that flashed up from the day he was arrested he was a tanned, muscular young man with a full head of bushy black hair. But the wretch who walked across the compound in handcuffs was portly, bald and pale. The headlines and accompanying crime scene photos for Eddie were decidedly gruesome, and police officers who had worked on the case described in horrific detail the sights they had been confronted with at the storage unit now commonly known as Eddie's Larder. Hands with no flesh left on them, rotting faces covered in flies and bite marks, a small camping stove where Eddie had sautéed the spleens and kidneys of previous victims, and forcibly fed them to his latest prey as they struggled helplessly in their chains.

Eddie's personal officer was a sombre-looking guy named Lez Trent who barely looked at the camera as he spoke. A middle-aged CO who had been working on Eddie's wing since his arrest twenty years previously, he wore the look of a jaded, cynical man beaten down by decades in the prison service. He was clearly uncomfortable with being on camera, and as he shifted awkwardly in his seat during the interview, I wondered what had possessed Aisling to recruit him. There must have been other guards from Eddie's wing who were more charismatic and camera-worthy. It was only when Lez began to recall his first day on the job, which just so happened to have been Eddie's first day in prison, that the reason became clear.

"I was new," Lez said, looking down at his feet as he spoke. "I'd had the training and that, but nothing can really prepare you for someone like Eddie. He was causing a disturbance in his cell, shouting and raving. My SO told me to get in there and sort him out. I didn't think it was safe, but I didn't want to go disobeying orders on my first day. So I went in, alone. The SO got the sack for what happened next."

Lez held his right hand up to the camera to reveal his missing pinky finger and the mangled skin where it ought to have been. "Bit it clean off," he said. "The man's an animal."

G wing gave a collective wince, everyone sucking air in through their teeth and scrunching up their eyes. I found myself making fists with my hands and Bodie looked as though he might throw up.

Ollie Barnes was still in the line-up, so I guessed Aisling didn't always get what she wanted, after all. A very nondescript-looking man in his forties, even the headlines about him that flashed up were boring in comparison to the others: *Disgruntled Accountant Charged With Poisoning, Barnes 'Snapped' Claims Lawyer*. There was very little reaction, beyond a cursory booing from the crowd. In amongst a line-up of child killers and creatively macabre criminals, Barnes just wasn't twisted enough to make an impact. Aisling was right: no one gave a shit.

His PO wasn't much better, in terms of piquing interest. Mikey Sawyer, a young correctional officer whose only connection to Barnes was that he supervised the library duties that the killer undertook. It wasn't much of a story, and even the inmates lost interest and started chatting amongst themselves.

After Ollie came Dil Travis, a cult leader who had convinced his flock to collectively shuffle off the mortal coil by downing a concoction of poisons as part of a cleansing ritual. After they'd signed over all their earthly possessions to his church, of course. He'd then done a runner with their money and headed over to America where he had been busy recruiting more followers when the extradition order came. Long-haired, bearded and barefoot, he purported himself to be a messiah, and had clearly modelled his aesthetics on Jesus, despite claiming that the carpenter's son had been a false prophet.

They couldn't make a murder charge stick, seeing as his followers had willingly taken their own lives and he'd been very careful to make sure that he himself had had no hand in the physical mixing and distributing of the poison, and that each and every one of the deceased had written a suicide note before partaking. They got him on tax evasion in the end. But for the purposes of *Justice Live*, it didn't matter what his conviction was for. He was a killer, everyone knew it, and the voting public don't care much for legal loopholes and technicalities.

His PO was Stewie Carter, a smart-looking man of around twenty-five who spoke softly and avoided using any profanity, substituting swear words for saccharine alternatives like 'doo-doo' and 'fudge' during his interview. His auntie had been one of the three dozen suckers that Dil had duped into taking their own lives. Stewie described her as: "A good Christian woman who was led astray and taken advantage of," and told the audience, "I just pray with all my heart that she has found peace with Jesus now." I already knew he'd be a hit with the older, religious viewers and couldn't help but admire Aisling's tactics.

Erin thrust a doughnut in a paper bag at me as the next commercial break began. "Take this to Squinty, will you?" she asked. "He'll go ape if he misses out."

I nodded and headed to the staffroom where Squinty was reclining on the sofa watching the twenty-four-hour news channel.

"From Queen Bee," I said, handing him the bag. He sat up and peered at the sugary treat inside.

"Blinding." He grinned and took a big bite. Jam ran down

his chin as he continued to speak with his mouth full. "How's the big show?"

"Pretty twisted," I replied. "Kinda interesting in a macabre sort of way, though."

"Yeah, well," Squinty continued. "I bet it's not as interesting as what's just been on the news."

"Oh? What's that then?"

"They've got the arsonist. You know, the one who burned those disabled kids alive. Well, actually they've got two of them – brothers, they are. They're not sure which one actually started the fire, or if it was a joint effort, but they were both identified by witnesses. 'Spect the older one will be coming our way soon enough. The younger one too, but he's not quite eighteen yet."

"Jeez." I shuddered a little. "Seventeen? What possesses a seventeen-year-old to do something like that?"

"Twelve it is now," Squinty said. "Twelve kids dead. The three that were in hospital didn't make it. Twelve kids and two of the staff. Fucking evil bastards they are, don't care how young. Old enough to know right from wrong far as I'm concerned. Hope they come to G wing, I'd love to let Lardarse get his greasy mitts on them."

"You're dreaming," I said. "They'll be straight in with the VPs."

"Yeah, I know." He sighed a little. "Fucking shame really. Oh, look. Here we go." He turned the sound up on the TV as the hourly round-up of top stories began. "Look at them, fucking evil scum. You can see it in their eyes."

I watched as the anchor cut to footage of the brothers being arrested, but I didn't see evil in their eyes. Instead, I saw two young boys being wrestled from a squalid bedsit not fit for a dog. I saw a man who was little more than child himself trying to be brave, shouting assurances to his younger sibling as the police bundled on top of him, pinning him down. I saw a curly-haired boy, with a kind heart and so much potential, crying in fear and gasping for breath.

I saw Vincent and Danny.

3

Back in the dining hall, the next section of *Justice Live* had already begun but I could hardly take it in. My mind was racing, searching for an answer. Trying to convince myself that the police must have made a mistake. It couldn't have been Danny, he couldn't have been involved. Not Danny. Not the quiet, unassuming kid who wanted nothing more than to play pool or chat with me over a cup of tea. Not the sweet, polite boy who offered to help the younger kids with their algebra and whose face lit up every time his beloved older brother turned up to collect him. What could have happened in my absence to lead to this?

Even Vincent, despite his notoriety as a gang leader, had never struck me as a cold-blooded killer. True, he wasn't averse to violence if it benefitted him in some way, or if it was directed at his rivals. But to set fire to a children's home? It wasn't the Frank Street Boys' style. They were territorial, drug-running petty criminals who sometimes crossed the line into assault and criminal damage, but only in retribution for wrongs done to them by others. As bad as his reputation was, I couldn't imagine Vincent having had a hand in this.

I tried to concentrate on the next lot of inmates entering *Justice Live*, but it all seemed so unimportant now. One by one, Mo introduced a string of killers whose atrocities had once been the talk of the nation for a few weeks, but who hadn't achieved the lasting notoriety of others such as Eddie, Finn and Harvey.

Georgie Hunt, who had raped and killed his stepdaughter in Hallow just a few years ago and his PO Josh; Hayden Matthews, the psychopath found guilty of torturing and beheading an elderly woman in her own home and his PO Dan; Kieran Brooks, briefly famous for the kidnap and dismemberment of his boss' wife, accompanied by his PO Benji, whose brother's wife's cousin had once cleaned the victim's house; Peter Stapleton, once dubbed the Manchester Maniac thanks to a killing spree thirty years prior that saw five prostitutes ending their days at the bottom of a river, along with his PO Jensen who looked like he was fresh out of training and had no connection bar having worked on Stapleton's wing; and finally Reggie Strange, a man whose name seemed to fit him perfectly. No one had ever been able to ascertain precisely what he was trying to achieve by abducting women and then simply making them sit on hilltops for several hours while he stared at them intently before letting them go, but it seemed he had never had any intention of killing them. Not until he tried to grab a self-defence instructor who was on her way home from teaching class and got a kick in the balls and a black eye for his trouble. Perhaps he was humiliated, perhaps he was just angry, who knows what goes on inside a mind like that? But either way, he snapped. When he'd recovered enough to walk, he kept to the shadows and followed her home, returning half an hour later with a can of petrol and a box of matches. She and her husband were charred to a crisp in the house fire that eventually brought Reggie's weird abductions to a tragic end. His PO Geoff had been one of the firefighters who tackled the blaze. The injuries he sustained trying to rescue the homeowners inside put an end to his firefighting career, and he turned to corrections instead.

The commercials rolled again, and G wing began to speculate as to who the last inmate might be.

"Must be a big one," Greavsie said. "Got to be the one they're putting in that special cell, that's why they're leaving him till last."

I already knew, of course, who the headliner was going to be. When he finally came on-screen, I was at last able to put my swirling thoughts of Danny and Vincent aside for a little while. My curiosity about the man Dax had warned us so strongly about had me glued to the screen.

Harvey Stone had an entire thirty-minute segment to himself. Well, he had to share the limelight with Dax a little, but there was no doubt that *Justice Live* considered the Playground Slasher to be their main attraction.

The first thing that struck me when I watched the footage of his arrival at max was how utterly normal he appeared. Short back and sides, thick-rimmed spectacles, average height, average weight, there was nothing distinctive about his appearance at all. He walked with a slight, barely perceptible slump to his shoulders. Had he been dressed in a shirt and tie instead of a brown prison jumpsuit, he'd have looked every inch the archetypal, world-weary middle-aged man. The sort of guy who would go unnoticed everywhere he went.

It made my skin creep a little to imagine how many mundane, routine encounters he must have had with unsuspecting members of the public during his three-year reign of terror. Countless shopworkers must have taken his money, packed his groceries, perhaps even passed comment with him on the weather, never knowing that the unassuming man in front of them had committed such unspeakable acts. Dax was right, I realised in that moment. No computer-generated monster could ever compare with Harvey Stone. It was the hidden evil, the one that moves amongst its prey masquerading itself as average and mundane, that was the real stuff of nightmares.

He was flanked on all sides by guards as he mooched across the compound. The others had been escorted by only one CO, but the producers must have taken Dax's warning that he must he never be alone with anyone, not even for a minute, seriously. Either that, or it was a stunt designed to portray him as the most dangerous of the twelve. Knowing the show as I do now, I'd bet on the latter.

The statements from his victim's families were as tearful and heartfelt as all the others, and the accounts of their injuries from the officers and coroners working on the cases were as stomach-churning as Finn's or Eddie's. But there was another aspect to Harvey's introduction that set him apart from his counterparts, and that was Dax.

Dax Miller was clearly born to be on camera. To compare his interview to those of the other POs would be to compare a Hollywood blockbuster to a Wednesday afternoon production by your local church's am-dram club. He had the looks, he had the range and now, thanks to Harvey, he had the spotlight.

"I've known Harvey Stone since we were both kids," his monologue began, and an old class photo came on-screen. "We went to the same school, Fir Bank Primary." Soft, sad piano music played as the camera zoomed in on the photo. "He was always a little… strange. Even back then." The rows of grinning young lads in short trousers and serene-looking girls in blue checked dresses began to blur as the shot focused on a tall, weedy kid with thick spectacles and a glassy stare. "He was always coming out with odd comments, y'know? Dark comments. The other kids thought he was funny, but it always made my skin crawl a little. He was popular, even though he was kinda odd. He was popular, and I wasn't. I was the kid who always came last in everything, the one who didn't have the right shoes, or the right lunch box, because my parents couldn't afford to buy me what the other kids had."

The camera panned across the photo, this time settling on a short, fat kid who had Dax's grey-blue eyes. "No one wanted to be my friend, y'know? And Harvey, he took advantage of that. It's no exaggeration to say he made my life a living hell. It got so bad that there were days when I really felt like I didn't even want to get out of bed." He looked directly at the camera and swallowed hard, his voice cracking ever so slightly. "Some days I didn't even want to be alive."

The scene changed to a still photograph of a generic school field with children playing football in their PE kits. "So one day," Dax continued, "I was playing football out on the field. All by myself, just kicking the ball against the fence. But I kicked it too hard and it went behind the science labs. I ran to get it back, and there was Harvey, crouching in the bushes with one of the hamsters from the reception class. He had his hand around its throat, really tight, and he was just... smiling. I could tell that it was dead straight away."

"He turned around and saw me standing there and his face was just anger. Just pure rage. He told me if I ever told anyone what I'd seen he would cut me. I was scared, just so scared. I couldn't understand why he would want to do something like that. But I never told. And I think, looking back, that's one of the biggest regrets of my life. Maybe if I'd told someone what I'd seen, maybe then he would have been on the radar, you know?" A solitary tear ran down his cheek. "Maybe even he'd have got some help for whatever was going so wrong in his head." His voice cracked and broke, and he grabbed a tissue from the table in front of him and dabbed at his eyes. "Maybe... maybe those beautiful little girls wouldn't have had to die."

They cut back to the stage, where the audience were silent and Mo Wilson looked respectfully sombre, keeping his excessively white teeth hidden for once. "Heartbreaking stuff," he said after a brief pause. "I'm sure I speak for all of us when I say we all feel your pain, Dax." The crowd gave a low rumble of agreement. "That had to be a tough story to tell, let's show our support for the incredibly brave Dax Miller!"

Now the crowd roared with cheers and applause and shouts of "We love you, Dax!" and all thoughts of sadness were forgotten. Mo began his recap of the twelve inmates and their crimes, but by the time he'd read out the phone numbers to call to cast your vote, the 'winner' was already a foregone conclusion. I understood now why Reynolds had been so confident about the outcome. They couldn't rig the vote itself, but they could steer the audience very strongly in the right direction.

4

There was a half hour interlude while the public jammed the phone lines voting in earnest. *Justice Live* handed over to their sister show *Behind the Bars*, which featured a young, bouncy aspiring comedian who used a multitude of terrible puns and interviewed so-called experts in order to 'delve into the psyches of the inmates'. It was all fluff and filler and I couldn't concentrate on any of it. I popped back to the staffroom to see if Squinty had any more info on the Felton brothers' arrest, but there was nothing new to report.

"Older one'll be here tomorrow, I expect," Squinty said. "Can't see 'em getting bail."

"They wouldn't have anyone who could pay it for them if they did," I replied and Squinty frowned a little.

"How do you know?" he said.

I was going to have to say it sooner or later, I realised. Besides, keeping it in wasn't doing me any favours, my head was a mess. "I know them," I sighed. "From the youth centre I used to work at. Vincent's a gang leader, but he's not a bad guy." Squinty raised his eyebrow at me. "Okay, he *is* a bad guy, but I never thought he was a killer. And Danny? Danny was always such a sweet kid, I can't believe it was him."

"Always the ones you don't expect," Squinty said sagely. "I mean it, think about it. Every time some bastard does something heinous and they interview his neighbours, they're totally shocked, aren't they? And they always, *always* say he was a quiet, polite man, kept himself to himself. You never hear 'em saying they'd suspected he was psychopath for years, do you?"

"I guess," I said, but I still couldn't bring myself to believe it. "But, Danny and I were close. He used to come every day after school, we'd play pool and chat about his day. I really thought he was going to be okay. I thought he'd stay clear of all that gang shit, maybe even get out of Hallow. I was coaching him for his exams, he was set to do really well. Shit, I feel terrible now. I should never have left."

"How'd you mean?"

"I let him down. I said I'd be there for him through the exams, but I just left when a better offer came along. What if that was the last straw? What if he just thought fuck it and followed in his brother's footsteps?"

"Beanie, be rational. If all that was standing between him and that bottle of petrol was you having a game of pool with him, then he was always a lost cause."

The door squeaked a little as Bodie opened it and stuck his head round. "Sorry, Cal," he said. "Erin wants you back, the lads are starting to get a bit rowdy."

"Coming," I said.

"Don't dwell on it, mate," Squinty called out as I left the staffroom. "It's not your fault, right?"

* * *

"What was that about?" Bodie asked when we were out of earshot.

I explained what had happened, and about my relationship with the Felton brothers. He whistled and put a hand on my shoulder. "That's rough," he said. "I can see why it's getting to you. But, you know Squinty's right, yeah? It's not your fault."

"Yeah, I know," I replied, but I wasn't sure I meant it.

The finale of the first ever *Justice Live* was about to begin, and if the inmates of G wing were getting hyped up, it was nothing compared to the crowd around the stage. The whooping and excited screaming was audible from inside Whitefield, even with all the doors and windows closed. When Mo walked back onstage, it reached fever pitch.

"And now, ladies and gents." His smile was so white the spotlights reflected off his teeth. "It's the moment of truth! The votes are in, the results have been counted and verified, it's time for me to announce the name of the very first criminal to experience justice – live!"

"Har-vey, Har-vey, Har-vey," the crowd chanted, as though they were calling the name of a rock star, and G wing joined in. The camera cut to inside max, panning across the cells showing each inmate in the main area as they waited nervously for the result to be called. A heartbeat sound played subtly in the background to ramp up tension. When the scene cut to Harvey's cell the whole crowd booed. He wasn't waiting anxiously beside his bars like the rest of his counterparts. Instead, he was sitting on his bunk with his nose in a book, seemingly oblivious to all that was going on.

"*Justice Live* inmates," Mo's voice rang out inside max. "This is Mo. The public have voted, and the results are in." Again the camera panned across the cells. Some of the inmates made faces, or stuck their middle fingers up at the camera. Others, like Eddie the Eater, looked more unsettled. "I can now tell you that the first monster to face public justice will be…" The pause went on so long as to be uncomfortable. "Harvey Stone!"

The crowd went wild. G wing jumped out of their seats, fists punching the air as they cheered.

But Harvey didn't flinch. He simply put down his book, folded up his spectacles and placed them gently on the table beside him. He sat on the edge of his bunk, waiting patiently as if for a cab to arrive.

"Harvey Stone." Mo spoke directly to him, but there was

no acknowledgement in Harvey's eyes. "The guards are coming to get you."

Four unnamed guards entered Harvey's cell along with Dax. They cuffed his hands behind his back and he was escorted past the other cells and out into a reinforced Perspex tunnel that had been erected after my visit to the compound. The tunnel led across the courtyard to the chamber rooms, and went right through the crowd.

The audience were almost feral in their bloodlust. They screamed obscenities, banged on the walls of the transparent tunnel, threw tomatoes and eggs that exploded against the Perspex and left red and yellow residue dripping down its sides. Dax swaggered a few steps ahead of Harvey and the four guards flanking him, blowing kisses to the women who shouted his name and winking at the camera every time he noticed it pointing in his direction. Stone just looked straight ahead, not even glancing at the baying mob. He didn't so much as jump when their edible missiles hit the walls.

When they reached the chamber rooms Reynolds was there, wearing a white lab coat and a smug smile. He gave a slow nod to the four guards holding Harvey and they tightened their grip, intending to wrestle him into the VR chair. But Dax held his hand up to them. "No need, lads," he said, giving them each a brotherly clap on their shoulders. "No need. He'll play. Won't you, Harvey?"

Harvey gave no response to Dax, but when the guards let go their grip on him he duly walked to the chair and sat himself down, leaving the viewers to coo in awe over Dax Miller – the man who could control the monster. The four guards attached the restraints and wires slowly and silently, each movement exaggerated for the camera. Reynolds flicked a large wall switch (another dramatisation, the simulation could easily be started by a simple keyboard press) and the program began.

The split-screen view began with Harvey on the right and the first-person perspective of the simulation on the left. Harvey's expression was blank, his eyes closed and facial muscles relaxed as though he were asleep. The tunnel came on-screen, and as it had in the run-through the creature emerged from the darkness ahead.

The live audience gasped at the sight of it and even some of the hardened crims of G wing looked a little freaked out when the tiny hands began to protrude from its distended stomach, until Fuller broke the tension by shouting to Erin, "Hey miss, look. It's your boyfriend!" causing them all to erupt into guffaws.

"Well, at least he's better-looking than you, Fuller," Erin retorted with a wry smile and the laughter among the inmates continued.

"Ha ha, she got you, mate," Greavsie said. "Proper mugged you off there!"

I half-expected Fuller to fly at Greavsie, it was well known he couldn't stand him, but he took it in good humour for once.

The creature moved closer and closer, until you could even make out the fingers on each flesh-wrapped hand, but Harvey's expression didn't change, and the camera didn't move. By now, the first-person view should have been hurtling through the tunnel away from Reynolds' nightmarish creation. But Dax was right – he wasn't scared.

"He's not running," I whispered to Bodie. "He's supposed to run."

There was a slight flicker on the screen. Harvey's face disappeared, leaving just a full-screen view of the simulation, and the creature was suddenly a few feet further away than it had been before. Nobody else seemed to notice, but I knew what had happened. They'd cut to a pre-recorded run-through because Harvey wasn't playing ball. Now the camera spun around, and the simulation continued with a shaky run down the moss-covered tunnel into red-tinged darkness.

On and on through the brown, rat-filled sludge, round bends and past the rotting corpses of what I could only presume were the creature's previous victims, all the while the heartbeat in the tunnel grew louder and the monster's rattling breath seemed to come from every direction.

Eventually, the tunnel opened out into a large stone-walled room. Rusted, blood-covered hooks were suspended from the ceiling and the floor was littered with lumps of bloody flesh. The camera spun around, revealing that the way back out of this dead end was blocked by the fast approach of the creature, its spindly limbs outstretched as it reached for its victim.

Yet still, no shots of Harvey's face. I could only conclude he remained completely unperturbed by the experience, and was mocking them with his serene expression. I wondered if Reynolds would now accept defeat and do what Dax had implored him to – crank up the juice to elicit some screams and save the show from disaster.

The creature had Harvey cornered now, trapped with his back to the wall and surrounded by the ominous metal hooks that swayed and creaked despite the absence of any fresh air. A sound like ripping fabric rang out as two scaly, clawed hands burst from the ground beneath him and tightened around his feet, holding him fast.

The creature reached forward, maggots dripping from every facial orifice, and leisurely took hold of the jagged, curved hook to Harvey's right. Reaching around the avatar's body, everyone watching winced as it became obvious what it was about to do.

Finally, the split-screen returned just in time for the world to witness the Playground Slasher's face as he was penetrated through his shoulder by the cold, serrated steel of the meathook. His expressionless face at last broke into a grimace, and he let out a guttural yell as the tip was pushed slowly through bone and sinew. To the viewers, he was reacting to the horrific torture being inflicted via VR, but I saw something different.

He was shaking, but not with terror. His body tensed and then juddered, his neck muscles taut as his jaw clenched and his hands balled into fists. The second hook speared his left shoulder blade, and again his body stiffened and convulsed.

It wasn't the contents of the simulation causing his reactions, it was just the electric shocks. And I betted Reynolds had had to crank them much higher than he'd anticipated.

'A scream is a scream,' Dax had said. But he was wrong. There was something missing. The screams that eventually came from Harvey when he was hoisted into the air by his impaled shoulders and the creature set about slicing slowly into his flesh with a variety of serrated blades were enough to please the crowd, but they weren't the screams Reynolds had been hoping to invoke. There was no terror, only pain. The same result could have been achieved without the VR at all, and at a fraction of the cost and effort. Harvey Stone wailed, and writhed, and cried, but as Dax had predicted it was all just a biological response to physical stimuli. They hadn't broken him psychologically in the way they had intended.

Not that the audience cared, or even noticed. As his screams rang out, the crowd became rabid in their frenzy. Grown men jumped up and down hugging each other, as though their team had just scored the winning goal. Women shrieked themselves hoarse, clapping and dancing in primal exaltation. A grey-haired lady dressed in a long, pastel pink dress raised her hands in the air and gently sang hallelujah, tears of pure joy running down her wrinkled cheeks. I can't have been alone in finding the scenes of celebration more disturbing than the images of Harvey's torture.

5

When the whole horror show finally ended, we had quite a job getting an overstimulated G wing back to their cells and settled for the night. Erin suggested we should all go for a pint or two, and we readily agreed. There was no escaping *Justice Live*, though, it was the only topic of conversation among the other pub goers, and even the taxi driver that dropped me home at almost 1am could talk of nothing else.

I crept into the apartment, expecting Mel to be sound asleep and wanting nothing more than to slink into bed, close my eyes, and forget about the show, and about Vincent and Danny, for a few hours. But she was waiting for me in the lounge, her hands wrapped around a mug of hot chocolate.

"Oh, thank God," she said, putting down her drink and heading toward me, arms outstretched. "I've been waiting for you. How was your night?"

I shrugged. I was exhausted and didn't want to get into it all. "Alright, I guess." I replied.

"Did you manage to watch it?" she asked. "Wasn't it awful? And all the people going mental in the crowd – God, it makes me feel sick. It was even worse at the party, they were all congratulating each other, and I had to pretend to be happy about it too. There were press everywhere, I swear I spent my whole night with a camera in my face."

"Must have been tough for you." I tried to sound sincere,

but it came out as sarcastic and Mel slowly withdrew her arms, looking hurt.

"I know it's probably nothing compared to what your night was like," she said, "but I'm just saying – I missed you. I wish you'd been there with me."

"From the sounds of it, I'm glad I wasn't," I replied. "Anyway, I'm knackered. I'm going to bed."

I knew I'd upset her. When I turned from her and headed for the bedroom I knew she was struggling not to cry. I knew she would likely be awake most of the night, wondering what on earth had turned me so cold. I knew, but I didn't care. Looking back now, I realise I hadn't cared in quite a while, at least not like I should.

I don't know if she came to bed that night, but when I got up the next morning she was busy making scrambled eggs and coffee. She smiled and wished me good morning but I could tell from the blotches on her face and the swelling around her eyes that she'd been crying. I pretended not to notice, I was too consumed with what might happen in the day ahead to address the problems between us. I ate my breakfast, picked up my bag and keys and kissed her on the head as I left for work as though nothing was wrong, and she let it happen.

I arrived at Whitefield to hear the news I'd been expecting: Vincent Felton had been ghosted into the VPs overnight. Woken from his bed in the holding cells at the police station at 3am, loaded into a van with no warning or explanation, and ushered on to the wing at Whitefield under cover of darkness, and while everyone's attention was still focused on *Justice Live*. It was standard practice for prisoners whose arrival, or departure, might cause a stir.

Squinty must have already told the others about my connection to the Feltons before I arrived, because everyone stayed conspicuously silent on the subject of Whitefield's new high-profile arrival. I was grateful not to have to hear judgements and aspersions over morning coffee, but I struggled to keep my mind on the job that morning, watching the minutes tick by until lunchtime.

As soon as my lunch break started, I headed to the VP wing. I knew the guards on duty a little, but only by way of the odd passing comment in the staff room or foyer. They weren't supposed to let anyone on the wing, but I pleaded my case and they seemed satisfied that I wasn't intending to off their new prisoner.

"Might actually help," Lewis, the elder of the two, suggested. "He won't talk, not at all. Not even to his lawyer. We've been asked to try to build a relationship, try to make him trust us so that he might open up. Cops are pretty sure it was his brother that did it and he's keeping quiet to protect him, but unless he spills the beans he'll be in here for life as well. Maybe he'll tell you something?"

"It's worth a shot," I conceded, though I hoped to God they were wrong about Danny. What I wanted to hear from Vincent's lips was that his brother had nothing to do with it. I wanted to hear that Danny had been at home studying and the witnesses who claimed to have seen him leaving the building just before the fire broke out had all been mistaken. But of course, we don't always get what we want.

I followed Lewis past the row of cells inhabited predominantly by men who had committed the most unspeakable of crimes. Abusers, rapists, child killers with the odd minor celebrity or prison snitch thrown in. Any prisoner thought to be in serious danger from the inmates in gen pop, either because of their crime or their notoriety, ended up here for their own protection.

His cell was the second to last on the left. Lewis pulled down the hatch and knocked on the door. "Someone to see you, Felton," he said.

"I already told you, I don't want a lawyer," I heard Vincent reply.

"Not a lawyer," Lewis said. "An old friend of your brother's, apparently. Just so happens to be a CO too." He stepped aside and gestured to me to move forward. "I'll leave you to it then," he said to me. "But make sure you let us know if he says anything."

I nodded and peered through the hatch. Vincent was sitting on his bunk, looking the other way and pretending not to care that he had company. The leader of the Frank Street Boys, a young man who had spent years building his reputation and commanding respect, and fear, from his cohorts, yet he looked so small and so out of his depth in the bleak, unforgiving cell.

"Hey, Vinnie," I said, and he turned to look at me at last.

"Beanie?" He stood up and came close to the hatch, eyeing me with a sneer. "Fuckin' hell, man. Spooner said you was a screw now." He spat on the floor by the door. "I couldn't believe it. I used to think you were alright, shows you can be wrong about a person, eh?"

"I get it," I said. "You think I've sold out, right?"

"I think you been sniffin' too much rich pussy," he replied. "Made you forget all the things you used to tell Danny."

"What things?"

"Oh, just little things like how you'd help him, how you'd be there for him. How Whitefield was a trap an' you wanted to help kids like him avoid it, how you was a kid like him yourself once. But look, here you are with your hands on the fucking keys locking up your own kind. You make me sick."

"I'm sorry I didn't come back to see him," I said. "I really am. I thought about him all the time. I'm worried about him."

"Yeah, well," Vincent continued, "it's his own fault, innit? Soppy little bastard. I always told him, you can't trust anyone but blood. No one else'll be there for you when the shit gets real. But he's got a big heart, hasn't he? Too fucking trusting. Anyway, he knows it now. He knows I was right. Cos who was still there for him, after all the pie in the sky bullshit turned to dust, eh? Who was still there after you went, and the centre closed, and Mum died—"

"Your mum died?" I felt sick. On top of everything else, Danny had had to grieve for his mum. I knew what that was like, I knew exactly how it felt. I could have been there to help him pick up the pieces, to stop him making grief-fuelled mistakes like I had, but I wasn't.

"Overdosed. Stupid bitch," Vincent replied. "But I kept him safe. I kept him fed. An' when he failed his exams, I kept him going. He knows now, see? He knows there's only one person in this world who really cares about him."

"I don't believe you," I said, deciding in that moment that the only way to get anywhere would be to play hardball. "I don't believe you care about him at all. If you did, you'd tell the cops what happened so he doesn't have to spend his life in prison for your crimes."

"Fuck you, Beanie," Vincent began shouting, and Lewis made his way up the corridor towards us. "Fuck you! Don't you ever come near me or my brother again, you piece of fucking shit!" He picked up his toothbrush and threw it against the wall, then he tossed his mattress onto the floor and began pulling at the metal bed frame, trying to rip it apart in his anger.

"Went well, then?" Lewis said with a wry smile as he closed the hatch on the cell door.

* * *

I didn't feel like going home when my shift ended, not least because I didn't know how I could even begin to explain the tempest whirling through my mind to Mel. Vincent had confirmed my worst fear: my absence had hurt Danny and perhaps even contributed to the trouble he was now in. I'd let him down because I'd put my future with her ahead of my values, and there was a bigger part of me than I liked to admit that blamed her for that.

I desperately wanted to feel better about my choices, so I decided to head over to the rehab centre to see Nate, and remind myself of all the good Whitefield was doing for Hallow and the fact that I was a part of that. The programs didn't run on Sundays, and it was technically Nate's day off, but I knew he'd be there. He had no partner, no children, and seemingly no interests outside of the work he was so passionate about.

I found him tinkering around with the carpentry program, he was always trying to improve on his creations. "Hey," I said, knocking softly on the door so as not to startle him. "Sorry, am I interrupting?"

"Nah, nah. You're all good," he said, smiling. "I'm done, just waiting for it to compile. Hey, you want to split a hot dog?" The microwave he'd installed on a small, high shelf above his desk pinged and he pulled out his snack.

"No, thanks," I said. He shrugged as if to say 'your loss' and bit into his greasy, unappetising meal, puffing his cheeks out a little at the heat of it. "Have you been over to the compound today?" I asked. "Were they happy with the show?"

"Depends what you mean by happy," Nate said. "Ratings-wise, they're ecstatic. Smashed every estimate, and the media coverage has been record-breaking. But Aisling's on the warpath anyway."

"Because of Harvey's simulation?" I asked.

"You got it." He nodded. "Didn't quite go according to plan, did it?"

"No. But, do you think anyone watching really noticed?"

"I doubt it," Nate said. "But that's not the point. She noticed, so Reynolds is in the doghouse. Plus she's still pissed off about Barnes being in there, so she's on a new mission now and heaven help anyone who stands in her way."

"What new mission?"

"The children's home fire. She wants the culprit on the show, in place of Barnes."

6

I got to work early the next morning after a night spent tossing and turning, wrestling with unwanted mental images of Danny strapped into that damn chamber chair. He was due to turn eighteen in three months' time, and I had no doubt that unless Vincent stepped in to clear his name Aisling would get her way and his coming-of-age party would involve a special edition of *Justice Live*.

I waited in the car park for almost half an hour before I spotted Lewis pulling up in his grey-blue saloon. I jogged over and accosted him before he could even get out of the door.

"Hey, I need a favour," I said, trying to look as calm and casual as possible. "I need to see Vincent again today."

"Oh no." Lewis got out and slammed his car door. "No fucking chance, mate. Took hours to calm him down yesterday. You're lucky I managed to bullshit the SO about what set him off, or we'd both have been hauled up in front of Captain Wanker. Not happening."

"Please, Lewis," I pleaded. "It's really important. I've got some information he needs to know."

"The only thing that bastard needs to know is not to push me any more," Lewis replied.

"A note then," I argued. "Could you give him a note?"

Lewis exhaled loudly and gave a sarcastic chuckle. "You don't know when to give up, do you?"

"I can't give up," I said. "Not on this. Please, I know Vincent. I know he loves his brother. If he knew what I know, it could be the thing that makes him talk."

Lewis gave a low growl followed by a sigh of resignation. "Alright," he said. "I'll slip him a note for you. But if it all kicks off again, it's on your head."

"I'll take the risk," I said. "And thank you."

I tore a page out of the small notebook I kept in my pocket and hastily wrote my message to Vinnie:

I've got inside info. Whoever is found guilty for the fire will be sent to Justice Live. Please, Vincent. Do the right thing by Danny.

Lewis looked at it, and whistled before sticking it in his pocket. "I hope you know what you're doing," he said sternly before heading for the gatehouse.

* * *

Free flow had just begun and I was supervising the movement of inmates from their cells to their designated work areas when Lewis appeared on G wing and made a beeline for me.

"Your boy says he'll talk," he told me. "But only to you, and only if you're alone."

"Okay," I said, feeling elated that my message had finally made him see sense. "Where?"

"We're doing this kosher," Lewis replied. "We'll go see Captain Wanker, let him know the score. But nothing about the visit, or the note, alright? I've got kids to feed."

I agreed, and we headed off to see the governor hoping he wouldn't delve too deeply into our accounts. Luckily, once I explained my prior connection to the Feltons he didn't ask any more questions. In fact, he was delighted. The children's home fire, and the two young brothers who stood accused of starting it, was currently the most high-profile case in the country; the chance to be instrumental in bringing it to a close was positive publicity for Whitefield, and therefore for him. He agreed to allow me to speak with Vincent alone, in the exercise yard as he had requested, with the caveat that I must immediately relay any and all information I received.

I waited on the empty basketball court, praying that Vincent would simply confess and end both Danny's nightmare and my own crushing guilt. Two guards from the VP wing escorted him to me with his hands cuffed behind his back and attached with a chain to his shackled ankles. He looked deathly pale.

"You can leave us," I told them, and they nodded and backed away, positioning themselves out of earshot, but close enough to run in and assist me if things turned nasty.

"You wanted to talk to me?" I asked Vinnie.

"What you said, in your note." He was trembling and fidgeting in his chains. He spoke almost in a whisper, voice cracking as if he barely had the strength to form the words. "Was that legit, or are you bullshitting me to get me to talk?"

"It's legit," I replied. "I wish it wasn't. I have a friend who works for VirtReal, he didn't know I knew you when he told me. So it's strictly confidential information. I just thought you ought to know. I thought I owed it to you and Danny to make sure you had all the facts before you decide what to do."

"I didn't see the show," he said, not making eye contact. "I was being arrested. Is it as bad as people say?"

"Worse," I said as sombrely as I could.

"Okay, Beanie," he said. "I'm gonna do what you want me to do. I'm gonna tell them I did it. Just me. I'll stand up in front of any judge in the land, look them in the fucking eye and tell them I burned kids to death for kicks, and Danny was only there because he tried to stop me."

"Is that the truth?" I asked.

"Does it matter?" Vincent replied. "One of us is going over there, right?" He nodded his head towards the *Justice Live* compound. "And it's up to me which one it is. So I choose me. End of."

"He was involved, wasn't he?" I asked, knowing it was true even though I didn't want it to be.

"Like I said," Vincent stared at the wall, jaw tense, "it was all me."

In that moment, he seemed to me a scared child. A child who had seen too much, and been loved too little. A child who had been forced to take responsibility too early and had now become a man with too much weight on his shoulders.

"That's the official line," I agreed. "And that's what I'll tell them when they ask me. But there's something else, Vinnie. I know there is. And you need to get it off your chest. If you want to tell me, it won't go any further."

"Bullshit," he said. "You'll run off squealing to the cops like a little piggy. Someone has to pay, so I will pay. That's all that matters. Danny's innocent, I'm a monster."

"I don't believe you're a monster."

"Nah? Well, you must be an idiot then, Beanie. I've done some proper fucked-up shit, and don't pretend you don't know that. I've cut men for looking at me the wrong way. I've smashed faces, I've fucked up people who've crossed me so bad their own fucking mothers wouldn't recognise 'em."

"Alright," I said, "you've done some bad shit. But who was it who picked Danny up every day when your mother was too drunk to know her left from right? Who was it who cooked his favourite dinner when he'd had a bad day? Who protected him from bullies, scared away the monsters in his closet, read to him until he fell asleep? Who has looked after that kid all these years, and who is it that's now lying to save him?"

"You can't prove I'm lying. No one can."

"I don't want to," I said. "I want it to be the truth. I want to believe you're solely responsible. I want to be able to dismiss you as the monster you claim to be, the monster the world will see you as. But I just can't. Come on, Vincent. Don't you want even just one person in this world to know the truth about you?"

"You swear, on your life, on your fucking life, Beanie, that you won't ever tell another soul?"

I nodded.

"It was Danny, Beanie. It was Danny. I wasn't even fucking there."

7

I listened, horrified, as he laid out the whole tragic tale. After the centre had been shut down, Danny had become withdrawn and lost all motivation. He failed his exams, just like the long line of Feltons before him. With no prospects, and nothing to do with his days, he begged his older brother to give him a position in the Frank Street Boys.

"Thing is, Beanie," Vincent said, "I was losing control. Malachi and his damn Ringers, they were coming after our turf and some of the boys were starting to say I didn't have the balls to take 'em on. If I could have, I'd have given Danny an easy ride – put him straight in on a cushy number, like being a lookout or something. But I couldn't be seen to play favourites, I was barely holding on to my guys as it was. And truth be told, they didn't think he was right for the gang. I had to make him prove himself to them."

"Initiation?" I asked.

"Yeah," Vincent nodded. "And I thought I had the perfect solution. If I could get Danny to make a move against the Ringers, the boys would be satisfied that I was taking action. But I didn't want him in any danger. It had to look impressive, and do 'em some real damage, but I didn't want him actually going toe to toe with any of them. So I came up with the idea of attacking their stash. They were after the Moorings, cos everyone knows it's the best place to score, and they wanted to take our clientele. Only, they don't deal spice. They deal meth and crack, and that shit'll destroy people."

I'd seen my fair share of lives destroyed by spice, but it didn't seem like the time to bring it up.

"No one was supposed to get hurt, Beanie. You have to believe me. I wouldn't have asked Danny to do that, he's not strong enough to live with it. I knew where they kept their gear, and I knew no one would be there cos I'd been watching them. Proper Mickey Mouse operation they are, don't even assign a proper lookout for their stash when they're out dealing. They were begging for it really. So I figured, get Danny to torch their hideout and destroy their income at the same time. Two birds and all that, right?" I nodded, seeing his logic, but not liking where this was going. "Do you know why they call themselves the Ringers, Beanie?" he asked. I shook my head. "Cos from their place, you can hear those bells ring out every Sunday, loud and clear."

"Church Street," I said, the whole mess falling into place in my mind.

"Yeah. Don't suppose you noticed the boards on the windows of the house next door, when the children's home was all over the news."

"No," I said. "No, I didn't."

"It's a squat," Danny said. "Roof half-caved in, full of rats. Been empty for years, apart from Malachi's gang and their merchandise. I don't know how he fucked it up, I went through it a hundred times. Those old houses, they have basements. Rare as you like round here, but that particular row was built with 'em, no one knows why. Anyway, they have entrances in the backyards. Most of them have been bricked up, or covered over with gardens, years ago. But no bugger had done anything with that fucking squat in decades, least of all bothered with the garden. I'd scoped it out for him, it still had its original wooden hatch – can't miss it, I told him. How was I to know the bloody children's home still had one too?"

"Fuck," I said, "he got the wrong building."

"Guess there's things you don't get from studying books," Vincent replied. "I should have gone with him. I would have gone with him, but then the boys would've said it didn't count. He needed to have the glory. Stupid sod didn't even realise until it was on the news, he thought he'd pulled it off. Can you imagine what he went through, when he saw those burned kids?"

"Jesus. I can't even begin to," I replied. "But, it wasn't intentional, Vinnie. That means it wasn't murder, not technically."

"Does it matter?" he snapped. "Murder, manslaughter, arson. What do words matter? Which word is going to stop him being strapped in that chair, eh? Which word is going to bring back those kids? Ain't no words going to save my brother, Beanie. That's all on me."

He was right. There was nothing a lawyer could argue that would save Danny from *Justice Live*, not with the media focused on the case and Aisling Swann on a personal mission. I thought about Dil, the cult leader convicted on tax evasion. People didn't care about semantics and technicalities. No matter what Danny's conviction was for, he'd still be the monster who burned those kids alive, no fancy courtroom talk could stop that.

"So I'm gonna confess," Vincent continued. "All they've got on him is witnesses who saw him nearby. I'll say he followed me and tried to stop me. I'll say I threatened him to keep quiet. And you won't say a damn word against it, right?"

"Alright," I agreed. The VP guards came wandering over, our signal that we'd had long enough to talk. I stood and watched for a few moments as they led Vincent back into the building. I couldn't help but admire him, even as helpless and bedraggled as he looked. He was a criminal; a violent, drug-dealing thug. But he was also a man of honour, willing to put himself in harm's way for the sake of another. And I'm ashamed to say, I think that made him more of a man than me.

As soon as Vincent was back inside, Captain Wanker emerged from the main building and headed straight for me.

"Well?" he asked. "What did the bastard have to say for himself?"

"He confessed," I said. "He started the fire. His brother tried to stop him. He'll give a statement, and he'll plead guilty."

"Ha!" The governor looked positively elated. He put his hand on my shoulder and gave me a condescending pat. "Good work, Roberts. Good work. I always did have a good feeling about hiring you. Shows I've got an eye for a good officer, eh?"

The state Whitefield was in when I applied, he'd have hired an amoeba if it'd agreed to work overtime, and we both knew it. But I just smiled politely.

"Was there anything else?" he asked. "Any hint of motivation? Accomplices?"

"No, sir," I lied.

"Ack, well. The confession is the main thing. I'll call the boys in blue right now, get them to come take an official statement. I guess I better notify his lawyer too, poor sod. Imagine having to try to *defend* that piece of scum! There's bound to be a press release too, once the formalities have been dealt with." He adjusted his shirt and puffed up his chest. "I might even make it on to the six o'clock news!"

8

Vincent's confession was headline news for a few days. The media delved into every aspect of his past, trying to paint a portrait of the man behind the killings. Trying to turn the brothers' troubled upbringing into a sensationalised, easily consumable product for the masses. Facts gave way to fiction, conclusions gave way to aspersions, and by Tuesday afternoon everyone in the country had a firm opinion on a man that they, in reality, knew nothing about. When my own connection to the Feltons came out, I even had to fend off reporters on my way into work. I wanted nothing to do with the media circus that seemed hell-bent on crucifying him for public amusement; particularly because I knew how unjust it really was.

But by Thursday night the papers and talk shows had turned their attention back to *Justice Live* in anticipation of its second live broadcast. Dax Miller was on the cover of every women's magazine, mostly in shirtless poses, and each of the guards seemed to be so busy doing the talk-show circuit that I wondered if any of them had actually worked a shift that week at all.

They became instant celebrities. Every teen magazine boasted quizzes to discover *Which guard is your perfect match?* or *Which guard would want to date YOU?* Even the broadsheets seemed to be obsessed with their personal lives and backstories, albeit in a more intellectual, deconstructive way so that their readership could convince themselves they weren't just reading glorified gossip columns.

And it wasn't just the guards. Every television network seemed to be trying to cash in on UView's golden show. The schedules were packed with true crime documentaries delving into every facet of the inmates' crimes and prior histories, families of the victims gave interviews to every media outlet and vloggers and bloggers talked of nothing else. Short of becoming a recluse and eschewing all forms of communication with the outside world, it was impossible to escape the behemoth that was *Justice Live*.

When Saturday evening rolled around again, the second live show was just as hotly anticipated as the launch had been. This time, instead of watching the arrival of the inmates and learning about their crimes, the public would get to see highlights from the twenty-four-seven recording of prison life.

Mel and I were existing in a strange sort of limbo. We both knew things between us weren't as they should be, but neither of us appeared to have the energy, or the inclination, to address the problem. Instead, we seemed to have silently, telepathically agreed to continue on with our usual routines as though nothing had changed between us. We ate dinner together, we chatted about our days, we even had sex, but it was all painfully superficial. I told her about Vincent's confession to me, leaving out the truth behind his decision, and she listened sympathetically as you would to a stranger relaying their ailments. She made the right noises, but her heart wasn't in it.

We were broken, and I didn't know how to fix us. Worse, I didn't know if I even really wanted to. So we poured out our wine and sat down to watch *Justice Live*, physically almost touching but emotionally continents apart.

The crowd were just as frantic, and Mo was just as enthusiastic as he had been the week before. The first half of the show, which was interrupted every seven minutes for advertisements, gave the viewers exactly what they wanted – 'behind the scenes' footage from the week just gone. And it was instantly clear to me that Nate had been correct in his assertion that the guards in max would be working to a very different agenda than those of us in Whitefield.

The twelve inmates (eleven, really, seeing as Harvey was kept apart from the others at all times) racked up more fights and incidents in a week than the entire population of G wing would in a fortnight. If we could keep reasonable order at mealtimes and free flow with ten times the number of criminals to supervise and a much lower ratio of staff to prisoners, then defusing tensions and de-escalating situations between such a small number of inmates should have been a cakewalk for such supposedly experienced officers. Yet despite the fact that there was one guard on duty for every inmate, they seemed to be incapable of preventing violence breaking out. Anyone with any knowledge of corrections could smell the bullshit a mile off.

But it made for good TV, there was no doubt about that. Eddie the Eater threatening the Sussex Strangler over a can of tuna; Finn Tulley spitting on Dax Miller and getting bundled to the ground by an excessive number of officers; Reggie Strange slipping on his arse on a newly washed floor and then attacking the Manchester Maniac with his own mop when he laughed at the killer's misfortune. None of it needed to happen, all of it was easily avoidable with the number of staff on duty. So there were only two conclusions I could draw: either conflict was allowed to escalate, or it was actively encouraged to.

In between the scenes of fighting and threats, the guards were given plenty of airtime during which they were portrayed as the tough-but-caring men Aisling wanted them to be. In a scene that quickly became one of the nation's 'favourite moments' (as voted for by readers of the leading television magazines), Carlos was comforted by Lez when he 'opened up' about the frustrations he felt as Franco's personal officer.

"I just want to help him," Carlos sighed, staring into his morning coffee as they sat around the Formica table in their small staffroom. "I feel like he could be a good man, if he could just let go of his past and try to make a change. But no matter what I do, he just throws it back in my face." He looked up, and the camera zoomed in on his face to reveal the water pooling in his eyes. "It's so hard sometimes, when all you want to do is make a difference to someone's life."

"I know, mate. I know." Lez put his pinky-less hand on Carlos' shoulder. "But hey, you know what? You are making a difference. I believe it, I know it."

Carlos just shrugged and Lez grabbed his other shoulder and forced him to look directly at him. "Listen," he said, authoritatively and with a dramatic pause, "you just need to believe in yourself. You're a good officer. You're a good man. And I'm damn glad you're here." Carlos blinked fast and nodded slightly. "Hug it out?" Lez asked, and the two men stood up and embraced.

The audience gave a collective "Ahhh" as the camera cut to scenes of the crowd watching the footage on a large projector screen. I'd never seen such a sugar-coated, badly scripted crock of shit in all my life. But that didn't stop the media harping on about their 'bromance' for the next week.

Other highlights from the week included cult leader Dil giving an impassioned speech to granny-killer Hayden about the importance of 'allowing the healing light' into your soul, and a six-a-side basketball match between the guards which was a thinly veiled excuse to show them topless.

Of course, there were plenty of scenes of Harvey Stone to keep the viewers happy too. Though it seemed the laissez-faire attitude that allowed trouble to erupt between the other eleven inmates on a regular basis was not applied to Harvey. The Playground Slasher was treated with as much caution as if he were an unexploded bomb, despite the fact that he had not yet displayed anything other than a calm, resigned and frankly boring demeanour. He was mostly kept isolated in his cell, and the cameras caught nothing more interesting than him reading, sleeping, or simply staring straight ahead with a faraway look in his eyes – leading columnists and bloggers to speculate that his mind *is ablaze with gruesome plots*. On his daily trips outside for exercise, he was escorted by three officers and remained cuffed even as he did his slow, meandering circuits of the yard. He ate alone. He showered alone, save for the accompanying guards. Not once was a single word from his lips broadcast, giving more fuel to Dax's claim that he was dangerous to listen to.

After the week's highlights came the prolonged build-up to the results of the public vote. To nobody's surprise, Finn Tulley was chosen by a landslide. The two child killers were always going to be the first to face the public's wrath, you didn't need any kind of psychology training or fancy algorithms to work that one out.

Although to those on the inside of *Justice Live*, Harvey's chamber experience had been a failure, the audience hadn't noticed – perhaps because they were unaware of how the inmates were *supposed* to react to the torturous justice they were served. But when Finn Tulley's name was called, they soon found out.

9

There was no calm composure from the killer of little Jessica. When Mo called his name, he did not wait by his cell door with quiet resignation as Harvey had done. Instead, he picked up his mattress and tried fruitlessly to barricade himself in with it, retreating to the back of his cell, dropping to his knees and gripping the metal frame of his bunk so hard his knuckles turned white.

The guards made short work of bursting into his cell and wrestling him into his cuffs. He refused to stand, writhing and screaming as they dragged him along the floor to the Perspex tunnel. He thrashed, swore, tried to kick and bite the officers – all behaviours that under other circumstances would result in a swift injection of a sedative to calm him down. I wondered if that was his intention, if perhaps in his desperation to avoid the horror he was doomed to suffer he was trying to force the staff to give him liquid anaesthesia. Unfortunately for him, what would be an inconvenient way of behaving in any other prison environment was in this circumstance precisely what the producers wanted.

A child killer, reduced to being dragged along the ground as he pleaded and shook with terror – Aisling must have been jumping for joy.

He was finally hauled to his feet and forced to walk through the crowd, and his journey through the tunnel was

222

not one of dignity and acceptance as Harvey's had been. He jumped and screamed as the missiles of tomatoes, eggs, and a bottle of what looked suspiciously like piss hit the Perspex right beside him. Wild-eyed, he scanned the watching crowd with a furtive, terrified urgency.

He did not calm down once he reached the chamber. He wailed and bucked as six officers forced him into the chair and attached the restraints, Reynolds standing close by trying to look respectfully sombre, but failing to contain the hint of a smirk that twitched at the edges of his mouth. When the checks were complete, Titch nodded to Reynolds to signal that it was safe to proceed. With a theatrical flourish, and far too much glee in his eyes, Reynolds flipped the unnecessarily prominent switch and for a few moments Finn stilled, suddenly immersed in the all-encompassing world of VirtReal's simulation.

Finn's chamber program took place in what could be described as a modern version of the Roman Colosseum. When the first-person view of the simulation came on-screen, it was clear he was in the sawdusted circular centre of a large auditorium, packed to the proverbial rafters with noisy spectators. Alone and exposed, his glances around the ring revealed that the walls between him and the audience were far too high to climb. The only exit was an iron portcullis and it didn't take much imagination to realise that it would soon be raised to allow some form of horror to enter the arena with him.

In the chair, he panted and tensed and the pulse of his heart was visible in his taut neck as he waited in terrified anticipation for his fate. It was the build-up, and as Reynolds had explained to us when we watched the run-through of Harvey's program, it was all-important for provoking the heightened state of panic and fear that would ensure the victim felt the coming pain all the more acutely.

Trumpets sounded and the crowd roared in unison at the heralding of the impending 'games'. It was only when they leapt to their feet and began chanting that I noticed that their eyes were unusually large. Not comically, or supernaturally so, but each member of the CGI audience was in possession of a pair of slightly oversized eyes that seemed just a little too big for their faces and, as a result, made their gaze appear more menacing and intense.

Then came a slow, scraping sound that seemed to fill the whole arena as the portcullis began its dramatically slow ascent and the viewers waited with bated breath to see what devilish terror would emerge from the dark passage behind. Cheers and screams of delight rang out as a mass of creatures, each no bigger than a small domestic cat, swarmed forth with astounding speed.

The creatures, devised no doubt by Reynolds' warped and sadistic mind, appeared to be unnatural chimeras that resembled some form of long-snouted rodent with six legs and no eyes. Obviously blind, the furless spider-rats (as they would be referred to by the media, despite having too few legs to be arachnids, and being closer in shape and stature to an armadillo than a common sewer rat) surged forward, filling the area, their long noses quivering as they searched for their prey.

Finn's body twitched in the chamber chair as his avatar tried in vain to outrun his pursuers. Within seconds, they had him surrounded and he screamed and stomped as wave after wave of the creatures sunk their teeth into his bare feet and tried to climb up his legs. He batted and swatted, jumped and kicked and the crowd cackled manically at his futile attempts to push back his tormentors. He was already close to being overwhelmed by the sheer number of them, and had almost lost his footing and fallen into the heaving mass of snouts, legs and teeth, when the portcullis rose for a second time.

Four large wolves dashed into the arena with clear and purposeful direction. The spider-rats seemed to be expecting them, and parted to allow them through. The snarling canines were upon Finn in less a second, giving him no time to do anything other than succumb. Each took hold of a limb, causing him to scream as their sharp teeth tore through the skin and sinew of his hands and feet and their strong jaws clamped firmly around his bones.

Slowly and with choreographed synchronicity, they each pulled at the limb they held until Finn was spreadeagled face up on the dusty floor. His face forced to look up at the ceiling, the first-person viewpoint now revealed the huge mosaic eye that looked down upon him. With speckled blue corneas and an unusual, slightly angular pupil, the replica of little Jessica's most unique feature was made up of dozens of large, tinted mirrors reflecting Finn's tortured avatar back at him.

Two spider-rats simultaneously jumped up onto his chest as the stoic, steadfast wolves held Finn still despite his attempts to thrash against them. Wasting no time, the creatures scuttled up to his face and began to nibble at his eyelids. The close-up of yellowed teeth and spiky, furry tongues that filled the screen made Mel look away and put her hand to her mouth, and even I felt a little queasy.

With the lids chewed off, and Finn utterly unable now to close his eyes against the onslaught of horror, the spider-rats that had waited patiently around his star-shaped body scurried forth and began to consume him. Finn could do nothing but scream, unable to look away from the reflection above his head as he was forced to watch the creatures burrow through his abdomen. In many ways, it must have been a blessed relief when they finally consumed his eyes.

10

The Finn Tulley that emerged from the chamber chair was a shell of his former self. Within seconds of the program ending and his restraints being loosened, he began to sob uncontrollably. When the guards tried to get him up onto his feet, he projectile-vomited all over the chamber chair and trembled violently in their grip as he tried to stand but his legs gave out. The camera quickly cut away back to Mo Wilson and the whooping crowd, not giving the viewers too much time to dwell on the obvious signs of extreme shock, and likely long-term psychological effects, that their chosen victim was now suffering.

Of course, it was widely argued that any trauma Finn, or any of the *Justice Live* inmates, would undergo as a result of his chamber experience was nothing compared to the horror they inflicted on their victims and their families. It was a justification that didn't sit too well with me, even in a case such as Finn's. So the prospect of an innocent man, such as Vincent, being destroyed in that way was utterly sickening.

Yet there was nothing I could do about it. At least, nothing that wouldn't result in an even worse outcome. Vincent was right; it was him or Danny. There was no happy ending to be had for the Felton brothers, only a choice to make as to who would live the horror story and who would be left to wrestle with regrets. Vincent had made that choice, and I had to respect it.

It took six weeks for the case to come to trial, an unusually long time for a Hallow-based case, especially given Vincent's guilty plea. It was painfully obvious that they were awaiting Danny's eighteenth birthday in order to try him as an adult. During that time, I was allowed to visit Vincent on a weekly basis and I did my best to try to make things a little more bearable for him. A little extra money on his canteen, a few comic books and pastries, none of it was anywhere near enough to assuage my own guilt, but it was all I could do. I watched him grow more and more fearful, and less and less the self-assured gang leader I had once known. But not once did his resolve to save Danny weaken.

When the day came, the trial was broadcast not only on Court TV but on several major networks too. I couldn't bring myself to attend in person, even though Vincent asked me to. I couldn't watch it happen right in front of me and say nothing; watching it on the television was hard enough. True to his word, Vincent pleaded guilty and sat stoically listening to the accounts from coroners, police officers and witnesses that described the suffering of the children he had confessed to murdering.

Danny's face was ashen throughout, and more than once he broke down into tears. The media claimed it was because he was horrified by his brother's crimes, and full of empathy for the victims. I knew, of course, that it was guilt. Gut-wrenching, life-changing guilt that would never leave him nor let him rest. He might not be heading for *Justice Live*, but he would still suffer torment for the rest of his days.

Danny was convicted of 'gang activity', as were all the Frank Street Boys when they were hauled in days later. Part of Henman's Zero Tolerance scheme was the criminalisation of belonging to, or having any association with, a gang – regardless of whether the defendant had actually committed a crime. It made the police's job much easier, there was no need to prove much beyond a connection to a known gang, and eyewitness testimony was sufficient evidence to convict. The sentence was the same for all young men convicted of gang activity – they were required to undergo the National Service program. So Danny would serve his two years in a VR simulation in just three days of real time and then he would walk free, physically at least.

Vincent's guilty verdict carried with it twelve consecutive life sentences. He would never leave prison, not until the day came to carry him out in a box.

I don't know how he found the strength to get to his feet. I don't know how he managed to keep his composure and walk from the courtroom in chains with his head held high. But he did, and I watched with an admiration I could speak of to no one.

* * *

When I arrived for my shift the next day Erin was waiting for me in the staffroom.

"Hey," she said, handing me a mug of coffee. "I made you a cuppa. Best down it quick, though, Captain Wanker wants to see you in his office ASAP."

"Me?" I asked, feeling slightly panicked. "Why? What exactly did he say?"

"He said, and I quote," Erin cleared her throat and affected a deep, gruff tone, "'Tell Roberts to come to my office as soon as he gets in.' That's the extent of my knowledge, I'm afraid, Beanie."

"Shit," I said, taking a slurp of the coffee and burning my tongue in my haste. "What have I done wrong?"

Erin just shrugged so I abandoned my drink and headed to the warden's office, praying Lewis hadn't turned grass and ratted on me for tipping Vincent off about *Justice Live*.

His secretary ushered me into the small, stuffy office from which all major decisions about the running of Whitefield were made, and I was surprised to see Aisling Swann sat beside the governor.

"Ah, Roberts." He was smiling. My heart slowed a little, at least I knew I wasn't in trouble. "Fantastic to see you. This is Aisling Swann, UView's brightest and most respected producer. She's the head honcho over on the compound."

I was about to say that we'd already met, but when Aisling held out her hand for me to shake and said, "Charmed," I realised she didn't remember ever seeing me before.

"Aisling has a very exciting proposition for you, Roberts," Captain Wanker continued. "One I think you'd be a fool to turn down." The look in his eyes told me that was less a suggestion, and more a direct order.

"It's Cal, isn't it?" Aisling asked, getting up from her seat and perching herself on the edge of the table as she looked me up and down and smiled.

"Yes, Ma'am," I replied.

"Oh, you're *precious*!" she enthused. "Oh, Stewie, you told me he was good but you didn't tell me he was precious. Yes. Yes, you, my boy, are exactly what I'm looking for. You grew up in Hallow, am I correct?" I nodded. "Ah, that's just wonderful. I bet it was hard, wasn't it? Poverty, filth, disease?"

"Well, I—"

"Yes, I can only imagine what you've been through. What you overcame, to be who you are today. And yet here you are, a beacon of kindness and morality. And a shining example of what a young man from Hallow can accomplish if only he puts his mind to it! Yes, that's the angle. Hallow's our lowest demographic, you know? In terms of active viewers."

"By 'active' I assume you mean viewers who phone in and vote?" I asked.

"Very astute." Aisling beamed unnaturally wide. "He's astute too, God love him. Yes, you're quite right. Hallow watches, of course. Everybody watches! But they don't participate, and it has been bugging the hell out of my team, trying to figure out why that may be."

"Probably because they don't have money to waste on reality show phone-ins," I snapped, before I could help myself. I instantly regretted it, but Aisling seemed in that meeting determined to view anything I said or did as a positive.

"Oh, the passion." She clapped her hands together. "Yes. Keep that. Keep it exactly like that. Because it's you, Cal. You're what's missing!"

"I'm sorry, Ms Swann," I said, "I'm not sure what you're getting at."

"Your boy, Vincent," she said, leaning forward and looking me straight in the eyes. "He's going to be replacing Ollie Barnes on *Justice Live*, as of next week. It's going to be huge. For the first time we will have an inmate whose crimes are so recent the bodies are barely cold. Stewie here was kind enough to tell me all about the quite extraordinary relationship you have with him, and your astounding bravery and tenacity in forcing him to confess."

"I didn't for—"

"It's quite the tale. You are a hero, young man. And you deserve to be celebrated as such. In recognition of your outstanding contribution to English justice I, Aisling Swann, on behalf of UView, Fanning Corp and VirtReal, would like to offer you the coveted position of Vincent Felton's personal officer."

"What?" I couldn't believe what she was saying. "Are you joking?"

Captain Wanker picked up on my tone, and widened his eyes at me. But Aisling chose to interpret my shock and disgust as flattered surprise. "Oh, come now, don't be modest," she replied. "You'd be an asset and you know it. Frankly, I can't think of a better person for the job."

"I don't, I mean, I can't."

"Take some time to think it through," she said. "It's a life-changing opportunity, I don't expect you to be able to fully comprehend all the benefits in an instant! I mean, quite apart from the extremely generous salary, and limitless potential for additional earnings from magazines, television interviews and the like, there's also the small matter of worldwide fame. Not to mention the adoration of millions of lusty fans.

"And if all that isn't enough to float your boat, consider this: you, Cal Roberts, can be a true inspiration to an entire generation of Hallow kids. You can give them ambition, passion, goals! Hallow is shockingly under-represented on television, you know it, I know it. Everyone knows it! But you, you can redress that balance. Vincent represents the very worst of Hallow, he embodies the criminal, sadistic underbelly that the public at large are afraid of. But you, you represent the very best of Hallow! You can show the country, nay, the world, that Hallow is more than just filth and crime. And in doing so, you can help shape its future!"

It was a ridiculously exaggerated pitch, but she did have a point. Vincent's conviction did nothing to improve Hallow's reputation. I'd even heard talk among the pig-ignorant rich elite that Mel associated with of 'savages that kill their own kind' since the children's home fire. The gulf between us and the razzles was wider than ever. They seemed to now regard Hallow as its own country, and its residents their own species. A better representative of Hallow in the public eye was sorely needed. But I never imagined that could be me.

"Can I go speak to Vincent?" I ignored Aisling and asked the warden directly.

"Fabulous idea," Aisling interjected before he could respond. "It's all about strengthening that relationship. My staff broke the news to him this morning, I'm sure he'll be very glad to know there will be a familiar face around."

"I haven't said yes," I replied.

"Yet." She smiled. "You haven't said yes, yet."

"By all means," Captain Wanker added, trying to pretend he still had some sort of authority in the face of Aisling's bulldozing. "You have my permission to speak to Felton before your shift begins."

I thanked him and turned for the door. "Hey, Cal," Aisling

called out to me, and I turned around to see her smirking like the cat who stole the cream. "Welcome aboard, darling."

Her arrogance incensed me, not least because her 'offer' felt more like an inevitability than a choice. Already, I was struggling to see how I could say no when the warden so obviously wanted me to agree, and would likely make my working life a living hell if I didn't. But, I realised as I headed to protective custody, he wasn't really my boss. True, he could fire me from my position as a CO if he wished, but it was Doug who signed the bigger portion of my pay cheques – the ones no one at Whitefield, save Nate, knew about. And as one of *Justice Live*'s major investors, surely Doug could find a way to halt the notion if he were so inclined?

Vincent was sanguine when I arrived at his cell. He'd known the transfer was coming, thanks to me, and was resigned to his fate. Much to my dismay, though, the prospect of me accompanying him over to the compound lifted his spirits.

"You're gonna say yes, right?" he asked, coming right up to the hatch and eyeing me with desperation. "C'mon, Beanie. Tell me you're gonna say yes."

"What difference would it make, really?" I reasoned. "Me being there isn't going to stop them putting you in that chair. The only difference is I'll have to help them do it."

"It would make all the difference, man. All the fucking difference. Having someone around who knows me, someone who doesn't think I'm scum."

"We'd be filmed, all the time," I said. "I couldn't give you favours, or even…" I lowered my voice to a whisper. "*Discuss* things. I'd have to be a bastard to you."

"But I'd *know*, Beanie. I'd know. Whatever you have to do or say to me, just fucking do it and say it. I don't care. I'd know we had this between us, this secret. I'd know you were on my side." He sighed and ran his palm across his head. "I know I'm like some big bad gangster man that people are afraid of, but I'm not that all the way through. I swear to God,

232

sometimes I just feel like a fucking kid. A kid who made some mistakes and can't outrun them. The whole fucking world hates me, every single one of them. Except Danny, and you. And I can't be with Danny, not ever again. So if there's a chance you could help me, even just a bit, I'm begging you to take it, man."

How could I say no? How could I let down another Felton brother? I felt sick. The last thing I wanted to do was get involved with the twisted carnival that was *Justice Live*, but how could I leave Vincent to face it alone when it was in my power to make a difference? I couldn't tell him I just didn't want to, that was for sure. But what if I couldn't take the job for reasons beyond my control? He couldn't blame me for that.

After my shift ended, I rushed out of Whitefield and headed to Doug's office, certain he'd agree that the whole thing was a terrible idea and find a way to bring the entire preposterous notion to a grinding halt.

11

"Well." Doug poured me a glass of Scotch and sat back in his chair, chuckling. "You're just the gift that keeps on giving, aren't you?"

"What do you mean?" I'd explained the whole situation and was naïvely expecting him to pick up the phone with urgency to put a stop to it all.

"Honestly, I don't think I've ever been so impressed. I mean, I *could* have got you in there myself, obviously. But, I didn't think you'd go for that, what with your moral objections. This is all your own steam, you know? I mean, I may have steered you into Whitefield, but you've made your way to the top of the tree all by yourself and that is something to be very proud of. I never dreamed my little idea would bear such fruit."

"What fruit?" I asked, confused. "Doug, it's not my aim. I mean, I didn't do it on purpose, I don't even want it."

"Why not?" he asked, lighting one of his oversized Cuban cigars. "That bitch Aisling is right, you know. You'll do more good for Hallow with the platform she's offering you than you could in a thousand years working in Whitefield. Just insist she keeps that inspirational angle of hers going, you can make all the do-gooding statements you want once you get a media presence."

"I don't *want* a media presence."

"Look, kid. I'm going to level with you." Doug leaned forward and I knew instantly that I wasn't going to like what he had to say. "*Justice Live* is the main focus of my investment. You know that. It's the part of the whole scheme that's actually making money, and it's the part that's needed to keep the rehabilitation programs you're so enthusiastic about going. Having you on the inside at Whitefield is nice, but it's nowhere near as useful as having you observe what's going on in the compound. You can be my eyes and ears. Watch that bitch, and her cronies, let me know what they're up to. Because, and I know the VirtReal execs would agree with me here, those UView bastards can't be trusted. Now that the rehab programs are established, there's really nothing of value you can give me, information-wise, from your current role. But this," he let out a low whistle, "this is gold to me. Primo insider knowledge. I'll double your salary."

"I don't care about the money," I protested, but it fell on deaf ears. As far as Doug was concerned, every man had his price and he could buy anyone, and anything, he wished.

"You're going to be famous, Cal," he carried on, ignoring my distress. "Rich and famous, and an icon to millions."

"Ha." The fatal flaw in Doug's musings hit me suddenly and I almost shouted *Eureka*. "That's exactly why I can't do it, Doug. I can't be famous, it'll blow our cover. Those guards, they can't sneeze without some pap taking a picture. You already warned me against going to any work-related functions with Mel, this'll be even worse. They'll follow me home, they'll take candid snaps of us having breakfast. The whole world will know I'm dating your daughter and Aisling will know I'm spying on her."

He wasn't phased, not even slightly. "So you'll move into the guard's quarters," he said. "It's really no big deal."

"You want me to move out? Leave Mel?"

"Just for a couple of months, maybe less. She'll understand, I promise you. She's a Fanning, don't forget. She grew up watching her mother making sacrifices for the good of the company, she knows the score. After a while I'll throw some big party, celebrate some milestone for *Justice Live*. We'll invite all the guards as well as all the execs, and you'll get introduced to Mel and fall madly in love. A whirlwind romance, the papers will love it. You can move back in to the apartment. We could even hold a wedding; the bids for the live coverage would be out of this world."

So not only had I not succeeded in putting a stop to my transfer on to the sickest reality show in history, I'd somehow ended up temporarily losing my home and hurtling towards a televised wedding. As meetings go, it couldn't have been much worse.

Mel raised only cursory objections to my moving out. Perhaps Doug was right and her upbringing had taught her to accept such things as a necessary means to an end. Or perhaps she didn't really care if I went. Perhaps she was secretly pleased to be rid of me for a while. The way things had been between us of late, I couldn't blame her. I tried to be optimistic about it, even as I packed up the few possessions that actually belonged to me and prepared to leave the home that she had built for us. Some time apart might reignite the spark. I knew I had been taking her for granted, not appreciating her in the way that I should, so maybe losing her for a little while would make me remember why I fell in love with her in the first place. And if it didn't – well, that would be an eye-opener all of its own.

She embraced me and kissed my cheek as I left and I tried to drink in the scent of her and the feel of her skin against mine.

"I'll miss you," I said.

"I know," she replied. "But will you miss me enough?"

12

"So this is where you'll be sleeping." Serena, Aisling's latest assistant, opened the door to the small, sparsely furnished bedroom that would be my home for the time being. "You can customise it however you want, of course. Just let one of the crew know if you'd like any additional furnishings, they'll be happy to organise that for you."

"It's fine as it is," I said, hauling my suitcase onto the bed. "I don't need much."

"Well, you've got a sink in the corner," Serena continued. "Which I gather is something of a novelty round here. Would you like me to demonstrate how it works?"

"I know how to work a fucking sink!" I snapped at her, unable to contain my anger at the ignorance and condescension of the spoilt little razzle girl in front of me. She visibly recoiled, but quickly replastered a professional-looking smile onto her face.

"Okay." Her voice was nasal, and overly high-pitched. "Well, I'll just leave you to get settled in then. The rest of the guards are out at a photo shoot, but they're due back before lunch so you'll get to meet them then."

"Whatever." I turned away from her, still enraged by the suggestion that someone from Hallow must be unable to cope with turning on a tap, and she hastened out of the room. I unpacked my meagre possessions quickly, eager to get to exploring the rest of the living quarters before my new co-workers arrived home. When I got to the small Versace toiletry bag that Mel had given me for Christmas, I pulled out my toothbrush and went to place it on the sink, but the sink was nowhere to be found.

"Shit," I muttered to myself, suddenly flummoxed. "Where the hell is it?" The room was ten by nine, at most. The bed was against the left-hand wall, and the right-hand side of the room was lined with a mixture of low and high cupboards. I opened all the doors, nothing. "Where the fuck is this sink then?" I yelled in exasperation.

"Mr Roberts." Serena must have been waiting close by, because she appeared in the doorway with a smirk on her face. "Would you like me to demonstrate how the sink works now?"

I nodded sheepishly and she stepped forward into the room and reached underneath the wall-mounted desk to pull a small lever. The top of the desk retracted to reveal a small basin underneath. "Having running water this side of the river is not something the producers want to draw attention to," she told me. "So all the sinks in the compound are kept out of sight from the cameras."

"I didn't think there were any cameras in here." I panicked slightly, wondering if I was being watched.

"There aren't," she assured me. "Not in the guard's private quarters. But from time to time a camera crew may come in here to film 'off duty' footage, by prior arrangement, of course. So they thought it best to keep the sinks hidden, just like the showers in the unit."

"I thought they didn't show the washroom because they can't broadcast nudity," I said. "You know, for public decency."

Serena laughed. "You won't find much in the way of decency around here, I assure you."

"I'm sorry," I said, mortified at how I'd spoken to her.

"When you asked if I wanted you to show me how the sink works, I thought you were being rude."

"I get it," she said with a smile. "You're sick of people making assumptions about you because of where you come from."

"Yes," I agreed enthusiastically. "That's exactly it."

"Funny how you do it to other people yourself then, isn't it?"

She strode out with her head held high, leaving me to feel thoroughly ashamed of my own prejudices.

I finished unpacking and headed out into the communal area. We had a large lounge, furnished with leather sofas and an enormous wall-mounted television, a well-stocked minibar and a kitchenette, which contained two fridges that were packed with all manner of meats, vegetables and cheeses. To the side of the kitchenette, a silver door led to three separate bathrooms each with its own shower, bath, toilet and bidet. In comparison to the bathroom in Mel's apartment they were a significant step down in comfort and style, but to anyone who lived in Hallow they would be the height of luxury.

I was contemplating grabbing a beer from the minibar to steady my nerves when I heard a gaggle of male voices approaching.

"I swear to God, man, she was totally up for it. I could have had her right there if it wasn't for you twats mucking up my game."

"Yeah, in your dreams, Titch. She was looking at me."

"Never mind the fucking pussy, where's that runner with my burger? I'm wasting away."

Dax was first through the door, entering the room with his usual swagger. Behind him were Titch, Lez and Carlos, swiftly followed by the other seven. They were all talking and laughing, slapping each other on the shoulders or giving each other the finger as their banter filled the room with raucous noise. But they all stopped abruptly when they spotted me.

"Well then," Dax said, walking over to me and throwing a muscular arm around my shoulder. "We meet again. Lads, this is the new guy, Cal. Let's show him some fucking hospitality, eh?"

They all spoke at once, a mixture of hellos, what's ups, and alright mans. Each of the now-famous men either shook my hand or patted me on the shoulder. They seemed friendly enough, though I noted that Lez seemed to be eyeing me with suspicion.

"What do we know about him then, Dax?" he asked as though I wasn't in the room.

"Not much," Dax smiled. "But I expect we'll find out. As for us, Cal, there's only one thing you need to know. We stick together. Like fucking family, right?" The rest gave low grumbles of agreement. "What happens between us stays between us. That's the golden rule. A man needs a bit of privacy, if you catch my drift. And there ain't much privacy in our lives any more. So, you gotta rely on your brothers here to keep your secrets, and you gotta keep theirs. Am I clear?"

I nodded. The concept of closed ranks and secrecy was nothing new. It was standard prison rules, among both prisoners and staff. What happens in prison stays in prison, and you don't lag. Inmates don't rat on inmates, and guards don't rat on guards. From Dax's little speech you'd have thought the notion was some special, inner-circle agreement. But in reality it was an unspoken code in all prisons, and probably all workplaces. I couldn't see why he thought it necessary to explain.

"You'll soon realise just how quickly our lives have had to change." Dax carried on with his monologue. "Fame is something that nothing can prepare you for. The constant pressures, the lack of privacy. The offers, the opportunities…"

"Some of us have wives and girlfriends," Titch piped up, and I started to catch the drift.

"A man's gotta blow off steam, though, right?" Dax's arm was still around my shoulder, and the weight of it was beginning to hurt. "And his brothers – well, they understand that."

"Don't go selling stories about what we do in our spare time, and don't go running off to Aisling moaning if any of us piss you off," Jensen chimed in from the sofa. "That's basically what he's saying."

"I was going for nuance, you twonk." Dax whacked him softly round the head.

"An' I was saying it straight," Jensen retorted. "Now can we *please* have some fucking lunch?"

"Alright, piggy. Chill your trotters." Dax strode over to the still-open front door and gave a loud whistle. "Oi, Serena," he shouted to the hassled assistant as she scurried across the courtyard. "Any sign of Matt? We're famished over here."

A few moments later Matt, who I soon learned was the newest runner on the show and thereby everyone's personal errand boy, arrived with arms full of paper bags.

"I didn't know what to get for you," he told me apologetically. "So I just went for a cheeseburger, hope that's alright?"

"That's great," I said, unwrapping the unexpected treat and tucking in. "Thanks, I appreciate it."

"Just so you know, Cal," Matt continued, "we're filming your arrival after lunch. So if you could be in uniform and out by the gates with your suitcase by 2pm that would be super."

"But, I've already arrived," I protested. "I've already unpacked!"

Dax chuckled and flapped his hand to swat away the soggy lettuce that had fallen from his burger. "Oh, Cal," he said. "Lesson number one. You ain't done anything until you've done it seven times for the cameras."

13

"Make-up! *Maake-uup!*" Aisling screamed across the courtyard at the UView staff that were milling around by their caravans. "Somebody get make-up over to that van. Felton's got a black eye, I need it covered up stat."

"Don't mind her," Matt said as he escorted me to the compound entrance. "She's a bit highly strung."

"Yeah, I noticed," I replied, watching with astonishment as the production staff scattered like insects to rush to Aisling's bidding.

"So, Felton's in the van already, just outside the gate," Matt said. "We just need to get you in there with him and then we'll shoot the arrival."

"Why have they put him in a van?" I asked. "He's only coming from the other side of the wall, it'd be quicker to walk."

"Something about sympathetic aesthetics, or was it synchronised aesthetics? I don't know. I just do what I'm told."

"And why has Vinnie got a black eye?" I asked. "He's been in protective custody."

"A parting gift from someone, perhaps?" Matt offered. "It's only just happened, by the looks of it, just a bit red and puffy. It's going to come up into a real shiner, though. He says he walked into a door."

"Don't they all." I reached the van and waited patiently for the harassed make-up artist to finish daubing flesh-coloured goop onto Vincent's face before getting in beside him. "You alright?" I asked him. He replied with a shrug.

There were three loud bangs on the side of the van, and the driver started the engine and rolled us forward all of six feet until we were through the gate. Dax and Carlos opened the doors and made a big show of shaking my hand and helping me out of the vehicle. Carlos took my suitcase with one hand, and embraced me with the other.

"I'm Carlos," he said, even though we'd already been exchanging life stories over greasy burgers not half an hour before. "It's an honour to meet you, we're very glad to have you on board."

"If you need anything, *anything* at all, I want you to know you can always come to me," Dax said with gravitas. "It's a tough job, but we've always got each other."

"Um, thanks," I replied, trying but failing not to glance at the camera that was pointed at my face.

"Cut!" Aisling screamed from her chair a few feet away before getting up and coming over to me, sidling up a little too close. "Cal, darling, do you think it might be better to say something along the lines of how honoured you are to be here? How much respect you have for the other officers?"

"I thought you wanted me to act naturally?"

"Yes," she said. "Absolutely. Say it *naturally*."

She ushered me back into the van, which then reversed to its original position and the whole charade began again. It took five takes for me to say what I'd been instructed to say in a way that sounded natural enough to please Aisling. The walk across the courtyard took three attempts, mostly because I wasn't walking 'authoritatively' enough for her liking. I had no idea how exactly I was supposed to walk authoritatively but eventually she seemed satisfied with my affected gait and we finally made it to the main door into max.

Inside, the other guards and inmates (with the exception

of Harvey Stone) were milling about in the communal area awaiting our arrival. Almost as soon as we had stepped through the door, Bruce Knox got up from the sofa where he had been sitting reading a magazine and strode towards us. None of the guards made any attempt to stop him.

Before I could properly react, he drew back his fist and threw a punch in Vincent's face. I thrust out my arm to try to deflect his blow, but was too late.

"That's for those poor innocent kids, you scumbag," he yelled. The other guards piled on top of him, pinning him on the ground and wrestling him into cuffs.

"Fantastic!" Aisling's voice rang out from behind the two-way mirrors. "Now somebody wash the make-up off Felton, quickly."

A young female crew member scurried in through a concealed door brandishing a wet flannel.

"Are you alright?" I asked Vincent.

"Yeah," he replied, shaken and bewildered. "He barely touched me."

The girl with the washcloth looked at me nervously and I realised she wanted me to do the deed. "Alright if I do this?" I asked and Vincent nodded, although he looked as confused as I was.

"I better get that bloody chocolate you promised me now," the Sussex Strangler called out from the floor, where Jensen and Marv still sat atop his restrained body.

14

"Is anything real?" I asked Carlos once the whirlwind that was Aisling Swann had finally finished directing the guards and inmates and flounced off back to her office.

"How'd you mean?" Carlos asked as we flopped down onto the armchairs in the staffroom – the one place where there were no fixed cameras.

"I mean, that." I gestured at thin air in frustration. "That whole farce in there. Stand up, sit down, punch this guy, swear at that inmate. I thought this was supposed to be reality TV."

"It is," Carlos replied. "Mostly. I mean, eighty per cent of the time it's sweet as. Easiest fucking gig I ever had. Like now, with 'em all in their cells there's naff all to do 'cept sit around scratching our balls. Trouble is, that doesn't make a show, does it?"

"Are you saying there's no trouble, no fights or dramas among the worst killers in the country unless Aisling sets it up?"

"Why would there be?" Carlos leaned forward and grabbed a digestive from the table in front of him, shoving it in his mouth whole and spraying crumbs as he continued to talk. "I mean, think about it. They've got it cushy too, apart from the chamber shit, of course. And that's the other thing, none of 'em want to be voted for that, do they? And who gets voted, now that the kiddy killers have all been in? It's whoever got the most camera time that week – absolutely guaranteed. So, they don't want to go doing things that'll bring attention to themselves, do they? That's why we have to sweeten the deal a bit for them sometimes, if we can't get them riled up ourselves."

"You're telling me Bruce Knox was so desperate for a bit of chocolate he was willing to risk getting voted?"

"Course not," Carlos laughed. "Fuck me, that'd have to be some world-class chocolate to be worth that, eh? No, there's no risk this week. Which means we have to be extra careful, they might start thinking this is a good time to push our buttons."

"No risk?"

"Come on, your boy Felton's getting the chamber this week. Ain't nothing going to stop that. One of them bastards could knife me in the face and it'd still be the kiddie cooker who gets ninety-nine per cent of the votes. So watch your back this week, carefree inmates are unpredictable."

"Noted," I said.

"Not that you'll be here much this week anyway, they'll have you on the circuit."

"The circuit?"

"Talk shows, daytime TV, magazine shoots. A new guard, it's a big deal. Trust me, teen girls will be pinning your ugly mug up on their walls by Wednesday."

"I doubt it," I said, glancing down at my less than athletic physique.

Carlos just chuckled. "You'd be surprised."

Dax waltzed in with a look on his face that I couldn't quite read, part arrogance and part frustration. "There you are, Roberts," he snapped. "Come on, it's time to meet the real monster."

"Stone?" I asked.

"Of course Stone. You can't call yourself one of us until you've survived an encounter with that bastard, can you?"

It seemed a pretty dramatic way of describing being

introduced to an inmate who was kept secured behind bars for ninety per cent of his day, but I'd already started to realise that Dax was dramatic by default. He seemed to think himself the star of his very own show, always talking in sound bites and affecting a swagger even when there were no cameras rolling. Everything about him was exactly what Aisling was trying to get from us all – natural, in a very exaggerated and screen-ready way.

I followed him past the main cells where the inmates tried to pass the long hours any way they could. I glanced in at Vincent, who was hunched on his bunk with his head in his hands. His cell was next to Dil Travis, the cult leader whose long unkempt hair and wild eyes made him look like a psychotic version of Jesus, and who was furiously scribbling in a notebook with a pencil so well-used that barely a stub remained. Perhaps he was writing his own bible, or maybe just a list of what he wanted to order from the canteen with his spends. Whatever it was, his hand flew across the page in his haste to accomplish his task.

"Hey, new guy." Kieran Brooks gave a sharp whistle and called out from his cell across the room. "How about you bring me in some burn, eh? I'll put on a show for ya, let you be a hero for the cameras."

"How about you shut the fuck up, Brooks?" Dax yelled without even glancing in the killer's direction.

"I wa'nt talkin' to you, sir," Brooks shouted back. "So why don't you just suck my dick?"

"Maybe I'll snap your fucking spine in two so you can suck your own." I was shocked at Dax's threat, not because I'd never heard a CO verbally abuse an inmate – I'd worked with Lardarse, after all – but because everything would have been caught on camera. I'd imagined the guards of max would be whiter than white, at least in the areas that were constantly filmed. But what Dax said next just left me confused. Before even taking a breath he quickly continued, "Jennifer Alsop, one-one-three Weston Way," and proceeded to escort me through the two sets of doors between the main cell block and the washrooms.

We turned right at the showers, heading down the corridor towards Harvey Stone's solitary cell. "What was that?" I asked Dax, unable to fathom what I'd just heard.

"They can't broadcast any personal information about anyone who isn't part of the show," Dax explained. "So if you want to say something that you don't want going out to millions of viewers, throw in someone's name and address."

"Oh," I replied. "I guess I've got a lot of tricks to learn."

"You don't know the half of it," he said before placing his hand on my shoulder in a manner that I guessed was supposed to seem supportive but in fact felt patronising. "But don't worry, I'll teach you everything you need to know. This corridor, for example, there's no mics down here."

"No mics?" I scanned the ceiling and noted the cameras in the corners. "Why not?"

"Because of my siren song, of course." Harvey's voice echoed from the secluded cell at the end of the passage, though I was not yet close enough to see him in the flesh. It occurred to me in that second that I had never heard him speak before. All the hours of footage of him in his cell or the exercise yard and yet not once had he been broadcast speaking. "I'm quite a legend, you know, something of a Pied Piper, so Dax would have you believe. It's quite an extraordinary power he's bestowed upon me; the mere whisper of my words are enough to corrupt the most steadfast of ears. Of course, it's a legend that benefits dear Mr Miller most auspiciously."

"Shut the fuck up, Harvey," Dax bellowed as we approached the bars. I found myself pausing involuntarily when I noticed the elongated shadow of the Playground Slasher spread slowly across the floor in front of his cell and creep up the wall as his feet shuffled towards the bars. Like all things feared but half-unseen, the monstrously misshapen silhouette loomed larger than the man himself and caused me to shudder in anticipation of coming face to face with its creator.

"I don't bite, Cal," Harvey said with a small chuckle, causing me to wonder for a moment how he knew that I was hesitating when he could not yet see me. I quickly realised I was casting my own shadow on the shiny, well-polished floor and chided myself for letting him get under my skin before I'd even been introduced. "That particular kink belongs to our now toothless cannibal friend, so I'm told. Took that poor officer's finger right off, if you can believe that. I, of course, wouldn't make such a wager. Too many variables. Too many... egos."

I stepped in front of the bars and got my first look at Harvey in real life. He was shorter than I had realised, no more than five-seven, five-eight at a push. I'd seen his face hundreds of times on TV, or in the newspapers, I could have picked him out of a line-up of a hundred guys with the same short black hair and thick glasses, so familiar was I with the eyes that now scrutinised me. But I'd never seen him smiling before. Not just smiling, in fact. He was positively beaming as he reached a hand through the bars, angling for me to shake it. Dax shook his head, and I stepped backwards rather than take Harvey's hand.

"Very wise," Harvey said with clear amusement in his voice. "Perhaps I am proficient in some sort of ninja nerve grip that would render you paralysed with a mere shake of my hand, eh? Or is it the germs you object to? All those little microbes and parasites too small for the eye to see just waiting to abscond from my skin and lodge themselves in your lymph nodes, or perhaps your respiratory tract."

"Shut it," Dax snapped at him, and then turned to face me. "To answer your question, that's why there's no mics down here. Because Harvey spouts such mountains of shit."

"Really?" Harvey replied. "I must confess I thought spouting, as you put it, 'mountains of shit' was precisely what the entire reality television genre was based on. Pay him no heed, Cal. He's never been the sharpest of minds. You, I am sure, are astute enough to realise that there is less fallout from 'shit' than there is from truth."

"You see?" Dax said. "This is why we don't let him talk to anyone alone. He's fucking psychotic. He'd have you believing night was day if you let him get a word in edgeways, trust me. He's a cunning little bastard."

"A cunning little bastard?" Harvey chuckled. "I quite like that. Would that I could be a callous, hulking brute like you, Dax. But I suppose cunning little bastard will serve me just as well. Better, perhaps. It is, after all, more in keeping with the almost supernaturally evil persona you have created for me."

"Whatever, you fucking dickless freak," Dax snapped. "Come on, Cal. That's quite enough of this twat for one day. Let's leave him to his psychosis."

"And here I was thinking you might have come to take me dancing." Harvey smirked. "Or have I trodden on your toes too many times now?"

"Fucking looney tunes." Dax tapped the side of his head with a fingertip. "It'd be sad if he wasn't such monster with it."

Dax started to walk back along the corridor, and I turned to follow.

"Mr Roberts?" Harvey called out, and I stopped and turned to face him. "Don't mind Dax and I, we've something of a chequered past. We've played these games since boyhood, and still I can't work out the score. But I just wanted to say good luck to you, in your new role. Please accept my heartfelt best wishes for the path ahead, from one victim to another."

15

"What do you think he meant by that?" I asked Carlos, who had made the mistake of asking me about my encounter with Harvey while my mind was still swirling.

"I dunno, man." Carlos shrugged. "What does he mean by anything? Dude's a fruit loop. If I had to guess I'd say he meant 'I'm a fucking psycho who wants to mess with your mind'. Seriously, don't even think about it. This is exactly why Dax says not to speak to him."

"It was just such an odd thing to say," I protested. "It was like he knew something, something about me, something I don't know myself."

"Fuck, man." Carlos shook his head and poured me a coffee. "Don't let Dax hear you talking like that, he'll be straight to Aisling saying you're not mentally strong enough or something. I mean it, forget everything that fucker said. And stay away from him, don't want you going loco on us like that CO at his old prison did."

"Okay," I said. "You're right. I'm just going to forget it – he's crazy. End of."

But I couldn't forget it. Something about the Playground Slasher's words had filled me with a silent unease that I couldn't quite place. An insidious feeling of being in the dark, or being deceived. I carried on with the rest of the shift, which was pretty much just twiddling our thumbs and passing the odd comment to the inmates given that they were all in their cells now until dinner time. I tried to talk to Vincent, but he wasn't in any mood for conversation. I couldn't blame him, every guard and inmate had made it perfectly clear that his visit to the chamber on Saturday was a foregone conclusion, as if he didn't know that already. I could only begin to imagine the terror of that anticipation, and I wouldn't have been surprised if he had regretted his decision to protect Danny during that long week of dread.

Dinner was a very different affair in max than it was in gen pop. There was no canteen, for one thing. Instead of the usual nightmare of trying to organise hundreds of inmates to walk, queue and eat in a semi-orderly fashion, the meals were delivered on a trolley by a runner, and the inmates were released from their cells in two groups to eat in the communal area. Apart from Harvey, of course. Dax snatched his tray from the trolley, lifted the lid to reveal a rather watery-looking cauliflower cheese and yelled loudly, "George Mason," before spitting onto the cheesy goop and continuing with, "Seven Birch Drive," as he replaced the lid. He shot me a grin, and a wink, before disappearing through the doors towards Harvey's cell.

"Shouldn't someone go with him?" I wondered aloud. "I thought no one was supposed to approach Harvey alone."

"No one *except* Dax," Titch replied. "Dax only trusts Dax." He dropped his voice to a whisper. "Nonsense, if you ask me, but that's the way it goes."

Vincent was part of the first six allowed out of their cells to eat at the tables, but he barely touched his food. The other inmates jeered at him in a nice little show for the cameras that would end up being broadcast on Saturday.

"Don't like the food?" Kieran quipped, nudging him too hard in the ribs. "I'm afraid they don't serve crispy kids here."

"Yeah," Franco joined in, with his mouth full of cauliflower cheese. "No deep-fried kids! Geddit? Like deep-fried squids?"

"Fucking kiddie cooker." Eddie tutted.

"You're a fine one to fucking talk," Franco laughed. "Thought you were a connoisseur of human flesh, sure he wasn't cooking 'em up for you?"

"Watch your fucking mouth, Franco." Eddie waved a plastic spoon at him, trying but failing to look menacing. "I've never hurt a kid in my life and I never would. Besides, I like my meat rare."

"He prefers finger food," Bruce called out from his cell. "Isn't that right, sir?" He waved his pinky fingers at Lez who just shook his head and rolled his eyes.

"Very funny, Knox," he said. "Never heard that one before."

Watching the exchange, another of Harvey's strange comments came to mind. Hadn't he said something cryptic about Lez's missing finger? Somewhere in amongst his garbled metaphors and pseudo-intellectual psychobabble hadn't he implied there was more to the story?

The idea played on my mind all through dinner, and by the time we finished our shift and headed back to our quarters I had resolved to ask Lez about it if the opportunity arose. There were several large pizza boxes on the kitchen side when we got in, and the other guards wasted no time in grabbing themselves slices from the boxes and bottles of beer from the fridge.

"Here." Carlos grabbed two beers and handed one to me. "But don't go getting pissed tonight. Look." He pointed to the small cork noticeboard above the microwave where a list entitled *Cal's Itinerary* had been pinned up in our absence. "You've got *Teen Dream* at 8am."

"*Teen Dream*?" I asked

"Photo shoot," Carlos said. "They're one of the largest teen magazines, you'll get a nice little bonus out of it."

I scanned the long list of appointments on my itinerary and discovered I had six photo shoots and two talk shows over the next few days, not to mention the big one – the live *Behind the Bars* interview after Saturday's main show. "This is all a bit much," I said. "I mean, I'm a CO not a bloody celebrity."

"You are now," Carlos replied. "Or at least you will be by the time you drag Felton kicking and screaming to his chamber program. If you want my advice, just enjoy it. There's plenty of perks."

"And pussy," Titch interjected, grabbing his second beer already.

"I'm not... I mean, I can't..."

"Gay or taken?" Lez asked, raising an eyebrow.

"Taken. But... I'm not supposed to let on."

"Didn't I already tell you?" Dax wandered in from the bathroom and Marv hastily moved out of the large armchair to allow him to take up what I soon realised was his spot. "We're brothers. We have a code. What happens between us stays between us, and we don't spill each other's secrets, or indiscretions. In fact, it's the secrets that keep us tight. If you're not prepared to share yours, then how can we trust you with ours?"

"And if we can't trust you," Lez said, "that's going to make life very difficult indeed."

The atmosphere of camaraderie suddenly turned sinister with Lez's vague and thinly veiled threat hanging between us. All eyes were on me, and I cursed myself for my folly. I had hinted at a secret I didn't want to spill, a secret I thought I couldn't spill if my status as Doug's spy on the inside were to remain unknown. I couldn't blame them for being suspicious; they were right to be, after all. But I needed to think fast, give them enough of the truth that they would believe that I had given them trusted information, but not so much as to actually blow my cover.

"Alright." I held my hands up in a 'surrender' pose and feigned a sigh. "I guess since we're all going to be living together, I might as well just tell you. But you have to swear it doesn't leave this room, alright?"

Dax leaned forward, gently twisting his bottle of beer so that the half-drunk liquid sloshed against the glass. "There isn't a man here who couldn't ruin all his brothers with a well-timed word in a journalist's ear," he said, before taking a long swig and then tossing the empty bottle onto the floor. "It's what the military call 'mutually assured destruction', but I like to think of it as insurance. A man's word is easily broken, I'd rather have his secrets than his promises."

"I can respect that," I said, nodding solemnly although in reality it all sounded like overly dramatic macho bullshit to me. "Well then, here's mine: I'm dating Melody Fanning."

"Doug Fanning's *daughter*?" Dax chuckled and tipped his fresh bottle toward me in a gesture of respect and congratulations while the other guards let out whistles and whoops. "My my, Roberts, you are a dark horse, aren't you?"

"Wait," Stewie piped up. "Ain't you from Hallow?" I nodded and he screwed up his face. "I don't buy it, why would a rich bit like Melody Fanning go for an unwashed oik from Hallow?"

"Maybe she likes it rough," Dax said with a salacious, knowing wink. "Plenty of 'em do."

"Dax has got a thing for posh pussy," Carlos explained. "And surprisingly the feeling seems to be mutual. Don't think you've scored as high as a Fanning, though, have you, Dax?"

"Nah," Dax said, downing the bottle of beer and gesturing at Marv to toss him another. "Not yet anyway." There was a hint of a threat to his tone that set me slightly on edge.

"Why the big secret then, Roberts?" Lez asked. "Does old man Fanning not approve?"

"He doesn't know," I lied. "Because Melody thinks he wouldn't be too pleased, or at least wouldn't *have* been."

"What do you mean?" Titch asked.

"She's actually one of the reasons I took this job," I continued, quite enjoying spinning a yarn now that I had got into my stride. "This is her daddy's pet project, she thought me being involved in it would make him more inclined to give me a chance."

"I expect the extra moolah won't hurt either," Josh suggested. "Your bank won't know what's hit it after Saturday."

"I even got a call from mine after Finn's show," Titch laughed, "concerned about the 'unusual activity'."

"What unusual activity?" I asked.

"The fact my account actually had some fucking coin in it for once, I expect." Titch guffawed and several of the guards joined in.

"Man." Dan shook his head ruefully. "I've gotta get Hayden in that chamber soon as. It's my daughter's birthday next month, I want to get her a pony or something. Show that bitch-ass mother of hers I can be the favourite parent too."

"Is it really that lucrative, being the personal officer on a chamber show? I didn't think they paid us extra for that."

"UView don't," Titch replied. "But their wage is only the tip of the iceberg, mate. It's the magazines, radio shows, all that shit. If your con is this week's hot ticket, then so are you. And seeing as how they can't leave the premises to go to the studios, you're the next best thing to the bastard himself. It's a proper cash cow, if you know how to milk it."

"Yeah," Lez replied. "Why'd you think Dax is looking so fucking sour all the time? He's not going to get his hands on those magic udders again any time soon if Harvey won't play ball."

"You mean, the way he reacted to the chamber?" I asked.

"Yeah," Dax grumbled, gritting his teeth slightly. "I told that twat Reynolds his program wouldn't work, remember?" I nodded my head, recalling Dax's predictions when Nate and I had been shown the chamber program. "Someone like Harvey, they just don't scare easy. He's got no emotion, no fucking soul. I warned them, but they didn't listen to me. And now Aisling says he can't go in the chamber again until she's certain he's going to give the viewers what they want. And there's no negotiating with him, there's nothing he wants. So I can't even bribe the bastard to act scared."

"It's worse than that," Lez chipped in. "The only thing Stone wants is to piss you off, Dax. There's nothing you could offer him that's worth more than that."

"You got that right." Dax sighed and put his right foot on the table in front of him, reaching forward and pulling something out from inside his boot. I gasped slightly when I saw a flash of silver and realised what it was. "Relax." Dax scoffed at me, my shock must have been obvious. "It's just my grandad's old hunting knife. I like to keep it with me, for nostalgia."

The hilt was golden and shiny, with the initials *JM* engraved on it. The blade itself gleamed and reflected shards of light as Dax tilted it to and fro to show off the curved, razor-sharp edge. I highly doubted that knife had ever even seen the insides of a supermarket-bought chicken, let alone been the instrument of a wild animal's demise. Middle Englanders weren't exactly known for their strong ancestral ties to carving up wildebeests or wolves. In fact, there was barely any wildlife or open countryside left at all, and there hadn't been for generations. More than likely, the knife had been given as some ridiculous 'what do you get the man who's got everything' type present and spent the next fifty years sitting in a display cabinet until JM's headstrong grandson inherited it.

He used the knife to flick the cap of his beer bottle off and took a long swig as he eyed me up and down. "So," he said, "Melody Fanning, eh?"

I just shrugged, realising all at once that in bringing up my relationship with Mel I had inadvertently engaged in what amounted to a pissing contest. The knife display had been Dax asserting his alpha status after having his pride wounded by the new guy's 'conquest'. I had no interest in participating.

"Well," I said, hurrying to change the subject and shift Dax's focus away from me. "I've told you mine. Seems only right I hear some of yours now, in the interests of brotherhood and all that."

"Sounds fair," Carlos said, and the others mumbled agreements.

As the beer flowed and the conversation became more

raucous and less inhibited, I was regaled with tales of indiscretions big and small. Most of them were the usual fodder of drunken one-night stands, I laughed and nodded in all the right places, but they were of no interest to me. There was only one secret I really wanted to hear. I had to know if the niggling feeling I had that there was some truth to Harvey's words was right. The only person who could tell me that was Lez.

I counted eight beer bottles by his feet, and calculated that he ought to be drunk enough by now not to take offence at my question, as long as I phrased it flatteringly.

"What about you, Lez?" I asked.

"What about me?" he asked. "I ain't got no secret sordid exploits to confess to, the tabloids bought those stories off the gold-digging bitches already."

"You just don't strike me as the kind of guy who would let a crim get the best of him," I said.

"I'm not." Lez frowned, wondering what I was getting at. "Those bastards know better than to mess with me."

"So what happened to your finger then?" I worried he might get angry, but his face remained calm.

"I thought that was common knowledge," he said dispassionately.

"Oh, come on," I prodded. "You couldn't overpower Eddie? You took your eye off the ball and let him get the better of you? I've seen you work, you're a pro. There's no way."

"Of course I can overpower that twat," Lez said, starting to rise to the bait.

"So what happened to your finger?" I asked again.

"I lost it," Lez replied. "In a card game."

I hadn't expected that. Lez recalled the whole incident in graphic detail, from how he had got into serious trouble with the 'wrong sort of players' to how they had jokingly offered to write off his debt in exchange for his finger, not expecting him to agree, and the sickeningly vivid description of how these wannabe gangsters had tried to cut off his pinky with a

Stanley knife, but had struggled to get through the bone and resorted to a meat cleaver.

"Joke's on them now, though," Lez grinned, holding up his hand and looking at his missing finger with pride. "This little baby has made me richer than any of them."

"You mean, you were chosen because of it?"

"Of course," he replied. "Who better to be the personal officer of a cannibal than an officer with a missing appendage? Aisling was over the moon when she saw my application, makes for a great story, doesn't it?"

"Yeah," I agreed. "A really great story."

The only question was, how did Harvey know it wasn't true?

16

When I awoke the next morning, my mouth felt as though it were full of sawdust and a worrying wave of nausea overcame me when I tried to sit up, causing me to reach for the small waste bin by the side of my bed in case the contents of my stomach refused to stay put. How much had I had to drink? I decided it was better not to try to count in case knowing the total made me feel even worse. After a few moments, the hot, dizzying sensation subsided and I managed to sit upright, my head pounding. I picked up my phone and squinted at the screen through the blurry haze of my early morning hangover.

"Shit," I muttered out loud when I realised I had missed five calls and seven text messages from Mel the night before.

"Oh shit indeed," announced Carlos, throwing my door open with a grin and thrusting a mug of coffee at me. "*Teen Dream* just pulled up outside. Ready to be the next pin-up boy?"

The photographer looked horrified when she saw me stumble unshaven and red-eyed out of the guard's quarters, but she affected a professional smile and bid me good morning before fiddling with the lens of the camera. No doubt she was trying her best to use whatever filters and photographic trickery she had at her disposal to help negate the sheer wreckage of my appearance. I complied with her various instructions, posing and pouting on command though all the while struggling with the sloshing sickness that lolloped in my stomach. When she had finished angling my limbs and demanding smiles from me, she offered to show me the pre-filtered shots she'd taken. I declined; if the wretch in the mirror was anything to go by, no one ought to see those pictures at all, and certainly not before they'd been heavily doctored by the very best editing software known to man.

After she had bid me a very curt and professional farewell, I headed back to the guard's quarters and downed several cups of black coffee before heading over to the cell block to start my shift. My phone buzzed urgently in my pocket as I made my way across the courtyard. It was Mel again. I dismissed the call, feeling guilty that I hadn't yet called her back or responded to any of her messages. I needed to be less hung-over before I could give a good enough account of myself to prevent her from getting even madder at me than she must already be.

"Here comes next week's pretty boy," Lez smirked as I entered the small staffroom to collect my equipment from my locker. "Enjoy your first modelling gig?"

"I think I'd have enjoyed it more if I'd drunk a little less," I said.

Lez just shrugged. "Should have just kept drinking," he replied. "Postponed the hangover."

"We've got to do Harvey's shower this morning." Titch accosted me as soon as I reached the cells.

"Why?" I asked, confused.

"Dax has got a big meeting with Aisling or something," he said.

"So why didn't it just get rescheduled?" I queried, knowing Dax was very particular about who could do what when it came to Stone.

"Harvey's kicking up a stink," Titch sighed. "Harping on about human rights and all that."

"Fuck me." I shook my head. "Human rights? Comes to something when a murderer has more rights to a shower than a child born in the wrong part of the country."

"What can I do?" Titch shrugged and gave a small tilt of his head. "It is what it is."

A standard razzle response, they were water off a duck's back to me by now.

"I would have thought him kicking off would have been exactly what UView wanted, bit of action from him for a change."

"Yeah, except he's not *doing* anything except spouting off loudly. Like, literally nothing. He's on strike. Won't move from his bunk or open his eyes, he's just lying there reciting the terms of peace conventions and prison regulations. And there's no audio – so he's actually even more boring on camera than usual."

"Alright," I said, "if we must, we must."

Harvey was pleased to see us, knowing that his little protest had born fruit. He was calm and compliant as we attached his chains at the wrists and hands and led him to the shower block. Once inside, we unshackled first his hands and then his feet to allow him to remove his jumpsuit. We were quick to restrain him again as soon as he was naked, attaching one handcuff to the water pipe so that he could move around within the shower cubicle a little, but could not reach outside it.

"Cover for me for a few minutes?" Titch asked, pulling his phone out of his pocket and waving it at me. "I've reeaallly gotta make a call."

"What?" I was incredulous. "No one but Dax can be alone with Harvey, you know that."

"Oh, that's just Dax spouting bullcrap, trying to make himself the big man," Titch replied. "Look at him." He gestured to the shackled Harvey. "What's he gonna do? Splash your shoes? I'll only be a minute."

Without waiting for me to object, Titch slipped quickly out of the fire door and left me alone in the camera-less shower room with the Playground Slasher.

17

"Well, well." A slow smile spread across Harvey's face. "Alone at last, Mr Roberts."

I ignored him and pressed the button to activate the shower before standing back and folding my arms, staring straight ahead and avoiding eye contact.

"Oh, come now." He tutted a little as he began soaping his body with his free hand. "Aren't we going to converse at all? Do you really believe I'm that dangerous? I thought you were cleverer than that. That little fellow has the measure of it, and I'd never have guessed he'd be more insightful than you are. Perhaps my ability to detect a keen mind is waning somewhat."

"What do you mean?" I hadn't meant to respond, but somehow I couldn't stop myself.

"I mean, there are things you'd love to ask me, now that you have the chance. But Dax has spun a tall tale, created a legend. The titchy one is right, it simply suits his own ends. I can no more talk you into madness than I could lure a randy sailor to the rocks. But if you're the type to believe in myths and half-truths, what can I do? I'd thought you smarter, that's all."

"How did you know Eddie didn't bite Lez's finger off then?" I asked, giving in to my burning curiosity.

"You don't know?" He gave a little snort. "I'd have thought that much was obvious. Dax created a legend for his own benefit, that's true. But that's not to say it doesn't provide

263

me with some perks as well. No audio recording near my cell being one of the most interesting."

"How does that benefit you?"

"Oh, come now, think about it. Say you were on shift and you wanted to tell that Titch fellow something, something you were bursting to say but something you didn't want the world to know. Where might you do it?"

"Outside your cell," I said slowly, the realisation of Harvey's prime position dawning on me.

"And if I repeated it to anyone?"

"I'd say you were a raving sociopath, a pathological liar, an untrustworthy murderer with a history of causing trouble among prison staff with your cunning words."

"Precisely." Harvey smiled. "Who but the basest imbecile would take my word over that of a respectable, honourable man of the law? Who would side with a man who has ripped the hearts from seven beautiful children over a hero such as Dax, or Carlos, or even yourself?"

"You talk as though you're trying to make me doubt you."

"Why should I care if you doubt me or not? What impact does your opinion of my words have on my existence? I simply tell you this to demonstrate the fragility of truth. For something we supposedly hold so sacred, we do precious little to protect it from distortion. Those seven girls, for example, were neither beautiful nor innocent – at least not while they were alive. But they have now become eternally, irrefutably both, entirely because of my actions."

"Are you really trying to suggest you did them a favour?" I asked, incredulous at the suggestion.

"Not at all. I had no intention of doing *them* any favours. The favours I did were for the ones they tormented."

"What?" I shook my head, he really was as crazy as Dax said.

"If there's one thing I can't stand, Mr Roberts, it's a bully."

"You're trying to tell me those seven little girls – those sweet, innocent, defenceless little girls – were bullies?"

"Oh yes," he said matter-of-factly, as if he were confirming some unquestionable truth. "To you they may have looked sweet and innocent, but I can assure you that is not how they appeared to the poor wretches they targeted with their vicious words and hateful actions."

"They were kids!"

"That's an adult perception talking. Tell me, Cal, was there ever a child who haunted your nightmares? A child who made your heart race and your breath quicken when you spotted them out of the corner of your eye? A child with the power to make you so miserable that you dreamed of disappearing into a cocoon and emerging as someone completely different? Someone stronger, taller? Someone who could destroy that little bastard where he stood?"

Yes. I thought back to my early childhood, before the disaster, before Hallow, and there was one name that sprang to mind: Charlie Bexwell. He was an evil little shit who liked to cast his net of misery wide, causing as much pain and humiliation to as many kids as he could. He was a year older than me, and had one of those faces that seemed to be permanently cast in a sneer. I was too scared to use the toilets at infant school in case he came roaring out of a cubicle and pinned me on the ground, just like he had on my very first day. I was so terrified that I wet myself in class rather than use the latrines. I hated that kid.

"Yeah," I replied, not going into detail. "There was. What of it?"

"Were you to have visited that little boy's mother – because he was, after all, a little boy to her, even if he was a hulking, intimidating aggressor to you – I bet she could have shown you pictures of a sweet, almost angelic child that would have rivalled those of Sophia Lawrence or Dolene Foster." To hear him speak his victim's names so casually made goosebumps rise on my flesh. "Beauty, Mr Roberts, is in the eye of the beholder. But so is fear. One woman's little cherub is some poor young child's waking nightmare. And one man's violent killer can also be a tormented little girl's saviour. I'd show you the thank you notes I received from a young girl whose life had been made a misery by Sophia, if they hadn't been confiscated from me. She was quite candid in her gratitude."

"Sophia Lawrence was nine years old," I said slowly. "Even if she was a bit of a bully, she could have grown up to be a good person. Maybe even a great person, who knows what she could have become? But you robbed her of that chance."

"Perhaps," Harvey shrugged. "Miracles do happen, so they say. But at nine years old, she was a bitch. And in all likelihood she would have remained a bitch into adulthood, tormenting peers, co-workers, partners and eventually her own filthy spawn, who would then go on to perpetuate the cycle. Lacey Dixon, on the other hand, now she *is* a good person. Had her suffering continued, perhaps she would never have gained the confidence to put herself forward for the accelerated programme at school, or compete in the gymnastics tournaments. Perhaps even, she would have been so victimised and so traumatised that she wouldn't have made it to adulthood at all, then the world would have its 'sweet' Sophia Lawrence, but her victim's story would have come to a tragic, and entirely avoidable, end."

"That's some very twisted, spurious logic," I said, appalled at Harvey's justifications and feeling I was in the presence of a true cold-blooded psychopath.

"But it *is* logic." Harvey smiled. "Uncomfortable as you may find it. My only crime, when it comes down to it, is the ability to see past the trappings of the present. Once you see the elements, the atoms, the strings themselves that hold the world around you together, you can navigate truth and fiction as though it were mapped out on GPS."

"Whatever," I said, growing tired of his narcissistic ramblings. "All I wanted to know was how you knew about Lez's finger."

"No." Harvey picked up the bar of misshapen, strong-smelling soap in the shower dish and began rubbing it slowly over his torso. "That's not all you wanted to know. It was simply the – rather pedestrian – question you employed to try to find the deeper answer. What you really want to know is how I know so many things about so many people, despite my complete isolation from the world. That was the question I was answering. Oh, and incidentally, the answer to the question you'll *really* be dying to ask me come Saturday is exactly the same."

"What question?" I asked. Harvey just smirked, and I realised I'd been drawn in again. "Fine," I snapped at him, pushing the button to switch off the water and throwing a coarse, stiff towel at his naked body. "Well, I'd say it's been an enlightening chat but all I've really learned about you is that you're a delusional, hypocritical psychopath who eavesdrops on the guards, and frankly, I knew that already."

"I'll take psychopathic eavesdropper," he said, wrapping the towel around his middle to cover his pathetic, wrinkled genitalia. "Not a bad moniker. Factually correct, at least. But I can't agree with delusional or hypocritical."

"Well, if you knew were you delusional you wouldn't be delusional," I replied.

"Fair point," Harvey conceded. "We'll just have to agree to disagree on that one. But I am no hypocrite, you'll come to see that for yourself in time."

"Of course you are!" Despite myself, I was getting riled by his blatant lies. "You say you can't stand bullies, to the point that you use it as a twisted justification for playing out your little butcher fantasies, but you were a bully. Everyone knows that. You made Dax's life a living hell!"

"You disappoint me, Cal," Harvey said, shaking his head sadly. "I had an inkling you saw things more clearly than the other Neanderthals. I suppose I was wrong, which makes me worry for that poor boy of yours."

"What boy?" He was tying my mind in knots, taking the conversation down different rabbit holes deliberately, making me chase his answers. I knew it, but somehow I couldn't stop pelting after him regardless.

Harvey sighed, and rubbed his temples, like an exasperated professor trying to explain a simple concept to an imbecile. "I thought," he began slowly, "that you of all people would understand the way in which blame is assigned according to the story one wishes to tell. After all, you're complicit in helping those Felton boys rewrite their narrative, aren't you?"

"I..." My mouth went dry. How did he know?

"Oh, don't have a coronary." He waved his free hand at me dismissively. "I don't *care*. I was merely giving you an example you could relate to. Consider, if you will, if two uneducated, unwashed louts from the armpit of Hallow are able to persuade the public, and the courts, that black was white and innocent was guilty, how easy is it for the likes of Ms Swann and her army of media manipulators to write a history that suits their angle?"

I suddenly realised what he meant. "You're saying you weren't the bully, Dax was?"

"Yahtzee!" He smiled and clapped his hands together. "You got there in the end. It makes no difference, of course; truth is what people believe it is, not what actually occurred. Although, you'd do well in this instance to take heed. Leopards don't become zebras just because the producers paint some stripes on them."

I didn't know whether I believed him or not. On the surface, Dax seemed like the stronger, more aggressive one and it wasn't hard to picture him picking on the weedy, prepubescent Stone. But it was Harvey, not Dax, who had grown up to be a monster. It made no difference who started what when they were snot-nosed kids in the playground, the fact remained that it was Harvey Stone who ripped those little girls from end to end, and even the most bleeding-heart liberal couldn't justify that, no matter how many times he'd been given a wedgie in his youth. Even if Dax had been the 'bad guy' of the two back in the day, he wasn't now. Mass murder trumped stealing lunch money in anyone's book.

"See what I mean about the irrelevance of truth?" Harvey

tilted his head as he looked at me, as though he were adjusting the angle to better see my thoughts. "You've already weighed and measured it, and decided it makes no bearing on the present, beyond some amateur psychobabble about me internalising my victimhood only for it to fester until I became a perpetrator in order to try to find the power and control I had sorely lacked in my formative years. Nonsense, of course. Am I right?"

I nodded warily.

"But here's what's going to bother you in the days to come. Here's what's going to sneak into your paranoid, unsettled thoughts at 3am when the shadows contort on the walls and the noises outside are almost explainable, but not quite." He leaned closer to me and lowered his voice to a whisper. "Which one of us tortured that hamster?"

18

Titch stumbled in through the fire exit looking sheepish, and his presence broke the eerie silence left by Harvey's last question and snapped me back to reality. We got him clothed and marched him back to his solitary cell, the click of the door as it locked him in his lair reminding me that he had no power, not really. At least, not beyond spouting clever words and posing unanswerable riddles.

But still, I couldn't seem to push his words out of my mind, no matter how hard I tried to rationalise them.

By the end of my shift, I had come to the shaky conclusion that I was simply too immersed in this strange, self-contained and decidedly artificial little world. Understandable, even Whitefield could feel like a reality all of its own when you were in the middle of a long shift; the petty concerns and politics that were so amplified within a closed environment could start to feel much more important than they objectively were. But when I was at Whitefield, I walked out of the gates and back into the real world when my hours were up. Here, I was totally immersed. No wonder I had lost perspective a little. I needed to remind myself that this was not real life, that there was another world outside the compound, one that Harvey Stone had no impact on.

I needed to reach out to that world, to anchor myself. I

rushed back to my room and called Mel. She answered on the first ring. "Cal! Oh thank God, I was getting worried."

The sound of her voice made me wish I was with her, which took me a little by surprise. As we had been distant of late, I had begun to wonder if our differences would prove too great in the long run. But when I heard her speak, I felt a pull towards home that I hadn't been expecting. "I miss you," I said, and I meant it.

"Why didn't you answer my calls yesterday?" she asked, the relief at hearing my voice quickly turning to irritation that I had made her worry.

"I'm sorry, it was just really busy. Settling in, learning the ropes, you know what it's like."

"Yeah," she replied. "Yeah, I get it." Though the tone of her voice told me it wasn't a good enough excuse in her eyes. "Never mind, I'm just glad you're alright. So, tell me everything! What's it really like there? What are the other guards like? What's Dax like in real life?"

I tried to ignore the fact that she had asked specifically about Dax, and the queasy feeling that gave me after his lecherous comments about her last night. I began telling her about my arrival, and the farce of reshooting 'spontaneous' moments over and over again. She laughed and gasped in all the right places, and with her encouragement I found myself unable to stop talking about all the things I had seen and learned over the last twenty-four hours. Apart from my conversations with Harvey. I didn't mention those. I don't know why, perhaps I was embarrassed at having been so intrigued by such a monster. Or perhaps he was already getting under my skin.

"Well," she said as our conversation dwindled to a natural close. "I'm pleased you've settled in alright. Miss you, though. It's going to be surreal seeing you on TV on Saturday."

Saturday. I felt a wave of nausea. Saturday was coming, and there was nothing I could do to prevent it. Nothing I could do to save Vincent from whatever horror Reynolds and his underlings had concocted. He should be my focus, his welfare should be foremost in my thoughts, not the ravings of a dangerous madman. He was the whole reason I was here, after all. I owed it to him to do whatever I could to ease his fears and make his life more tolerable.

I tried several times over the next few days to talk to him discreetly, but it was next to impossible in such a goldfish bowl of an environment. I was worried about his mental state: the closer we came to Saturday's show, the more withdrawn he seemed. "I don't think he's coping," I said to Carlos, nudging him and gesturing to the cell where Vincent sat motionless, staring at the blank wall and rocking, ever so slightly.

"So?" Carlos shrugged, "Who gives a shit?"

I did, but I couldn't let on. To everyone else, Vincent was a sadistic bastard who had deliberately burned vulnerable children to death; of course they didn't care whether he was suffering, they felt it was deserved. But to me, he was possibly the most selfless and honourable man I had ever known, aside from all his previous gang-related activities, of course. As I watched him descend further and further into an anxious abyss, at times looking almost catatonic with fear, I felt impotent and ashamed, unable to save him from this terrible injustice.

19

By the time Saturday night rolled around, I was starting to think that perhaps getting it over with would be the best thing for Vincent. Surely, the reality of the chamber couldn't be as bad as the anticipation? He wasn't a weak man, I reminded myself. Sure, the last few days had him scared but it was likely fear of the unknown. I was scared myself; I'd never been on live television before. In the outside world, Vincent had been someone to be feared. A leader, a criminal, a man who didn't tolerate disrespect or shy away from confrontations – violent or otherwise. In all likelihood, he'd be relieved when he discovered the program was nowhere near as bad as he had built it up to be.

"Alright, guys?" Matt the runner rapped gently on the staffroom door, stepping in tentatively as he did so, the huge corporate-friendly smile he was wearing a direct contrast to his nervous, timid gait. "Aisling's asked me to come and brief you on a couple of things ahead of the show, Cal. Would that be okay?"

"Sure," I replied. It wasn't like I could say no.

"Super." Matt studied his clipboard. "So, first thing to be mindful of, and this is relevant to all you guys, not just Cal, is the size and nature of tonight's crowd."

"No shit," Dax grunted, twirling the tip of his knife on the coffee table in a move that was rehearsed to perfection so that

273

it seemed absent-minded. "I saw 'em lined up outside the gate a while back, there's more than there even was for Stone." He sounded pissed off about that.

"Quite." Matt tried, and failed, not to keep flicking his gaze towards the shiny 'heirloom' Dax played with. I tried to imagine what must be running through his mind. Should Dax have a weapon, in here? Ought he be confiscating it, reporting it? Which would anger Aisling more, him turning a blind eye to Dax's contraband, or him upsetting her star guard just before the big live show? He clearly couldn't decide, so chose to carry on with the task he'd been instructed to do, rather than risk upsetting the apple cart. "To that end, UView want to assure you all that we have drafted in extra security, and even commandeered some of the guards from Whitefield to help out. Therefore, we are confident that despite the larger number of spectators, there is no increased risk to yourselves or the prisoners."

"What did you mean by the 'nature' of the crowd?" I asked.

"Well," Matt cleared his throat, "Felton's crime was very recent, and very emotive. Feelings are raw. And… well, it occurred locally. Therefore, it's likely to feel very personal to the audience. There may even be friends and family of the deceased children present, for all we know."

"Jesus." Carlos whistled. "A crowd of unwashed Hallow hooligans out for revenge. No offence, Cal."

"None taken," I said, but I was lying. The crowd was always predominantly from Hallow, given our location on the very edge of the river. Entry was free, so it had become a form of communal entertainment. Aisling may have bemoaned the fact that Hallow residents rarely picked up their phones and parted with their cash in order to vote, but they gave her a whooping crowd each week to bolster the atmosphere and aesthetics that she was always so concerned with. She relied on them. Carlos' casual derogatory comment reminded me that although I was geographically back in Hallow, I was still surrounded by razzles whose prejudice against their southern neighbours was never far from the surface.

"Yes," Matt nodded, ignoring our exchange, "like I say, with the increased security it shouldn't pose an issue. But, it may be wise to be mindful of the depth of local feeling surrounding this one, okay?"

We all nodded, and Matt continued. "So Cal, I'm going to take you along the route in a moment, just so you're completely au fait with it, alright? Plus we need to make sure you've memorised the code for the chamber door. Aisling wants you out front leading him in, and because of the high-profile nature of this one, she'd like Dax to be your second, if that's okay?"

"Fine by me," Dax said, trying to sound nonchalant, but I caught the glimmer of excitement in his eyes at the prospect of more camera time.

"Great." Matt smiled again. "Cal, would you mind coming with me for a quick run-through before we open the gates to the crowd?"

I duly got to my feet and followed him to Vincent's cell. He harped on about how Dax and I would go in when his name was called and attach the cuffs, being mindful of the positions of the static cameras in order to ensure the best angle. But I wasn't really listening, I couldn't take my eyes off Vincent. He was staring straight ahead, his arms covered in gooseflesh and his left knee jiggling, ever so slightly. I wanted more than anything to show him my support, to remind him that even if the world hated him, I was on his side. But I couldn't.

As Matt led me outside and along the Perspex tunnel, pausing repeatedly to highlight the best places to look directly at the cameras, I wished with all my being that there was something, anything, I could do to reduce Vincent's suffering.

Harvey's cryptic words came back to me in a flash: 'the question you'll *really* be dying to ask me come Saturday'. I hadn't had a clue what he was on about at the time, but now I knew exactly what that question was. How was he so unaffected? How was it that the horrors in the chamber did nothing to elicit any fear from him? Did he have some insight that could help Vincent? He'd hinted that he'd already given me the answer, hadn't he? Something about the answer to both questions, the one I had already asked him and the one I would want to, being the same. I racked my brain, tried to pick through my memory of his odd, rambling metaphors for something that might be applicable. I'd asked him how he knew about Lez's finger, that was the question. But, being Harvey, he hadn't given me a straight answer. Instead, he'd said something about strings and atoms and truth being like GPS. Damn it, that didn't mean anything at all. At least, not to a sane person. Maybe it was just as Dax said it was: he was simply too cold and emotionless to feel fear or remorse.

We reached the chamber door, and Matt watched me punch in the code with a solemn nod. "Perfect," he said. "You're gonna do great, Cal. Now, as soon as the chamber program is over, I'll open the door to the camera run on the right-hand side of the room, and lead you through the warren and out the back to the limo. Then it's just a short trip across the river to the *Behind the Bars* studio, okay? Your driver's name is Josef, he'll wait in the studio car park until you're done and then whizz you back home."

Home. It seemed an odd way to describe this macabre, artificial place filled with killers and chameleons, but I suppose it was apt. I was, after all, fully ensconced in all its horrors and deceptions now.

20

As I made my way back to the main building, two waving figures dressed in the navy-blue security uniform caught my eye. "Bodie?" I muttered out loud, recognising the messy hair as he jogged towards me followed by a shorter officer with a big grin and brown ponytail. "And Erin?"

"Hey, Cal." Bodie panted a little as he reached me.

"What are you two doing on security?" I asked.

"They wanted volunteers." Erin beamed. "We thought it could be fun, front-row view and all that. Plus we wanted to be able to cheer you on on your big night."

"Oh," I said, noticing how Erin placed her hand on Bodie's shoulder as she bent forward a little to get her breath back. "Well, thanks, guys. I appreciate it."

"You must be hella nervous," Bodie enthused. "Millions of people watching you. I'd be bricking it."

"Yeah." I hadn't been thinking too much about the viewers at home, I'd been more focused on the idea of getting through the crowd, and trying to help Vincent. "More worried about that lot waiting to get in, though. They reckon it's a huge crowd tonight, and there could be trouble."

"Never fear, Beanie boy." Erin grinned. "That's what we're here for. Well, us and about another fifty security officers."

Bodie nodded. "They're definitely worried about this one," he said, opening his jacket slightly and beckoning me to look. I peered inside, and noticed the shiny grey hilt of a gun protruding from his waistband.

"Jesus," I hissed. "They've given you guns?"

Erin nodded. "All the security guards have them," she said.

"Do you even know how to shoot?"

"Did a VR course this morning," Bodie replied. "Erin's a much better aim than me, but I passed anyway."

"So you've never actually shot one in real life?" I asked, wondering if any of the fifty or so goons milling about with firearms stuffed in their trousers had any real-life experience at all, or if UView had decided to arm a bunch of glorified nightwatchmen who had done little more than play a shoot-'em-up game and send them to roam free amid a huge angry mob.

"No," Erin replied. "And hopefully never will. They're just a precaution, not to be used unless absolutely necessary."

"Sorry, Cal," Bodie said, noticing the look of bewilderment and panic I couldn't keep off my face. "Didn't mean to make you more worried, I thought it'd make you feel safer, knowing the security was armed."

"Yeah," I said, forcing a smile. "Of course it does."

"Anyway," Erin changed the subject, "what we really wanted was to ask if you wanted to go for drinks after the show, celebrate your big night?"

"Oh," I said, "I'd love to, but I've got to go do that *Behind the Bars* talk show straight after. Not sure when I'll be back."

"No drama." Erin shrugged. "We'll be in The Parrot until late, just pop along when you're back if you fancy it. Figured we'd go for an old-person's bar, less conspicuous, now that you're a star and all that."

I winced a little. *A star.* I supposed I was, or at least would be after tonight. I wasn't yet sure whether that was a good thing, or the worst possible outcome. On the one hand, stars shone. They lit up the night sky, provided guidance to those who were lost and in need of direction – and that was always what I'd aspired to do. But on the other hand, stars were only serene and stoic from a distance. If you looked closer, they were nothing more than swirling, burning, chaotic masses of gas and fire that would one day crash and burn, causing untold devastation. It's funny how our perspective of things changes depending on our proximity to them.

Back in the cell block, it was dinner time and the trolley was wheeled in full of plastic trays. I looked for Dax but he was nowhere to be seen.

"He's with Mo," Titch commented, noticing me scanning the room. Nobody touched the trolley until Dax had taken Harvey's food from it usually. "Recording some sound bites."

I saw my chance and grabbed a tray. "I'll take Harvey's," I said, moving swiftly before anyone but Titch, who I knew to be a firm disbeliever in the whole 'Stone is a siren' legend, could register what I was doing. I hurried down the corridor to his cell, and wasted no time on pleasantries.

"Okay, Stone," I said as I approached. "You were right, I need to ask you a question."

"But I already gave you the answer," Harvey said, his eyes fixed on the hatch.

I let out a huff, unlocked the hatch and shoved his tray in gracelessly. "No more cryptic mind games. Just give me a straight answer. How do you do it?"

He took his tray slowly, sliding it from the hatch and placing it on the table with deliberate lethargy, making me wait. Then he turned to face me and looked me straight in the eye.

"Do you know how I know you're authentic, Cal?" he asked.

I rolled my eyes. He was meandering again, trying to force me down another rabbit hole, trying to make me chase another wild goose. "Forget it," I snapped, and turned away. I didn't have the time or patience to be a pawn in his sadistic little mind games.

"It's because you don't glitch," he called out, and I stopped in my tracks.

"What do you mean?" I stepped back to face him again.

"When something isn't real, there's always a glitch. As

if the act of pretence is so all-consuming that occasionally it flickers, strains at its edges. You see it all the time with people, if you look closely enough. A momentary lapse in their affected expression, a huffed word almost unheard when they think they're alone. If someone is faking, there's always a moment or two where the truth spills through the seams quicker than they can stitch themselves back up. The same is true of the chamber.

"I told you before, once you see what things are made of, once you know what holds them together, the whole becomes merely the sum of its parts. The illusion unravels and is laid bare for you to see. Tell your boy to look for the pixels, the rest will follow."

Dinner was in full swing when I sneaked back through the door. Vincent sat staring at the tray in front of him, fork in hand but making no attempt to eat. Probably for the best, I thought. Vomiting on live television wouldn't be the worst experience he'd have tonight, but it certainly wouldn't make the night any better for him. Though Harvey's words might.

I didn't fully understand still, but perhaps Vincent would once he was in the chamber. I'd been in several VR simulations recently, by virtue of helping Nate develop the training programs, and I'd never noticed any glitches. But then, I hadn't been looking for them. If it was possible to distance yourself from the horror around you by concentrating in this way, then I wanted Vincent to have the best possible chance of alleviating at least some of his suffering. There was nothing I could do about the electric shocks – they'd get him screaming one way or another, just like they did with Harvey. But perhaps, if the Playground Slasher's tip meant that Vincent's show was a damp squib, then they'd shy away from using him for the chamber shows in the future, just like Stone.

I dashed into the staffroom, pleased to find no one else was in there. I grabbed a pen and a Post-it note from the small wooden desk in the corner and scribbled: *Look for glitches and pixels.* It wouldn't mean much out of context, I knew that. But maybe, just maybe, Vincent would recall the strange advice once he was in the program, and it would suddenly make sense.

In the communal area, he was staring into space, fork still poised in mid-air, the slop of tonight's unnamed stew untouched in its compartment on his tray. I strode up behind him, affected a sneer for the watching cameras and colleagues, and with the small note balled up in my hand, slammed my palm down on the table next to Vincent's elbow.

"Not hungry, Felton?" I snapped at him, and he turned to me, his face unable to hide a wrinkle of confusion at my uncalled-for spite. While the other inmates erupted into jeers and laughter, I discreetly poked Vincent's elbow with my pinky finger and slid the note out from my palm and under his tray. He looked me directly in the eyes, and I knew he understood. He got up to scrape his untouched dinner into the bin, palming the note as he did so. I hoped to God it was enough to help him, even just a little.

21

When Mo called Vincent's name the crowd outside went wild. I approached his cell slowly. "It's time," I whispered.

"I know," he said, looking up at me with defeated resignation and sticking his hands out in front of him so I could cuff him. He didn't struggle as Finn had, or look stoic and resolved like Stone. He kept his gaze straight ahead, as I had advised him to do, but from the look of concentration on his face, and the heavy rise and fall of his chest, I could tell that it was taking every ounce of his focus just to keep putting one foot in front of the other. We made our way through the door and slowly down the Perspex tunnel, trying to ignore the crowd and keep our eyes on the chamber door as it loomed ever closer.

It was impossible not to hear the screamed insults and crowing chants coming from the crowd; we were almost nose to nose with them, after all. Just a thin transparent layer separating us from the hoard of furious onlookers who would, I had no doubt, tear Vincent to shreds within seconds given half the chance.

Burn in Hell Kiddie Cooker and *Fry you F*cker!* were just some of the handmade placards held aloft by the mob. Just as we were turning the last corner, almost close enough to reach out and touch the door, an almighty thud made me jump so hard I bit my tongue. I looked up, panicked, thinking for a split second that it was a bullet, probably shot by an overenthusiastic security guard. Even Dax was shocked by the loud, unexpected bang that echoed through the tunnel. "Shit!" he yelled involuntarily. The censors didn't have time to bleep it out.

But it wasn't a bullet, it was a bloodied missile of animal guts and dripping offal that had been launched at Vincent. The red stain streaked down the side of the Perspex, and I could just make out what looked to be stringy, sausage-like organs half-splattered and stuck to the side of the tunnel right next to my head.

"You alright?" I turned and asked Vincent. He nodded, but he shook like he had a fever of a hundred and four. "Nearly there," I whispered, trying fruitlessly to comfort him. 'There' was, after all, worse than 'here'.

I punched in the code, and the door opened with a loud creak which was clearly an intentional addition – the building was brand new and hadn't yet developed any of the knocks or creaks that come from frequent use. Reynolds waited inside, wearing a lab coat and a sombre smile. He gave me a slow nod, which I had been instructed to reciprocate, and then I took Vincent's arm and led him to the waiting chair. I gave his elbow a subtle, friendly squeeze – for all the good that did. He didn't fight, or yell, instead he duly sat in the chair of his own accord; a man resigned to having no control over his fate.

Dax and I attached the restraints and wires, Reynolds loitering behind me to make sure I did so correctly, and perhaps to ensure I didn't 'accidentally' forget to attach the electrodes.

With Vincent strapped in, breathing raggedly and clenching and unclenching his fists in a vain attempt to calm himself, Dax and I stood back, taking up our positions in the two far corners of the room. I folded my hands behind my back as was protocol, and tried to retain a respectful professionalism. Reynolds smiled, and flipped the switch.

As the screen came to life, my heart sank with the reality of Vincent's situation. It was bad enough watching the torture of heinous killers, but it was unbearable to watch such things happen to an innocent man. It took all my willpower to not look away as the screen began to shake.

Vincent's avatar was lying face down on a dusty wooden floor. He glanced around tentatively, trying to make sense of his surroundings. It looked to be an old, decrepit farmhouse. The air was clouded, musty and thick. Vincent pressed his palms to the floor, trying to lever himself up, but he couldn't. He turned around, and the first-person camera revealed the cause. His legs were unnaturally bent, the left one sticking out to the side and the right one stuck in a strange, obtuse angle so that it seemed to be set in a permanent kicking motion. Below his knees, the cotton trousers were torn clean off, and red rivulets ran from open wounds as shards of bone protruded from each of his calves. It looked as though his lower legs had been pierced and crushed by some sort of unholy machinery. I wondered what Reynolds had envisioned making such a mangled mess of his subject's legs. A bear trap? Perhaps some sort of industrial grinder? It didn't matter. Regardless of what had caused the injuries, the outcome was the same. Vincent's legs were useless to him.

In his chair, Vincent shrieked with pain as Reynolds cranked up the current to the electrodes attached to his lower limbs at the same moment that his mutilated legs came into view.

Vincent scanned the room in panic, looking for the danger he knew must be present, but he saw nothing except several small doors, one of which opened into a narrow hallway. It was only when he chanced to glance up that the thick, coiling smoke that snaked across the ceiling left everyone in no doubt as to the nature of his suffering. The crackle started then, as though waiting for the billows of black to be noticed before beginning its refrain. Distant, at first, like the comforting rhythms of an open fire on a winter's day. There was no way to tell which direction the whispered rush of flames was coming from, which door might be concealing an inferno behind its fragile timber frame.

He began to drag himself toward the open door, panting with the effort of heaving his body with just his arms. After he had made it a few feet, there was a loud crack as a beam overhead gave way and crashed to the floor beside him, covered in flames. The fire was on the floor above, and the ceiling was about to give way. He screamed with pain as the flames from the burning beam beside him spread and licked at his sides, Reynolds giving him a blast of electric to make the pain real. He redoubled his efforts, wriggling across the rough wooden floor, hauling his useless legs behind him as more and more of the burning timber crashed down around him. He barely made it through the door when the whole ceiling fell into the room in a smouldering, flaming mass.

In the narrow corridor now, the air was thick with choking black smoke and Vincent began to cough. Reynolds sent current to the pads on his chests, causing him pain with every breath he took against the poisonous fumes. Ahead, there was a shard of light and as he drew closer I could see daylight. An open door to the outside. On and on, the corridor getting hotter and darker, Vincent screamed every few seconds as another burst of flame appeared as if from nowhere, singeing and scorching his tortured flesh.

Outside there were fields, and trees, and the cool breeze of a summer's day. He ploughed on, trying to ignore the rising heat and blinding pain. Closer, closer and now a figure became visible. A young blonde girl, dressed in a chequered blue pinafore dress, played hopscotch just outside, seemingly oblivious to the burning building behind her. She had her back to the house, skipping forward over the numbers as Vincent finally reached the exit and pulled himself over the small step, collapsing in a panting heap on the grass outside.

"Are you alright?" The little girl's voice was soft and tinkly – like the tiny bell on a kitten's first collar. Vincent looked up at her as she turned to face him, and then he screamed.

Her face was barely a face at all, so much of it was missing. The skin that remained was blistered and puckered and covered only a small part of her skull, the rest had melted away. She titled her head, looking at Vincent with her one remaining eye, and he recoiled in horror as it swelled and swelled, the pupil getting larger and more distorted as the whole eyeball began to protrude out of her face. With a tiny 'pop' it exploded, white and green liquid oozing from the now empty socket and sliding down her red and charred face.

He threw his arms over his eyes, and lay on the ground sobbing. The girl stood over him still, and slowly more and more figures began to appear above him until he was surrounded. Around a dozen children, all covered in scars and blisters. Some had lost so much of their flesh they looked more like skeletons than living human beings. Behind them, two smartly dressed nurses appeared, small cloth hats tied atop their hairless, fleshless scalps.

"It's time for your medicine now, Vincent," the taller of the nurses said in an authoritative tone. She pulled a large glass medicine bottle from her pocket and unscrewed the lid slowly, fixing Vincent with a stony, resolute stare as she did so. She turned the bottle upside down, pouring its contents all over Vincent's helpless body. The camera zoomed in to allow the viewers to see that the label on the bottle read *Paraffin*.

"Stand back a little now, children," the other nurse instructed her charges. "Let us administer the treatment." She produced a box of matches from her pocket and pulled one out slowly, holding it up so that Vincent had plenty of time to anticipate what was coming next. He pleaded, writhed, screamed for mercy. But the watching children just smiled serenely, their blackened and lopsided faces all around him.

She struck the match, and dropped it from head height onto Vincent's body. Reynolds turned the dial sharply as the paraffin ignited, sending more and more volts coursing through Vincent. He bucked, convulsed, wailed and screamed with the agony of it all. Even as I watched him thrash, I could hear the jubilant cheers of the crowd outside.

I was the first to notice the wet stain creep across his groin as his bladder emptied involuntarily. When the program ended, and his convulsions subsided, I tried my best to manoeuvre myself in front of him and hide it from the cameras, but it was no use. As soon as Dax and I had loosened his restraints and helped the shaken, broken inmate to his feet, there was no disguising it and I knew he would have to walk back through the tunnel to the laughter and cackling jeers of a crowd overcome with joy at his added humiliation.

I had no time to settle him back in, offer him any comfort, or get him fresh clothes, as Matt appeared in the hidden doorway and ushered me into the rat runs to be whisked off to the *Behind the Bars* studio in the waiting limo.

22

I stared out of the window at the lights and buildings as they whizzed by in a blur, a multicoloured haze against the night sky. I tried to fathom all the lives that those endless lights represented. All those houses, all those families, all those televisions, all those people who knew so little about me, or Vincent, or Danny, but who now discussed us with mouths full of greasy snacks, sure and certain in the opinions they had formed. Perhaps they laughed and crowed at Vincent's fear. Perhaps through some of those windows, in the glow of some of those lights, women cackled as they raised gin and tonics to their lips, recalling the long streak of piss that snaked down the kiddie cooker's trousers. Perhaps little kids, allowed to stay up late by their irresponsible parents, guffawed and jumped up and down with primal glee at the sight of a grown man's embarrassing bodily functions.

In that moment, I hated them all for their ignorance. Hated them all for their callous, cruel amusement at another's misfortune and suffering. Hated myself, for allowing an innocent man to undergo such torture and humiliation just to protect my own selfish feelings – I didn't want to be faced with the guilt of abandoning Danny, didn't want to have to see that young, promising lad suffer that way and know I could have prevented it if only I'd made different choices.

When we pulled into the studio car park, two young

women with clipboards and lanyards rushed up to the limo and ushered me into the building without so much as a hello. I followed them at a brisk pace through labyrinthine corridors, one of them tucking stray locks of hair away from my face and pulling at my shirt to straighten it as we went. There was no time for any preamble, the show went out live straight after *Justice Live*, which meant it had already been on air for thirty minutes by the time I arrived. As we approached the main studio, Jaxon Miles, the androgynously dressed, emaciated presenter, was trying to fill the wait between guests with his banal anecdotes and innuendoes. The woman to the right of me raised her hand at a technician, who raised his hand at someone else until eventually the silent signal reached the person whose voice was in the host's ear, and he stood up with exaggerated aplomb and made my introduction.

I was propelled forward by adrenaline, the whistles and claps from the studio audience muffled by my heart thumping in my ears. Jaxon walked towards me, hands outstretched, teeth on show, and drew me into an unexpected bear hug. He was about six inches shorter than me, and I got a mouthful of over-sprayed long curls when he squeezed me close.

"Oh my," he said, pulling back and looking me up and down before turning to the camera. "He's a big boy, isn't he?"

The audience chortled and wolf-whistled and I tried to keep smiling and acting cool, though my guts were churning. Jaxon turned and flounced back to his swivel chair, his impossibly pert buttocks bouncing in his ultra-tight leather trousers. "Take a seat, take a seat," he said, gesturing to an oversized armchair. "We don't bite. Unless you pay us extra."

It wasn't a real interview – Jaxon Miles doesn't like to share the limelight. He wasn't interested in asking me any pertinent questions, settling instead for showing the audience stills of me with my mouth open or in a half-blink and captioning them with heavy innuendo, to rapturous applause and squawking laughter. My segment came to an end and I was herded offstage in something of a daze, more than a little bewildered at the fact that I seemed to be appreciated more for participating in the 'comedy' of this show than I ever had been for any of the truly important community-minded jobs I had done in my life. It felt as though the world had its priorities upside down and twisted beyond recognition.

23

I made it back to Whitefield just before midnight. I thanked the driver as I exited the limo just outside the gates, but I did not head to the *Justice Live* compound. Instead, I carried on down the road, and took a right turn into the narrow street that played host to several different second-hand shops and some exotic food stores. Just off the street, almost tucked away on the edge of an alley, was The Parrot: favoured drinking place of retired men and middle-aged couples, and anyone who wanted a quiet pint away from the garish, lurid noise and spectacle of the young people's bars.

When I entered the musty, dimly lit pub I was pleased to see Nate and Squinty sitting with Erin and Bodie in an upholstered booth, at least a dozen empty glasses discarded on the table in front of them. Erin spotted me first, and gave a huge, animated wave as she nudged Bodie in the ribs and nodded her head towards me. She looked different, away from the prison. Her cheeks were rosy from the alcohol and her long hair flowed freely down her shoulders as she laughed and slapped the table in response to something Squinty had said. She looked happy, really happy. Bodie beamed at me, getting up and gesturing for me to take his seat. "Pint, Cal?" he asked, indicating that he was off to the bar.

"Please," I replied.

"Well, here he is." Squinty clapped me on the shoulder.

"Man of the hour! The latest celeb, the cat's whiskers. How does it feel to be an icon, Beanie?"

"I don't know," I said. "I mean, it doesn't feel like anything."

"Did Reynolds do that program by himself?" Nate asked, straight on to the techy talk as always.

"I don't know, I guess so."

"Thought so." Nate downed the foamy end of his pint, put down his empty glass and reached across the table to take the fresh pint Bodie held out to him. "Shoddy."

"It did the job," I said ruefully, recalling Vincent's tortured screaming and taking a long swig from the glass Bodie had thrust in front of me to try to numb the memory.

"It was rough round the edges," Nate said, shaking his head. "Trouble with Reynolds, he's sloppy. Puts all his effort into the shock-value stuff, doesn't like troubling himself with the nuts and bolts of the program."

"So why don't you take over the chamber programs?" Squinty asked. "If you could do a better job?"

"Because I'm not a sadistic, vindictive bastard," Nate replied. "I'll stick to teaching woodwork to reprobates, thanks."

"Speaking of sadistic, vindictive bastards," Erin said, holding her glass aloft. "This is a double celebration. Not only do we say 'hello' to Beanie the star, but we also say a big fat good fucking riddance to Lardarse!"

Bodie and Squinty cheered, and clinked their glasses against Erin's. "Lardarse?" I asked. "He's gone?"

"Fired," Erin said, unable to keep the grin from turning into a giggle.

"Don't look so surprised, Cal," Bodie said with a wink. "I told you he would be."

I recalled the look in Bodie's eyes after Lardarse had upset Erin that day, the steely determination with which he had declared he would get him sacked. I'd thought that was just heat-of-the-moment stuff, one of those things people say when they're angry but don't really manage to achieve.

"No?" I said. "Really? You got him canned?"

"What can I say?" Bodie splayed his hands and shrugged. "I'm a man of my word."

"It was magnificent," Squinty said. "Sweat Sack here, he was like a ninja. Biding his time, watching. Then, when the moment was just right, he called Captain Wanker up on threes on some ridiculous made-up request just in time for him to witness Lardarse attacking Greavsie, totally unprovoked."

"Well," Erin smirked, "all the officers present stated it was unprovoked."

"Who were the officers present?" I asked.

"We were," Erin and Squinty said in unison before erupting into laughter.

"And Greavsie provoked him as a favour?" I asked.

Erin nodded. "He's the bloody toast of G wing now," she said. "Honestly, when Lardarse was escorted off the premises, the inmates went nuts – it was like Christmas."

"I bet," I said, smiling at the thought of Greavsie being the man of the hour. He was a good guy, it seemed fitting. It was justice, of an orchestrated sort. Sometimes karma needed a little helping hand.

As the beer flowed, I found myself relaxing muscles I didn't know had been tensed. It was a relief to be in such easy company, to be unwatched and unjudged. Just after 1am, Bodie turned to Erin and put his hand on her shoulder. "We should get back," he said gently. "You told the babysitter 1.30 at the latest."

She nodded, and downed the dregs of her glass while wrestling her coat on. I noted Bodie reached behind her to help her with the second sleeve, and she didn't react.

"It was so great to see you, Cal." She kissed me on the cheek, her breath warm and her lips cold and wet from the lager. "Do it again soon, yeah?"

"Definitely," I said, and I meant it. Their company had been the perfect antidote to all the stress, guilt and farcical charades of the evening. Bodie pulled me in for a bear hug, patting me solidly on the back with three flat slaps, that unspoken indicator of male camaraderie.

I watched them exit the pub, Bodie holding the door open for Erin, then turned to Squinty and Nate. "*We* better get back?" I asked. "Did I miss something?"

Squinty grinned wide. "They think they're being discreet," he replied. "But everyone knows. Neither of them are the secret-keeping type, they're terrible at it!"

Bodie and Erin? I was surprised at first, I didn't think she'd go for someone as overtly nice and – I felt disloyal even thinking it – boring as him. "How did that happen?" I asked. "Was it because he got Lardarse fired? She doesn't strike me as the damsel-in-distress type."

"She's not," Squinty said, his expression turning serious. "And she'd have your balls for the suggestion of it, Beanie boy. He's a good guy, that's all. I'm happy for her, she deserves to be treated well, given a bit of respect and consideration. She doesn't need 'rescuing', just companionship."

I paused for a moment, reflecting on Squinty's uncharacteristically poignant words. My relationship with Mel suddenly consumed my thoughts. Weren't we based, entirely, on having rescued each other? Me, the knight in shining armour who rode in to save her from her attackers; she, the grateful, delicate princess whose love elevated me out of squalor and into luxury? Was that the problem, was that why I felt resentful? Were we keeping score, subconsciously? My one good deed versus her years of giving me the life I could never have dreamed of achieving on my own, although at times it was a life I wasn't sure I wanted at all. Or was it just me that felt that way? Perhaps, like Erin, she didn't need or want a rescuer or provider, perhaps she just craved a companion. I thought of the conversation we had had on launch night, all she had wanted was to stay home together, just *be* in each other's presence. She'd wanted me. Just me. And I'd already been so consumed with disdain and resentment for the extravagant world of her childhood and family that I hadn't appreciated the pureness of that simple wish.

I needed to call her. The revelation struck all at once, sharp and urgent in my beer-fuddled mind. I had to tell her what I'd realised about us, and about myself. I stood up and made my excuses, thanking Nate and Squinty and promising we'd get together again real soon. With the memories of all my own bitter, cynical assumptions about Mel weighing on my conscience, I hurried down the moonlit street towards Whitefield, desperate to get behind my own little locked door and make the contrite call I knew was way overdue.

24

The guard at the *Justice Live* gates didn't seem to care about the late hour I was arriving back at, and I was grateful not be questioned. He just gave me a nod, and let me straight into the compound. No need to sign in, no need to show ID, another perk of celebrity.

I meandered my way across the courtyard, empty and desolate now that the crowds had been dispersed and the stage dismantled. Only a few food wrappers scuttling in the breeze and a slight smear of blood still present on the asphalt gave hint to the spectacle that had taken place here just a few hours before. Most of the buildings were in semi-darkness, the only lights coming from the staffroom next to the cell block where the off-camera night-shift guards were counting the hours until dawn, and the lurid glow of the security lamps and illuminated fire exit signs.

I was almost at the door to the guard's quarters when something unexpected caught my eye. A light I hadn't seen before, not until I'd turned past the cells and hit just the right angle. A light in one of the chamber rooms. I frowned a little, but concluded it was probably Reynolds working late, his eyes full of determination and his black heart full of glee as he keyed in his little codes and watched his sadistic fantasies of torture and dismemberment come to life on-screen.

But when I entered the living quarters, I could tell

something was amiss. It was only just gone 1.30am, on a Saturday. Yet there was no one drinking in the living room, and no evidence that anyone had been. Dax et al never cleared up their own detritus – that was what runners were for – yet there were no discarded bottles, no lumps of cigarette ash on the carpet. I stepped into the hallway past the lounge and noticed several of the bedroom doors were ajar, with the beds inside neat and unslept in. I counted them, and ran through whose they were. Lez, Dax, Marv, Carlos – where were they? Out on a bender? Or maybe...

I thought about the light in the chamber room, how quickly I'd assumed why it was on. I'd probably been right, of course, but I knew I wouldn't be able to rest now unless I checked, so I ventured outside again and headed for the chambers.

The main door was locked, but Matt had made sure the code was as familiar to me as my own birthday prior to the live show. I opened it cautiously, not wanting to startle Reynolds into thinking I was an intruder and calling the over-armed and undertrained security. From the main corridor, I could see the four chamber rooms ahead, each separated by a Plexiglas screen that meant once you were in one chamber you could see into the other three. This was so Reynolds could supervise work on four programs simultaneously, and make sure his underlings were fully focused on the task in hand. I could tell from the sliver of light visible under its door that it was chamber three that was currently in use. I eased open the door to chamber one, and slunk inside trying to stay in shadow. If it was just Reynolds working late, then I didn't want to make myself seem like a paranoid busybody. I'd just take a peek, note that my initial conclusion was correct, and go back to my room to call Mel. If it wasn't Reynolds, if it was in fact an intruder or some nefarious late-night visitor, or even Aisling doing some kind of check or plotting some sort of scene, then I definitely didn't want to be seen.

Inside chamber one, I pressed myself up against the tall control cabinet and leaned my head forward so that I could see through the large window and into chamber three. There they all were, the missing guards – everyone except Titch. They were all crowded around the chair, laughing and jeering. Their bodies blocked my view and at first I couldn't see who or what was the source of entertainment. Reynolds was with them, still bedecked in his white lab coat. He fiddled with the control panel, casting quizzical looks at Dax after each turn of a dial or press of a button. Dax was clearly running this show – he gave nods or shakes of his head in response, and Reynolds acquiesced to his unspoken requests.

What were they doing? I leaned forward further, squinting a little in an attempt to see more clearly. In between Marv and Carlos' shifting torsos, I thought I caught a flash of an arm strapped tightly down, tense and taut. They had somebody in the chair. But who? I strained to see behind them, but it was no use. Whoever it was, they were surrounded by a circle of a guards who watched their plight with glee.

As luck would have it, Marv pulled his carton of cigarettes from his pocket and stuck one between his lips. He touched Carlos on the shoulder with one hand as he pulled out his lighter with another. Carlos nodded, and Marv headed for the door in pursuit of his nicotine fix. As he stepped away from the others, I could at last see who was strapped in the chair – it was Harvey Stone.

His body was tense in its restraints, but the Playground Slasher's expression remained calm and neutral. When Marv opened the door to the soundproof chamber, the noise inside spilled out. I could hear the rumble of the guard's chattering amongst themselves, and above that Dax swore loudly. "Nothing. Fucking nothing!" he raged, and I watched as he punched the wall of the chamber.

"What about heights?" Reynolds asked, calmly and cheerfully, as if trying to pacify a toddler. "We haven't tried heights yet."

I realised all at once what they were doing. They were trying to find a program that would break Harvey, trying to uncover his fears so that he could be put in the live show again, and Dax could get his week in the spotlight, and the pay cheques that came with it. But I knew it was a fruitless endeavour; Harvey had told me as much himself. Although I hadn't understood his method well enough to help Vincent employ it, I had no doubt that Stone was telling the truth on that one – he was able to distance himself from the program, to prevent the total immersion that everyone believed was inescapable. It didn't matter what they put into that computer, his response would be the same.

"Fuck it, I'm done for tonight," Dax snapped. "Just give him the juice."

The door closed behind Marv, cutting off the sound. I held my breath as his footsteps padded down the corridor, past the slightly ajar door next to me, and out of the building. When I turned my attention back to chamber three, I was glad not to be able to hear the noises inside.

Reynolds turned the dial sharply, pushing it much further than he had done for Vincent earlier that night. Too far, surely? Harvey bucked and thrashed as the savage current coursed through him. His hands gripped the chair, but his chest arched up and slammed down repeatedly, every part of him convulsing. His mouth opened wide in a scream before snapping shut as his teeth clenched and chattered and frothy foam began to appear between his lips. The guards were laughing, hard.

After what seemed like an age, Reynolds flipped the switch. Harvey's muscles ceased their spasms and he flopped in the chair, limp and listless like an unstuffed rag doll. Dax removed the headset and spat in Harvey's face. He drew back his fist and punched him squarely in the stomach six times, before pulling his hunting knife from his boot and running it slowly across Stone's neck. He was saying something to the restrained and beaten killer, spouting threats no doubt. But despite the unholy ordeal Harvey had just endured at Dax and Reynolds' hands, a slow smile, smug and victorious, crept across his face and he stared Dax straight in the eye, not even blinking.

Lez and Carlos, sensing their comrade was on the edge, quickly grabbed Dax and pulled him away, even as he shouted and raged at Stone.

My heart thundered in my ears, head swimming with what I had just witnessed. This was torture, pure and simple. This was an abuse of power on a scale that put Lardarse to shame. I couldn't be a bystander to this; I had to put a stop to it. But how many were involved? They couldn't have brought Harvey here unseen – quite apart from the night-shift guards, there were cameras trained on Harvey's cell. So someone in the production crew had to be helping, at least one someone, and maybe even more. Perhaps it wasn't even clandestine. Perhaps Aisling had sanctioned their little experiments, in her ruthless quest for ratings. But, even if she had, she wouldn't want it getting out. I'd go to Doug, he wouldn't want Fanning Corp associated with anything like this, he'd shut it down – he'd threaten Aisling, if she was involved.

I sighed with relief at having a plan, at having a saviour. Doug would sort it all out, all I had to do was get back to my room and send him an email, then I could rest easy knowing I had done the right thing. I was congratulating myself on my ingenuity when a strong, greasy hand reached through the darkness and settled on my shoulder.

"Well, well." I turned around to come face to face with Marv, his expression dark and his breath smoky and sour. I hadn't heard him come back in from outside, I'd been too consumed by my own thoughts. He must have noticed the slightly open door and decided to investigate. "Is this a rat I see, cowering in the dark?"

25

Marv flicked on the light, revealing all that was in shadow – including me. I felt naked and exposed as he banged on the window and everyone gathered in chamber three turned around to see me, Marv's hand still gripping my shoulder.

"What the fuck?" Even though I couldn't hear the words coming from the soundproof room, I knew what Dax was saying. He and Lez stormed through the door and headed my way.

"What the fuck are you playing at?" Dax yelled at me as he entered chamber one and pushed Marv aside to square up to me.

"Found 'im hiding in the dark," Marv said, sounding very pleased with himself. "Watching."

Dax stepped back and looked me up and down. "It's not very brotherly, is it, Cal?" he sneered. "Sneaking around, spying on your friends."

Were we friends? I didn't think so, and his demeanour certainly wasn't friendly at that moment, if it ever was at all.

"I just saw the light on," I said. "I thought you guys were out on a bender or something, thought it might be an intruder."

Dax and Lez burst into a laughter, a raucous, forced and over-exaggerated chortle that sounded more menacing than mirthful. "And what were you planning to do if it was?" Lez asked. "Take them on?" It was a slight on my scrawny and less than muscular limbs. "Weren't you worried they'd snap you?"

I smiled, pretending to appreciate the joke. "I dunno, I'm half-cut," I said. "Dutch courage, I suppose. Maybe I'd have tried to whack them with one of these." I picked up a stapler from the small admin desk next to me, and they laughed. "Just as well it was only you guys, really."

"Yeah." Dax dropped the fake smile. "Only us. No need for any heroics, eh? No need to go calling for security, no tragic tales to go whining to your posh pussy about, nothing to worry Aisling with. Only us. A total non-event, wouldn't you say?"

"Absolutely," I replied, thinking about the implications of what he'd just let slip. 'Nothing to worry Aisling with.' So she hadn't sanctioned this, it was just Dax's little ego trip, and he'd roped the sycophantic Reynolds, and God knows how many others, in on it too.

"I'm glad we agree." Dax put his arm around my shoulder. "On a totally unrelated note, there's something I've been meaning to show you." He pulled his phone from his pocket and started scrolling through the photo gallery.

"Oh," I asked, feeling suspicious. "What's that?"

"It's just something I find useful to keep in mind, something to help me focus on the job. I mean, this place, it's sort of in a vacuum, if you get me? It's easy to forget who these inmates really are sometimes, what they're actually capable of. When you see them day in and day out, eating their sad little dinners, playing fucking canasta or watching cartoons, shuffling about in chains and jumpsuits, they seem so…" He searched for the right word. "Benign. You could even start to feel sorry for them, if you're not careful. Ah, here we are." He thrust his phone in front of my eyes, I moved my head back a little to better focus on the image, and instantly wished I hadn't.

A girl's body filled the screen in Dax's hand, her face pallid and contorted in terror. Jaw already frozen open with rigor mortis as she lay lifeless on the dewy grass; short floral summer dress split open at the front and tainted with a large crimson stain. Dax put his fingers on the screen, and pulled them slowly apart, zooming in again and again until I could see that the stain wasn't a stain at all. It was a tear, not just of the dress but of the child beneath it. It was a gaping chasm, dark red and hollow, the pointed, fractured shards of the girl's ribs lining its edges. He swiped right a little, and I gasped when I saw them there, beside her body. They were the lumpy mound I had taken at first glance to be just a clod of earth, or a pile of leaves. They were her organs, neatly piled one atop the other like the removed pieces from a game of Operation. He zoomed again, and my stomach lurched with burning bile when I saw the flies, swarming around the discarded meat, laying eggs on the little girl's ripped-out heart.

"Crime scene photos," Dax said sombrely. I had no idea how, or why, he had got hold of them, but I didn't ask. "This one is little seven-year-old Delilah Giles, Stone's fourth victim. I mean, as a man, Christ, as a *human*, when I look at that image I can't think of a single thing the bastard who did this to her doesn't deserve to suffer, can you?"

I glanced through the window at Harvey who was being released from his restraints and pulled to his feet by the other guards. His stare was fixed on me, looking to me to see my reaction to the torture I had just witnessed inflicted on him. But now all I could think about was how the girl in that picture had suffered, how she must have screamed for mercy – but found none. How her last moments were filled with terror and unimaginable pain, and how those beady, glassy eyes were the last thing she ever saw. I shuddered and turned my back on him. "No," I said to Dax, sincerely. "No, I can't."

"Good man." Dax winked at me, and patted his phone as he put it back in his pocket. "Always useful to remember who the real bad guys are, eh?"

Marv and Lez exchanged dark looks. "Dax," Marv began tentatively. "What are we—"

"Cal's sound," Dax snapped back, shutting him down.

"But—"

"He's. Sound." Dax sounded irritated now. "He knows the score, right Cal?" I just nodded, not knowing how else to respond. "See? I trust him. And I *know* he wouldn't want to upset me by betraying that trust." It was more of a threat than a statement.

I was glad to get back to my room and close the door on the evening and all its confusion. Vincent in the chamber, the talk show, drinks with the others, it all seemed like weeks ago now. The whole night had been such a roller coaster, it was hard to process any of it, not least what had occurred in the chambers after dark. I looked at my phone, it was gone 3am now, and my desire to call Mel had waned. I'd resolved to be honest, attentive, a proper partner to her, not a jealous rival. But how could I do that without telling her what had happened this evening? I couldn't, not while it was all that was consuming my mind. I'd have to wait until I'd sorted my own jumbled up thoughts out first, *then* I could focus on being a better man for her.

I lay awake, running it all over in my mind. At the time, I thought I was examining the situation from all angles, trying to make an unbiased and logical decision on what to do. But with hindsight, I can see now that what I was really doing was finding a way to justify doing absolutely nothing. Harvey Stone was a monster, there was no disputing that. I should never, ever have let him have my ear, not even for a second. Dax had done me a favour by showing me that photograph – he was right: within these walls it was easy to forget the reality of the man Stone was outside of them. I felt disgusted at myself for ever entertaining the thought that he might have useful or insightful things to say. Of course he'd been playing me, that's what he did. The first conclusion I came to that night was to have nothing more to do with him. I wouldn't speak to him, certainly wouldn't listen to him, and I would never allow myself to be alone with him again.

Of course, as a nice little by-product, that meant I wouldn't

304

have to face him knowing he knew I'd done nothing to right the wrongs that were being done by Dax and the others.

So what of those wrongs? What they were doing to Harvey was an abuse of power, a misuse of facilities, a sackable offence for sure, but perhaps morally it wasn't quite so black and white as it had seemed to me at first. Hadn't I been congratulating Erin and Bodie for setting Lardarse up and getting him fired just a few hours ago? They'd used dubious means to get the result, but there was no doubt his comeuppance was heartily deserved. Was this any different? Surely, Harvey more than deserved what he got; if his victim's families knew, they'd probably call Dax a hero. The public wouldn't bat an eyelid either, if anything they'd just be disappointed that it hadn't been televised. Did Dax and the others deserve to lose their jobs, just for giving the murderous, twisted bastard a bit of off-the-record justice? If I called attention to it, the producers would be forced to take action whether they wanted to or not, and the only person who would benefit from my whistle-blowing would be Stone himself. But if I kept quiet, he would also be the only person to suffer.

By the time the sun came up, I had convinced myself that turning a blind eye was not only the easiest way to proceed, but also the morally right thing to do.

My conscience temporarily sated, I waited until 8am and picked up the phone to call Mel. There were so many things I wanted to say, things I should have said there and then. I should have told her I saw it now, saw that my own reverse snobbery had driven a wedge between us, and I'd looked upon her with envy and disdain for things that were no more her fault than Hallow's troubles were mine. She was a good person, a warm, sweet person who didn't care where I came from – only that we were going forward together, and I shouldn't have let my own prejudice blind me to the value of that.

But when she answered the phone, she was so happy to

hear from me, so quick to tell me she missed me and loved me, that it all went unsaid. I realised from the affection and concern in her voice that I didn't need to say it all, didn't need to lay myself bare and admit my faults, after all. I could just keep my resolve to be a better partner from here on in, without having to bruise my ego by facing up to past mistakes and asking for another chance – she was already giving me far more of them than I probably deserved. I didn't need to say it all, but I probably should have while I could.

26

On shift that day, there was tension in the air. The others moved around me, not sure what to say. They gave each other knowing glances, and shared whispers that stopped abruptly when I walked by. I tried to ignore them, chalking it down to guilt and nerves on their part. In broad daylight, and with dozens of cameras trained on us, they had no power to intimidate me and were probably worried that the sober light of day might give me the desire to squeal on them. I wasn't going to, but I saw no reason to assuage their fears just yet. Let them stew for a while, perhaps it might cause them to be more careful in the future, knowing now that their careers and reputation were balanced delicately in the palm of my hand.

Titch, of course, was utterly confused by the strange atmosphere and hushed conversations going on around him, having no notion of what had happened overnight. He frowned at me, and beckoned me into the staffroom. "What's going on?" he asked me. I shrugged. "Oh, come on," he hissed. "Something's happened. I may be daft but I'm not fucking stupid. Where were you last night?"

"*Behind the Bars*, and then out with some mates," I replied.

"What about after that, what about when you came back?"

"What about it?"

"Did you go somewhere you shouldn't have done?" he

asked, and a prickle ran down my spine. Did he know? Did he know what they were up to?

"Like where?"

"I dunno, like another part of the compound."

"So, like the chamber rooms or something."

"Yeah. Just like the chamber rooms. Or something."

"Perhaps," I said, eyeing him with curiosity.

"Oh, fucking hell. Let's stop dancing around, Cal," Titch replied. "Do you know what I'm driving at, yes or no?"

"Yes," I said. "I'm pretty sure I do. I didn't think you were… in on that particular event."

"I'm not," Titch said. "I want no part of it. They know that, I made it clear right from the start."

"From the start? How many times have they done it?"

"Dunno, like I said, I want no part of it."

"But you must have some idea?"

"Well," he said, not meeting my gaze, "sometimes it's very quiet in the evening, no one drinking in the lounge, you know?"

"How often is it very quiet?"

"Once or twice a week, ever since Harvey's live chamber bombed."

I gave a low whistle. So it was a regular occurrence then, yet despite their best efforts Dax still couldn't break Harvey.

"Are you going to squeal?" Titch asked, looking a little nervous. He'd be in trouble too if I turned rat; he'd known all along, after all.

"No," I replied, and he let out a sigh of relief.

"Are you going to join in?" he asked warily, and I was taken aback by the question.

"No," I said. "Of course not."

"Oh, that's great." He smiled and nodded his head enthusiastically. "That's really great. I didn't think you were like that, like them, I mean. It'll be nice to have some company when they're all, y'know, busy."

Just then, Lez strolled into the staffroom. He looked less

than pleased to see the two of us talking alone, no doubt concerned that I might be trying to convince Titch to join me in spilling the beans. I shot him a wry smile, enjoying the shift in the balance of power while it lasted.

For the rest of the shift I tried to focus on Vincent. He was clearly struggling with the psychological after-effects of the chamber program, and his own pain and humiliation. He lay on his bunk in the foetal position, and refused any breakfast. I couldn't be seen to give sympathy on camera, but I had good cause to take him to the showers to get cleaned up given that he was still wearing the urine-stained jumpsuit he'd had on last night, and the smell was beginning to permeate the air.

"On your feet, inmate," I yelled exaggeratedly and poked him gently with my baton. "You smell like a piss house; you're coming with me for a shower. Stat."

At the sound of my voice, he looked up slowly and I gave a slight, inconspicuous wink when his haunted eyes met mine. With a weak nod, he hauled himself to his feet and presented his hands to be cuffed. The other cons harangued him with shouts of "Piss pants" and "Better tell Mummy you wet your nappy again" as I led him across the cell block. The guards joined in, and I forced myself to laugh along for appearances.

But once inside the shower block, away from the scrutiny of the incessant cameras, I closed the door behind us, uncuffed his hands and pulled him into a hug, not caring about the stench of stale ammonia. He wept and shook in my arms for a long minute, before suddenly pulling away and looking embarrassed.

"It's alright," I said softly. "I'm so sorry about what happened."

"It's not your fault, Beanie," he said, hurriedly wiping away the last of the snot and tears from his face with the filthy sleeve of his jumpsuit. "Better me than Danny, eh? That's all I could think, that's all I kept trying to tell myself the whole time. If it wasn't me it would be him."

"Did it help?"

"At first," he said, staring at his feet. "Until it got too bad. There was a moment when…" His eyes filled with tears again, and I waited patiently for him to find the strength to say the next words. "There was a moment when it was so bad, the pain and the fear, when I, I would have traded with him if I could. That's the worst of it, Beanie. I thought I was so strong, such a good big brother, but when it came to it, I'd have seen him suffer rather than take one more second of it myself."

"Vincent," I said softly, "the pain is designed to send you out of mind, temporarily at least. You can't blame yourself for having a perfectly natural biological response; it's just survival instinct. The things that run through your mind when you're enduring that kind of trauma, you can't dwell on them, they're not you."

"Yeah, sure," he said, sounding unconvinced.

"Come on." I handed him soap and towels. "Let's get you showered. You'll feel better once you're cleaned up. As long as you keep your head down now and don't get much camera time, there's no reason why you should be voted again. The other guards are all trying to push their inmates into the spotlight, if you and me just stay boring and sedate, the public will lose interest in you."

That seemed to comfort him a little, and he proceeded to shower and change before I escorted him back to his cell, his head held a little higher than before.

By the time I clocked off for the evening, I was exhausted from the lack of sleep the night before and desperate to be alone with my thoughts. Someone, probably Matt, had laid out boxes of fish and chips on the kitchen side for all of us, but I wasn't hungry. I went straight to my room, crashing down on my bed with relief, and succumbed to a deep sleep even before I had summoned the energy to change out of my uniform.

27

I woke with a start when my door flew open, the light from the corridor piercing the dark stillness of my bedroom. I didn't know what time it was, or how long I'd been asleep, but I had neglected to close the curtains, and through the window I could see the moon high in the sky. They stormed in, Dax reaching me first and pressing a firm, tobacco-stained hand over my mouth, pushing my head down into the pillow.

"Wakey, wakey," he sneered at me. "Me and the boys have got a little surprise for you, Cal. You up for a midnight stroll?"

My answer was not required, neither was my compliance. Lez and Marv hauled me up by my arms and marched me forward, my feet struggling to find purchase and dragging on the floor. Laughing, Carlos and Dax grabbed a leg each, and I was carried unceremoniously out of the quarters and across the courtyard to the chamber rooms.

"What the fuck are you—" I tried to protest, but Dax twisted my ankle hard and hissed at me to shut my mouth. I tried to thrash and wriggle, but they held me fast.

"Got a live one 'ere, lads," Lez announced as we reached chamber three, where Reynolds and the other guards, except Titch, were waiting.

"Just get him in quick before my fucking back gives out," Marv complained.

I was bundled into the chair. Before I could move a muscle,

there were hands all over me, holding me tight in place while Dax and Lez attached the restraints.

"You don't have to do this, Dax," I yelled as he came towards me with a sinister grin on his face and the headset in hands. "I'm not going to tell on you!"

"Oh," he said, lifting my head and forcing the device on. "I *know* you won't, Cal, I know you won't. Fire it up, Reynolds."

Reynolds pressed a button, and the chamber room flew away, leaving me in darkness.

I was standing in a lavishly decorated hotel hallway, the floor a shiny marble and the walls a tasteful off-white. Tall exotic houseplants thrived in ornate pots, each positioned precisely the same distance apart from the other along each side of the lengthy passage. The doors to each room were made from a superbly polished wood, and each had solid gold numbering. The hum of a ceiling fan, and the slight chill of air con, told me I was abroad, somewhere hot and sunny and full of wealthy tourists.

I stood still for a while, scared by my own disorientation. Why couldn't I remember where I was, or how I got here? The last thing I remembered was being strapped into the chamber chair by Dax and the others. Was I still there? Was this a chamber program? How could it be, when this was nothing like a nightmare? I looked around again at the plush corridor. I must be on holiday, and I must be with Mel because I could never afford to set foot in a place like this otherwise. But I couldn't remember making plans, or packing cases, or even taking a flight. Had I had too much ouzo, or sangria, or whatever the local tipple was in whatever country I was in?

I felt around in my pockets for a key card, praying there would be a room number printed on it so I would at least know where I was staying within the building, even if I had no clue whereabouts on the globe I might be. To my relief, I found it in my back pocket and saw it was still in its little white envelope with *Room 276* handwritten on the front. I was on the right floor, at least.

I started down the corridor, passing door after door until I reached room 276. The *Do Not Disturb* sign was hung over the knob, perhaps Mel was having a nap and I'd gone out for a walk alone and got sunstroke without her there to nag me to wear a hat. Or perhaps we'd just arrived and were both jet-lagged – that could explain my confusion, couldn't it?

I swiped my card and as the door beeped open I heard Mel's unmistakable light and airy giggle and smiled at the familiar, reassuring sound of the woman I loved. I was about to call out to her, confess my confusion and wait for her to laughingly explain that I'd had a skin-full, or bashed my head by the pool or something like that, but then I heard a different sound. A moan, long and low followed by a sharp, high gasp and a breathy cry of "Oh God, yes."

I stepped forward, past the large yucca plant that had been obscuring my view of the queen-sized, satin-quilted bed, and there she was. My Melody, laying naked on her back, legs wide and eyes tight shut, groaning and gasping as a man with thick muscles and prominent tattoos lay on top of her, pounding into her, making her sing for him.

"Oh, Dax," she gasped with pleasure, and I felt my blood run cold. The man turned his head, looked directly at me with a wink, and I let the key card fall from my hand and hit the floor as I stood staring at Dax Miller as he fucked the only precious thing in my life with his filthy cock.

"Share and share alike, eh, buddy?" he said to me, still thrusting. He patted Mel on her perfect bottom and whispered, "Flip over for me, baby." She nodded and, totally ignoring my presence, turned over onto her front. In my head I was running at him, pulling him off her, smashing his smug fucking face into the floor until his skull disintegrated in my hands, but shock was holding me prisoner, causing a paralysis of sorts that left me stunned and staring.

But as she completed her manoeuvre, I noticed something. Something small and seemingly insignificant that changed everything all in an instant. Melody, my Melody, had a small brown mole on her left ankle. The Melody sweating and writhing with Dax did not.

"A glitch," I said to myself, as reality suddenly started flooding back. "A mistake."

Mel was self-conscious about that mole, the one tiny blemish on her alabaster skin. She hated it, though I told her over and over again that I thought it was cute. She hated it so much that she never wore sandals, not unless they were the strappy kind and she could position them so that the offending mark was covered by leather or buckle. There wasn't a picture in existence in which it was on show. Only I, her parents, and her former lovers knew it was there.

I stared intently at her bare, flawlessly white ankle and a strange thing began to happen. It flickered, just a little. I relaxed my eyes, tilted my head slightly and it flickered even more. Suddenly, I could see pixels dancing on her skin, I could see the frames shifting making each movement jerky and unrealistic. I could see that she was CGI.

Harvey's words came back to me again – "once you see what things are made of" – and now I could understand. Mel's image had been created from public photographs, her voice from videos or recordings, she was just a mock-up, a sham. I had found the mistake, and from that one wrong pixel the whole illusion had unravelled. If she wasn't real, then neither was the image of Dax, neither was the hotel around us. I surveyed the room, and what had looked authentic and immersive just moments before now looked jagged and fake. The moving image of the two bodies rocking and thrusting together now held no detail, it was just a blur of different coloured pixels, like some amorphous lump of throbbing goo.

I was in a chamber program, I knew it now. What's more, I had conquered it.

The hotel disappeared as suddenly as it had appeared, and I was back in chamber three surrounded by clapping, guffawing colleagues who patted me on the shoulder and – bizarrely, I thought – offered me congratulations. They couldn't know that I had seen through the program, that was certain. If they could tell what I had been able to do in there, then they would already have known about Harvey's 'talent', making all their efforts a waste of time. I knew now why no chamber program could break Harvey Stone.

My restraints were removed, and Dax took my hand, shaking it vigorously.

"Welcome to the brotherhood, Cal," he said. "Excuse the explicit content, eh? Just a bit of a laugh between lads, you know how it goes."

"He's done it to all of us," Stewie chimed in.

"Think yourself lucky you've got a girlfriend," Marv remarked. "I had to watch Dax doing me mum!"

They all laughed even harder, Carlos was almost bent double wiping tears from his eyes. "Oh, mate, that was a classic that was," he managed to say.

"So this is some kind of initiation?" I asked.

"Got it one, brother," Lez replied.

"Why tonight?" I asked. "I mean, I don't get it. Why, after what happened yesterday?"

"Titch told us what you said," Dax smiled. "He told us you're not going to squeal. That makes you a comrade, brother. But, you know what else it makes you?" I shook my head. "It makes you an accessory. It's like I was saying before – mutually assured destruction. You've got as much to lose as we have now, that's how we know we can trust you."

"Enough of the bloody mushy stuff." Marv rolled his eyes. "Someone wake up Titch and let's go celebrate."

"Jaspers?" Carlos offered.

"Damn tooting," Dax said, taking my hand and helping me out of the chair.

28

Jaspers was an upmarket strip club north of the river, the kind where they put free hors d'oeuvres out on the tables but the drinks cost triple and the girls' pants get stuffed with fifties. Dax dropped five hundred pounds for a private 'dance', and Marv bought champagne for everyone in a drunken fit of generosity. The atmosphere between us had shifted, I could tell by the way they all let their guard down in front of me now. I hadn't realised before, but there had always been a stiffness to their interactions with me, an air of mistrust. Now, by virtue of the strange initiation they had concocted, the barriers were broken. It was as though they believed some magic spell, some sacred unbreakable oath, had now bonded me to them. It seemed a little naïve on their part, I thought. I was no more trustworthy today than I had been yesterday, but I'll admit it felt heady to truly feel accepted into such an exclusive clique.

Over the next few weeks, I settled in to the feeling of belonging and began to enjoy the ease and security of being one of the boys. There were the odd nights when it was just Titch and me, of course, but we didn't speak of what we knew was going on across the courtyard and that seemed enough to keep our consciences at peace. Most evenings were filled with beer and banter, and when the alcohol ran dry, we were driven out of the compound by our thirst for more and often ended up in high-end nightclubs or river bars, drinking and causing an uproar until we eventually collapsed into our limo, trying not to vomit on its plush interior.

Things were better at work too. As the weeks passed, Vincent seemed to recover from the trauma of his chamber experience, and started to relax and even socialise a little with the other inmates. He seemed to strike up a rapport with Dil, the nefarious cult leader, and they often played cards together during free time. It helped that my prediction had proven correct, there were plenty of altercations and dramatic scenes going on with other cons, some real and some scripted, which meant Vincent was rarely on camera and therefore never came close to winning the weekly vote.

Most deals between personal officers and their inmates were done in the showers. Invariably, the screw would offer perks, or goods, to their nominated prisoner in exchange for an orchestrated drama that would lead to them to secure the vote. The inmates weren't stupid, of course. No amount of extra TV time or even extra phone calls home was worth being at the mercy of Reynolds and his itchy electrocuting finger. But there were ways around that. Lez had shown us all how to subtly disconnect the supply while attaching the pads and connectors. "It does rely on their ability to act, though," he cautioned. "They've got to scream like they're getting the volts, or the jig will be up for all of us."

He'd managed to get Eddie to bite him on camera in exchange for extra puddings and a small bottle of whisky, although the aging cannibal had had his misgivings.

"No fucking chance, mate," he'd said when Lez initially broached the subject. "They'll take me fucking dentures away!"

"Don't need dentures for whisky and extra trifle." Lez shrugged. "In fact, when was the last time you got served anything other than slop anyway?"

"Not the fucking point, sir. Not the fucking point," Eddie replied, shaking his head.

"Well," Lez said, pulling up his sleeve. "Put it this way."

He raised his arm to his mouth and bit his own arm so hard that blood dripped onto the shower room floor. "Either you bite me on camera, go the chamber with no juice and get your little goodies in return, or I'll waltz out there, show this wound to the cameras and tell 'em you just bit me in here and you'll go the chamber with full voltage and no little luxuries to show for it afterwards. Plus you'll lose your dentures either way. Your call."

"Fucking fine, you filthy bastard." Eddie knew when he was beaten, and proceeded to launch at Lez later that afternoon, in perfect position to be captured by camera six, and sank his teeth into the scheming guard's shoulder. Lez got three magazine features and a spot on breakfast television out of that little bargain, as well as the usual tabloids and *Behind the Bars* interviews. But he still wouldn't get a round in at Jaspers.

The only fly in the ointment that could potentially upset my current equilibrium was Harvey. I had so far managed to avoid seeing him ever since that night in the chamber rooms. It wasn't too hard, Dax dealt with him for the most part and I'd been careful to be otherwise busy whenever it was time to commandeer someone to accompany him for exercise. With his cell tucked out of the way of the main action, there was rarely any need to even be in his vicinity. I didn't want to be confronted by him, I knew he'd have a thought or two about my silence, and I had made peace with my inaction and didn't want him planting any of his seeds of doubt in my contented mind.

But I couldn't avoid him forever. About four weeks after my strange and disturbing 'initiation' in the so-called brotherhood of guards, I was milling about near Vincent's cell, chatting with him about the football scores, when the dinner trolley arrived. I hadn't realised Dax had left early for a cameo appearance in some unfunny sitcom. If I had, I'd have made sure I wasn't around. Titch nudged me, Harvey's tray in his hand, and my heart sank.

"Be my second?" he asked. How could I say no? I was clearly at a loose end. I followed him, hoping if I stayed a step or two behind, Stone might not notice me there.

Titch whistled, as if calling a dog, when we neared the cell. "Dinner," he stated abruptly as he shoved the tray into the hatch.

"How kind." Harvey's voice echoed in the corridor. I hoped that would be it, but before Titch could step away, the monster was at the bars. He knew, of course, that if Dax wasn't bringing his tray then there should be two of us, and craned his neck to see who Titch was being accompanied by.

"Ah, Mr Roberts." He smiled, his tone congenial and sinister all at the same time. "Forgive me for not being ready to receive you, I was rather engrossed in my reading."

I just grunted, and started to turn away.

"I'm rereading *Hamlet*," he called out. "One of Shakespeare's finest, wouldn't you agree?"

"Dunno." Titch shrugged. "We did *Macbeth* in my school."

"Another good choice." Harvey nodded. "But I just find there's something so compelling, so relatable about the tragedy of our dear indecisive prince. Don't you, Cal?"

My name from his lips made my spine prickle, and although I didn't intend to respond I found myself saying curtly, "Never read it."

"Something is rotten in the state of Denmark," Stone proclaimed dramatically. "But alas, our would-be hero prince is too caught up in his own existential crisis to do what he knows to be right."

I couldn't help but look back at him over my shoulder, catching his gaze as he shot me a pointed look, leaving me in no doubt of his double meaning. "Perhaps," I retorted, "he feels things are already exactly as they should be."

"I suppose he may convince himself of that, for a while at least." He smirked and turned the page. "But fate has a way of moving her pawns where she needs them to be. I guess we'll have to wait and see how it all pans out, won't we?"

I cursed myself for getting roped into taking his tray. As much as I tried to dismiss his words, they played over and over in my mind and I was condemned to trying to deconstruct them in the small hours of the night, when restful minds are at peace.

Harvey's words weren't the only thing I was trying to exorcise from my mind, of course. But I'd been doing a pretty good job of separating the Mel whose voice I heard on the phone each evening from the image of her CGI replica writhing and groaning with Dax. I couldn't get the sordid picture out of my head, but I had managed to compartmentalise it to an extent. Speaking to Mel didn't create an association between her disembodied voice and the unwanted pornographic memory. But I wasn't sure if my mental gymnastics would pass muster if I were to see her in the flesh.

It had to happen sometime, I knew the plan was being formed outside of these walls. Nevertheless, I was still taken aback when Mel called me excitedly one evening, just as I was about to hop in the shower and settle down for a drinking session with the others.

"Guess what, Cal?" She sounded fit to burst, and didn't bother to wait for me to guess. "It's happening, next weekend. The party!"

"Oh," I said, feeling excited and panicked all at once. "So soon?"

"You've been gone nearly two months, Cal!"

"Oh, yeah. I guess time flies when you're busy."

"So anyway, Daddy says *Justice Live* has won some entertainment award or something, so it's the perfect opportunity for him to throw a celebration where we can 'meet'. Fantastic, right?"

"Right," I replied quickly, not wanting to seem anything less than enthusiastic. My worries about seeing her were not her fault, not at all. I just had to try to get out of my own way and put the memory of Dax's cruel creation out of my mind.

"If all goes well with the press, Daddy reckons you can move back home in a couple of weeks!"

"A couple of weeks?" I asked. "Doesn't that seem a bit rushed, for a couple that have supposedly just met?"

"Whirlwind romance," she said matter-of-factly. "And to be fair, you practically moved in pretty much straight away when we actually met."

I couldn't argue with that. Who can argue with Doug Fanning at all? I'd been sending him my weekly emails, telling him everything was going great and his investment was in safe hands, and he was delighted. As far as he was concerned, I was on the up and up, and with the quite obscenely large cheques I'd received for my various interviews and appearances, I was definitely now a man of independent means. I was no longer struggling to win her daddy's approval, I had it in spades. There was no reason for Doug to create any obstacles, no reason at all for him not to help us on our way to happiness.

29

The limo pulled up outside the lavish country club, which Doug had commandeered for the evening. I surveyed the guys nervously as they fiddled with the stiff collars of their starched shirts and pulled on their suit jackets. I was concerned about the amount of champagne that had already been consumed on the journey, and the prospect of several more hours of their drinking. They had all sworn to keep my secret, assuring me they would play along and pretend I had never met Miss Melody Fanning until this very night. But alcohol loosens tongues, and I was anxious.

The paparazzi's cameras started flashing even before the car came to a stop. "Showtime, boys," Dax said with a wide grin as he opened his door, the first to exit the limo, as always. We gave it our best swagger, all remembering to smile at the cameras and pause periodically to allow them to get a clear shot, just as Aisling had instructed.

Once inside, Doug greeted each of us with a warm handshake and a hearty congratulation, deliberately leaving me until last.

"Cal Roberts!" he enthused as he took my hand. "Ms Swann has told me so much about you. It's a pleasure to have you here, young man."

"Thank you, sir," I replied, conscious of all the eyes on us and hoping I was acting well enough to fool them all.

"Am I right in thinking that you used to be a youth worker in Hallow?" he asked. I nodded, thinking it was best to keep my verbal responses to a minimum to avoid saying anything I shouldn't. "Excellent," Doug proclaimed loudly. "What noble work. I wonder, would you be willing to lend some of your expertise to my daughter? She's in fashion, you know, and she's particularly interested in the young demographic in Hallow. She's always looking for ideas that might appeal to them."

"Of course," I replied. "I'd be delighted."

It was a flimsy excuse; the type of outfits advertised in Mel's magazine would cost an average Hallow resident a year's wages. But it worked. Doug led me through the well-dressed partygoers, all busy sipping champagne and trying to impress new connections. We weaved through them all, Doug managing to avoid conversation with the many ambitious executives who tried to catch his attention as he passed, and eventually I spotted her. Standing at the back of the room, taking elegant sips from her half-full flute as she talked with her mother, she looked radiant and graceful. My heart sped up, as though I were really about to speak to this unattainable woman for the first time.

When she noticed me, she tried but failed to contain her special smile – the one that bloomed across her face involuntarily whenever she was just too happy or excited to remember to aspire to serenity. The smile I loved the most, because it wasn't one she allowed many people to see. We shook hands as Doug 'introduced' us, and she spoke to me as though I was a stranger, but her eyes sparkled and in them I could see familiarity; I could see my home. I was more than a little relieved that the sight of her made me long for her, with all that had happened since I last saw her I had worried about how I would react. Our conversation was superficial, there were too many UView people around for us to risk hinting at our real connection, but I delighted in it anyway. In many ways, it felt like a fresh start. A chance to forget all my previous mistakes, a chance to put my own prejudice aside and begin again, as equals now that I had more than enough money to support us without relying on Doug. For an exquisite, magical half-hour I was full of hope and anticipation, certain that my destiny was finally falling into place, and I had become a good enough man to deserve it.

But all too soon Dax Miller sauntered over to us and wrecked my peace of mind.

He approached with all the arrogant confidence of a man who is entirely comfortable in his own skin, and has become accustomed to being admired, and even lusted over, by others. Paying no care to the fact that Melody and I were mid-conversation, he sidled up to her and passed her one of the two flutes of champagne he was holding. "Melody Fanning, I presume?" he said, smiling.

I expected Mel to be polite but shoot me a look to indicate her annoyance at the rude interruption. That's what usually happened at these functions when we were approached by someone she didn't really want to converse with. But she smiled back, sincerely. Not her fake high-society polite smile, but a look of genuine pleasure. Then I noticed the slight pink bloom that appeared on her cheeks, and as she took the champagne he offered with one hand, her other involuntarily moved to her hair, smoothing down a stray lock.

She was attracted to him. If only she'd been more able to conceal herself, if only I'd been less familiar with all her subtle gestures, movements and expressions. If only I hadn't noticed the tiny, almost inconsequential spark that passed between them, maybe that wouldn't have been the end of my hopefulness. It wasn't that I didn't trust her, or that I thought she'd go with him given half the chance, she wouldn't. Mel just wasn't like that. She loved me, and she was faithful – I didn't doubt either of those facts. Rationally, a small glimmer of attraction for someone else is hardly unexpected. It's not as if I had never felt that way about another woman since I'd been with Mel. I would never act on it, and neither would she. Had it been anyone else she eyed with a lustful favour, it wouldn't have mattered. But seeing her swoon, even just slightly, when he spoke to her caused the walls I had built in my mind to explode, and I could no longer keep the image of the two of them together in its own compartment. Instead, it spilled out and covered all my thoughts and memories of Mel, like some creeping oil slick marring and corrupting everything it touched.

Another of Mel's acquaintances approached and engaged her in an unbearably sterile conversation about Fanning Corp's performance on the stock market and the impact of the Dow Jones on his own investments. Dax manoeuvred himself to stand behind her, a little too close, and raised his eyebrow at me. I felt sick. It was impossible in that moment to picture anything other than the two of them naked together, Dax eliciting groans of pleasure from Mel's lips. I watched as he smirked, knowing exactly what memories he was triggering for me. He winked at someone across the room and I followed his gaze to see the guys all bunched together, sniggering into their drinks. They were all picturing the same sordid image as I was, and Dax was revelling in it.

I think that might have been the first moment that I truly hated him. It's hard to be sure, there had certainly been many times when I had been appalled or disgusted by his behaviour, and there was the little matter of wanting to smash his skull in during the program he subjected me to. His treatment of Harvey had horrified me, at first. But those images of his victims that Dax had shown me had done precisely what he'd intended them to do: they'd shifted the focus of my outrage and disgust away from the guards' actions and on to Stone. In reality, one abuse of power does not justify another. Any court of law would tell you that. But he'd managed to confuse me, blurring the lines between right and wrong and convincing me of the karmic nature of his actions. It's easy to accept what you are told if believing it means you don't have to take action.

The 'initiation' had also been perfectly timed: the shock of my own ordeal replacing what I'd witnessed the night before at the forefront of my mind. Mistreatment, swiftly followed by the reward of friendship and acceptance, and topped off with the excesses and luxuries celebrity allowed. It was all so calculated, so manipulative. Yet somehow I hadn't seen the truly controlling and sadistic monster Dax really was.

But now I could see it, plain as day. The look of pleasure on his face knowing he was inflicting torment on me. And if he took this much satisfaction in tormenting a supposed 'brother', how much did he get from the torture of his lifelong enemy?

I conjured up the image of the two little boys, Dax and Harvey, in their grubby primary school uniforms and remembered the stories I'd been told of their childhood. I could see the playing field clearly in my mind, the small patch of trees in which one boy was crouched and shrouded in the undergrowth, doing unspeakable things to an innocent creature. Only this time, when I looked closer at the vision, it was Dax with hands around the hamster's neck.

30

Somehow I made it through the rest of the party, even managing to kiss Mel on the cheek for the cameras as Doug had instructed. In the limo back, I pretended to be far drunker than I was and feigned sleep so I wouldn't have to talk to anyone. Once back in my room, I formulated my plan.

I had a significant advantage, one that Dax didn't know about, in the form of Doug Fanning. I was grateful to my past self that I had kept our prior relationship to myself, even when confessing to the boys about my attachment to Melody. As far as they were concerned, I had met her father for the first time that night. Doug had wanted me on the inside to let him know what went on behind the scenes. Well, did I have a hell of a story to tell him.

I smiled to myself in the darkness, looking forward to the revenge tomorrow would bring. It all seemed too easy; Doug wouldn't want Fanning Corp associated with this kind of misconduct. He'd threaten to pull his funding, and Aisling would have no choice but to fire Dax, and perhaps the others too – though I was fairly sure they'd been swept along for the ride by Dax's hatred of Harvey. No matter, the purge would come swiftly. The power was mine, and it had been all along. Dax's biggest mistake was to cross me, and he'd pay for it dearly.

I slept later than I had intended. Fortunately, we'd all been given the day off following the party – presumably, Aisling was well aware of what free access to champagne would do to her 'stars', or perhaps she was hung-over herself. She'd certainly been putting it away all night. I'd avoided her as much as possible, but it was impossible not to hear her lamenting the current lack of truly evil killers in the news. "Oh, for a really good old-fashioned psychotic reign of terror," she'd enthused to a couple of execs over her champagne. "Where are all the modern-day Bundys, Shipmans or even Mansons? Don't get me wrong, darlings. I'm delighted with the show's success, but you know me, I'm always looking to the future. I want to mix it up, get some fresh blood in there before the ratings start to wane. But there just aren't enough truly grotesque murderers out there. It's terribly frustrating."

It was gone 10am when I woke up, but my resolve remained as strong as it had the night before, even now that the effects of the obscenely expensive alcohol had worn off. I picked up my phone and called my secret weapon.

"Cal!" Doug was in a good mood. "My boy! Have you seen the papers this morning?"

"No I…" I decided against letting on that I hadn't even got out of bed yet. "I haven't had a chance yet."

"They *love* you!" he enthused. "Both of you, as a couple! They've even got a nickname for you."

"A nickname?"

"Calody! Get it? Cal and Melody – Calody. I tell you, they are so excited about that chaste little kiss you let them photograph. This is going to be gold, Cal. Your romance is going to raise the profile of both *Justice Live* and Fanning Corp. I've already got the glossies calling me asking for exclusivity if there's a wedding."

"Jesus," I replied, shocked at how quickly my personal life had become public property.

"I know! Fantastic, isn't it?"

"Yeah," I said dubiously. "Really fantastic. But listen, that's actually not what I was calling about."

"Oh?" Doug sounded concerned.

"I have something important I need to speak to you about, something that's going on here that I don't think you'd be too pleased about. I need to see you, to make sure you're in the loop."

"Right." Doug huffed out a sigh, and I felt a little guilty at having burst his bubble of elation. "Well, I'm heading into the office to deal with a few things anyway, meet me there. We've 'met' officially now, so it won't look suspicious. People will just think you've come to ask me permission to take my daughter out or something."

"Yeah, okay," I said, wondering if Doug thought we'd suddenly gone back to the 1940s. "I'll be there in an hour."

He was sitting at his desk rifling through mounds of paperwork when I arrived. He eyed me with concern and stopped what he was doing to give me his full attention. "What's going on, Cal?"

"Okay." I took a deep breath, feeling suddenly nervous. Righteous fury had carried me this far, but it seemed to have deserted me at the door. "I'm sorry to be the bearer of bad news, Doug. But there are some very serious abuses of power going on at *Justice Live*, and I think as its major investor you ought to know exactly what's going on when the cameras aren't rolling."

I went on to explain it all. Dax's torture of Harvey, the misuse of the chamber equipment, the fact that Reynolds and the other guards were in on it, and that there must be some of the night-shift guards and camera operators who were complicit too.

"So you see," I said at last, "it's not even just a case of one bad apple – half the damn barrel is rotten."

"Oh." Doug exhaled long and loud and raised his hand to put his palm on his chest. "Thank Christ. Jesus, you had me really worried for a while there! I thought something terrible had happened."

"What?" I asked. Had he even *heard* me?

"Don't get me wrong, you're exactly right to tell me – it's what I pay you for, to be my spy on the inside. But you really got my nerves on edge with the way you did it. Save it for your weekly update next time, eh? You nearly gave an old man a heart attack. Do you know how much I would lose if I had to go into battle with UView over something? I thought you had news that would mean I'd have to pull out my investment or something like that, the legal minefield is unthinkable."

"Are you kidding me, Doug?" I ranted. "You do need to pull your investment, or at least threaten to. You need to shut this down, now!"

"Why?" Doug asked, as if it was the most reasonable question in the world.

"Because of everything I just told you! It's torture, it's abuse of power, it's evil and sadistic and the public would be outraged!"

"Really?" Doug asked, sitting back in his chair. "I mean, yes, it is torture. But, isn't that the whole point of the show? Isn't that why people tune in in their millions, why they pick up their phones and spend their money casting their vote, why the advertising slots are at an absolute premium? So, what makes it okay for Harvey to be tortured on Saturday evening, in front of millions, but not okay for it happen on Saturday night off camera? Why is one morally justifiable, and the other abhorrent?"

"They're both abhorrent, if you ask me," I said. "But at least the public vote is fair, this is just victimisation."

"Ah, well, I'm afraid you've lost any rights to claim moral superiority to the viewers. You voted with your feet when you chose to join the show. So, that's rather a moot point," Doug said. "Here's the real issue, Cal. Or rather, here's why it's not an issue. Who cares?"

"What do you mean?"

"Who actually cares, Cal? Aside from yourself, obviously, and perhaps a few bleeding hearts out there who never watch the show, and therefore never contribute to its profits anyway.

Do the parents of his victims care if he suffers? Do the viewers? No, they actively want him to. You know all the families of the little girls he killed were asked their feelings about Stone being on *Justice Live* before the line-up was decided?"

"No," I said quietly. "I didn't know that."

"A matter of courtesy," Doug continued. "Obviously, it was going to mean dredging things up, showing the victims' faces again and all that. Do you know what every one of them said, to a man?"

I shook my head, this was not going the way I had envisioned it at all.

"They said: good. Torture the bastard, make him suffer, make him pay for what he did to our precious little daughters. Make him pay in pain and fear, make him wish he'd never been born. I don't suppose they'd have any objection to a few unscheduled trips to the chamber, would they?"

I shook my head again.

"In all honesty, Cal, I wouldn't be surprised if Aisling gave it the green light anyway. You say they're testing out programs to try to find one that will actually scare the bastard? Even if she doesn't know what they're doing, she'd be the first to congratulate them if they succeeded. He's supposed to be her biggest draw, and she can't use him. So, that just leaves the misuse of equipment…" He shrugged. "All employees make a little extra use of company equipment when the boss isn't watching. Perks and all that. If I fired every guy who photocopied his arse for a laugh, I'd have no staff left."

"This isn't like using the office photocopier," I protested. "It's not even in the same league."

"No," Doug said, with a sharp edge to his tone. "It isn't in the same league. *Justice Live* is the big league, and it keeps getting bigger. Confidentially, Cal, I'm set to make more out of that show than half my businesses together. You know me, I do what needs to be done. If there was a real cause for concern, I'd get the hell out, whatever it cost me. But I can't justify the loss of billions, and that's what we're talking about, for the sake of a mass child murderer that everyone wants to see hung, drawn and quartered anyway. That's the bottom line, Cal. I'm sorry if you disagree, but that's where I stand."

So that was it. The bottom line – of course it was. It was always about the bottom fucking line, wasn't it? Always about the money. There's a saying in Hallow, 'A razzle always wants more', and it certainly held true here. Doug was making more money than he could ever spend, more money than his descendants could ever spend in a hundred years. Yet he could not countenance seeing even a drop in that vast ocean wasted on decency.

I left without saying another word, too afraid of what might come spilling out if I did. Why should I be surprised? Across the river from Doug's gilded office block there was poverty; abject poverty. There were people, *my* people, forced to choose between having a meal or having a wash. The Doug Fannings of this world could end that in a heartbeat if they so desired, if they chose humanity and compassion over their goddamn bottom line. But Doug was right: no one cared. No one cared about Hallow, no one cared about Harvey. Trying to find an ounce of fairness or morality in this fucked-up world was like trying to catch the wind in a jar.

Despondent, I walked the streets for hours not wanting to go back to *Justice Live*, but not having anywhere else to go. I ran through the whole thing in my mind, over and over. I thought about going to the press, but I had no proof and anyway, as Doug had pointed out, the public would probably just be pleased that the Playground Slasher was getting his just deserts.

As dusk fell and my rage burned out and turned to a dull, hollow ache in my stomach, I was forced into self-reflection. No one cared, so why did I? The answer was as selfish as Doug's reasons for not doing the right thing, when you looked at it objectively. I'd known about this for weeks, and managed to make peace with it. The reason it now filled me with anger and a drive for retribution was actually nothing to do with

Harvey. I didn't care that he had been tortured, I only cared that I had. Dax had played me for a fool, manipulated me into silence and then teased and taunted me with my own fears and nightmares. That was why I wanted to bring him down. I wasn't altruistic, or selfless, or a hero for the disadvantaged and downtrodden. I was none of the things I had spent my adult life trying to be, none of the things that I thought I ought to be in order to atone for the mistakes I made as a boy. Mistakes that cost Curly his life. Somehow I'd convinced myself that I was a force for good in the world now, someone who stood up for what was right. But looking back, I had always let the knife strike someone else rather than myself. Curly, Danny, Vincent, Harvey – there were things I could have done along the way, things that I knew were right even though they were hard. But I didn't, instead I always took the easy route, the one that gave me what I wanted and damn the consequences for anyone else. I stared at my rippling reflection in the dark, polluted waters of the Thames. 'I am not a good man,' I whispered to its fragmented form.

31

I had to go back eventually. Disheartened, disgusted as much by myself as everything else and exhausted from my regretful musings, I slunk back into the compound with my tail between my legs. There was nothing to be done now, nothing but to get out of this pit of vipers and frauds and back to Mel, hoping against hope that all would be well between us once we were back together. If it wasn't for the promise I'd made Vincent, I'd have quit altogether there and then. But I couldn't let him down, I couldn't abandon another Felton to whatever the gods had in store for them. For once, I had to keep my word, no matter how much I wanted to walk away and never look back, and that meant getting on with the job I was there to do.

Once I got into the mindset, it was surprisingly easy to present a fake version of myself to the others. I pretended to laugh at their jokes, pretended to want to 'hang' with them, pretended I was part of the pathetic 'brotherhood' they harped on about. But in my head I responded to their juvenile banter with sharp, devastatingly witty cut-downs and composed the list of insults I would hurl at them if only I could say what I truly felt, without any fear of the repercussions. The only one I had even a smidgen of respect for any more was Titch, and if I'm honest I'd have hated him for being complicit if only I hadn't done the same myself.

Fortunately, even though I was still living on the compound

I was able to escape it almost every evening thanks to Doug pushing the 'Calody' phenomenon for all it was worth. Mel and I met for swanky dinners or trips to the theatre nearly every night and were followed by paps everywhere we went. When it was just the two of us, a candlelit table between us and glasses of Merlot in our hands, it was easier to forget my rage. Although my regard for Doug had plummeted, Mel was only her father's daughter in public. In private, she was still the sweet, funny girl I had fallen for and the more time we spent together the more I was able to put aside my hatred for all her family stood for, and the images Dax had planted in my mind. I remembered instead the nights spent watching trashy TV in bed, a pizza box between us and sloppy, tomato-stained kisses. Her laughing so hard that she snorted, and then laughing even more at her own embarrassment. Those moments were Mel; those moments were who she was when she could be free of society's expectations and conventions. And those were the moments she only shared with me. If we could just get those back, it would all be alright. I could endure the days at *Justice Live* if only I could go home to that at the end of them. I could keep my promise to Vincent and still be happy. Fortunately, Doug had managed to persuade Aisling that allowing me to live off-site with Mel would boost ratings and publicity, given how obsessed the press currently were with our 'whirlwind romance'. There was no rule or convention our illustrious Ms Swann wouldn't break in pursuit of viewing figures.

On the day I was due to move back home to Mel, I woke up feeling more positive and content than I had in weeks. I got out of my bed for the last time, pulled the lever to reveal the hidden sink for the last time, and ate breakfast with Dax and his minions for the last time. I checked each thing off in my mind as I did it, happy to say goodbye to them all. From now on, I would arrive for my shift and leave as soon as it ended. I needn't encounter any of the other guards in private at all, every interaction I had to have with them would be on camera. They would be nothing more to me than co-stars on a film set, and I couldn't wait.

There was an air of frivolity on the cell block that morning. The UView producers had decided to add a ping-pong table to the communal area, in the hope of getting some decent footage. It had been hard to generate much in the way of 'compulsive viewing' of late, with the inmates doing very little other than watching TV or playing cards. There hadn't been so much as a spontaneous argument between them, and we were quickly running out of things to bribe them with in order to get something worth broadcasting.

Vincent was as close to ecstatic as I had ever seen him, and I soon learned why. It turned out that the former gang leader was something of a whizz with the ping-pong bat, which wasn't something I'd ever have predicted. It didn't take long for the others to realise that he was the one to beat, and they all lined up to take turns trying to best him. Each round was played for a tin of tuna – the most prized item in the canteen by virtue of its protein content, and by the time Eddie took up the bat to have his shot at dethroning the champion, Vincent already had ten cans to his name.

"Come on then, you toothless wannabe," Vincent bantered amiably, and I was pleased to see him finding some small joy in this detestable place.

"I was pinging pongs when you were still pissing your nappy," Eddie retorted.

"Hang on," Franco piped up. "That was only the other week wasn't it?"

Everyone laughed, and to my delight, Vincent joined in. This was good, this was very good. If he could laugh at the incident now, then he must have been able to distance himself from it and put it behind him. I was proud of him.

The pair began their match, and it became apparent that the aging cannibal was something of a ping-pong aficionado himself. He lacked Vincent's speed and stamina, but he made up for it with a precise aim and a wallop of a serve. The game went on much longer than any of the previous ones, and everyone watched the two avidly as the ball ricocheted back and forth between them at an ever-increasing pace. It was too close to call, there would be no winner until one of them made a mistake. They couldn't keep the furious speed up forever. The rally continued, the whole cell block silent apart from the rhythmic bonk-bonk of the little white missile hitting the table.

Vincent sent the ball shooting towards the right-hand side of the table, and Eddie expertly tapped it back across the net to the opposite corner. Vincent wasn't quite quick enough, he'd been expecting the ball to bounce to his left. He reached out in desperation, swinging his bat with all his might. The sound of the door to the corridor opening as Dax walked in broke his concentration for a split second, and he only managed to hit the ball with the tip of the bat, sending it speeding across the room instead of to the other side of the table.

Dax wasn't paying attention, he had a script in his hand for some guest appearance he was due to make and was mouthing his lines silently as he came through the door. The ball bounced past the cells, and came to a rest just under Dax's raised foot. He slipped, his feet sliding out from under him as his back hit the floor with an almighty thump. The paper went flying, Dax's legs were akimbo in the air, and he lay on the floor for a few moments, shocked and stunned.

The whole room, guards and inmates alike, erupted with uncontrollable laughter. It was impossible to keep a straight face, even for Vincent who clamped his hand over his mouth trying not to show his mirth as he waited to see how Dax would react. I held my breath, I expected him to go ballistic. As he got to his feet, I tensed, worried I might have to try to intercede to stop him attacking Vincent. His face was granite as he righted himself, but the pissed-off look disappeared quickly when he realised all his 'brothers' were chortling at his misfortune. He broke into a grin and joined in with the laughter, congratulating Vincent on a 'good shot'. *Very clever,*

I thought, *very restrained. Everyone loves a man who can laugh at himself.* Dax was playing to the audience, and knew which reaction would serve him best. Vincent looked relieved, and apologised despite Dax's friendly reaction. Dax saw a photo op, and shook his hand, reassuring him there were no hard feelings before challenging him to a game to show the world how easy-going and forgiving he could be.

I could see right through him, I knew he was already imagining the footage and the camera stills, and how his tough-guy-with-a-big-heart performance would win him even more adoration. But nevertheless I was relieved that he had chosen to go down that route; the prospect of leaving Vincent here with Dax angry at him would have made me too uneasy to enjoy my move back home. As it was, when I packed my bag and left the compound at the end of my shift that day, the mood amongst the inmates was perhaps the best I had ever known it.

32

It didn't take me long to adjust to being back home. Within a few days, it felt as though I had never left and Mel and I settled into our routines as before. There was only one real problem, and although I knew it was born of my own weakness I couldn't seem to rise above it. We weren't having sex, and I couldn't bring myself to admit why. Every time Mel tried to touch me intimately, the chamber program and all its twisted images of her and Dax consumed my thoughts, and my body refused to proceed. The first night, I told her I was exhausted. The second, I said I'd had too much wine. The third, I blamed a stressful day at work, and so on and so forth. Eventually, she stopped even trying, the constant rejection making her too hurt and humiliated to continue.

Perhaps I should have told her what Dax had done, perhaps the truth would have hurt less. But I was trying to protect her, in my own twisted and illogical way. She would have been devastated to know that those brutish, drunken guards had been picturing her that way, distorting her image into something seedy and dirty. I reasoned that keeping quiet was the lesser of two evils, and apart from the lack of action in the bedroom, we functioned pretty much as we had before. But as the weeks passed, the crack between us widened. It happened slowly, so slowly that it became a chasm before I realised exactly how far apart we'd drifted.

At the same time, I noticed Vincent begin to withdraw again. The happy, confident man who had whipped almost everyone's arse in the ping-pong tournament couldn't even be persuaded to pick up a bat. He stopped coming out of his cell for meals, stopped playing cards with Dil, even stopped spending his canteen money. I wondered what could be wrong, he'd been nowhere close to winning the vote since his first live show so there was no reason for him to be worried about that. Was it that I wasn't around as much? I tried asking Dil, figuring that if any of the inmates had any insight it would be him.

"It's just a funk, man," he said, brushing his long, unruly hair. "Happens to all of us sometimes, stuck in here. Just gets to you, from time to time. He'll be alright, he's got a strong energy. He just needs to learn to harness his inner joy and manifest it, and then he'll be right as rain again."

I didn't hold much stock in Dil's pseudo-hippy nonsense, but perhaps he did have a point in there somewhere. It was natural to have peaks and troughs, prisoners often went through periods of depression, especially the lifers once the initial few weeks of their sentence had passed and the reality that this was going to be the rest of their lives sunk in. Mostly, they came through it with time, found their place in the pack and carved out a purpose for themselves within the prison walls. I tried to talk to Vincent when we were alone in the shower block, but he wouldn't even meet my eye. He mumbled he was fine, just tired. I wasn't sure I believed him, but what could I do? I asked him if he wanted to see a psych, but he was vehement in his refusal, so I had no choice but to hope Dil was right and he'd snap himself out of this cloud once he'd worked through whatever it was that was getting him down. Truth be told, I had my own problems to worry about anyway. I needed to put my energy into my home life, try to bridge the gap between Mel and me that my inability to be truthful had created.

That Sunday morning I lay awake as the dawn broke outside, contemplating ways I could make the day special for

Mel, and hopefully get across in actions what I was unable to express in words: I love you; I still want you; it's not you that's the problem, it's me. And, most desperately: please, please don't give up on us yet.

I was just calculating the logistics of taking a picnic somewhere scenic enough to be romantic, but populated enough to be able to get a decent coffee, when my phone rang.

"Cal." It was Matt, and his voice sounded urgent. "I know it's your day off, but this is important. Can you come in, right now? We need you for a reaction shot."

"Reaction to what?" I asked, sitting bolt upright in bed. Mel picked up on my tone and touched me lightly on the arm, her face full of concern and questions.

"Felton slit his wrists."

33

I dashed out of the limo and ran past the security guards who opened the gates when they saw me coming. Aisling was screaming at her latest assistant in the car park, waving a lit cigarette dangerously close to the poor girl's long brown curls.

"Aisling," I panted as I ran up to her, not bothering with politeness. "What the fuck happened?"

"Cal, darling!" She turned to me, beaming. "Thank you so much for getting here so fast, sweetie. Y'know I had my doubts when Doug wanted you to live off-site, but you've proven yourself alright."

"Cut the shit," I snapped. She initially looked shocked, but her gasp of surprise soon turned into a slow smile of satisfaction. I got the impression she was sick of sycophants and appreciated someone with the guts to say things straight. "What the fuck happened to Vincent, is he alright? Who was on duty? Have they been fired? Prosecuted for negligence?"

"Oh, I love the passion, Cal. Keep that going. He's fine, darling. The care bears have got him over in the medical wing." She pointed towards the wall that separated *Justice Live* from Whitefield. "It looks worse than it is, but we need to film you finding him before the blood dries too much to look authentic."

"How can you film me finding him, if he's over in medical?"

"We'll edit the footage so it looks like it was you. The

night-shift guard who actually found him was about your height. Well, only a few inches different anyway, won't be able to tell from the back. We'll splice you in, no issue at all."

"How did he do it? What did he use? Why didn't someone stop him?"

"So many questions," Aisling grumbled. "He stole a plastic spoon from his dinner tray, snapped it so it was sharp and then just sawed away." She gave a small shrug, as if she was discussing nothing more serious than a rain shower on a sunny day. "It was hardly a major incident really, barely a sharp implement at all. He must have gone at it for quite a while and eventually hit an artery or something I suppose because it's one hell of a mess in there. So you need to get in there and shoot that bloody scene so we can get the cleaners in."

I scowled at her, but she pretended not to notice and waved me along with a friendly smile. Inside the cell block, the inmates had been left locked up in their individual cells to allow the camera and sound crews to set up their equipment at the best angles – for important scenes like this, the static cameras were considered insufficient.

My shock and horror when I saw the state of Vincent's cell wasn't feigned. I'd seen cells covered with blood before, I'd even held an inmate's arm together as his arteries pumped and gushed covering me in the sticky, metallic-smelling liquid. These scenes weren't uncommon in prison, sadly. It always made me feel like a failure, to have missed the signs that something was so dreadfully wrong that the troubled con could see no way out of his situation. I always looked back and wished I had been more vigilant, even when I knew that the ratio of guards to prisoners made it impossible to pay special attention to everyone who might need it. But here I was responsible for just one prisoner, a prisoner who had cameras on him twenty-four hours a day, and I had still failed to realise just how serious his plight had become.

"Can you call out?" one of the camera guys asked me.

"What?" I said, still trying to process the scene in front of me.

"So, we need you to jog towards Harvey's cell from the sofas, as you reach it call out: 'We need medical, stat.' Okay?"

"This is sick," I snapped. "A man is lying in a hospital bed because no one on duty noticed that he had made himself a blade, or what he was doing with it, and you're here trying to recreate it for entertainment!"

"Aisling's orders." He shrugged. "It's all we need from you, Cal. We've got the live footage, just need a shot of you running in to splice into it. It won't take a minute."

"You're going to show the actual footage of him doing…" – I waved my arm towards the blood-stained cell – "doing *this*? On prime-time television? And you don't think this is sick beyond belief?"

"We're going to put a viewer discretion warning on-screen first," he said defensively, as if that made it alright.

"Fuck me." I could feel myself losing my temper. "It's like trying to reason with a bunch of automatons. Don't any of you give the tiniest shit?"

"Cal." Titch appeared by my side and touched my arm gently. "Calm down, mate. It's alright. He's going to be alright, you know? They got to him as quick as they could when they realised, saved his life. It's fucking awful, I know. But he is going to be alright. Let's not piss off Aisling, eh? Her coming in here giving everyone hell isn't going to help anything."

I took a deep breath and nodded. "Alright, just get it over with," I said, realising that Titch was right. Causing a problem wasn't going to help Vincent. I shot the scene as requested, storming off to the staffroom as soon as it was done. The truth was, I was angrier at myself than I was at the guards who had been on shift, or the guys in the control rooms who could see every cell on camera simultaneously and yet hadn't spotted what Vincent was doing quick enough. I had known something wasn't right with him, I'd known it for weeks. One day he'd been fine, relaxed and joking about – seeming as though he'd really settled in and was making the best of being stuck here. Then all of a sudden he'd withdrawn, retreating into himself again like he had on his first week here, when he was anticipating the chamber.

The chamber. A warm shiver crept up my arms and slalomed down my back, a dreadful possibility hitting me all at once. The last time I had seen Vincent happy was the afternoon he tripped Dax over. Dax had laughed, at the time. But I hadn't seen Vincent smile, or play cards with Dil, or even eat with the others at the table, ever since that day. I'd been ignoring it, hoping it was nothing. Hoping that if I buried my head in the sand yet again, the situation would somehow disappear.

Had something been going on in my absence? What had Dax been up to on all the nights I lay beside Mel, unable to touch her without his image burning my mind? While I was across the river in my luxury penthouse, wrestling with my own ridiculous and superficial worries, had Dax been doing the unthinkable? I hadn't wanted to accept it was a possibility, although every ounce of logic screamed at me that it was the most likely scenario. Even at that moment, confronted with the bloody evidence of Vincent's collapsing mental health, I couldn't make myself believe it, not without confirmation. But I couldn't lie to myself any more either, I had to know for sure no matter what the consequences might be. There was one man I knew would know, and what's more, he'd be all too pleased to tell me.

I left the staffroom and headed across the cell block. Luckily, there was still so much bustle and chatter as the camera crew packed up their stuff that nobody noticed me slip quietly through the door and into the corridor. I rushed to Harvey's cell, not bothering to greet him.

"What happened to Vincent?" I demanded. "Have they been doing something to him?"

"Well, good morning, Cal." He stood up from his bunk

where he had been reading and stepped slowly towards me. "Are you worried that your own choices have come back to haunt you? Perhaps," he said with a glint of mirth in his eyes. "Is this the part of the story where the flawed protagonist realises that inaction can have as many consequences as action?"

"What do you mean?" I asked, grabbing the bars and shaking them fruitlessly. "Tell me what you mean, you motherfucking psycho!"

"'First they came for the Communists...'" He began to recite the old poem with dramatic aplomb. "'And I did not *speak out*.' Oh, you kept your silence, didn't you? Because I am a monster. It never occurred to you that the man you and I know to be innocent is, in the accepted canon, also a monster."

"The chamber." My worst suspicions were confirmed, and I felt a deep, lurching nausea in every cell of my body. "They've been doing it to him, what I saw them do to you?"

"Alas, poor Yorick." Harvey tutted. "Dax is not one to take a public slight lightly, or let disrespect go unchecked. Are you really surprised? When have you ever known a tyrant to be restrained in his tyranny? Yes, Cal. They've been doing it to him. While you've been schmoozing with the ski set and dining on caviar, that innocent boy has been tortured to madness."

"Fuck!" I kicked the walls, gripped at my hair. "I'll kill them! I'll fucking kill them!"

"There, Cal," Harvey enthused. "That's it. There's that hero's spirit, that righteous anger. But don't waste it here, don't burn it out on inanimate tiles and your receding hairline. Sit with it, Cal. Keep it in, let it fester and grow in your belly. Revenge is a dish best served cold. Take it from someone who knows. Take a breath, take a seat. Consider your next move carefully."

PART 4

JUSTICE LIVE

1

I take one last look at Mel sleeping soundly in the armchair before I close the door and head out into the night. I wrench my hood up, pulling the drawstrings to hide my face as much as possible and keep my gaze focused on the pavement to avoid making eye contact with anyone. I'm too well known to go unnoticed if I don't take precautions. There are no press hanging around outside our apartment tonight, they're all at the compound vying for the best pictures. I head to the taxi rank and take the first cab in line, mumbling the destination to the driver and keeping my head down. As we speed across the river I check my pockets again, even though I've done it at least five times already, and pray Aisling is as good as her word.

There had been no point going to Doug after Vincent's suicide attempt. He'd already made it abundantly clear that he didn't care about the suffering Dax was inflicting on Harvey, there was no reason why he should feel any differently about Vincent. They were both child killers as far as he knew, and not worth the cost of kicking up a fuss for. I'd thought about going to the press by myself, blowing the whistle to one of the tabloids, but I dismissed the idea quickly. Would I even be able to find a journalist who saw my side of things? I suspected not, they cared about their readership's engagement just as much as UView cared about its ratings, and public opinion would undoubtedly be that the two murderers deserved everything they got.

That had left me with only one option – Aisling Swann herself. While I still wasn't sure she'd actually care about either of the inmates' suffering, I knew she wouldn't want a scandal. I was the media's golden boy at the moment, thanks to my relationship with Mel. If there was ever a time to cash in on my fifteen minutes of fame, it had to be now. She knew I had the reporters' ears, she knew I could get an interview on breakfast television at the drop of a hat, I had plenty of ways to get my story out there if I chose. She didn't need to know that I had already considered the implications carefully, and decided against it.

She listened, her face expressionless as if she wasn't sure how to respond. "I see," she said quietly when I had finished telling her of the abuse I had witnessed, and of the certainty I had that the same thing was happening to Vincent and had been the cause of his attempted suicide.

"You have to stop this, Aisling," I said, as forcefully as I could. "I've come to you first out of courtesy and respect, and to give you the chance to do the right thing here. But believe me, I will go the press with this and damn the consequences if you turn a blind eye."

"Of course I'm not going to turn a blind eye," she snapped. "What do you take me for? But situations such as this are delicate. There are a lot of people's – innocent people's – careers at stake here, not to mention the future of the rehabilitation programmes that are doing so much good for the community of Hallow. We both know they only exist because of *Justice Live*; we need to take decisive action, of course. But we need to do it in a way that protects the show, promotes it even."

Only Aisling Swann could be thinking of gaining exposure and promotion at a time like this. Most producers would have been focusing on damage limitation, but not our Ms Swann, oh no. To her, everything was an opportunity if only you could find a way to exploit and film it.

"What you need to do is sack Dax, and his cronies," I replied, firmly.

"Indubitably." She nodded her agreement. "That is without doubt the course of action I will be taking. But I can't help but feel that simply calling them in here right now and giving them the boot wouldn't be the most productive idea. Certainly, doing it behind closed doors like that would make the whole thing seem clandestine and seedy."

"It *is* clandestine and seedy."

"In reality, yes. But it doesn't have to look that way on television. What if we could bring them down publicly? If I just go sacking the nation's favourite guards without providing evidence of their wrongdoing, people will stop watching in protest. But if they saw the proof themselves, perhaps a televised confession, they'd be right behind my decision. And of course, it would improve the ratings and get everyone talking – which is always a happy by-product."

We both knew it was less a by-product and more the main aim, but I let it slide.

"In fact," she got up from her desk, lit a cigarette and started pacing around the room, "we could use it as an opportunity to do a big glitzy relaunch! All new guards, except for you and the short one, of course – and it goes without saying you'll be the new number one, Cal darling. The public will love you even more for your integrity and bravery, I'd be a fool not to promote you. Perhaps even swap out a few of the duller prisoners for some spicier ones. There's a pyromaniac in Lincolnshire who is an absolute scream, always pulling pranks on the guards. I couldn't get him for the original line-up because he was in intensive care after that little cell fire he started, but he must be mostly recovered by now. Yes, we'll turn this terrible incident into something wonderful!"

I didn't really care how Aisling went about doing what needed to be done, just so long as she did it. Why should it matter if she got something out of it? Sure, it was a little distasteful, but the whole show revolved around exploiting the inmates' misery so it was a bit late to go moralising now. Let Aisling have her 'prime footage' if it made her happy, all I cared about was bringing Dax down and that was going to be a hell of a lot easier with her on side. So I listened as she ran through every idea that popped into her head, dismissing most of them before she'd even finished her sentence. It was like watching a mad professor at work, she paced and smoked at three times her normal speed, verbalising everything and yet somehow saying nothing that made any sense. It seemed that this was her way of brainstorming, speaking and retracting her thoughts in a way that appeared chaotic, but which ultimately allowed her to pull together a plan that she convinced me was watertight.

"I suggest you go home now," she said at last, after we had ironed out all the details and she was satisfied I knew exactly what I had to do. "And give me your pass while you're at it."

"What?"

"No offence, Cal darling, but you really aren't the most natural of actors. If you go waltzing back in there and try to pretend everything's normal, those boys are going to see straight through you. It's best if you take some leave, it's easily explainable with Vincent in hospital. I can just say I advised you to take a break while your inmate wasn't here. Plus it means you won't be here in the days leading up to Saturday's show – no chance of you being accused of setting anything up if you weren't even on the premises, hmm?"

It made sense, I could see that. The prospect of having to act natural around the others wasn't a pleasant one either; she was right, I wasn't good at pretending. So I handed her my security pass and she shook my hand. "I'll be in touch as we discussed," she said with a wink.

2

I fiddle with the burner phone in my hand, anxiously checking the screen, willing it to beep with the message I'm relying on. It's 8.55pm, the cab pulls up outside the pub down the road from Whitefield. I need that code. I need it now. "C'mon, Aisling," I hiss at the phone. "What are you playing at?"

I chuck some banknotes at the cabbie, barking at him to keep the change, and stride purposefully into The Parrot, making sure he sees me enter. As soon as he pulls away, I walk straight back out and dash down the urine-scented alleyway that runs beside it. The noise of the crowd gets louder and louder as I approach the prison, but I don't head for the main gates where security jostle with the disgruntled would-be spectators. Instead, I take a sharp left through another alleyway, this one running between a row of residential gardens and the west-side wall of Whitefield. It's overgrown, and brambles whip at my hoodie as I pull my sleeve up over my hand and try to bat them away, barbs getting stuck in the fabric.

I reach the almost completely obscured back gate, the one I hadn't known was here until Aisling had shown me on the map. "It's not in use," she said. "It was supposed to be for tradesmen, deliveries and such, but they couldn't get the planning permission to install a driveway up to it. The neighbourhood homeowners kicked up a stink about pollution and noise or something. They had to abandon the idea and expand the main car park to accommodate deliveries instead. It's not guarded, because it's never unlocked and hardly anyone is even aware that it's there."

"How do you know about it then?" I asked.

Aisling smirked a little. "I'm planning a special. A 'great escape' to mark the one-year anniversary, when we get there. Can you imagine? One of our inmates at large in the community? A nationwide manhunt, with a premium number to call if you spot him? Cash prizes for information, on the news tickers twenty-four-seven, then the glorious recapture and chamber extravaganza! All completely safe and controlled, of course. We'll have a tracker on him, and he'll follow our predetermined escape route. So, I've been scoping out the wider grounds, looking for the best way to get him out secretly, while still catching it on camera. That gate is perfect."

I rolled my eyes. How bloody typical of her. "Where does it lead?" I asked. "If you're using it to enter the prison, I mean."

"Ah," she said. "Well, that's the best bit."

3

9pm. I can hear the roar of cheers and applause as Mo announces Finn's return to the chamber, thanks to a little bit of entrapment Aisling orchestrated earlier in the week. She used some footage of Finn looking at a newspaper report that Dax had thrust in his face – a report with a picture of his victim wearing a little white dress – and cut it together with footage of him masturbating in his cell. The two sequences occurred weeks apart, but with editing and the addition of fake timestamps, it looked as though, upon seeing the picture, he had immediately retreated to his cell and begun to jack off. That's the beauty of prison uniforms, they are all dressed the same way every single day, which allows UView the freedom to effectively change time without the usual continuity issues.

At last, the phone buzzes and a six-digit code appears on its screen. I swallow hard and take a deep breath before pushing aside the ivy that has begun to strangle the walls and entering the code into the semi-rusted keypad. There is a small click, and the gate pops open ever so slightly. I push it, just an inch or two, and peer through, my eyes flicking up to the CCTV camera I know to be positioned halfway up the wall, and trained on this very gate. There is no blinking light. Aisling has disabled it, just as she promised. I exhale, feeling for the first time that I can trust her to uphold her part.

It had all sounded so easy and simple when she outlined

it in her office that day. But once I was home, and on leave with little to do except stew over every minute detail of our plan, I realised how much depended on her being able to carry out the subterfuge she had promised, and I wasn't sure how far she could be relied upon. One working camera, one missing code or one unexpected security guard and it would all go wrong.

I squeeze through the gate, pushing it open only as far as is absolutely necessary, and survey my surroundings. I can tell straight away that I'm in the very arse-end of Whitefield's grounds. Beside me is the unused back door to the storage rooms where the maintenance staff keep the spare tools and chemicals. No one goes in there except to grab the odd industrial-sized bottle of bleach, or a new set of mop heads to restock the main maintenance cupboards with.

There is only a narrow space, less than two feet wide, between the walls of the prison and the barbed-wire-topped concrete wall to my left, and it clearly hasn't been traversed in years. The weeds are even thicker here than in the alleyway, and I try not to picture the rodents I feel certain must frequent the overgrown path ahead.

I stay half-bent, in a sort of running crouch, as I push on through the weeds and webs, keeping below the barred windows just in case by some twist of fate a random guard chooses this exact moment to venture into the dusty storage rooms. When I reach the end of the path, I take a left and squat down behind the large luminous-yellow clinical waste bins that sit tucked away close to the medical wing. I risk a peek around them, looking down the length of the prison. I can see the car park full of staff vehicles, and I know there will be security on patrol there, thanks to the large number of people currently jostling for a view next door. Luckily, I don't need to get any closer to the prison entrance. I can stay here in the shadows until Aisling plays her next card.

"I'll create a distraction," Aisling said with a wave of her hand when I'd pointed out that while the semi-obscured delivery entrance to Whitefield might not be guarded, the side gate between the prison and the compound most certainly was.

"I don't think you yelling at cameramen is going to quite cut it, Aisling," I retorted.

"No," she said with a wink. "But a bomb threat might."

4

After a quick glance towards the car park to check the coast is clear, I lunge forward from behind the bins and flatten myself against the opposite wall, sidestepping slowly until I reach the gate that acts as a quick cut-through between Whitefield and *Justice Live*. I can hear the guards on the other side, chattering inanely about home brew and football games. Their radios crackle with a steady stream of routine commands and information as various ambient patrols confirm their locations, or receive orders to deviate from their prescribed route.

9.05pm. The crowd are reaching fever pitch now as Finn takes his walk through the tunnel. A cacophony of jeers and screamed obscenities, punctuated by the occasional sharp thud as various homemade missiles hit the Perspex. The burner phone in my pocket vibrates with the next code, the one for the gate beside me. But it's useless while those guards remain in place.

I listen intently to the muffled, static-filled noises coming from their radios, trying to block out every other sound. I squint involuntarily, as if narrowing my eyes makes any difference to my ability to focus on just one sound in an onslaught of noise. *Come on, come on.* What is she playing at?

Just as I'm starting to think she's failed, the guard's radios crackle urgently, and the voice that booms through is clearer, and far more urgent than before.

"All guards, we have code red at entrance one. Suspect potentially carrying explosive device. All guards to position zero. Repeat, all guards to position zero. Suspect is a white male aged thirty to forty wearing brown duffel coat and sunglasses."

"Fuck," one of the guards on the other side of the gate swears loudly, and I hear their hasty footsteps as they leave their positions and head towards the crowd. I struggle to breathe, an unexpected rush of panic taking me over. I am both relieved that Aisling came through with her plan, and terrified at the same time. Until this point, I could have turned back. At any moment I could have changed my mind, backtracked to the outer gate and simply sneaked back through and gone home. I may even have got back before Mel so much as stirred. But once I go through this gate, there's no way back without being seen. In a few moments, the bomb scare will be revealed to be a hoax, and those guards will be back. There is currently nowhere in the country with more eyes on it than the compound behind this wall. This is the point of no return.

I think of Vincent lying in the medical unit somewhere nearby, driven to the brink of insanity by Dax's cruel power-trip games. I think of Harvey, and the years-long grudge Miller keeps indulging. Sure, Stone is a monster, there's no denying that. But what of the man who delights in tormenting the monster? How is he any less abhorrent? Worse, what if Harvey is telling the truth about their school days? What if Dax has always been a sadistic bastard? What if he killed small animals and tormented his classmates as a child, and never outgrew that lust to make others suffer? What if he is, even if only in part, responsible for creating the monster?

Someone like Dax should not work in corrections. Regardless of the truth of Harvey's claims, or whether or not their childhood encounters had helped shaped him into a killer, I have seen enough with my own eyes to know that irrefutable truth. And now that I know it, I have two choices: proceed through this gate and make damn sure everyone else knows it too; or turn a blind eye yet again and watch

Dax's toxic, deranged egomania destroy others over and over again. If I'd have acted sooner, if I'd refused to turn a blind eye to his torture of Harvey, Vincent would never have had to suffer it. That is a guilt I will never be able to assuage. Just like Curly's death when I was still a child, it will haunt me always.

"No more," I whisper as I punch in the code and slowly open the gate. "No more regrets I can't live with any more."

5

Once inside the compound, I move swiftly. There's no point now in doing anything else, if the distraction Aisling created isn't enough to keep eyes away from the dark recesses between the side gate and the guard's quarters, then nothing will save me from being caught. Speed is what matters now, getting what I need and reaching the back of the shower block before the hoax is discovered.

To the side of the block where the guards live, there is a large waste bin. I lift up the black bin liner inside it and see the square plastic key card and package containing the walkie-talkie, just where she promised they would be. I retrieve them, getting my arm covered in slimy bin juice in the process, and deposit the burner phone in its place before replacing the bag. Almost there, and I can just make out the crackle of radio as the security guards begin to return to their former positions having received the all-clear from command.

I'm going to make it, just. I shove the unnamed key card into the slot next to the fire door and mentally shush it as it beeps and the LED turns from red to green. I slip through into the shower block, taking care to close the outer door securely, but quietly, behind me. Away from all danger of cameras or patrols, at least for the moment, I stare at the walkie-talkie in my hand. It should be set to broadcast to one of the guard's radios, and only one. If Aisling got it right, any message relayed on this device will be heard only by Dax Miller.

I reach beneath my shirt, finding the button on the concealed microphone hidden there and pressing it. I tap it a couple of times to make sure I can hear the slight echo it creates. From now on everything I say, or hear, will be recorded by Aisling and played back to the nation. All that is left now is to hope that the least predictable pawn in our game plays by the rules.

Harvey hears me coming as I tiptoe down the corridor towards his cell. I know because his shadow grows larger on the floor as he approaches the bars.

He doesn't speak, and that gives me some small reassurance that he has understood Aisling's instructions and plans to adhere to them. *Why wouldn't he?* I reason. He wants what we want, after all, to bring down Dax Miller. This little scheme will benefit him most of all, and he is, if nothing else, a smart man. He may have no love for me, or for Aisling, but he has the brains to know when co-operating is in his own best interests. The enemy of my enemy is my friend, so they say. Sometimes you have to side with the snake to take down the wolf.

He smiles and nods his head slowly at me, communicating his compliance without words. I point to my chest, indicating the microphone. He rolls his eyes and nods again, indicating that he knows full well what the plan is. He holds out his hands in anticipation, and I gently open the hatch and place the walkie-talkie inside. He picks it up and holds it to his face, then stares first at me and then the locking mechanism on the door. I swallow hard, insert the key card into the slot and watch the light turn green as Harvey's cell door unlocks. I step back against the wall, hoping I haven't just made a big mistake.

Harvey presses the button on the walkie-talkie. "Good evening, Mr Miller," he says into it. "This is your friendly neighbourhood psychopath. I appear to be in possession of a communication device, and I can't help but feel that from your point of view, that is a very bad thing indeed. Over."

His grin broadens as Dax's voice comes over the airwaves, sounding harassed and confused. "What the fuck are you playing at, Stone? How did you get a goddamn radio? You piece of shit."

"Oh dear," Harvey smirks, "am I going to be in trouble?"

I hold my breath, hoping our guesses at what Dax's reaction will be were correct. We're relying on the fact that he is too much of an egomaniac to bother calling for backup, so sure and confident is he in his own dominance. So sure and confident is he that Harvey is safely trapped behind bars.

I hear footsteps thundering towards us, and quickly step into the store cupboard next to Harvey's cell, pulling the door almost closed so that I can just see the corridor through a small crack. Sure enough, Dax storms towards us, face red as beetroot and eyes ablaze with fury.

"Give me that fucking thing now, you spineless little cunt," he yells as he approaches the cell. "And you better tell me who gave it to you so I can kick their arse in sideways too."

He's so wound up, so consumed with anger at Harvey having upset the equilibrium of his evening, that he fails to glance down and notice that the little LED on the keypad is blinking green, not red. Harvey kicks at his unlocked door, just as Dax reaches it. It hits him in the face, and he stumbles back with the shock of the blow.

Now, I say to myself. Now I am supposed to leap out, push Dax into the open cell and lock him in, then confront him and force him to admit to what he's done. There is no reason why he won't confess it all to me, Aisling reasoned. Harvey and I both already know about his little late-night 'entertainment', and with no audio recording in Harvey's cell he should see no danger in talking about it.

But before I am even out of the door, I can see that something is going very, very wrong. Harvey should be out of his cell, standing to one side to allow me to bundle the dazed and stumbling Dax in there, even helping me if necessary. But he isn't. Instead of dashing from his cell, he quickly reaches under his mattress and pulls out something golden and shiny. I recognise it in a fraction of a second, it's Dax's 'antique' hunting knife.

Harvey lunges forward with a loud roar that sounds like some ancient battle cry. Before I can even begin to process what he's doing, or how and why he came to be in possession of the blade, he swoops forward and buries it up to the hilt in Dax's stomach.

Dax bends double, spluttering and wheezing, and Harvey maintains his grip on the hilt, twisting it with a maniacal glee before pulling it out with gusto and smiling at the unstoppable flow of blood that pours from his victim's abdomen. I try to move, knowing I should tackle the knife from Harvey's hand and call for help, but I am paralysed by the spectacle.

"I believe we can call that checkmate?" Harvey says as Dax collapses to the ground, coughing blood and gulping for air. "It has been a pleasure playing against you all these years, but I think we can both agree the better man won."

Dax looks up at him, his face contorted with agony as he writhes on the ground.

"Here, I'll prove I'm the better man, Dax. Remember little Bubbles? Remember how you tortured him? Well, that's where you and I differ. You see, I don't torture animals. I put them out of their misery." He raises the blade above his head and brings it down decisively on Dax's temple, piercing the side of his skull and immediately silencing his coughs and splutters.

I am still frozen, watching with horror and unable to make my body listen to pleas to run, or fight, or do something, anything, other than gawp like a rubbernecker at a car crash. It's less than a second later when we hear the door to the shower room open, and Bodie bursts in, pausing with shock when he sees the bloody tableau before him. I panic, Bodie isn't supposed to be here. He must have been called upon for security duty again. Of all the guards in all the world, why did it have to be Bodie who stumbled upon this scene?

Harvey acts quickest. While Bodie tries to process what is happening, he reaches down and pulls at the knife still embedded in Dax's skull. I realise in an instant what he's going to do, and try to shout to warn Bodie but I can't find the air in my lungs to make a noise. Harvey's on his feet now, blade in hand. A surge of adrenaline courses through me combined with a wave of memory and regret.

Here we are again. A good man with a good heart, a bad man with a sharp blade, and me – the one who brought the whole situation into being. All I know is that this time, the outcome can't be the same. I cannot let Bodie die because of my naïveté, I cannot see the light fade from his eyes the way it did from Curly's. I cannot be the one to survive my own mistakes while others bear the consequences.

Harvey's running towards Bodie. I sprint after him. He's ahead of me but I'm younger and faster. In the corner of my eye, I see Bodie reach for something in his pocket, but Harvey has already drawn back the knife. I scream. Channelling every ounce of strength and regret I hold into my legs and arms, I fling myself forward at Bodie with my hands outstretched and knock him off his feet and onto the floor just as Harvey thrusts the blade forward. Bodie falls in a crumpled heap, and a sharp pain tears through me as Harvey's knife pierces my back.

I fall, face forward, onto the ground beside Bodie. But Bodie is already scrambling to his feet and pulling his gun from his pocket. I turn my head to see Stone lunging forward again, but Bodie doesn't hesitate this time. He pulls the trigger, the deafening shot turning noises of the world to a ringing bell in my ears, and Harvey drops instantaneously, a small round hole smoking slightly in his forehead.

I try to speak, but Bodie shushes me gently, calling for backup and an ambulance on his radio. "Stay with me, Cal," he says, shaking me as I feel the need to close my eyes become all-consuming. "Stay awake!"

But I can't.

6

There is no pain. That's the first thing I notice when consciousness begins to pull me from the void. Why is there no pain? For a moment I wonder if I'm dead, but I quickly dismiss the notion. I think therefore I am; ipso facto if I am querying my existence then I must still exist. I should open my eyes, that might help explain things.

Slowly, reluctantly, I begin to prise my lids apart, disconcerted by the brightness and unable to make out the truth of the shapes and colours that surround me. I look to my right hand, aware of something touching it, and see the cannula piercing my skin and the thin, transparent tube connected to it. That's why there's no pain, I realise. Whatever the liquid is that is seeping down the tube and into my veins, it is keeping me from experiencing the reality of my wounds. With that realisation, I know I am in a hospital bed and suddenly the strange beeps and chatterings around me make sense. What doesn't make sense is the fact that I can't raise my left hand to push my hair out of my face. I try again to move it towards me, and a loud, unexpected clink confuses me further. I turn my head to look at my arm, still struggling to focus. I squint against the glare of the daylight, and at once see the source of the problem. I am handcuffed to the bed.

"Wha fuc?" I try to speak but it comes out garbled.

"Awake now, are we?" a stern voice says to me, and I look up to see a uniformed police officer at the foot of my bed.

"Whas going on?" I demand.

"I am not at liberty to discuss that right now," he replies. "You are not in any fit state yet to answer questions, therefore I cannot discuss the incident with you in case your lawyer makes accusations of coercion or impropriety. And with that slimy bastard, you can bet he bloody would too."

"What slimy bastard?" I ask, trying desperately to haul myself into a sitting position. "What lawyer? I don't have a lawyer! What the hell is going on?"

"Cal!" A familiar voice calls out from behind the curtain, and the fabric is quickly pushed aside. "Cal, you're awake. Don't worry, it's okay." Bodie hurries into my cubicle, takeaway cafeteria coffee in hand, and shoots a dark look at the officer.

"I haven't said a word," the policeman says, holding up his hands in mock surrender.

"Bodie," I say, still trying to sit up. He holds out his hand to stop me and instead raises the head of the bed so I am sitting upright.

"Don't try to move," he says. "You've had surgery, the knife pierced your spleen. It's all fixed now, but you must rest."

"What is going on, Bodie?" I plead. "Why am I handcuffed? Where are Harvey and Dax?"

"They didn't make it," Bodie says solemnly. "You saved my life, Cal."

"You're a good man," I croak. "A bit of a stay in hospital is a small price to pay for your life."

He looks at the floor, his face ashen. "I'm sorry," he says.

"For what?" My panic rises with the sympathetic look on his face. "For God's sake, Bodie. Please, tell me what's happened?"

"You're under arrest," he whispers. "Or at least you will be once they decide you're awake enough to read you your rights."

"Under arrest?" I know I'm yelling, but I don't care. "For what?"

"Conspiracy to murder, aiding and abetting a known felon and assault."

"What?" I can't believe what I'm hearing. I should be a hero, not a suspected criminal. Bodie sits beside me, and gently tells me all that has happened while I have been unconscious. By the time he finishes, I'm wishing I had never woken up.

At first, as he tells me of the crimes I'm suspected of, I am confident that it is all just a mix-up that will be easily clarified once I give my statement. After all, I have the microphone recordings, and Aisling and Bodie's testimonies to back me up. But once all the details have been shared with me, a sickening truth seeps into my heart. There is no misunderstanding. I have been set up.

I've got to hand it to her, she's a genius. Aisling managed to convince me she was helping me to achieve my goal, when all the time she had a much bigger plan of her own. She never wanted Dax exposed, and I feel like an idiot in hindsight for ever believing that she would. The aim of the scheme was not to film his confession, but to televise his death and gain another high-profile criminal to add to her twisted carnival – me.

The evidence against me is irrefutable. My security card, the one I had willingly handed over to Aisling, had been used that morning to access the staffroom. Given that I was on leave, I had no business being there. There was no audio outside Harvey's cell, hence the hidden device I had worn to record Dax's confession. The only problem was, it had never been connected to anything. The words that could prove my story were never heard by a living soul – except me. The camera footage showed me sneaking in through the shower room and heading straight for Stone. When I reached Harvey's cell, the cameras show me handing over a wrapped bundle which I know to be the communication device, but everyone else has already decided was Dax's knife. Without the benefit of audio, the cameras tell a very simple story. I approached Harvey's cell, handed him a weapon, unlocked his door and stood back while he lured Dax to his death. Even my leap to save Bodie can be easily misinterpreted as a charge forward to attack him to allow Harvey to escape. Even Bodie's statement can't help me. He can only tell them what he saw and heard, and he arrived too late to see anything other than Dax dead on the floor and Harvey attempting to escape. He believes me, I know he does, but the police don't want his opinion, only his witness testimony.

I have been screwed. Outplayed by a devious, duplicitous mistress.

"I suppose you can at least testify that I wasn't attempting to assault you," I say. "I know that's not much in the light of the other charges, but…"

"Cal," Bodie says softly. "The assault charge isn't about me. It's about Mel. They found the sleeping tablets in her system. I'm sorry, Cal. But she's pressing charges."

Of course she is. Of course I've fucked every single thing in my life up in one fell swoop. She must hate me, and I can't blame her.

"She left a letter for you," he continues. "It's with the nurses. I… I don't think it's a love letter."

"No," I say, grimacing as I attempt to shift position. "I don't imagine that it is."

"I'm sorry to be the bearer of bad news," Bodie says, and I laugh at the understatement. Bad news. More like apocalyptically disastrous news. "But, there is someone here who says he can help. A lawyer. He says he knows you, he's been here for two days – waiting for you to wake up. I think he's in the canteen, he gave me his cell number, shall I call him?"

"I don't think I know any lawyers," I say, wondering who on earth it could be. Perhaps someone who had represented some kids from the centre and remembered me? "But I think I need all the help I can get."

Bodie nods, and makes the call. A few minutes later, the curtain opens again as a man in his late twenties wearing a smart, tailored suit and sporting thick spectacles steps into the cubicle cautiously.

"Hey, Cally-baby." He smiles tentatively, and I look more closely at his face to see the slightly sparkling blue eyes and lopsided dimple I used to know so well.

"Jay?" I can't believe my eyes. "You're a lawyer now?"

"Yeah." He shrugs and pulls off the thick glasses. "These are just for show, by the way. They're not prescription. Just thought they added an air of intelligence to my otherwise far-too-attractive-to-be-a-real-lawyer appearance."

I huff a small laugh, despite myself. Same old Jay.

"Listen." He looks uncomfortable. "I saw this business in the news and I thought maybe you could use some help. Maybe even a friend. But I understand if you don't want me here."

"No," I say, softening to the familiarity of his voice and allowing the good memories to overtake the bad for once. "Stay. Please."

"I'm sorry for what happened back then," he whispers. "I was a twat. Still am probably, but hopefully a bit less of one."

"We were just kids," I say, and the truth of that statement sends warm prickles down my arms, as if allowing that grace and forgiveness for Jay makes it real for me too. "We didn't really understand what we were getting into."

I think of Danny, how I was so quick to excuse his actions as naïveté. How obvious it was to me that he was a kid with a good heart and great potential who had simply got short-changed in life and got mixed up with things he didn't really understand. If I could see that, why hadn't I been able to see that the same was true of Jay, and me?

"But," I carry on, "I'm not sure you know what you're getting into now. Have you seen the charges? The evidence against me?"

Jay reaches into his briefcase and pulls out a file with my name on. "Sure have," he says.

"Then why on earth do you want to defend me?"

"Cos I figure it's all bull and you've got a very different version of events, am I right?"

I nod, feeling choked up. Would I have thought the same, if the roles were reversed? If Jay had appeared on the news accused of all these crimes, would I have instantly assumed he must be innocent? I don't want to dwell on that question too long, I'm scared I might not like the honest answer.

"Thank you," I say, as sincerely as I can.

Jay grins and holds out his hand. I take it, and in that vigorous shake we erase the bad blood, the blame and distrust of our adolescence and we are who we once were: friends against the world.

"Right then, you wanker," Jay says, pulling up a chair and spreading the paperwork out on my hospital table. "Let's get you off, eh?"

7

Jay doesn't get me off. I don't think there's a lawyer in the world who could, not with the combined forces of Doug Fanning, UView and VirtReal all gunning for me. The 'Golden Triumvirate' have an inordinate amount of power and influence – the type of power and influence that is able to sustain itself by virtue of the media it controls and the institutions it helps fund. I accepted that even before the trial began. The whole world believes I conspired with the Playground Slasher to murder Britain's favourite celebrity guard, and the only evidence to the contrary is my word that Aisling set me up, and the convoluted story of Dax's cruelty which all the other guards have vehemently denied, even Titch.

I will never be a free man again. I know this as surely as I know that the sun rises in the east. It doesn't matter, not any more. Even as the judge hands down the ludicrously severe sentence I am at peace because, although this verdict is wrong, nevertheless the world around me is at last as it should be. I did not commit these crimes, but I have committed others. And my real sins had far graver consequences than the death of a serial killer and a sadistic narcissist. I turned a blind eye to another's suffering, and in doing so allowed harm to come to an innocent man. I didn't act when I knew I should, and if my punishment is to remain static and inactive now for the rest of my life, then it is no more than I deserve.

I see myself now, not with the rose-tinted view of ego nor the dysmorphic veil of self-loathing, but with a clear neutrality. People have suffered needlessly because of me and for me. From Curly and his mother Patty, to Mel, Vincent and even Harvey. All the self-discovery and soul-searching in the world won't change that. And there's the rub; there's my greatest mistake. I have worried so long about the things I cannot change, the things in the past. I've dwelt there, in part because I can take no measures to alter its horrors. Harvey was right, I have been a man of procrastination and inaction, trapped in despair for the things I cannot change instead of shifting my focus to the things I could have prevented.

I saw all this, all at once and with an epiphany of self-realisation, when I finally found the courage to read Mel's letter.

I couldn't face opening the handwritten envelope for several days. The nurses had placed it by my bedside, and I had lain staring at it, imagining the words of hatred and blame contained within. I knew she had left me, I didn't need to read her goodbye to know it had been said. I assumed that her letter would be full of vitriol, an outpouring of furious anger at my crimes and the way I spiked her drink.

But I was wrong. Not about her leaving me, of course. Only a fool would stay with someone who had drugged them to try to create themselves an alibi, and Melody Fanning is no fool. No, it was her reasons that cut me to the quick.

I am sure you had good cause to do the things you did, she wrote, *and you will wonder why I am not prepared to hear them. The worst thing about this is that my refusal to listen to your side of the story will reaffirm your prejudice. Because you are prejudiced, Cal. You have never trusted me, I see that now. Nothing I could ever do would change how you view me. To you, I have always been and will always be a rich, spoilt razzle. You love me, I am certain of that, but love is not strong enough to make you let go of that deep-seated resentment you hold. You have never really seen me as I am, or listened to my ideas without assuming my bias.*

That's the true irony of it, Cal. Can you see it? All these years you have been so sure that your background was an obstacle to me, but in reality it's my background that bothers you. We are from two different worlds, but I welcomed you to share in mine and you refused to believe I could ever understand or be part of yours.

She was right. I knew it in an instant. It was the strangest, most heartbreaking and yet most liberating realisation I had ever had. I had lost her, but yet I hadn't really. I couldn't have lost her, because I had never really known her. I had loved her, cherished her, protected her, but I hadn't known her. It was an image of her that I had known, an image I created from my own prejudices and stereotypes. I hadn't listened, or seen, deeply enough to separate her from her background. Every frustration I had ever had in our relationship came from a place of resentment, from an assumption that she thought herself superior.

It was me, all along, who had been the arrogant, prejudiced presence in our lives.

There is no time to waste now. The van is waiting outside the courthouse to take me back to the *Justice Live* compound, this time in a jumpsuit and chains. Once I'm there, it will be impossible to speak to Jay privately. I turn to him, still sitting beside me with his head in his hands as the prosecution celebrate their victory.

"I need to talk you," I say. "Alone."

He looks up at me and nods, then goes to speak to the judge. After a minute or two of heated exchange, he grabs my arm. "We've got ten minutes in a private room," he hisses. "And it wasn't easy to get."

As soon as Jay shuts the door to the small, sparse room reserved for lawyer-client discussions, I waste no time. "Are you still my lawyer?" I ask him.

"What? Of course I am."

"I mean it, now that the case is over, are you still legally my lawyer? Do we have that attorney-client privilege they always talk about in the movies?"

"Yeah." He nodded. "I'm lodging an appeal, so I'm still your lawyer. But I'm your friend too, if you want to tell me something in confidence that's where it will stay."

I take a deep breath, and look him straight in the eyes. "The Felton brothers," I say, "the ones involved in the children's home fire. There's something I need to tell you. I need you to help Vincent."

I explain the whole sorry story of Danny's mistake and Vincent's sacrifice and Jay listens stoically before getting up from his chair and pacing the room.

"Fucking hell, Cal," he says at last. "You don't half get mixed up in some convoluted unprovable shit, do you?"

"I'm not asking you to prove anything," I say. "Vincent doesn't want Danny in trouble, he made the choice to take the fall. I just want you to make it easier, if you can."

"Pretty sure I could get him moved to a criminal psych facility," he shrugged, "if he's agreeable. It'd be a damn sight better than *Justice Live* and that fucking chamber, but still no picnic. But if I can argue that he wasn't of sound mind when the first trial occurred, I might be able to get him a better sentence on reduced capacity – he could be out in a few years if he toes the line and demonstrates recovery."

"That would be amazing," I say, jubilant all of a sudden despite my impending lifetime of incarceration.

I stare at him, this childhood friend from long ago when memories and regrets were made in equal measures. I see a man. A man of action and justice, a man who until just a few weeks ago I had thought so badly of. Another person I had assumed I was morally superior to, and another one who has proven me wrong.

"You're a good man, Jay," I say with conviction. "Do me one more favour?"

"What's that?"

"Don't appeal my conviction. It's a dead horse and you know it. It'll just take your time and resources, and those can be far better spent on causes less lost than mine."

8

When the van pulls into the compound and the back door is flung open, I am surprised to see Bodie waiting to greet me, wearing a *Justice Live* guard's uniform and epaulettes that denote seniority. He waves the officer escorting me away, and enters the van to sit beside me. "I'm just going to brief him on the next shot," he calls out to the waiting camera crew. "Give us five minutes."

He pulls the door shut behind him, and turns to me with a sympathetic smile.

"Hey," he says.

"Hey," I reply, puzzled. "What are you doing here?"

"There's been a few changes," he says. "I'm sorry, they wouldn't let me come and see you on remand, you know, because I had to testify at the trial and all that."

I nod, wondering exactly what has been going on at the compound in my absence.

"So, they asked me to be your personal officer," he says, "because, well, because they think you tried to attack me."

Bodie had tried to insist that I was defending him, not attacking him. I saw it for myself when he was on the stand. But he'd been shot down by the prosecution. No words had been spoken between us before I launched forward, so he couldn't possibly know my intentions, they said. The jury was told to disregard 'conjecture' and 'misplaced loyalty' – so the footage was all there was to go on, and that could have been interpreted either way. In their infinite wisdom, the twelve citizens decided it was an offensive lunge, not a defensive deflection, and Harvey had stabbed me by accident as we both ran to take Bodie down simultaneously.

Bodie was something of a national hero now, credited with having thwarted Harvey's escape attempt and bringing him down before he could kill again. I shouldn't have been surprised that Aisling would want him on set, I was only surprised that he'd agreed.

"I said yes because I thought I might be able to make things easier for you," he says as if reading my mind. "I believe you, Cal, and I promise I'll do all I can to help in here."

I remember myself making the same promise to Vincent, and failing to uphold it. But Bodie is not me. He is a good man, a man of honour and compassion. I am in better hands with him than Vincent was with me, though I'm not sure I deserve it.

"Thank you," I say, and he reaches for my cuffed hands and squeezes them.

"There's more," he says. "Aisling wanted me to take Dax's place as senior guard, but I told her I couldn't work with the others. It was a bit of a gamble, but I knew she wanted to cash in on my fifteen minutes of fame so I thought I'd see how far she'd go. She sacked them. The lot of them. Brought in a whole new staff, so none of your ex-colleagues are here. Reynolds has gone too, officially he resigned but I have my doubts. I think she wants to clear the place of anyone who might give the game away about her little set-up. I managed to persuade Nate to come across from Whitefield and take actual charge of the chamber creations."

"How did you manage that?" I ask, remembering how much Nate hated the torture side of the VR projects.

"I convinced him he'd be able to do something really good if he came on board," Bodie says.

"What's that?"

"You'll see," he says with a grin and a wink. "Besides, someone's got to program your chamber, haven't they? And better him than Reynolds, right? You're okay with heights, aren't you?"

"Yeah," I answer, confused at the question. "Why?"

"We've spread a rumour that you're morbidly afraid of heights," he says, "even told the media about it. So act terrified on Saturday, okay?"

Saturday. My stomach flips over. It's Monday today, but the inevitability of winning the vote and hearing my name being called by Mo Wilson is already filling me with dread.

Someone bangs the side of the van, and a voice shouts, "Come on, time to roll."

Bodie gets to his feet and gestures to me to do the same. "Showtime," he says. "They're putting you in Harvey's cell, they think it's poetic justice or something. But don't worry, they haven't put audio in yet so we'll be able to talk privately until they do."

"And when they have?"

"Oh, I have my ways," he says with another overenthusiastic wink before the door opens and I am blinded by the spotlights trained on me as the cameras roll.

9

They say no one sleeps on their first night in prison, but I do. For a while at least. I'm too exhausted and overwhelmed to do anything other than lie down and stare at the walls of Harvey's old cell, knowing there is nothing else I can do. Ever again. I don't know how long I am asleep for, perhaps minutes, perhaps hours. All I know is that the compound is dark and quiet when I hear the thumping of footsteps and jangling of keys coming towards my cell.

The door is flung open, and three burly guards I don't recall seeing on my walk in stride in and drag me from my bed. I start to protest, start to question what they're doing, but the largest one hisses at me to shut up. "We've got a little surprise for you," he says without menace, but the words send shivers of dread up my spine and down my arms.

That feeling of impending doom only increases as they march me across the courtyard under cover of night, taking care to stick to the camera black spots, and I realise we are heading for the chambers. Not again, I think, not another bunch of corrupt, sadistic guards? Perhaps it is what I deserve. After all, I knew what was happening to Harvey and did nothing. Perhaps I deserve to feel the pain of the electric volts and the humiliation of being helpless at their mercy night after night just like I allowed him to. Just like Vincent had.

I don't fight as they bundle me into the chair and strap

me down because I know it is pointless. I cannot overpower them, any more than Harvey could fight off Dax and his minions. There are some battles it behoves one to know are lost before they begin. But I am surprised to note that once the headset and seat restraints are in place they step away without attaching the electrodes.

I'm even more confused when Bodie and Nate step into the room, smiling.

"Don't look so worried, Cal," Nate says. "You're gonna like this one, I promise."

Then the world turns black, and I wait nervously for whatever program Nate has cooked up to begin. Is he testing out my chamber for Saturday? Making sure I can act scared of heights so that he'll get away with giving me an easy time of it?

WYRDWORLD – VERSION CAL 1.0

The writing that appears on-screen makes me inhale sharply. It's the same font, the same layout as the game I so loved as a child.

Then the loading screen is gone and I am there. I am there in the village square, with the tavern ahead of me and the smell of horse shit on the breeze. I look down at myself and I am bedecked in the costume I chose for my character on that day in London nearly twelve years ago.

"Hey, Cally-baby." A stocky, bearded bard sidles up to me and slings an arm around my shoulder. "Surprised?"

"Jay?" I ask.

"Yes, it's me," he sings out of tune and we both laugh.

"How? Why?" I ask.

"Well, I hope you don't mind, but I've been collaborating and scheming with those mates of yours – Bodie and Nate. Nice guys, you did well there. Course, you'll never find a higher calibre friend than me, but they're not too shabby." He grinned. "Bodie knows you saved his life, and he feels fucking awful, between you and me. He hates what's happened to you, so does Nate. So they were asking me if they could do anything to make things a little more bearable for you. So, I told your programmer mate about the good times we used to have here, and the rest, as they say, is history." He gestures to the bright technicolour world around us.

"Nate did this?" I ask, feeling very touched. It can have been no mean feat to get hold of the old software and adapt it for the chamber machines.

"It gets even better," Jay says, "he's done some of the old computer wizardry on the coding, adjusted the time difference. Basically, you can play for much longer."

"How long?" I ask.

Jay smiles so wide I think his face might crack. "One night in the real world is twelve months here."

"A whole year?" I can barely believe it.

"And it's yours every night," Jay says. "For every day you spend in prison, you can spend a year here. You can build a life here, Cal. One where you're free. In time, you might even forget the real world. It'll be just like a strange dream once a year. It's your choice if you want to come here every night, of course, but if I were you, I'd take it. There's nothing out there for you any more. If it were me, I'd take my shot at virtual happiness rather than wallowing in real misery."

I nod, thinking it over.

"Only thing is," Jay says, "I'm afraid there's nothing any of us can do to stop you getting the chamber on Saturday. I'm really sorry about that."

"That doesn't matter," I say, remembering Harvey's cryptic advice and the way I had been able to see through the pixels of Dax's simulation. "I learned a trick, from Stone."

"Well, at least that twat was good for something, I suppose," Jay says. "C'mon, let's head to the tavern and get a drink."

Jay heads for the door of the tavern and I turn for a moment to stare up at the vivid powder-blue sky. I tilt my head, just slightly, and relax my eyes. I can begin to see the edges of the pixels.

"Come on," Jay calls to me, holding the tavern door open so that the scent of hops and stew spills out into the air.

"I don't deserve this," I say.

"I know, mate," Jay replies. "It's a staggering miscarriage of justice, and I'm so sorry."

I shake my head. "Not that. *This*." I gesture to the virtual world around me, so heady and seductive. It would be so easy. So easy to follow Jay into the tavern, so easy to escape reality. So easy not to face up to who I really am. I've done it my whole life, after all. I've told myself untruths, convinced myself I was a man of ideals and courage – but I wasn't. When the shit hit the fan, I took the easiest option, not the honourable one, every time. It stops now.

I stare at the sky again, I tilt my head and concentrate on the pixels, pulling them apart. I break the whole vista down into small, flickering blocks of colour that have no magic any more. It's time to stop pretending I am more than I am, time to look life square in the eye and admit my own imperfections. It's time to be real, no matter how it hurts.

ACKNOWLEDGEMENTS

I have been incredibly lucky to have had such amazing support from so many people. Without them, the journey from blank page to publication would never have happened.

Huge thanks go out to Cari, Lauren, Olivia and all the team at Legend Press for their belief in *Correctional* and for being such wonderful people to work with!

My outstanding agent Emily Sweet (who is just as lovely as her name suggests!) has, as always, gone above and beyond for me, and I can never express how much her support means to me.

I am forever grateful to Gil Kaye and everyone at the fabulous ingénu/e Magazine for their continued support in showcasing my work, and for being generally wonderful!

I owe an enormous debt of gratitude to Christian Pettit for his invaluable insights during the research stage, and for taking the time to answer all my odd questions!

As always, I am overwhelmed by the support and generosity of friends and family who have all given such fabulous input in all my writing endeavours: Melanie Sedlmayr, Wendy Burke, Mike Grant, Sharon Swann, G J Rutherford, Roberta Crosskey, Barbara Evans and Aisling Mills – thank you all, so very much.

My heartfelt thanks goes out to the darkly fabulous Lady Amaranth, for a lifetime of friendship and for all her support in recent years as well as the high school ones! I'll always be thankful I got to have you by my side during our early teens.

Of course, nothing means anything without my awesome little family and all the love, laughter and happiness they bring. My husband Kev, my daughter Mya and my son Riley – you are everything.